Ivan's Captive Submissive

Submissive's Wish, #1

By Ann Mayburn

Ivan's Captive Submissive

Published by Honey Mountain Publishing

**DISCLAIMER: Please do not try any new sexual practice, BDSM or otherwise, without the guidance of an experienced practitioner. Ann

Ivan's Captive Submissive

When Gia Lopez signs up for the Submissive's Wish Charity Auction she has no idea that she's about to be bought by a Russian Dom who will do anything to make her fantasies come true. Including staging an elaborate kidnapping that Gia believes is real. Ivan is instantly drawn to Gia and he wants to be the best Master she's ever had. As he spends time with Gia he begins to have intense feelings for the strong, independent, and sexy American woman. He's only won a week of her service but wishes to keep her forever.

Unaware of Ivan's true feelings, Gia fights her growing emotional attachment to him. All she wants is to settle down with a nice Dom in the United States, continue her career, and live a normal life. However, Ivan sets a plan into motion that will push Gia to all of her limits and take her on a global journey of self-discovery, extreme pleasure, and love.

Warning: Contains Erotic Spanking, Subspace, f/f situations, a devastatingly sexy Dom who knows what he wants, and a submissive who just might be ready to give him what he needs.

"The hours I spend with you I look upon as sort of a perfumed garden, a dim twilight, and a fountain singing to it. You and you alone make me feel that I am alive. Other men it is said have seen angels, but I have seen thee and thou art enough."

—George Edward Moore

Chapter

Gia Lopez stood in a staging area for the submissive auction with a line of women covered in sheer black robes. Her long, light brown hair was twisted back into an intricate braid that was a work of art, but she desperately wished she'd gotten plastic surgery to take care of her big nose before agreeing to this. The other women scheduled to be sold off with her were beautiful, each perfect and lovely in their own way.

She felt like a sparrow surrounded by peacocks.

While Gia possessed enough self-worth to admit she was cute with her dimples and big brown eyes, she'd never be breathtaking like the auburn-haired sex-bomb submissive next to her. Gia had a slender figure from her daily jogging, but with her small breasts she felt like a boy when compared with the curvy submissive.

Why couldn't Gia have gone after someone who wasn't a pinup girl?

Mistress Alice, a tall, blond Domme, walked down the line of submissives. They were gathered in what looked like a parlor with all the furniture moved out. Elegant watercolors still graced the walls and a tasteful chandelier bathed the room in a low, golden light. The door to the room where the auction would take place was currently closed, but from her orientation earlier, Gia knew that on the other side there was a curtained area to hide them from the audience. Then, the scariest of all, a stage where she would be sold to the highest bidder.

Mistress Alice paused now and again to point out something she wanted changed with a submissive's hair or makeup and took a moment to speak with each woman. Up at the front of the line, a few men in brown leather loincloths presented a nice visual treat as they were oiled up by a trio of giggling submissives.

Mistress Alice stopped before Gia and slowly inspected her from head to toe. When she spotted the gold barbells piercing Gia's nipples through the sheer cloth of the gown, she smiled. "Lovely touch against your nicely tanned skin. The gold works much better than silver."

"Thank you, Mistress Alice." Gia curtsied as she'd been trained, and Mistress Alice's gaze warmed.

The Domme tilted her head and studied Gia's face. "You're Mistress Viola and Master Mark's girl from South Carolina, Gia."

"Yes, Ma'am. Mistress Viola and Master Mark were my trainers."

"Lovely couple. I met them once at a Domme convention in Las Vegas. They told me to keep an eye on you, that you have quite a temper and are very high-spirited."

Gia flushed and dropped her gaze. "I'm working on that, Mistress Alice."

"Well, don't work on it too hard." She leaned closer and whispered, "Some of us like a sub with fire in their veins. We like the challenge and the constant battle for your submission."

Gia started as the other woman gently bit her earlobe before leaning back. "Am I understood?"

A soft rush of desire went through Gia and she licked her lower lip. "Yes, Mistress."

The desire unfurled gently in her belly as she relived her training and how she owed her trainers a debt she could never repay. It had been a unique experience to work with Mistress Viola and Master Mark. Together they'd helped her start her transformation into the kind of submissive she yearned to be. They'd also given her glorious orgasms that swept the world away and left her existing as a being of pure pleasure. Not only did they train her physically, they helped her learn how to love herself just the way she was.

Mistress Viola was a plump, curvy, delicious armful of woman. By today's standards she was considered overweight, but back in the 1950s she would have been the ultimate in female beauty. Gia had yet to see a man who didn't gravitate to Mistress Viola in a room, no matter how many other women were there. The fact that her husband, the more traditionally handsome Master Mark, loved her beyond reason helped more than anything else to make Gia believe that maybe there was a man out there who could love her just as she was and give her the confidence to become the woman she wanted to be.

Beautiful, elegant, and loved.

Well, she wasn't loved yet, but she would be. She had faith her Master was out there, looking for her. The thought of him being here tonight, maybe waiting for her in the audience, sent an ache of longing through her. The practical part of her mind scoffed at the idea of soul mates and fate, but the romantic side of her nature insisted anything was possible.

A petite mahogany-skinned woman who reminded Gia of a pixie came up to Mistress Alice and knelt at her feet. "Mistress, Master Martin wishes me to inform you we have fifteen minutes until we begin."

Mistress Alice nodded. "Thank you, Tilly." She smiled at Gia. "Have fun, sweet girl. Whoever gets you is going to have their hands full."

"Thank you, Mistress." Gia bent into a graceful curtsey.

The pair went farther down the line and Gia tried to slow her breathing. The redhead in front of Gia turned around and gave her a warm and dazzling smile. "First time?"

"Yes. Is it painfully obvious?"

"Yep. First timers are pretty easy to spot. You're the only ones who aren't excited. My name is Iris."

"Gia. Nice to meet you." Gia smiled and smoothed her hands against the sheer robe. "I take it by your lack of panic attacks you've done this before?"

"Oh, yes. This is my third time." Iris gave a dreamy smile. "After the first auction, I was bought by a lovely Dominant couple. At the second auction, I met my husband, who is also my Master."

Gia tilted her head in confusion. As far as she knew, this auction was for single, uncollared submissives. "If you have a Master, why are you doing this again?"

The woman laughed and fingered her collar. "Because he wants to win me all over again."

Gia couldn't help a small stab of envy. "That's very romantic."

A chime sounded three times, silencing all conversation. All of the submissives turned toward the sound, and the redhead leaned over to whisper into Gia's ear, "Don't freak out. Whoever you end up with is going to be one of the best Masters in the world. If you click, great. If you don't, then you will, at the very least, come away from the experience as a better submissive. Besides, all of the Masters have your fantasies available to them, and only a Master or Mistress interested in fulfilling your fantasies will bid on you."

Gia laced her fingers together, trying to keep her anxiety at bay. She didn't want to start shaking like a scared puppy. "That's what worries me." She lowered her voice and leaned closer to Iris. "I shared a bottle of wine, or two, with my girlfriend before I filled my form out, and I'm afraid the fantasies I submitted are a little more…frank. Let's just say I was super honest about what my deepest, darkest desires are. Like, embarrassingly honest. When I read what I had already submitted the next morning, I couldn't look myself in the mirror for the rest of the day without feeling like a pervert."

Iris giggled. "Oh, that does sound interesting. Care to share what one of those fantasies was?"

A stern man's voice rang out over the crowd. "Ladies, eyes on me."

They turned and Gia recognized Master Martin, the man who ran the Submissive's Wish Charity Auction and owner of this elegant mansion. Tonight, the distinguished man wore a dashing black tux with an expertly tied red and black bowtie that nicely set off his graying hair. His presence filled the room and all conversation stopped.

Raising his arms, he smiled. "Welcome to the twenty-eighth annual Submissive's Wish Charity Auction. Some of your faces are well known to me as members, and others are delightful new additions to our evening. Whether new or old, I encourage all of you to make the most of the opportunities presented to you tonight. Allow yourselves to embrace your submission and give yourselves the freedom to enjoy the fantasies your Masters or Mistresses create for you without useless shame or misplaced guilt. For the next week, you will be at your Masters' or Mistresses' beck and call. You will find yourselves challenged, pushed beyond what you thought you could endure but, in the end, it will all be worth it."

A nervous giggle came from a few of the submissives and Master Martin smiled, then his expression turned serious again. "Let me take this opportunity to emphasize once again that your happiness is the most important part of this auction. If you are purchased by someone you do not wish to have sexual relations with, you are by no means obligated to do so. The only thing the Master or Mistress that wins you gets is your company. It is up to them to try to seduce you and make you fall under their wicked spell."

Barely stifling a wistful sigh, Gia wondered if she was really ready for this. Yes, she'd submitted to Mistress Viola and Master Mark while training, but she'd never managed to achieve subspace. After listening enviously to the way the other submissives talked about it, she really wanted to experience it but, truthfully, didn't know if she could. She'd tried with a couple of local Doms she was friendly with back home in Myrtle Beach. While the sex had been great, she'd never even gotten close to achieving that floaty, orgasmic feeling the other submissives described. It made her feel like a failure as a submissive that she couldn't get into the right headspace for her Dominants.

Hell, if whoever won her here couldn't top her, maybe she should consider becoming a Domme.

Master Martin's deep voice interrupted her dark thoughts. "You will soon be blindfolded and ear buds will be put into your ears so you cannot hear. We want you to focus on yourself, on your goals, on what you hope to gain from this experience. Not on what is happening around you."

Gia shifted nervously and the air around her became charged and crackled with tense energy.

"Don't worry about how you'll walk or move around while blindfolded. You will each be escorted onto the stage by an experienced submissive." He looked up and down the line. "Any questions? No? Such a quiet and trusting group of submissives we have here tonight."

Everyone chuckled, then a curvaceous dark-skinned Dominatrix toward the back of the line raised her hand. "Master Martin?"

Master Martin smiled. "Our lovely Mistress Vivienne. What is your question?"

Mistress Vivienne smiled. "This girl"—she pointed to the petite woman with a riot cute dark curls in front of her—"is worried she may end up with some serial killer."

The submissive flushed beet red and seemed to sink in on herself. Gia felt sorry for her, but she'd been wondering about that as well. Of course, this auction had been running for twenty-eight years without incident, and everyone had been highly screened, but all it took was one bad apple to end her life. Great. Now she was nervous and scared. It seemed like her brain would never turn all the way off and let her relax.

She liked being in control of her life, leaving nothing to chance or fate, but being constantly on her guard was mentally and emotionally draining. She hated not having control over what was happening to her, which was probably why she had such a hard time submitting. It took trust in the unknown to let someone truly inside your mind and heart during a scene and to totally let go. So far, no one had managed to breech the walls around her soul. That was fine, she was in no hurry to get serious…though it would be nice to have someone to cuddle with at night and wake up to in the morning. Someone to share holidays with and someone who would not only satisfy her physically, but also intellectually. She thought about being in some faceless man's arms as they watched the sunrise over the Atlantic Ocean together and let out a sigh.

Master Martin cleared his throat and her attention returned to him. "As we have a larger than usual number of visiting submissives for this auction, I will reiterate what our members already know. There is not a single Master or Mistress out in the audience tonight I wouldn't trust my own submissive with…though I doubt any of them could actually handle Mrs. Martin." He waited for the polite laughter to die down before continuing. "Every single one of our bidders has gone through extensive background checks and have been members in high standing of their local clubs for a minimum of five years. While nothing in life is ever guaranteed, I take the safety of every man and woman here very seriously. Does that answer your question, darling girl?"

The blushing woman dipped into an elegant curtsey and said in a lightly accented voice, "Yes, Sir. Thank you, Master Martin."

"You are most welcome. Any more questions?"

"Sir?" A willowy woman with short blond hair held her hand up.

"Yes."

"Will I have access to my luggage at all times? I'm a diabetic and will need to be able to get to my medication."

"Of course. The suitcase we asked you to bring has all of your important identification, including your passports and medication inside along with a change of clothes. We've also included two thousand dollars, cash. If you feel uncomfortable and you'd like to leave, you can do so without having to rely on anyone to help you." An uneasy murmur went through the submissives and he gave them a bemused smile. "We haven't had a single submissive leave before their time was up, but we like to make sure that you feel as comfortable as possible."

"Any other last minute questions?"

Silence blanketed the room and Gia laced her fingers together again. Her background check had taken six months. By the time it was done, they knew everything about her—from who her best friend had been in elementary school to her preferences in food. She hoped the Dominants had to go through equally thorough background checks. This whole experience was so outside her comfort zone that it was quickly turning into something surreal, like a confusing dream where the scenes changed too quickly to really get a grasp on what was happening.

If it weren't for the fact the money raised from her auction would go directly to her charity of choice, she'd be tempted to pretend to be sick and run as far and as fast as she could. Then she'd probably spend the rest of her life kicking herself in the ass for missing the opportunity to serve a true Master, however temporarily. No, she wasn't going to chicken out. She wasn't a quitter and she certainly wasn't going to let her fear rule her now. Though the thought of hiding in a bathroom with a fifth of tequila to gain some liquid courage seemed like a great idea.

She was such a basket case.

When no one spoke up, Mr. Martin gestured toward the back of the room. "Let me introduce you to the men and women who will help you navigate the stage."

Laughter rang from the doorway at the back of the room, and a steady stream of elegantly dressed men and women came to stand before them. A lovely Latina wearing a golden cat mask that matched her elaborate gown stopped before Gia with a friendly smile. Taking a closer look at the gown, Gia was pretty sure she'd seen it on the cover of this month's edition of *Vogue*. A diamond collar with a small gold owner's medallion glittered around her slender neck.

"Good evening. My name is Harper and I'll be taking care of you, Gia."

Giving the other woman a tentative smile, Gia almost held out her hand in the traditional 'nice to meet you' handshake but remembered where she was and who she was with. While shaking hands might be the proper thing to do in the outside world, the BDSM community had its own rules on what was proper. In this case, she didn't know if Harper was allowed to touch another submissive without her Master's permission. Gathering herself, she smiled back.

"Thank you. If I throw up on you or pass out, I apologize in advance." Gia flushed in embarrassment at how uncouth she sounded compared to this elegant and sophisticated woman.

Harper giggled and pulled a black blindfold out of her elbow-length white silk gloves. "I'll make sure to aim you in the other direction at all times. Now take a deep breath before you pass out."

Gia did as she was told and took another, which seemed to help clear her head.

The tall female submissive attending the redhead next to Gia smiled at Harper. "Did you hear? The European delegation is in the audience tonight. Yummy."

Gia blinked. "The Europeans?"

Lifting the blindfold, Harper smiled. "Bend down a bit so I can tie this."

The cool cloth slipped loosely over her eyes and the other woman said, "The Europeans are here as part of a…well, kind of like a cultural exchange program. They send their top Dommes and Masters over here for training and we send our best Dommes and Masters over there for the same thing. I've heard they're strict, but amazing."

"And they are soooo hot," Iris said with a purr. "I love my Master more than anything in the world, but if I were single I'd be begging any one of them to take me like the willing slut that I am."

All three women laughed, then hushed when Master Martin looked their way with a raised brow.

Harper adjusted the blindfold until Gia couldn't see anything and said in a softer voice, "Okay, the ear buds are going back in. I can tell you from experience, once they're on, you won't be able to hear anything. I'm going to hold your hand the whole time, so if you start to get a little anxious, just give me a squeeze. Got it?"

"Yes, ma'am, I mean Harper."

The beautiful woman's laughter was the last thing Gia heard before Harper placed some ear buds in her hand and Gia put them in her ears. A gentle, classical piece of music played from the tiny speakers, but the soothing melody did nothing to calm her nerves. Feeling suddenly very alone and vulnerable, a wave of distress tightened her muscles and she reached out. Almost instantly, Harper's hand grasped hers, the smooth satin of Harper's glove giving Gia something to focus on. No wonder men liked the feeling of a woman wearing gloves. It somehow accentuated how much smaller a woman was, how finely formed.

Harper squeezed her hand twice and began to lead Gia forward then stopped again. With the ear buds in place, Gia couldn't have a conversation with the other woman and was left with her own thoughts. Once again, they moved forward, and then stopped. By Gia's estimate, each time they paused they waited a good five to ten minutes. She should be using this time to think, to compose herself so she presented the best image possible. After all, she only had one chance to make a positive first impression on some of the best Dominants in the world. Unfortunately, her mind refused to stay on one topic for more than a few seconds.

Her thoughts were chaotic, jumping from concern about her appearance to wondering if she needed a breath mint. A fine tremor went through her hands and she worried she'd be shaking like a frightened animal on the stage. Mixed in with that was the reoccurring fear that she'd sweat through her deodorant before they made it through the door and that she had some toilet paper stuck to her sheer robe. Opening herself to the potential, very public rejection of nobody bidding on her was so far out of her comfort zone that she didn't know how to cope with her rising panic. This was like stage fright times a million.

Someone removed one of the ear buds and Harper whispered, "We're going up on the stage now to wait. You look beautiful, and I have no doubt there will be a bidding war for you." She put the ear bud back in and Gia was left alone with her spazztic thoughts and the mellow strains of a violin concerto.

Harper gave Gia's hand a tight squeeze and led her slowly up a ramp. The carpet beneath her feet changed to a smooth, cool surface and she realized she was now on the stage. At least her big feet looked cute. As part of her welcome package to the auction she had a full spa treatment consisting of dozens of feminine indulgences she'd never experienced before, including a pedicure that left her with pretty rose pink toenails and baby soft feet. Spending that kind of money on pampering herself wasn't in her Ramen noodle budget, so she'd enjoyed the experience immensely. Every hair-free inch of her body below the neck had been polished until it gleamed like bronze.

She almost licked her lips, then remembered the Domme who had expertly done her makeup had threatened to flog her if she messed up her glossy pale red lipstick. Gia was to be perfect, and that meant controlling herself for the pleasure of the crowd as she stood on the stage at the auction. Right now, though, she was about to pass out from fear despite Harper's sure grip. They stood still, and the occasional brush of air from someone passing would tingle over Gia's overly sensitive skin. With her sight and hearing taken away, she became hyper aware of any stimulation around her.

The idea of doing the charity submissive auction had seemed like a dream come true at first. Gia had a low paying job as an architect with long hours and asshole clients. In this economy, she was lucky to have gained legitimate employment with health benefits anywhere after she graduated. True, her work only paid her enough to give her a roof over her head and other basic necessities, but she knew if she busted her ass, she could and would rise through the corporate ranks. Unfortunately, all that work resulted in a miserable lack of a social life and an even more abysmal love life. Yes, she played at her local club, but it was more physical than emotional. She always left feeling that there had to be more to BDSM than what she'd experienced.

When the Submissive's Wish Charity Auction came up, she'd jumped at the chance. If a Dominant bought her, the money would go to the charity of Gia's choice, and she would get ten percent of whatever was bid. Gia planned on using the extra money she made to put a down payment on a house. She was tired of living in an apartment complex where people fought or partied at all hours of the night. The thought of being able to sleep without being awakened by the sound of techno or Fanny's screaming because she caught Joe cheating again was heaven.

She already knew where she wanted to buy some land with access to the ocean so she could build her dream home someday. The money from the auction could make that happen years ahead of schedule. First, she had to appeal to someone enough to be bid on. When she'd first applied for the Submissive's Wish Charity Auction they told her some of the submissives offered never got bid on, and she shouldn't take it personally if it happened to her. She couldn't imagine how humiliating that would be and prayed someone would find her lean frame, bubble butt, and exotic looks appealing enough to make up for her lack of experience.

Gia stood with her back straight, her shoulders gracefully curved, and one leg slightly in front of the other, turning her body to a subtle angle. Mistress Viola had pointed out how it showed off Gia's long legs and big, round ass. At the time, Gia wasn't sure if she was offended or flattered, but now she tried to accept her bubble butt as part of the way God made her.

Taking in a deep breath, she slowly let it out and tried to focus on the positive. She'd beaten incredible odds to make it this far, so there had to be something inside her the Auction Committee found appealing. Hell, she hoped she was attracted to whoever won her. She liked big, strong men and the sight of a pair of broad shoulders and narrow waist always made her heart beat harder. With her luck, she'd be bid on and won for ten bucks by a skinny guy with dandruff.

A soft, satin glove-covered hand touched Gia's chin and brought her back to the present with a rush of nerves. Gia let out a soft moan. It must be her turn. The ear buds were removed, and a moment later, the blindfold was taken from her eyes.

Harper stood in front of her with a warm smile curving her full lips. She looked like a golden goddess, while Gia felt like a walking plague victim.

God, please let at least one person bid on her.

Just one.

Leaning forward, Harper whispered, “Breathe.”

Gia sucked in a deep lungful of air and immediately felt better, less faint. Harper gave her a moment, then gracefully helped Gia walk to the center of the stage. They were in what had to be a ballroom, lit so she couldn’t see anything about the crowd. It was just her and Harper standing in a pool of warm light, while an anonymous group of people inspected her from the shadows.

Harper held Gia’s hand out and cleared her throat. Flushing, Gia remembered to curtsey to the audience. A soft chuckle flowed through the crowd, and she blushed so hot even her ears burned. Obviously, they hadn’t missed her chagrined look.

A male voice filled the auditorium.

“Masters and Mistresses, may I present Gia. Joining us from South Carolina, she holds a master’s degree in architecture and is relatively new to the lifestyle. Her charity of choice is a no-kill animal shelter in Myrtle Beach where she has volunteered for the past three years. While she has been trained by the esteemed Mistress Viola and Master Mark on the basics of submission, she has much to learn. I’ve heard she’s a very eager student. We’ve also been warned she has a temper, so it will take a strong Master or Mistress to win her submission.”

The crowd laughed, and the murmurs through the audience grew louder. Gia flushed hot enough to melt the sun. She’d imagined she’d get up here, and the guy would point out that she had nice legs in spite of her chunky butt and she liked to give blowjobs.

Oh shit, were they going to talk about the sexual fantasies she’d written down for them? She thought they were going to be in the program next to a picture of her or something, not actually talked about while she stood here. Anxiety tightened her muscles and she worried people in the audience could see her hands trembling.

God, they were going to think she was a weirdo, a pervert, a freak, all those things she secretly felt about herself. No, she wouldn’t give into those negative thoughts. Mistress Viola had spent a great deal of time talking with Gia about her sexual needs. The one thing the Mistress had emphasized above all else was that Gia should be honest with her partner and herself about what her needs were, and not be ashamed of her natural desires. The mature woman part of her mind agreed, while the prim and proper portion insisted she was a sexual deviant and needed therapy.

Sure enough, the next words that rolled out of the auctioneer's mouth made her wince. "Gia is fond of forced seduction and abduction scenarios. She also enjoys relationships where the man is powerful, someone to be feared and respected, but gentle with her…to a point. She craves dominance and has yet to achieve subspace. Well, I'm sure we can help her learn how to fly."

More audience laughter, along with a few catcalls. "Her trainers, Mistress Viola and Master Mark from the South Carolina club, The Iron Fist, have said she can be a bit of a brat and will need a firm hand. At her core, Gia is eager to please and wants to be found worthy of your attentions."

Harper gave her fingers the barest squeeze and whispered, "Breathe."

Gia sucked in an audible breath, and the audience chuckled. She imagined how they were talking about her, commenting on her bony knees, her giraffe neck, her tiny breasts. Here, under the bright lights, all of her insecurities threatened to rise to the surface and overwhelm her. A man to the left commented on her pierced nipples, while a woman somewhere ahead of her made a nasty remark about Gia's small tits.

This was the single most embarrassing, humiliating, terrible experience of her life. Tears threatened to fill her eyes and she blinked rapidly. No, she wasn't going to cry. At least, not right now. When no one bid on her, she could let her tears flow.

“This lovely submissive has agreed to one week serving the winning bidder. Masters and Mistresses, let us start the bidding at one hundred thousand dollars.”

Gia swallowed hard as the first bid came in. She had no idea how the auctioneer could see who was in the audience, but the bids kept climbing. When the staggering figure of close to four hundred thousand dollars was reached she openly gaped.

Two men were bidding. One was an American from one of the New England states by his cultured tone. The other had a rough, almost bestial voice with a sharp, growling tenor to it and an accent she couldn’t place. Her few remaining brain cells that weren’t freaking out, tried to focus on the spot the voices were coming from. She could barely see the outline of what might be people sitting in chairs.

The man with the rough, accented voice roared out, “Four hundred and twenty-five thousand dollars.”

Silence hung heavy in the air. Even the auctioneer seemed stunned. It took him a moment to respond before he coughed and said, “I have four hundred and twenty-five thousand US dollars. Going once...going twice…sold!”

Gia stood there in total shock. Four hundred and twenty-five thousand dollars! That was a life-changing amount of money for the rescue shelter. She spent one weekend a month volunteering, so she knew exactly how far they could stretch it—definitely a new building, maybe even enough to purchase the plot of land behind them and turn it into a dog run. They could even add a full-time vet on staff with that kind of money.

With a gentle tug, Harper brought Gia’s thoughts back to the present in a rush. Harper smiled at her and led her to the edge of the stage. Her time with the winning bidder began right now. For the amount he paid for her, Gia wanted to show him the time of his life, to somehow be worth all the money he’d spent. Hell, she didn’t care if he was eighty years old with liver spots on his balls, she would do her best to rock his world in thanks for his amazingly generous bid.

The spotlights turned away and she blinked rapidly, trying to adjust her eyesight. They took a few steps and were almost at the main floor when Harper paused. A moment passed, then a man said something in what she thought was Russian or some type of Slavic language. She looked at Harper, who gave her a slight shake of her head. Great. Harper didn't understand what was going on either.

A second man approached and she could see him a bit better. His suit was tan and stood out in the dim lighting of the audience.

"Your new Master extends his greeting. He is pleased to have won your service. You will wait for him in one of the sitting rooms while he finishes his business here."

Gia took a deep breath. Okay, she was really doing this. Soon she was going to make her first impression with a Master, not just any Master, *her* Master. She needed to do this right, but she really wished she could see what he looked like.

She held her hand out and the man in the tan suit moved forward. He helped her down from the stage and released her once she reached the bottom. He motioned to her, and she followed him out of the auditorium past men and women whose attention had returned to the stage where the next submissive was being brought out. They went down an elegantly appointed hallway done in red tones until he stopped before a door with the number seven on it. He opened the door and held it for her.

"Please wait inside. He will be with you soon."

She wanted to ask who 'he' was, but silence seemed to be the best option at this point.

The man in the tan suit left quickly, and she turned to look at the room around her. To her surprise it wasn't some kinky sex room, but rather a small reading area. A fire crackled in the black marble hearth, and deep burgundy velvet chairs were arranged artfully before it. Books lined the walls, but she didn't think she could focus enough to read.

There was a gilt-framed mirror above the fireplace, so she took a moment to check her reflection. A few wisps of her wavy light brown hair had escaped her waist-length braid and she quickly smoothed them back into place. Her makeup was intact, and she did a quick check of her breath. Good to go there as well.

Not knowing what else to do, she knelt in the center of the room and waited for her Master as she'd been taught.

She'd scarcely settled and arranged her robe about her in what she hoped was a pleasing manner when the door handle turned again. It opened, revealing a massive, thoroughly intimidating man with dark hair that was cut so close on the sides it was almost shaved. A scar went down his cheek and bisected his lips before trailing down to his strong chin. He wore an impeccably tailored black wool suit that highlighted his fit figure. On his wrist gleamed a gold watch that probably cost more than her apartment building.

She'd been expecting some elegant, sophisticated man who reeked money and class. The man standing before her was plain scary. Despite his obviously high-end apparel, he somehow exuded danger. In a way, he reminded her of the proverbial wolf in sheep's clothing. He was a good five inches taller than her, with a body like a prizefighter. No pretty gym muscles here; this man had a barrel chest and massive thighs, not to mention huge arms.

Gia looked back at his face and forced herself to meet his eyes. To her surprise, he had the prettiest eyes she'd ever seen, Caribbean blue with hints of green here and there. They seemed out of place in his rough and imposing features. He had a solid jaw, good cheekbones, and a nose that was a little bit bigger than normal and looked like it had been broken more than once.

The man reached down and took her hand. As he pulled her to her feet, she had the impression of great strength. The hand holding hers was large, with scars across the knuckles. Whoever this man was, he'd been a fighter at one time. The scent of his cologne reached her and she took in a greedy lungful of the air around him. He smelled delicious, like leather and spice.

"My name is Ivan. I am your new Master's bodyguard, and I will be taking you to him."

His voice was a deep rumble, like rocks grinding against each other. She was surprised to find herself disappointed he wasn't the man who had bought her. Attraction raced between them and she looked away, embarrassed by her body's reaction to the man who was not her new Master.

Unable to help herself, she took another deep breath of his cologne and her overactive imagination began to conjure all kinds of kinky things. Glancing down at his big hands, she tried to imagine what it would be like to be spanked by someone as large as him, or what it would feel like to have all of that weight on her, pushing her into the mattress while he fucked her. Power and strength radiated from him in a way she'd never experienced with any Dom before, similar to the way Master Martin's presence filled the room but somehow…sharper.

Her nipples drew to hard points and she quickly looked away from him. She'd always had a thing for men's hands and his were inspiring an almost dizzying amount of lust. He moved his hands so they framed his crotch, and she realized with a start he thought she was staring at his dick. As she looked back up to his face, she found him smirking down at her.

Damn, totally busted like some kind of hoochie for checking out a guy who wasn't her Master.

She was such a lousy submissive.

Something in Ivan's gaze sharpened, and she looked away, unable to hide from his scrutiny. He removed his jacket and held it out to her, revealing a crisp white shirt that stretched out over his impossibly broad shoulders. “Your Master wishes you to wear this so you don’t get cold. Though your American fall is like the summer in Russia, that little scrap of nothing won’t protect you from the chill.”

Unsure if he wanted her to respond, she simply nodded and let him help her into the jacket. He looked down at her and gave her a small smile that made her heart lurch. With a gentle touch, he draped the heavy coat around her. It hung to almost her knees and held the scent of his cologne and natural musk. She pulled it tight and gave him a grateful smile.

“Thank you.”

“What is your safeword?”

She blinked at him and tugged his jacket closer. “Damascus.”

“Damascus? Like the city?”

“Yes, Sir.” He looked at her, obviously expecting more of an answer, so she babbled out, “My mother was part Syrian. We would visit there in the summer every other year when I was little.”

The man nodded and took a step back, obviously putting some distance between them. She worried he thought she flirted with him. All she needed was her new Master thinking she was the kind of submissive who would screw anyone who smiled at her.

Ivan gave her another searching look before he turned. She followed, trying to at least walk gracefully. Mistress Viola had once said a submissive should be like a living work of art, graceful and flowing, a pleasure to the eye and touch, a joy to behold.

While she would probably never be anyone’s joy to behold, at least she wouldn’t embarrass her new Master. With the big strides Ivan was taking, she wasn’t as smooth as usual. Instead, she clutched his jacket around herself and hurried after him. They passed a few other couples on their way through the mansion, including a Master who was rather vigorously fucking his new female submissive on the bottom steps of a set of stairs.

Lucky girl.

All too soon, they reached the front door. Ivan stopped and looked down at her bare feet. Standing this close to him made her feel small, feminine, and vulnerable. Without a word, he scooped her up into his arms as if she weighed nothing. She gave a somewhat undignified squeak and instinctively laced her arms around his neck. The sensation of his rock solid muscle surrounding her was arousing and made her feel safe even as she scolded her body for responding to the wrong man. She looked up at him as he carried her outside and studied his profile. He had the look of some old time warlord, the kind of man who conquered the world in his spare time.

No, she needed to keep her focus on her new Master, whoever he was. Making herself look away, she studied the drive in front of the mansion and the cars parked there. Ivan headed to the left and tucked her closer to his body as a stiff wind filled with the spicy scent of fall leaves tickled her nose. He radiated warmth and she removed her hands from around his neck before tucking them against his chest.

They reached a black limo and a tall, lean man in a silver suit stood beside it. He had dark brown hair, gray eyes, and a well-trimmed beard. When he spotted her, he didn't say anything, merely nodded at Ivan and opened the door before getting into the limo.

She pushed at Ivan's chest. "Please let me go, I need to properly greet my Master."

Ivan looked down at the pavement then back at her feet. "No."

Befuddled, she found herself in the limo before she knew it, with her new Master sitting at the front near the partition between the passenger section and the driver. She quickly took a seat at the long bench along the side of the limo, unsure if she should sit next to her new Master or wait for him to motion her over. He certainly didn't appear eager for her to join him. When she smiled and tried to catch his eyes, he looked away. Ivan climbed in after her and took the back seat between the two doors. As they pulled away from the mansion, she wished the week was already over.

Chapter

Gia's new Master said something to the driver before the partition closed, then turned to watch her intently. He had soft gray eyes and was handsome in a very patrician way, probably around fifteen years older than she was with a bit of silver at his temples. While he was a good-looking man, and he certainly gave off that dominant vibe she'd learned to recognize in Masters, she experienced none of the instant attraction she'd felt with Ivan.

She pulled Ivan's jacket closer, knowing it was a flimsy barrier between her and the men, but she was comforted by its coverage. The atmosphere in the limo was tense at best. With a bit of a growl in his voice, Ivan said something to her Master, who chuckled and replied in an equally cold voice. She'd never seen anyone display such a complete lack of emotion like these two men. They were icy, calculating, and totally scaring her.

Her Master said something in what she assumed was Russian, then pointed at her. Ivan shook his head and replied with notable anger in his features. To her surprise, her Master backed down, then gestured to her again and said something in a less confrontational voice. Ivan nodded, then she assumed translated what her Master had said. “You are to remain silent until we reach our destination. Your Master wishes to know what your safeword is.”

Pulling the jacket tighter, she tried to keep the tremble out of her voice. “My safeword is Damascus, Sir.”

The men spoke to each other again before Ivan returned his attention to her. “Your Master was wondering what blend of people were responsible for your unique beauty.”

She gave her new Master a shy glance, wishing she felt anything about him other than unease, but at least he was showing some interest in her. “Thank you, Master. I’m Spanish and Italian on my late father’s side and my mother was Syrian and Dutch.”

“Your parents have passed?”

She gave him a brief nod, not at all comfortable discussing this with him. Right now, she should be having some kind of wonderful and kinky sex with the man who’d bought her. Instead, she was being pretty much ignored by her new Master while his bodyguard did all the talking. That wouldn’t have been so bad except, every time she met Ivan’s gaze, the hunger she saw in his brilliant turquoise blue eyes made her sex contract with need.

Her past wasn’t exactly a fairy tale, and she really didn’t want to think about it right now. When she looked up, she caught Ivan studying her intently, and for a brief moment, his usual fierce, intimidating expression softened the slightest bit. She could see how, in his own rough way, he was rather handsome when he didn’t look like he was about to kill someone.

“My condolences for your loss,” Ivan said in a deep, sincere voice.

Turning away, she looked out the darkened windows so he wouldn’t see the tears filling her eyes. “I don’t want to discuss it, please.”

He grunted and resumed talking with her Master, giving her time to pull herself together. Their voices washed over her, and she heard her name mentioned occasionally, but she couldn't even begin to guess what they were saying. Feeling very alone and disappointed, she burrowed into Ivan's jacket and once again wished the week was over. Something in the men's voices caught her attention and she looked over to see her Master glaring at Ivan. The big bodyguard glared right back, and their blatant animosity caused the hair on her arms stand up. Her Master growled out something and looked like he was about to leap from his seat and throw a punch at Ivan.

Nervous that she'd be squished if the men started fighting in the close quarters of the limo, she attempted to diffuse the tension and cleared her throat. "So, how long until we get there?"

Master turned his glare on her and snapped something that Ivan quickly translated. "Your Master wants your eyes on the floor and your mouth shut. Do not look up or speak until you are spoken to."

Both men ignored her from that point on, and she sat as still as she could. Disappointment left a bitter taste in her mouth. She chided herself for having such high expectations and for wishing Ivan was her Dom instead of the cold, angry man who'd bought her. She didn't feel any sort of connection to her Master and could only hope that, once they reached their destination, she could find some way to please him.

Maybe he was having buyer's remorse now that he saw her in the light of day.

She peeked up at the men, trying to study them without being noticed. Once again it seemed as if Ivan sensed her every mood. He narrowed his eyes and studied her while her Master did something on his cell phone.

"You are fearful." He said this like a statement, not a question.

"I..." She licked her lips and fisted his jacket around her. "I've never done anything like this before. I'm just nervous."

Ivan gave her an almost smile, a bare curving of the corners of his lips that softened his face slightly, making him even more handsome.

"Do not be. If at any time you feel any pain or fear beyond what you are comfortable with, you will use your safeword, understood?"

"Yes, Sir."

"Do not be coward." Her Master spoke directly to her for the first time, though he didn't look away from his phone. To her surprise, his Russian accent had a bit of an Irish mixed with it, but his speech was choppier than Ivan's. "This is your fantasy."

Staring at her Master, silently begging him to give her some kind of connection to cling to and slightly offended that he called her a coward, she whispered, "Yes, Sir."

He ignored her and she swallowed hard to fight back her tears.

The tinting on the windows of the limo made it almost impossible to see outside, and apprehension tightened her stomach. Of course she didn't have to do anything with her new Master other than hang out with him, and she could contact Submissive's Wish at any point and she would immediately be taken home, but she didn't want to give up just yet. She would work hard to show her new Master that she was worth the money he'd spent on her and hopefully grow to like him. Or at least not be afraid of him.

Something about her situation kept rubbing her the wrong way and made her uneasy beyond her nerves. She thought they would go back to the city and stay at the fancier hotels, but they hadn't gotten back on the highway, which probably meant they were going somewhere else. Since she couldn't understand what the men said to each other, she had to read their body language, and currently the men were both projecting anger. It was in the stiff lines of their frame, the hostile way they snapped at each other, and the glint of aggression in their gaze. It made the hair on her arms stand up and she fought back a whimper.

What kind of messed up situation had she gotten herself into?

The men's conversation grew louder, and she risked a peek out of the corner of her eyes. Her Master was yelling at Ivan, and a second later, the bodyguard reached out and jerked her to his side. She yelped and clutched at Ivan's solid arm, utterly confused at the turn of events, while the men started to yell at each other.

The limo screeched to a halt. She would have been thrown against the floor if not for Ivan's strong arm gripping her to his side. Ivan pulled out a gun from inside his jacket and pointed it at her new Master.

At the sight of the gun she panicked and struggled to get away, but Ivan's arm was like a steel bar across her chest. "What the fuck!"

Master held his hands up and yelled at Ivan. The door next to her opened up, and a man dressed all in black reached in and dragged her out. She screamed and looked around, hoping someone would help her, but they were in the middle of a road bordered by empty grass fields and a forest off in the distance barely illuminated by the lights of the limo. There were no houses, nor anything else resembling civilization within sight.

The man who'd grabbed her wore a black ski mask and put her into a chokehold before growling into her ear in rough English, "Stay still and you not hurt. Fight, and I cut off ear."

Unable to help herself, she struggled against him like a trapped animal. He growled out something and tightened his hold until she was gasping for air and clawing at his arm. No matter what she did she couldn't shake him off. Her brain decided now was the time to remind her that she took salsa lessons instead of kickboxing in college.

"Don't move or I choke you out."

She froze and he eased his hold enough so she could draw in a harsh breath. If she was unconscious, her chances at escaping this awful situation went down to zero. A pitiful sound escaped her throat before she managed to choke it back. The pavement was cold against her bare feet, and she was all too aware of how little there was covering her body beneath Ivan's jacket.

Oh, God, what had she gotten herself into?

A roar began to fill the air, blotting out the sound of men yelling, and a large, black helicopter appeared and hovered above the trees.

Stunned, she barely resisted the man in the ski mask as he dragged her toward the helicopter now landing in the middle of the road. The rotating blades slowed, and she could hear Master yelling something from inside the limo. Ivan got out and laughed before slamming the door.

Ivan looked over to where she stood, still in a chokehold, and said something in a commanding voice. Her captor abruptly released her, then pushed her toward Ivan. She almost fell before Ivan's steady arm encircled her waist. He hauled her over his shoulder as if she weighed no more than a pillow and began to walk toward the helicopter.

Ivan yelled over the roar of the chopper's blades, his rough accent almost making his words unintelligible. "If you cooperate, you will not be harmed. You are my captive now."

Fearing what would happen if he managed to get her inside, she fought with all her might to escape, but it was no use. Ivan, if that really was his name, had her and he was not letting her go despite her attempts to kick and punch at him. Another man clad in black with a ski mask on helped Ivan haul her into the waiting helicopter. The moment she was through the door, the man in black put her onto a plush leather bench and snapped a seat belt around her waist.

Shaking with fear, she took a quick look around the sumptuous cabin of the helicopter and wondered what kind of kidnappers traveled around in a vehicle fit for a CEO. The back portion of the helicopter was as luxurious as could be, with tan leather seats and polished wood accents. The bench she was strapped to was more like a comfortable leather sofa. Across from her were two swiveling chairs. The soundproofing was amazing. The harsh pants of her panicked breathing were louder than the roar of the blades overhead.

Before she had a chance to really get her bearings, Ivan swung into the helicopter and sat next to her. The door was then closed and secured. A moment later the helicopter began to lift off. Feeling like she was either having an intense nightmare or a mental breakdown, she looked out the window and watched the limo, now almost lost in the darkness of night except for its lights, recede and swiftly disappear.

Ivan took her hand in his. “You are cold.”

She jerked her hand away. “What is going on?”

“Easy, *dorogaya.* No harm will come to you.” He took her hands back in his and began to warm them with a small smile. “This is a simple kidnapping and ransom. You will not be harmed.”

“Ransom? You’ve got the wrong girl. No one is going to pay money for me. I’m not rich and my aunts live on Social Security.” She began to shake and tears filled her eyes. “Please, there must have been a mistake. Please let me go.”

Ivan laughed and unbuckled her seat belt. Fearing what he was going to do, she tried to scramble as far away from him as possible in the small confines of the cabin. He easily hauled her back onto his lap, the hard press of his muscles securing her to him far better than any seat belt. To her dismay, her body warmed as he held her, and she couldn’t help but notice on a primitive level how good he smelled. Her fingertips were icy and she shoved them against his stomach, not caring if she froze the crap out of him.

“It is no mistake. Andre, the pitiful man back in the limo, will pay very well for your return.”

She tried to swallow back tears, but the enormity of the situation was beginning to sink in.

Making a soothing sound, he gripped her chin and forced her to look at him. His blue-green eyes seemed to glow as he examined her and she noticed he had faint scars all over his face to match the ones on his knuckles. Without a doubt, this was a dangerous man, and she was entirely at his mercy.

"Now, you will listen to me." His tone deepened, turned into a command that she was helpless against. The strength of his will pushed against her like a visible touch and she yielded to him. "You will cooperate and be a good girl, or I will make you hurt."

The breath left her body in a silent gasp, and now, the tears did fall. "Please, please let me go."

"That is not an option." He looked over at the silent man with the black ski mask watching them. "She's cold. Get her coat out."

Gia closed her eyes and prayed with all her might this was some kind of weird dream. Things like this didn't really happen, especially not to someone like her. She was boring, a good girl, a careful woman who had everything written down in her daily planner. Ivan moved her around on his lap, and his arms momentarily loosened before softness enveloped her.

She curled further into herself, keeping her eyes tightly shut. It was stupid and childish, but her panicky mind insisted she'd be safer if she couldn't see him. Her other senses were certainly enhanced, and she was all too aware of the growing bulge of his erection beneath her bottom.

Oh no.

"Gia, open your eyes."

She slowly shook her head, afraid if she moved her body too much, he'd become more aroused.

"Keeping your eyes closed will not make me go away, *dorogaya*. I am your Master now. You will keep yourself open and available to me at all times, or I will make you remember your place."

She whimpered, anticipating pain, but when he stroked her cheek with a surprisingly gentle touch she didn't know what to make of it. Slowly, and with great care, he traced her features, pausing to run his thumb over her trembling lower lip and wiping the few tears that had fallen down her cheeks. He made a soft, shushing sound when she tried to jerk away from his touch.

"You are a trained submissive, yes?"

Swallowing hard, she nodded, afraid of what he was going to say next.

"Then you will submit to me. Open your mouth and suck on my thumb."

It took her a moment to muster up the courage, but she did as he asked. If she kept him happy, he'd keep her alive. The taste of his skin against her tongue wasn't bad. In fact, he tasted rather good. When she didn't begin to suck right away he started to pet the inside of her mouth with his thumb, exploring her in a way that reminded her of a vet checking a dog's teeth. Not exactly sexy, but proprietary.

When she began to suck as he'd demanded the hot length of his cock against her stiffened further and her pussy clenched. More tears fell now, tears of humiliation and anger at her body's betrayal. She shouldn't be enjoying this, shouldn't be getting wet from bringing this man any pleasure. He'd taken her from her rightful Master and was probably some kind of psychopath. After he removed his wet thumb from her mouth, his hold on her eased enough so he could tease one of her nipples with his strong fingers.

She stiffened and tried to fight the pleasure flaring through her nerves, tried to argue it was merely a physical reaction that she didn't really enjoy.

Which was a lie so huge even she didn't believe it. For whatever fucked up reason, they had chemistry together, something that went beyond the normal level of heat with the men she'd dated. Of course it would be her luck that the only time in her life she felt like she found someone she could fully submit to, the only man who was strong enough to bend her to his will, was a criminal. A criminal who even now looked at her like she was the most amazing thing he'd ever seen.

With a pleased murmur, he circled her breast, awakening her body to his touch even as she hated herself for becoming aroused. Her gold barbell piercing seemed to intrigue him because he soon began to pull and twist on it. To her embarrassment, a whimper of need escaped before she could swallow it.

"You like my touch, don't you, my Gia? Your body recognizes I am your Master."

She wanted to argue with him, to tell him to fuck off, to kick him in the nuts, but she didn't dare anger him. First, because he could kill her, and second, because what he was doing felt so damn good, though she'd die before she admitted it. Her clit throbbed to the beat of her heart. She shifted on his lap, earning a groan as her butt pressed against his epic erection.

He stroked her nipple, now hard enough to cut glass, and pulled her toward him using that sensitive peek, making her arch up or risk being hurt. This exposed her other breast and he played with that nipple as well, making it as stiff and needy as the other. He easily cupped her whole right breast in his hand and squeezed.

"You have such nice, firm breasts. Now, open your robe for me or I will tear it off."

Her arousal cooled abruptly, and she pushed against his chest. "No, please don't make me do this."

"Dimitri, hand me the cuffs and the spreader bar."

"No!"

She opened her eyes, and Ivan's amused expression helped to quiet some of her fear. Then again, maybe the thought of torturing her amused him. She tried to swing at him, but he easily captured her hand and placed a gentle kiss on her wrist, sending confusing sparks of arousal through her. "Cooperate with me, Gia. You have no choice but to submit to my desires and right now my desire is to see your beautiful body bound and spread for me."

She began to cry again and watched as Dimitri pulled a set of fleece lined leather cuffs out of a storage cabinet situated between the two chairs across from her. Next came a small silver bar with two more leather cuffs attached to it. He tossed the cuffs to Ivan, who strapped them onto her wrists with little effort, then hooked them together so her hands were bound in front of her.

A metallic snick drew her attention away from the cuffs and she watched as Dimitri twisted the silver bar so it extended and tripled in size. Ivan spun her around so she was straddling his lap in reverse and the silky white fur of the knee-length coat he'd covered her with slid to the ground at her feet. When Dimitri approached her with the spreader bar she panicked, kicking out, barely catching the other man in the side of the face.

He made a startled grunt and Ivan tightened his hold on her.

"Stop fighting us. I do not want anyone to be seriously hurt during our play."

She was past words right now. Her terror at what kind of horrible torture they would do to her if they got the spreader bar on made her buck, kick, and try to bite anything that came near her. Ivan laughed and held her closer.

"That's it, Gia, fight me. Make me punish you."

"You bastard!" She continued to struggle, a fine sheen of sweat breaking out over her body as she desperately tried to get away. One cuff went on her right ankle, and Dimitri's strong hands grabbed her other foot. To her astonishment, he bit the sensitive inner arch near her heel. That sting made her settle long enough for him to get the other cuff on.

Defeated, she sagged in Ivan's grasp. "I'm sorry, please don't hurt me."

He stroked her arms and nuzzled his face against the side of her neck. “Gia, right now, you belong to me. Every inch of your body is mine to do with as I see fit. You have no choice in anything, but I promise you that, if you do as I say, you will have nothing but pleasure. Do not fear me, *dorogaya.* This is all for your pleasure.”

Blood rushed to her sex and she sincerely hoped that, despite being spread wide open to Dimitri’s gaze, he couldn’t see how wet she was behind the fine black mesh of her robe. Her arousal was the most humiliating thing of all. Despite the gravity of her situation, and the sheer evil of the kind of man who would kidnap and ransom a woman for money, she was growing needier by the second.

Ivan began to gently kiss the side of her neck, and the soft, delicious touches of his lips to her skin almost brought a moan to her lips. In a perfect world, Ivan would have bought her and she’d be back in the limo with him, having glorious sex, soothing the ache of her pussy with his hard cock. Instead, she had to view him as an enemy and escape at the first possible opportunity.

He continued to stroke her, soothing her body even if his touch only made her mind more conflicted. Part of her wanted to relax into his petting, to take whatever pleasure she could from this awful situation. Another part was afraid if she gave in to his unspoken demands, she’d only be opening herself for further hurt. After all, if they thought she was some easy slut, she might be passed around to her captors like a sex toy. Her hips shifted at the thought and she was not going to acknowledge how disturbingly hot that idea was.

His lips grazed her ear, and she tensed as her sex contracted against her will. That energy between them flared to life, and even though she was in a dimly lit helicopter flying to God knows where, she wanted him. His touch gentled but remained strong and demanding, coaxing feelings from her reluctant body that put all of her previous notions of arousal to shame.

The warmth of his breath bathed her ear as he whispered, “Don’t worry, beautiful girl. In addition to being an opportunistic extortionist, I’m also a Dominant.” He licked the shell of her ear, and she didn’t even bother to try to stop her moan. “In this case, I’m your Dominant and you are my beautiful, sweet, submissive who will serve my every need.”

She pawed weakly at his hand as he cupped her breast, pinching her nipple hard and making her yearn to close her legs. The man sitting across from them had a direct view of her most intimate parts, spread and displayed for him. She must look so wanton, squirming against Ivan and making the occasional needy whimper, her pussy wet and glistening with her need. Hell, she could feel her wetness dripping down between her butt cheeks.

He gave her breast a hard squeeze. “What do you say to your Master, girl?”

On the last word, his voice dipped to a low rumble that was almost like a growl. So demanding, so possessive. He had absolute control in this moment. She would be a fool if she didn’t capitulate to his demands. Being tortured didn’t interest her in the least. But being pleasured did.

“Yes, Master.”

With a contented sigh, he kissed her forehead. “My beautiful slave.”

His arms loosened until she could have pushed away if she wanted. No doubt he was testing her. She would play along and at some point he’d get careless and she’d escape. And so what if he turned her on. It was a physical reaction that couldn’t be helped.

Yeah, right.

He parted her robe and she tried to close her legs. She didn’t like being so exposed before the other man. While she’d already capitulated to Ivan, that didn’t mean she was going to be passed around like some party favor. He folded back the robe in a surprisingly artful manner, displaying her body and framing her.

"Look at this skin, like heavily creamed coffee." He ran his fingers down her ribs. "You need to eat more. Another fifteen pounds would fill you out."

She tried to keep her voice calm, but a bit of her anger seeped out. "I like how I am. Can we please not do this in front of...well, whoever the hell that guy is? I mean, are you one of those guys who can't get stiff without another guy watching?"

Ivan tensed behind her and she got a terrible sinking feeling in her stomach. Once again, her suicidal mouth couldn't help snarking off to her Dominant. Apprehension had her afraid to move, to even breathe. He remained silent and she risked a glance at the man in the ski mask. His blue eyes glittered intensely, his mouth set into a firm line. She was pretty sure he was pissed and closed her eyes, awaiting her punishment.

"*Malyshka*, let me assure you the only thing I need to get off are your sweet moans and tears. Now, because you are begging for it, I will give you a lesson on what my ownership of you means."

He shifted and she flinched, but he did nothing more than adjust his cock so it was seated between the cheeks of her ass, separated by her thin robe and his pants. "I'm sorry, Master. Please, don't hurt me. I'll do whatever you want."

"Hurting you doesn't interest me, Gia. I want to possess you, to dominate you, to make you my willing slave. I don't want to hurt you."

Oh, God, why did this psychopath have to be the one who knows the words that would open my heart to him?

He smoothed his hands over her hips and down her thighs, his pale skin standing out in contrast to her dark tan. She loved how big his hands were, the rough feel of his palms on her. Tingles ran through her at his touch. She longed to press her legs together, not so much to hide herself from the still silent man sitting across from them, but to find relief for her throbbing need with a hard squeeze of her thighs.

"Mmm, *dorogaya,* I can smell your wet cunt. Your body understands what your mind still refuses to admit. I am your Master; my desire is your pleasure. Your pussy, your tits, your mouth, they all belong to me and I will use them as I see fit. Do not worry, I will help you learn this lesson well."

"Yes, Master." Her voice stuttered on the last word and she hoped he thought it was from fear, not desire.

He chuckled, a dark, masculine rumble that made her body hum like a tuning fork. "So agreeable. You should have no problem with letting Dimitri eat your cunt."

Dimitri laughed while she gasped. "I thought you'd never ask. The sight of her sweet *pizda* has been driving me crazy."

She struggled against Ivan. "No, please, I don't want this. I only want you. Please don't share me."

Across from them, Dimitri dropped to his knees. As he approached them, she swallowed hard, disconcerted by the ski mask still covering his face. It somehow made him more intimidating. She began to cry, and Ivan ran his hands soothingly over her torso.

"Easy. You have no choice in this. I want to watch you orgasm on my lap while he eats your pussy, so you will do it. This is not a hardship for you and nothing to fear. I am your Master, and you will obey me."

Wanting to stop this, and not wanting to admit how much it was turning her on, she tried to press back into Ivan as Dimitri advanced on her. "Master, if you want me as yours, why are you giving me to him?"

"Because it arouses me to have you come undone while I'm holding you. Your face, your pleasure, your desire will all be open and available for my study." He leaned closer and whispered into her ear, "This is as close as I will ever permit another man to come to you, at my command and at my pleasure. If anyone touches you beyond eating your sweet cunt while I watch and with my permission, I will kill them for daring to touch what is mine."

Her response was lost as Dimitri knelt between her legs, moving the spreader bar so her feet sat on his thighs as he leaned forward. She watched, unable to look away, as his masked face hovered over her needy sex. He took in an audible breath and groaned before giving her labia a gentle lick, sliding his tongue between her nether lips with a skill that made her toes curl.

"Put your head back on my shoulder. I want to watch you."

Not liking how exposed the position made her, she turned her head away from him and hoped he wouldn't say anything. With a soft chuckle, he grabbed her braid and forced her to look back. The position he put her in strained her neck, but Dimitri was rubbing his thumb up and down the slit of her sex, following the motion with his tongue, and the sensation stole her thoughts. The contrast of the rough skin of his hand and the slick caress of his mouth had her body already hovering on the edge of an orgasm.

Ivan looked her over slowly, studying her eyes, her mouth, and her chest. His gaze went lower, and she looked down as well, wondering if the sight of her pussy being eaten like a juicy fruit aroused him. Ivan grasped her breast and began to thumb her nipple, watching the dark tip crinkle and elongate under his ministrations, the gold bar gleaming in the lights.

"Look at your breasts, so firm with nice, big nipples. And I love the toys you pierced them with for me." He wet his finger and returned to tormenting her breast, adding an unbelievable eroticism to the man licking at her pussy like it was his favorite treat. With Ivan whispering dirty things to her in his deep, purring, bass voice, she was straining to hold back. He had thick, firm lips, the kind she preferred. She wondered how he kissed. Even more, she wondered how he tasted.

"Eyes on me, slave."

She looked away from his mouth and back to his gaze. Intense lust radiated from him and she clenched her jaw, her back arching involuntarily as her orgasm threatened. The most basic and first command she'd learned during her training was never orgasm without permission. Now she struggled to fulfill that command even as she berated herself for doing anything to please her captor any more than necessary.

Ivan grasped the back of her head while Dimitri began to focus more on her clit, getting rougher and drawing sharp cries from her. He began to suckle the nub and she whimpered. With a knowing smirk, Ivan brought his mouth to hers, hovering over her skin so the scent of his cinnamon-tinged breath washed over her. "Are you waiting for my command to orgasm, *dorogaya*?"

She nodded and groaned against his lips, her body tensing up to the point of pain. Dimitri was now sucking rhythmically on her clit, while teasing the entrance of her sheath with his finger. He'd press in enough to start the feeling of being penetrated, then he'd draw back and leave her moaning in need.

Ivan tightened his grip on her hair until it hurt and yanked her head back, exposing her neck to him. "Beg me."

"Please!" The word burst from her as she dangled helpless in his grasp, her hands bound, her feet spread apart, and her pussy throbbing to be filled by someone, anyone. "Please, Master, may I come?"

He licked the seam of her lips, then commanded, "Climax for me, *moya sladkaya*."

She cried out when he pulled away, then Dimitri pushed two of his thick, wonderful fingers deep inside of her while he devoured her with big, greedy swipes of his tongue. The rough fabric of his hood scraped against her inner thighs as he finger fucked her with enough force to make her shake on Ivan's lap.

The first blissful contraction made her world go dark and she screamed, twisting and writhing against Ivan until he had to pin her to his chest. The sensations of being bound by his strength made the orgasm deepen, grow longer somehow. Then, Ivan bit the side of her neck and she shuddered, so overwhelmed by a deep emotional relaxation and pleasure that she could barely breathe. Each wave of her release pushed her deeper against Ivan until she wasn't sure where his body ended and hers began.

Through it all he kept talking to her in Russian, saying things she didn't understand, but in a tone of voice that was at once demanding and seductive. With one last gentle lick, Dimitri pulled back from between her legs and said something to Ivan that was almost a growl. Ivan snarled back at the other man and a moment later Dimitri began to uncuff her feet from the spreader bar.

She moaned in appreciation when her legs were finally moved back inside of Ivan's powerful thighs. The muscles burned and tingled, but the discomfort only made her snuggle closer to her captor. Her mind seemed to have gone on holiday, but that didn't really matter. Right here, right now, she'd found a small island of peace in the middle of the terrifying storm that had filled her life.

Ivan unhooked her wrist cuffs from each other, but kept the cuffs on—probably a symbol of her servitude to him. He removed a handkerchief from his inner pocket and gently cleaned her sex. Little tremors shook her and Ivan leaned forward, easily cradling her weight as he grabbed something from the floor. She opened her eyes enough to see him tucking the fur coat around her with an expression of great contentment. Warmth flowed through her, mixing with the soft blanket of pleasure surrounding her soul like the jacket surrounded her body. She was the one who made him smile like that, she was the one who now enjoyed his affectionate touches.

He caught her watching him and winked. "You pleased me very much, my Gia."

Smiling at him, she attempted to say something, then sighed and closed her eyes again.

"Sleep, *moya sladkaya*. Nothing will harm you while I am here."

Peace like she'd never known moved through her and she prayed she'd be rescued or ransomed before she started to view Ivan as something more than her captor.

Chapter

Ivan Ershov debated if he should wake the sleeping woman in his arms as they neared the hunting lodge where he was staying with a few of his Russian friends and other members of the European delegation. They were nearing the end of their tour of various US clubs, and as the grand finale, they'd attended the infamous Submissive's Wish Charity Auction where Ivan had found his Gia. The memory of her standing on the stage near him, trembling with fear, made him smile. The moment he looked into her big, expressive brown eyes he knew he had to have this woman. And so far she'd exceeded his highest expectations.

She snuggled closer against him, her brow drawn down in distress as something troubled her in her sleep.

He leaned closer and placed his lips against her smooth forehead. "Shhhh, easy, *moya sladkaya*."

With a soft sigh, she relaxed back into a deeper sleep. He studied her features, marveling at the exotic blend of people that had made such a stunning creature. She looked almost Indian, but she had the slightly almond-shaped eyes of her mother's Syrian people and a golden undertone to her darkly tanned skin. Normally he liked big breasts on a woman, but Gia's small mounds fit his hands perfectly, like she'd been made for him. And she was so expressive, wearing her emotions for everyone to see, or she was a fantastic actress.

While he enjoyed role-playing, he'd found it difficult to find a submissive who could fully commit herself to a role like Gia did. If they hadn't had more than two conversations reminding her about her safeword, and she hadn't responded so well, he'd almost believe she truly thought herself a captive. Such dedication to her role inspired him, and while she slept, he had Dimitri call ahead to the lodge and arrange a few surprises for his captive submissive.

Dimitri's deep voice cut through Ivan's obsessive examination of his new girl. He kept his voice low, but spoke in Russian. "You like this woman, don't you?"

Bemused at the slightly jealous tone in Dimitri's voice, he looked up and shifted his hand so it gripped her firm ass in a possessive manner. "Yes."

Swearing, Dimitri twirled the black ski mask on his finger. He was a handsome man in a stern way, around ten years older than Ivan, with silver flecking his coal black hair and a goatee. "Damn. She'd look lovely serving under high protocol. How much do you want for her?"

Laughing softly, Ivan stroked his knuckles over Gia's cheek. "No, all her training will be done by me. If you wanted her, you should have bid on her at the auction."

Dimitri shrugged. "I thought she sounded too high maintenance for me, but I had no idea she would submit so beautifully."

Ivan shrugged. "Your loss, my gain."

He tried to keep the anger out of his voice, a possessive resentment he'd never felt before when sharing his submissives with his friends. After all, they shared their submissives with him. Well, some of them did. His friends who'd married or permanently collared their submissives tended to be far more protective. Most would only allow their female subs to play with other women.

Not that Ivan had a problem with that in the least. He knew Gia liked women, had even trained beneath one, and the idea of watching her tease another woman to orgasm had his cock throbbing beneath her warm, sleeping form. The smell of her arousal still haunted him and he longed to slip a finger between her legs and sample her sweetness.

He'd had to listen to Dimitri brag about how good she tasted, how hot and soft her cunt was for the past hour and he was about ready to punch his friend in the face.

"She is mine, Dimitri. If you wish to play with her again, you would do well to remember that."

With a shrug, Dimitri sat back, then looked out the window. "As you wish. Just know the offer is out there. You know I wouldn't be cruel to her and there are plenty of submissives with us who would gladly attend to you."

Instead of replying, Ivan turned and looked out the window as well, then shifted Gia in his arms. The edges of the horizon had begun to brighten, faintly illuminating the forest below. They were on their way to a hunting lodge in the Allegheny Mountains. While the European delegation also had an entire floor at one of the hotels in Boston, and another in New York City, most preferred to spend their time at the mansion, and with good reason.

As the massive lodge with its twenty-two bedrooms and a fully equipped dungeon came into view, Ivan couldn't help a renewed rush of blood racing into his already aching cock. He couldn't wait to fuck his beauty. Now that he'd seen her orgasm and been able to detach himself enough to really pay attention to her body and responses, she'd never be able to fake her arousal with him. He'd run into subs who would sometimes fake their pleasure in a misguided effort to please their Master, not realizing they were denying both themselves and their Dominant a deeper pleasure.

They landed and Dimitri got out first, making sure he was out of sight by the time Gia roused from her deep sleep.

The whine of the slowing blades brought her awake with a jerk and she looked around in confusion before Dimitri closed the door again. Ivan gave her a moment to get her bearings, and when her gaze met his, he saw a heady mixture of desire, need, and unease. Unable to help himself, he shifted his hand so it slipped through the opening of the fur jacket. Blood rushed to her cheeks as he stroked his finger over her mound, teasing the small patch of short curls there.

"Good morning, Gia."

Her voice came out husky, and he wasn't sure if it was from sleep or the way her body was warming beneath his fingers. "Good morning. I don't suppose you decided to let me go?"

He was glad she still wanted to role-play with him. Smiling, he moved the tip of his finger a tiny bit closer to her slit. Her pupils dilated and her lips softened, inviting his kiss. He was tempted, but he had other plans for their first kiss. "Not until your ransom is paid."

She frowned, pressing her legs together in an effort to keep out his hand.

Unacceptable.

He moved her off his lap and she blinked in confusion as he removed the fur and tossed it onto the other seat.

"Bend over and place your hands on the chair across from me."

A tremor ran through her and he waited. Part of him wished she would disobey so he could punish her, but another part wanted to underscore the lesson he was about to teach her in a brutal manner. The morning light strengthened, and he took a moment to appreciate her flawless beauty. Mile long legs with the muscles of a runner, a high and tight round ass, and a slender waist that begged for his hands to grip it as he fucked her. She appeared so fragile, but he'd learned a long time ago that women were far tougher than most men gave them credit for.

Swallowing hard, he berated himself for getting so carried away about a submissive. Yes, she was extraordinary; yes, the attraction between them was more powerful than anything he'd felt before, but he wasn't some green Dom. He'd been in the lifestyle for ten years, was a respected member of the community in Moscow, and a Master at the art of making a woman his willing slave.

This tinge of nervousness running through him was something he tried hard to ignore.

"Pull your robe up. Show me my pussy."

Without having to be told, she also spread her legs, showing her wet cleft with its pouty inner lips begging to be sucked. Fucking Dimitri had gone on and on about how sweet her pussy was after she'd fallen asleep, and how hard and big her clit had gotten. Indeed, that firm, pink tipped nub stood out from the dusky skin of her pussy in a way that made his cock lurch.

He stood and moved next to her, smoothing his hand down her flank. "What did you do wrong?"

She froze beneath his hand. "I'm sorry, Master. Whatever I did, please don't hurt me."

"I told you, Gia, I will not hurt you. But I also will not have my submissive deny me her body."

She was silent for a moment, then sucked in a tense breath and said, "Yes, Master. Please forgive me."

He stroked down the slit of her bottom to her warm, wet pussy. Playing with her arousal-slickened lips, he smiled as she relaxed, then arched into his touch. She was so responsive and eager to please once he got past her initial resistance. Without preamble, he thrust two of his fingers into her, inwardly groaning at how fucking hot her cunt was. When she squeezed down on his fingers he clenched his teeth and tried to fight the urge to fuck her until she couldn't walk.

"Who owns this pussy?"

"You do, Master."

Her tight passage gripped his fingers in a rhythmic squeeze and his smile grew. So, his beauty liked domination. Good thing he did as well. "Whose cunt is this?"

With his thumb he began to massage her clit, loving how she bucked and moaned. "Yours, Master."

She tried to roll her hips, but he gave her ass a sharp slap with his other hand. "You will be still."

"Yes, Master." She'd begun to pant and her sheath spasmodically squeezed his fingers.

Ivan hooked his fingers and pressed down, looking for the ridges of her G-spot. After finding it, he began to massage that dense bundle of nerves. "That's right, Gia, it is my cunt and I will touch it, fuck it, and eat it whenever I want."

"Yes, Master." She added a plaintive, "Please."

He removed his fingers from her body and she gave a sound somewhere between a whimper and a moan. Moving out of her line of sight, he licked his fingers clean and delighted in the taste of her cunt. She had almost a red wine essence to her arousal, a heady blend of musk and salt that had him seconds from pulling out his cock and giving her the fuck she so desperately wanted. Then he caught sight of the two women waiting at the steps leading to the house and grinned.

Ivan had asked to borrow two of his friends' submissives to help him fulfill all of Gia's fantasies. He knew from Gia's bio that she enjoyed men and women and he was going to make sure she was satisfied in every way possible while she was his. With a start, he realized he indeed thought of her as his, even though they were virtually strangers. Good thing he was leaving for Russia next week or he might be tempted to stay with her, which would never work. They lived on different continents; he was a busy man, and she probably had a full life back in her hometown. Still, he allowed himself to indulge in the moment and imagine keeping her as his permanent submissive.

He glanced over at the woman who was becoming an obsession. "Pull your robe back in place, put the jacket on, and follow me."

She did as he asked and he caught her giving the women waiting for them a worried look. He didn't know why Gia was so tense. Ilyena and Catrin were lovely and accomplished submissives. Plus, they both spoke fluent English, so they'd be able to talk to Gia and calm her. They would bring Gia nothing but pleasure, just as he'd instructed. The thought of tall, fair Ilyena and the plump and blond Catrin with a dark-skinned Gia between them was the kind of thing men fantasized about. He wanted Gia to feel conflicted, to have to seduce her into being his willing captive. Now, after their rough evening, he wanted her pampered and well-rested for the night he had planned for her.

He opened the door to the helicopter and stepped out. Gia followed and yelped as her feet touched the cold stone of the landing pad. Cursing himself for being distracted and allowing his submissive to suffer unintended discomfort, he swept her up into his arms again. She shivered and he wasn't sure if it was from the early morning fall chill or her nerves. He knew she came from a modest background, so this whole experience must be overwhelming for her. All the more reason to get her into the house and introduce her to her own personal harem.

He nodded at Ilyena and Catrin as he passed and said in Russian, "Follow me."

They went in through the French doors leading off of one of the parlors and made their way into the main part of the house. This early in the morning everyone should be asleep, but he caught curious faces peeking out of doorways as they passed. Giving one of the staring submissives a stern look, he tried to not smile as she giggled at him.

Gia shifted in his arms. "Master, I can walk now." He looked down at her and she blanched. "I mean, if it pleases you, Sir."

"It pleases me to hold you."

She swallowed and nodded, taking quick glances at their surroundings as he took them to the special voyeur suite at the end of the first floor. A massive one-way mirror took up the entire connecting wall of two bedrooms. The furniture inside was arranged so the voyeur would have a perfect view of what was happening in the other room. In this case, Gia being serviced by Ilyena and Catrin while he watched from his bed and jerked off repeatedly.

Hopefully, by the time the afternoon rolled around, his burning need to be buried inside Gia would be under control enough to give her the kind of experience she deserved. Right now he'd fall on her like a rutting beast and ride her until she collapsed. While that would be fun, any man could fuck a woman. He wanted to make sex more than a meeting of bodies, but a meeting of souls.

He planned to take his beauty so deep into subspace she would never forget him as the first Master to truly dominate her. The thought made him feel possessive of her, and he held her closer, his heart lightening when she snuggled in his arms.

When they reached the door to her room he stopped and slid her down his front, letting her feel his erection, his need for her. He was also showing her he would not be ruled by his body. But, fucking hell, it was torture to step away from her and assume the stern expression her captor would have. If she was going to put this much effort into role-playing, he would do the same.

"Do what these women say. If I hear you gave them any trouble, I will make you swallow the seed of every man in this place." He gave her a cruel smile and enjoyed her dramatic shiver. "I only want those lips around my cock, so I will be forced to punish you further for sucking some stranger to completion before you've attended to your Master."

"Please don't share me," she blurted out.

Her big brown eyes filled with tears and she raised her hands toward him, taking a step forward and closing the distance between them. Unable to resist her silent plea, he held her against him and gave her as much comfort as he could without breaking his role. Slowly her shivering stopped and she took a deep breath. Her small ribcage felt so slight, so fragile beneath his hands and it made him feel strangely protective.

"I told you before, Gia, you are mine. I won't let anyone harm you and no man will touch you beyond making you orgasm against his mouth, and only if I allow it."

He looked up and caught Catrin and Ilyena giving him identical knowing smiles. They were always going on and on about how Ivan needed to find himself a good woman. Not liking what their happy looks implied, he silently snarled at them and they grinned back. He'd have to make sure their Masters beat them more often. Considering the women's Masters were waiting in the viewing bedroom for Ivan, he wouldn't have to hold that thought for very long.

He gently pushed Gia away and wiped the tear marks staining her face with his thumbs. "I will see you this afternoon. I suggest you get some sleep because I'm going to fuck you until your voice is gone and your limbs will no longer support you. Then I'm going to strap you into a sex swing and fuck you some more. I can't wait to get inside your tight little pussy."

She licked her lower lip and shifted, pressing her thighs together. He already knew that was one of her signals for being aroused and liked the subtle shift in her posture. Instead of shrinking in on herself, she stood at a graceful angle, posed to position her body in the most flattering way possible for those viewing her. Ivan would bet his corporate jet someone had taught her that lovely pose, and he wondered what other surprises she had in store for him.

"Now, come here and say goodbye to your Master."

She looked up at him from beneath her dark lashes and glanced away, then back again at him in a charmingly shy manner. He had to force himself to breathe as she reached up and cupped his face with both of her soft, smooth hands. The way she looked at his mouth made him aware of her intent, and he knew he should stop her. Their first kiss should be on his terms only, but he didn't have the strength to stop her, not when this was her first willing act to please him. She could have kissed his feet or employed any number of ways to show her respect, but she'd chosen instead to kiss him.

She had chosen their mutual pleasure over protocol. This was something to be cherished and rewarded.

At the first brush of her lips, they both groaned and his muscles ached from the effort to hold still. If he touched her, even to push her away, there would be no way he'd be able to resist taking her. Thankfully, she was satisfied with a soft, gentle kiss that spun through his blood like slow, sweet fire. He couldn't remember the last time he'd enjoyed a simple brush of the lips so much.

Stepping back, she gave him a worried, conflicted glance before opening the door and bolting into the room. Ilyena and Catrin went to follow her, but he stopped them for a moment.

"Remember, stay in character."

They both nodded, and he waited until the door closed to go into the viewing room.

As soon as he entered, his friends Alex and Nico turned from where they were standing in front of the one-way mirror and smiled. In his early forties, Alex had a long scar going down the side of his face from when he'd been in a knife fight. It gave him a sinister appearance that went well with his mafia background. Nico was a dark-skinned Russian with Somalian roots and a tall, strong frame. Growing up in the direst of poverty in the cold Russian city of Moskova, Nico managed to work his way out and ended up in Moscow where he now ran a successful pharmaceutical firm. Catrin, the curvy little blond submissive, was his wife. Ilyena belonged to Alex, but they were more of a casual, physical relationship rather than true love.

Alex turned back to the mirror and whistled. "Dimitri told me Gia was beautiful, but he didn't mention how exotic she was. A very unusual combination that works for her."

"Thank you," Ivan said with a small smile as pride filled him at the compliment.

Ivan strolled over to the bed and sat on the edge, pulling off his shoes. He'd been awake for close to twenty-six hours right now and his eyes were gritty from lack of sleep. That didn't mean he wouldn't staple his eyelids to his forehead if that's what it took to enjoy every minute of Gia's seduction, but exhaustion pulled at him.

The women went into the bathroom together, then Ilyena and Catrin came out a few minutes later and shut the door so Gia could have her privacy. Ilyena darted toward the mirror while Catrin stayed back by the bathroom.

Keeping her voice low, Ilyena said, "Master Ivan, are you sure she knows this is role-playing?" While they could hear her, she couldn't hear them, and she began to tap her foot. They all chuckled as comprehension dawned. "Oh, that's right, I can't hear you. Okay, well, Master Ivan, Catrin and I think Gia may believe she is actually being kidnapped. The way she talked, how she acted…she's scared. She begged us to help her escape."

Nico pressed the button next to the mirror that activated the microphone so they could talk. Ivan frowned. "Gia's a good actress.

I've reminded her of her safeword more than once, and she has not used it."

Catrin nodded, but her doubt was obvious. Neither Alex nor Nico commented, and Ivan scowled at their backs. Now that the seed of uncertainty had been planted in his mind, he tried to examine what had happened so far. Could it be true? Could Gia really believe she was actually kidnapped?

Disturbed at the possibility, he barked out to the men, "Get your asses out of the way and sit down. I want to see."

Throwing friendly insults at each other, they settled back and waited for Gia to come back out. It didn't take her long, and when she exited the bathroom she had her hair up in a towel and another towel wrapped around her body. Her skin was still flushed from the heat of the shower and she was even more beautiful without any makeup on. Her hesitant smile at the other girls settled his doubts. If she really thought this was a true abduction, she wouldn't be smiling at the women helping to hold her captive.

Moving almost as one, Ilyena and Catrin took Gia's hands and led her toward the massage table set up next to the bed. While Ilyena helped Gia up onto the table, Catrin lowered the lights until the room was bathed in a mellow glow.

Gia sighed and shook her head, then her voice came through the speakers. "If you won't help me escape, can you at least tell me about the man who has kidnapped me? Is he the kind of man who likes to hurt women?"

"Master Ivan?" Catrin almost looked over her shoulder at the mirror, but caught herself. "Of course not. He's a wonderful man."

Ilyena smiled, removed her blouse, and placed it on the bed. She caught Gia's confused look. "I don't want to get oil on the silk."

Catrin giggled and slipped out of her shirt as well, her big breasts wobbling with her movements. "I don't want my Master to beat me."

Gia leaned up on her elbows, the valley between her soft brown breasts mounded nicely against the surface of the massage table. "Ivan beats you?"

"No, silly. Master Ivan isn't my Master."

Ilyena quickly spoke up, "We belong to some of Master Ivan's friends."

Gia let out a sigh that held the unmistakable note of relief. "Oh, well, that's good. I mean, I wouldn't want to be interfering in anything you had with him."

"No, Master Ivan is very single."

Giving a dry laugh, Gia turned her head so she faced away from the mirror. "Great. I'm sure after I'm ransomed, I'll leave my number with him."

Catrin tugged the towel out from beneath Gia. The table was angled so the men had a side view, and the swell of Gia's firm ass made all three men groan in appreciation.

"Now that's an ass I would like to fuck," Alex muttered in a dark voice.

Ivan gave him a grin that was more of a snarl. "That ass is mine."

Laughing, Nico lifted his hands in their direction. "Shut up."

Following the pronounced curve of her ass with his gaze, Ivan adjusted his aching dick. "If you gentlemen don't mind, I'll be jerking off back here. After watching Dimitri eat her cunt and not getting anything other than blue balls, I need to let off some pressure."

Alex grunted. "Feeling a bit of pressure myself."

"Me too," Nico said as he shifted and stroked himself through his pants.

Ivan turned his attention back to the window, then clenched his teeth. Ilyena and Catrin were massaging oil into Gia's skin, making her body shine and highlighting the grace of her lean figure. Both women looked over at the mirror and gave their Masters hot, hungry looks. Ivan knew that after this, his friends would have their girls to fuck while he'd be left alone with his hand. Oh, he could use one of the always available submissives who traveled with them, or borrow one of the submissives from his friends who were into sharing, but the only woman he wanted was Gia.

Evidently, he wasn't the only one, because the ever-bold Catrin made the first move. She leaned over and licked a line over Gia's ass. "Mmm, vanilla flavored oil."

With a squeak, Gia almost rolled of the table. "What are you doing?"

"Giving you pleasure like Master Ivan instructed us to."

Flushing, Gia clutched the sheet beneath her to her chest. "Please, you don't have to do it. I won't tell. I'm fine."

Catrin giggled and boldly slipped her hand between Gia's legs, cupping her sex. "Mmm, nice and wet. Just relax, Gia, and let us take care of you. It would please me very much."

Gia moaned softly and glanced at Ilyena. "Are you sure we should be doing this? I don't think I should orgasm without Ivan's permission. I mean, I know he's just the guy who kidnapped me, but I don't want to do anything to make him mad. You won't tell him, will you?"

Even as Gia said that, she tilted her hips up at a needy angle. Ilyena smoothed Gia's hair back and placed a soft kiss on the other woman's shoulder. "Stop thinking so much and enjoy the moment. You have no control, no choice in this, so you might as well take as much pleasure as you can. If Master Ivan hasn't told you not to orgasm, I say have as many as you can."

With a soft whimper, Gia bit, then released her lower lip in a way that made Ivan almost desperate to kiss her. "I really shouldn't."

Turning in his chair, Alex gave Ivan a grin. "Looks like you'll be able to punish a naughty girl after this. I doubt she'll be able to withstand both Catrin and Ilyena."

Groaning, Ivan rubbed his dick through his pants. In the other room, Gia was shifting restlessly on the table as the girls worked her over. As they massaged Gia's feet, they both smiled at Gia's full-throated groan of pleasure. He made a mental note to see if Gia liked to have her toes sucked.

Ilyena stepped back. "Turn over, please."

Gia did and he swallowed hard at the sight of her dark, hard nipples pointing toward the ceiling. The little gold barbells piercing the tight nubs glinted with her increasing breath. Catrin moved up toward Gia's chest and began to massage her shoulders while Ilyena started rubbing oil into Gia's thighs. All the men in the room held their breath while Ilyena slowly worked her way toward Gia's cleft and Catrin began to smooth oil over Gia's breasts.

Ivan paced the room, unable to stand the need to touch his submissive. The way she quivered beneath the other woman's ministrations goaded him on like a bull seeing red. He stalked up to the window and gripped his hands into fists as Catrin played with Gia's nipples.

He groaned and turned to Nico. "I'm going in there."

"Wait!" Alex stood and physically blocked his way to the door. "For the love of God, man, interrupting them would be a sin. At least let us see her climax first. That way you can go in and punish her while we fetch our unruly submissives."

Ivan considered pushing him out of the way, but Nico spoke up from where he was still sitting. "Your beautiful girl looks like she's about to come despite her best efforts."

Alex and Ivan whipped around to face the window and made similar pained noises. Ilyena was busy thrusting her fingers in and out of Gia's pussy hard enough to make the other woman's breasts shake.

Catrin had begun to toy with Gia's piercings and Gia panted, her moans surrounding him and driving him beyond reason.

Ilyena swept her hair to the side and leaned down, moving her head so the Masters watching could see her tonguing Gia's aroused clit. The other woman seemed to enjoy Gia's pussy because she leaned closer so she could get a better angle with her mouth while she fingered Gia.

To Ivan's right, Nico began to move restlessly in his chair. "Alex, I say we let our girls play together tonight after we punish them for making Ivan's sub orgasm without his permission."

Alex laughed, a dark rumble that didn't bode well for Ilyena. "Agreed."

Gia arched her back, thrusting her pert breasts into the air. She grasped Ilyena's head and rocked her pelvis against the other woman's face. Catrin gave both of Gia's breasts a sharp pinch and Gia came with a wail, shivering and shaking as Ilyena continued to lick at her with wet, sucking sounds.

"Thank fuck," Ivan breathed out a second before he practically dashed out the door. Alex and Nico followed him, the men saying something in voices too low for him to hear then laughing. He reached the door to the room Gia was in and took a deep breath. So much for taking it slow. He was going to go in there and fuck that beautiful woman until she screamed his name like a prayer.

Ivan jerked the door open and stepped inside before roaring in Russian, "What is going on in here!"

Chapter

Gia shrieked as an enraged Ivan burst through the doors like a demon breaking out of Hell, scaring the shit out of her. Ilyena and Catrin screamed as well, and Gia tumbled off the table in her haste to get away from Ivan. Gone was the tender man who'd carried her into what amounted to her luxurious prison and in his place stood a big, pissed off Dom. There was no mistaking the proprietary way he looked at her, like he owned her. She cursed her body for finding that arousing even as she scrambled away from his wrath.

He began yelling at the girls in Russian. Catrin wailed something back to him while Ilyena remained silent. Gia glanced at the open door and began to creep toward it, hoping maybe he'd be so busy yelling at the other woman he wouldn't notice she was gone. Then again, she was nude, in an unfamiliar place, in a mansion full of criminals. Who knew what one of them might do to her if they found her before Ivan did.

It might be better to stay here.

Two more men entered the room, one a very tall and handsome black man and the other an older gentleman with strong features and commanding eyes. They both snapped something at Ilyena and Catrin, and the women hurried to kneel at the other men's feet. As soon as Catrin and Ilyena knelt in front of the new Doms in a position similar to the one Gia had been taught for presenting herself to her Master, she knew those men must be Ilyena and Catrin's Masters.

The tall, black man grabbed fair-haired Catrin by the arm and jerked her to her feet. His full lips drew back in a snarl and Catrin began to cry. She said something to him, obviously begging, and he grabbed her around the throat, bringing her close for a very thorough, very passionate kiss. Then he released her and muttered something that had the pretty blonde whimpering.

Gia crouched next to the bed, wanting to crawl beneath it and hide, but at the same time fearful of what would happen to the other women. Even if they wouldn't help her escape, they'd shown her nothing but kindness. Ilyena was being handled by her Master in a similar rough fashion. Catrin's Master had pulled her to her feet by her arm, while Ilyena was yanked up by her hair. Gia curled in closer on herself, frightened about what Ivan would do to her, but also terrified of what would happen to the other women. Ivan had joined the other men, ignoring Gia, and when he snapped at Catrin, the other woman choked back her sobs.

Screwing up her courage, hoping someone would hear her over the shouting and crying, Gia said, "Please, Master Ivan, they did nothing wrong."

Ivan turned toward her and glared. "Did you have an orgasm?"

"What?" She tried to think if he'd been in the room when she'd reached her peak, but her eyes had been tightly shut at the time, and the only thing she'd been paying attention to was the way Catrin and Ilyena worked her into a frenzy. "How did you know?"

Ivan jerked his chin toward the mirrored wall. "I was watching you."

The man with the commanding eyes said something to Ivan, and all three men laughed. Ivan moved closer, looking down where she cowered. Damn it all, of course he wouldn't have left her alone. She'd noticed the huge mirror when she first entered the room but, due to the positioning of the bed, she thought it was for people to watch themselves while having sex. It never occurred to her Ivan would violate her privacy like that. However, as a prisoner, she probably didn't have any right to expect any kind of privacy.

The two men and their very subdued submissives left the room, and Gia crossed her arms over her chest, the pleasant rush of her orgasm destroyed by Ivan's yelling. As irrational as it was, she felt violated by him spying on her. In a way, she'd trusted him, and he'd betrayed that trust. She stood, jerked the blanket off the bed, and covered herself with it.

With a deep chuckle, Ivan took another step closer and she backed up, trying to keep her chin held high. "I don't appreciate you spying on me."

A smile twitched the corner of his firm lips, but his eyes darkened as he slowly looked her over from head to toe. "Until your ransom is paid, you belong to me. You are mine to protect, mine to pleasure, and all of your cries of passion belong only to me." He moved closer still until his energy trembled over her skin like a warm breeze. "You knew having an orgasm without my permission would lead to a punishment. I would hate to disappoint you."

Swallowing hard, she fought the tightness of her throat. "You don't own me. You've kidnapped me."

He sat on the edge of the bed, the mattress dipping with his weight. "We can do this the hard way or the easy way, Gia. Either you come take your spanking like a good little girl, or I will be forced to take you downstairs and allow every Master in this house to have a turn spanking that pretty bottom of yours. Considering we have a number of sadists in residence, you would be wise to stop defying me."

The thought of strangers beating her, touching her, hitting her made her ill. Ivan waited patiently, his gaze never leaving her face. From the way he sat, the shirt he wore stretched over his wide shoulders, and she wondered if he had to have his shirts custom made in order to accommodate his big, bull neck. Looking down at his equally big hands, she tried to still the shudder of apprehension and desire. Later, when she escaped or was finally ransomed, she'd have to see a therapist to deal with these conflicted feelings. For now, she wanted to stay alive and unharmed.

"Promise you won't hurt me?"

Shit, she hated the tremble in her voice, but the reality was that Ivan could do anything to her he wanted. The weight of that knowledge settled in and started a low, warm burn in her belly. The fact that she found this situation arousing only deepened her self-disgust. She'd heard of Stockholm Syndrome, where the captive begins to develop positive feelings for their captors, even falling in love, but she never thought it could happen to her. While she didn't love Ivan, she was deeply attracted to him and his total domination of her.

His gaze softened and he motioned to her. "My Gia, there will be discomfort, even pain. Otherwise, it wouldn't be a punishment, but it won't be more than you can take. Now, come here before I make you wear weighted clamps on your nipples while I play with a magnet."

Hesitantly, she did as instructed. He had to pull the blanket from her hands, revealing her body to him an inch at a time. Once she was fully naked, he let out a low growl of pleasure and tugged her closer until she stood in the cradle of his heavily muscled thighs. He ran his hands down her hips before cupping her bottom, his grips almost big enough to cover the entire area of her ass.

“I don’t know who trained you or how you were trained but, for me, when it is time for punishment, you will beg for it.”

She stared at him. “You want me to beg you to spank me?”

He didn’t say anything, just locked his gaze with hers. She saw no mercy, no pity in the shimmering blue depths of his eyes. She shivered at the raw, barely contained desire reflecting back at her. Even without the restless way his hands massaged her bottom, she could feel his need for her, yet he wasn’t throwing her over the bed and fucking her. Instead, he was making her connect with him, like a good Dom would, and that scared her. Whoever Ivan was, he obviously knew his way around a submissive’s mind and heart.

Unable to face his gaze, she looked away. “Please spank me, Master.”

He laughed and leaned forward until his breath warmed her nipple. “You can do better than that.”

The all too pleasant warm rush of his heated breath on her tender bud made her wish he’d close the distance between them and put his mouth on her breast. She knew better than to move forward so his lips touched her flesh, but she was tempted. With a low growl, he briefly caressed the areola of her breast with his tongue, sending bright sparks of pleasure through her, making her greedy for more.

“Please, Master, spank me for coming without your permission. I’ve been a bad girl.” She licked her lower lip and loved the way his jaw tightened at the sight of her tongue.

He swallowed hard then said in a tight voice, “That’s more like it.”

He placed his lips over the tip of her breast and gently suckled her nipple, playing with the gold barbell piercing until she had to grab onto his shoulders for support. God, he was so strong. The muscles beneath her hands were rock hard slabs, highlighting his power over her. He switched to her other breast, and seemingly of their own accord, her hands moved to the back of his head, gently caressing the almost smooth skin of the back of his skull before playing with the longer strands on top. Her confused emotions swung between fear, self-disgust, and a pussy-clenching need for his touch.

Letting go of her now stiff nipple with a pop, he pushed her back a step. “Come on, *malyshka*, it is time for you to take your punishment.”

He helped her lie over his lap, adjusting her until her toes barely skimmed the floor and she was balancing most of her weight on her palms. He spread his legs wider, giving her a better base of support and pressing his cock against her stomach. She almost moaned at the sensation of his erection beneath her and the knowledge she was turning him on. Then shame set in as she realized she truly wanted to please him, wanted him to punish her so she could make up for her lack of control. She was a submissive down to the very marrow of her bones, and she was helpless against her desire to please the man she thought of more as her Master than her captor.

He stroked her back, murmuring something in Russian that sounded complimentary by his tone. Her skin was still slick from the oil and she hoped that would somehow lessen the impact of the spanking. Then again, a small, dirty part of her wanted it to hurt, wanted him to exert his dominance over her further. It wasn’t really her fault he turned her on. He knew exactly how to play her body and she had no choice but to endure the intense sensations.

The rough, utterly masculine quality of his touch across her bottom had her arching into his hand. She needed to let go of herself, to let her body lead her. Fighting him wouldn’t stop him from doing anything. He was going to use her as he wished.

To her shock, he swept one of his thick, rough fingers between the folds of her sex, gathering her arousal and spreading it around her labia. She tried to hold still, to not let him know how much he was affecting her. Unfortunately, her body seemed to have a mind of its own, and her hips tilted into his touch, giving him better access.

"Ahh, *moya sladkaya*, you are so wet for me. I want to drink this sweet honey and make you give me more."

He found the bump of her clit and began to rub that oh so tender bit of flesh in a way that had her toes curling. Passion burned through her, pushing away her fears and doubts and replacing them with the need to please her Master. Shifting beneath her, he thrust the thumb of his free hand into her mouth.

"Suck."

Eagerly opening for him, hoping that if she pleased him he'd let her come and forget about the spanking, she did as he said and groaned at the taste of his skin. To her dismay, he removed his other hand from her swollen sex and rubbed her ass. Goosebumps rose along her back and she drew in a deep breath through her nose, surrounded by his smell and taste.

The first smack caught her unaware, and she jerked her head away from his thumb with a sharp gasp. While she was sure he hadn't hit her with all his strength, it fucking hurt! He shoved his thumb back into her mouth, and she had to suck or choke. Another slap, this time on her right cheek.

"I love to watch your ass dance beneath my touch, Gia. Almost as much as I love how wet you are for me. Now be a good girl and keep sucking while I administer your punishment."

She nodded and moaned low in her throat as he used the hand against her face to cup her chin and support her head. While she licked at his thumb, he used his fingers to delicately caress her chin and jaw, a devastatingly gentle touch when compared to the harsh slap of his hand against her ass. Pain began to radiate through her bottom as he slapped her again and again, taking up no particular rhythm and leaving her constantly anticipating the smack of his hand.

Another slap, this time to the sensitive skin where her left thigh met her ass. It stung, bad, and she cried out around his thumb.

"Keep sucking."

She whimpered and tried to do as he asked, but the pain had reached the level where she couldn't hold back the tears. When the first salty drop reached his fingers he made a pleased murmur and spanked her harder. Hell, she didn't have to worry about the sadists downstairs, she had her very own right here. The way he made her suckle on him while submitting to his punishment tore at her mind, breaking down her mental barriers between pleasure and pain, right and wrong. She wanted to please him, to make him happy with her, but, oh, God, she couldn't stand much more of his stinging smacks.

With her breath hitching in her throat, she began to shriek every time he hit her, over and over again.

"Whose pussy is this?"

"Yours, Master." Talking around his thumb in her mouth made her voice sound garbled.

"Yes, it is."

With that he hauled her off his lap and threw her back on the bed hard enough to bounce, the stinging in her ass making her cry out. She landed among the mound of taupe and cream pillows, their softness cushioning her fall. Her whole body ached, the battling sensations of the pain in the ass and the throbbing in her pussy mingling until she fairly shook with need. The overload of feelings began to fog her mind, to take her to that place deep inside of herself that Ivan seemed to find with ease.

Ivan unbuttoned his shirt, and she sat up straighter, eager to see his body even as she scolded herself for wanting him. Inch by inch, his sculpted torso, covered in a soft mat of fur, was revealed. Most men with killer bodies like his waxed or shaved, but the hair on Ivan's body seemed to highlight the muscles, making him even more masculine.

Why couldn't he be the man who had won her at the auction? He was perfect. Pure sensual domination wrapped up in a bad ass package. It was almost unfair that he was so sexy. Women must be throwing themselves at him…yet he wanted her. At least temporarily.

Making a low, hungry growl, he came onto the bed and grabbed her ankle, hauling her toward him as if she weighed no more than the pillows surrounding her. Without preamble, he shoved her legs open, his broad shoulders stretching her wide. The soft, warm brush of his lips against her inner thigh had her moaning softly and she abandoned herself to his touch, letting him do whatever he wanted to her. It wasn't like she had much of a choice…or that's what she told herself when guilt at her lack of resistance tried to intrude on the moment. She ground her pussy against his mouth and he nipped her labia hard enough to hurt.

He smiled at her pained moan and looked up at her. "You have such a beautiful cunt. My cunt."

An altogether pleasurable shiver raced through her over stimulated nerves. Her ass burned and she shifted, trying to get more comfortable. Making a displeased sound, he slapped her thigh.

"Be still."

She froze. Then, unable to help herself, she arched as his mouth sealed on her swollen sex. He could hold her pussy in his mouth all at once, and his touch felt sinfully good. He didn't tease or nibble. Instead, he ate her with an aggression that curled her toes. He began to suckle that tender bundle of nerves, driving her crazy. She moaned and thrashed beneath his onslaught, unable to control her own body. His licks gentled, becoming soothing strokes that only served to drive her higher.

"Master, please, you feel so good. May I come?"

He didn't lift his mouth from her sex, only shook his head. She groaned in frustration and curled her legs around his shoulders, drawing him closer. Setting her heels against his back, she began to rock her pelvis against his greedy mouth, moaning with abandon as he pressed his thick tongue into her sheath. Her pussy clamped down on him, and when he pulled away, she moaned in distress.

Sitting back on the bed, he began to unbuckle his pants, then paused and looked at her where she was writhing against the comforter, her legs scissoring in an effort to alleviate the muscle-clenching need he'd unleashed in her. Damn, give the man five minutes eating her pussy, and she was ready to do anything and everything he wanted. Feeling wanton, she crawled across the bed toward him and sat back on her heels with her thighs spread, giving him an unimpeded view of her wet sex.

"How may I serve you, Master?"

He smiled, a slight dimple deepening next to his mouth that she hadn't seen before. "I want you to ride me, *dorogaya*."

Sliding out of his pants, he turned his hip so she couldn't get a good view of his cock.

Bastard.

"Close your eyes and do not open them until you are about to climax."

Confused, she did as he asked, feeling very vulnerable without her sight to aid her. A moment later the bed shifted, and with a gentle touch, he pulled her along with him until the crisp hair of his thighs tickled against her. His warm scent enveloped her and she yearned to feel his body pinning hers to the bed.

"Lift your leg."

She did as he commanded and he grasped her hips, moving her onto his lap as easily as a doll. A moment later, she heard the foil of a condom wrapper tear. When he pulled her closer the hard, very thick length of him rubbed against her slit and belly.

Dear God, the man was hung like a bull, too.

"Grasp my cock and put it inside of you, slowly. You have no choice. I am your Master and you will obey me."

She groaned and reached between them, her senses heightened by her lack of sight. The smooth, spongy tip of his dick sheathed in latex met her questing fingertips and he tensed beneath her, the already hard muscle turning to steel. She'd love to look at him right now, to see his expression and know if she pleased him. As messed up as it was, she wanted to make him feel good.

Lifting herself slightly, she rubbed the thick head of his erection back and forth through her slit, lubricating him and driving both of them crazy. He had much better patience than she did, because not once did he try to shove into her or jerk her down on him. Instead, he let her play and tease until she was panting.

Unfulfilled need made her aggressive, wanting him in deep right now. She placed the head of his cock against her sheath and prepared to slam herself down on him. He was thick, very thick, and it would hurt, but, fuck, she needed him to fill her. To give her an anchor to hold on to as she floated in the dark depths of her mind.

Before she could sheathe him, he gripped her hips and held her immobile, poised over his body.

Holy shit, he was strong.

Ever so slowly he lowered her until the fat mushroom cap of the head of his cock rubbed just inside of her entrance. The sensation had her eyes rolling back into her head and she gasped. With a pleased rumble, he lowered her a little more, now almost halfway inside of her. Then he pulled almost all the way back out and she groaned in frustration.

"Beg for it, my beautiful girl."

"Oh, God, Master, please fuck me. Please fill me up with your cock, ease the ache you've left in my body. I want to come with you inside of me. I want to feel you all over me, surrounding me. I've been good, please." She squeezed down her vaginal muscles, saying a thank you to kegel exercises, and delighted in his growl. "I want to milk that big dick of yours while you come inside of me."

She braced her hands on his chest and he removed his hands from her hips. "You please me very much, my Gia. Show me the beauty of your willing submission."

Tears gathered in the back of her throat at how soft his voice sounded, filled with emotions she didn't know if she was imagining. If she could see his face, she might be able to better judge his mood, but she didn't dare peek, not now, when she was finally going to get her release.

His erection slid through her wet, swollen tissues in a toe-curling sensation. He was much thicker than she was used to, and the way his dick seemed to rub her clit from the inside out with each inch, drove her out of her mind. She kept her pace slow, even though her legs shook with the effort. When her pussy finally came down all the way onto his pelvis, she almost opened her eyes in shock at the feeling of bare skin against her. Evidently Ivan didn't shave his chest, but he did shave his pelvic area. Smooth, satiny, firm skin caressed her labia as she ground herself against it.

Fuck, he was going to destroy her with pleasure.

Unable to resist the temptation, she reached between them and caressed the skin of his pelvis, loving how smooth it felt, how decadent. Stroking her fingers over his firm abdominals almost made her feel like she was reading some type of braille. All the ridges, bumps, and valleys entranced her. Her fingers soon found a faint trail of hair above his navel leading to the soft fur of his chest. She leaned forward and rubbed her face against him, loving the feel of his chest hair tickling her cheek.

Rolling her hips in a long, slow circle, she ground her clit against Ivan.

"That's my girl. Now, clamp down on me with that strong cunt of yours."

She did as he asked, and they both tensed at the sensation. For her, it made his cock feel even bigger, better. Beginning to move, she slid up and down his shaft. When she was coming down, she would relax, allowing him a smooth ride deep into her body, and when she drew away, she'd clamp down and torture them both.

All too soon, her orgasm began to push against her control, spurred on by the sexy sounds Ivan was making, the rough, almost growling noises in a tone so deep and low, the vibrations seemed to caress her body. He reached up and began to play with her nipples, making her arch into his touch.

"Please, Master, may I come?"

"No, not yet. Play with that pretty clit of yours. Show me how you like to touch yourself when no one is watching."

Too aroused to be embarrassed, she reached down and began to rub her clit between her thumb and index finger. It felt so good, especially when Ivan began to move beneath her, his short, hard thrusts pushing the air from her lungs. A moment later, he brushed her hand away from her pussy and began to manipulate that bundle of nerves in a much rougher manner than she was used to. It seemed to somehow reawaken the burning pain in her ass, making her once again aware of how sore and used she felt.

It was wonderful.

He rubbed his lips against her neck and murmured, "So perfect, so tight. You feel amazing."

He pulled at her clit and slid deeper. She tensed, shaking with the need to come. Finally, he gave her mercy.

"Open your eyes, Gia, and come for me."

She opened her eyes, hovering on the edge of her orgasm, feeling incredibly aroused and vulnerable. The moment her gaze locked with his turquoise one everything froze, and her soul cried out with longing. His eyes held an incredible mixture of fierce lust and a possessive demand that she lost herself in him. He tore down every wall between her soul and his without even trying.

The pleasure spiked and she struggled to hold his gaze, but the amazing surge of her release caught her in its sharp, crystalline talons. The contractions seemed to go on and on, making her collapse against his chest as she clenched around his wonderful dick. Goddamn, he even tasted good. As she licked his chest, she savored the heady, pheromone-laden sweat mixed with his delicious cologne.

He rolled them over so she was on her back and began to fuck her hard. Her body, so tender from her orgasm, seemed to sink into the mattress. He wrapped her legs around his waist and leaned up, easily supporting her weight as he slid her up and down his cock like his own personal sex toy. The best she could manage was to hold on, her muscles having gone on vacation and leaving her pleasure dazed mind behind. She rubbed her lips against his neck, licking the salt from his skin.

He was so masculine, so strong.

Nothing mattered but him.

Raining a trail of kisses over him, she eventually reached his mouth. When their lips touched he thrust hard into her, making her gasp and open for his tongue. She eagerly kissed him, loving his taste, the way he moved, and how he tensed up to the point where it almost felt like she was fucking a marble sculpture.

Their kiss deepened and his strokes grew less controlled, more erratic. He swelled deep within her, slamming her down on his cock until she fairly keened with an overwhelming urge to come. The knowledge that her Master was feeling the same thing she did, was enjoying this same bliss, stroked her the right way.

"Master," she panted against his lips. "Please come inside of me."

"When I come, you come."

"Yes, Master."

He said a long string of words in Russian she didn't understand, but boy, did they sound hot. Grasping her ass with one hand and her back with the other, he held her close and gentled their kiss. It was now a long, slow, delicious sensation that spun into her need for her orgasm. Eager to make him come, she squeezed down with her sex and released again. He made a choking sound, and she did it again, her pussy trying to suck his seed out of him.

It didn't take long before he bucked with his hips and growled out, "Gia, orgasm for me."

She clung to him, ridding out the initial hard burst of pleasure from her climax, the fact that she was only being held up by his strength, that she was only coming because he let her sending her deep down into her quiet space. Cradled in warmth, she floated, occasionally buffeted in the darkness of her mind by movements, while riding out those gentle ripples until stillness returned to her soul.

Here, in the quiet, everything was perfect.

She'd never felt so at peace before, so relaxed. It wasn't until she finally allowed herself to completely let go that she became aware the aches and pains caused by tension were disappearing. Nothing hurt now and she drifted.

She began to slowly surface from her dark ocean, drawn closer to consciousness by the slow, warm stroke of his hand over her hip. When she opened her eyes, she found Ivan had turned off the lights at some point and had them both snuggled together beneath the sheets, the comforter a heavenly weight on her body. She stretched, pressing her bottom against his semi-hard dick and sighing.

"Wow."

He chuckled behind her, wrapping his arms around her waist and chest, holding her close. "So, how do you like subspace?"

She giggled, the lightness of her soul lingering and filling her with a soft joy. "I liked it very much, Master."

"I must say, you pleased me greatly, Gia. Perhaps I won't accept any ransom offers and keep you for myself."

His words chased the tingle of pleasure from her blood, leaving her cold and the tension returning to her muscles. Oh fuck, she had to escape. Trying to keep the fear from her voice, she murmured, “Whatever my Master wishes.”

He didn’t say anything more, just continued to hold her. Then he began to stroke her arms, smoothing the tension from her limbs. Her lack of sleep and all the shit she’d had to endure soon caught up with her, leaving her exhausted. She snuggled against him, loving the press of his body against hers and hated herself for enjoying it.

The thought of leaving him made her heart hurt; even so, she began to plan her escape. Eventually, Ivan would leave her alone, and when he did, she was getting the fuck out of here.

Chapter

Ivan woke slowly, completely satisfied in a way he'd never known. It was like his body had let go of all of his tension with his orgasm. He'd grown so used to his muscles being tight, it had become an annoying background hum of pain. But now it was gone, all of it, and he had the woman sleeping next to him to thank for it.

He reached out, wanting to touch her warm skin, but found only sheets. With a start, he sat up and turned on the light. Pillows had been mounded next to him in a vaguely human shape, but Gia was gone. He checked the bathroom quickly and found nothing there. The sink was dry and so was the shower. Panic made his heart race as he realized Gia was missing.

After returning to the bedroom, he swore as he saw his clothes were gone as well. Thankfully she'd left him his underwear, but nothing else. He tried to rationalize that she'd gone to get something to eat, but he didn't think so. With a sickening lurch, his stomach tightened as he realized that maybe, just maybe Gia *didn't* know this was all a ruse.

Instant guilt made his chest tighten and he ran out the bedroom door, looking for some sign of her.

"Gia!" he yelled at the top of his lungs, praying she would hear him and come back. If she was really trying to escape what she thought was a real abduction, she could easily get lost and hurt. Hundreds of acres on all sides were nothing but forest. The temperature was going to be close to freezing tonight and he knew her life was in danger.

"Gia!" he yelled as he took a left and ran into his room long enough to throw on some pants, a shirt, two pairs of socks and shoes before grabbing his jacket. If he got hypothermia looking for her in his underwear he wouldn't be much good to anyone.

"Ivan," he heard a man yell in a tight voice. "Here."

He quickly made his way across the great room of the house, a huge affair with a two-story ceiling and lots of exposed beams. A gigantic river stone fireplace flanked the far wall, and various colorful carpets and padded furniture made up different sitting groups. At the end of the room, his friend Yuri was holding his crotch while the male submissive Yuri won at the auction looked on with worry and guilt.

With a groan, Yuri glanced at Ivan and said in Russian, "Are you missing a girl?"

Ivan nodded as guilt gnawed at him. "I've fucked up, big time. She doesn't know this is a fake abduction. She thinks I really did kidnap her and am holding her for ransom."

Yuri glared up at him. "Wait, you faked an abduction? Is that why you needed the helicopter to yourself last night? While I did enjoy the limo ride with my new submissive, I would have liked to get home sooner. And she wouldn't have kicked me in the balls."

"What happened?"

"I saw her going outside in what were obviously not her clothes, wearing only a pair of those flimsy shower slippers with some socks beneath on her feet. Of course, I wondered what the hell was going on, but I pretended not to see her as she snuck to the door. When I realized she was actually going outside in that ridiculous outfit, I went to stop her so I could get her a jacket. I thought maybe you two were playing a game."

Yuri's submissive, a handsome man with soft blond hair and a square jaw, interrupted them. "Hey, I don't know what you're talking about, but that girl is out in the woods. After she nailed Yuri, I mean my Master, in the nuts she took off. I was laughing too hard to chase her."

"Get some help. We need to find her before we lose all of our daylight."

Ivan vaguely heard his friends start yelling to each other about what was going on.

The submissive male nodded. "You're in luck. I'm a police officer and I'm trained in how to conduct a search. Let me get dressed and I'll get some of your people together."

With a sigh, Yuri finally stood. He captured his submissive's neck in a tight grip. "You're lucky they need you to find this girl, or I'd show you how much fun cock and ball torture can be."

The male submissive swallowed hard, but Ivan didn't stick around to watch. He needed to find Gia. Right before he left he spied a throw blanket over a chair and grabbed that as well. Rolling it as he jogged, he placed it around his neck and tried to figure out which way she went. He needed to get into her mind, reason out which way she would go.

A moment later Alex ran up to him with a backpack. "Hey, heard what you said. They have an emergency backpack in case someone gets lost."

"Thank you." He slipped the pack on and tightened it until it sat right. "I'm going after her. Hopefully, I can find her before nightfall."

"There's a thermal blanket in there along with enough food and water for a day. There's also a flashlight that's bright as hell and some other stuff. It should give us something to track. We're getting the helicopter ready just in case we can spot her before full dark falls. If you find her, stay where you are and point the light up into the sky."

"Thank you."

"Good luck."

Turning to the forest again, he tried to shut out all of his emotions and focus on the probabilities. He had a unique gift of being able to figure out the most likely scenarios, and it paid off in his military and civilian life. He knew she was a long distance runner, so she'd probably try to use that to her advantage, not realizing she was only putting herself in greater danger. Ivan didn't know these woods or this area, so he was as blind as she was to any pitfalls that could break legs or natural predators. He wasn't sure if they had bears here like they did where he grew up in Russia, but he had a feeling her greatest threat was going to be dehydration and hypothermia. Her entrance into the woods was easy to spot. Branches had been broken and the green smell of recently crushed vegetation still scented the air. Saying a quick prayer, he picked the route of least resistance through the undergrowth and trees.

Gia leaned against a moss-covered boulder and tried to slow her speeding heart. She knew better than to sprint, especially in a pair of flip-flops. Thankfully they were made of a soft terry type material on top so they didn't cut into her, but they sure as fuck made running awkward at best. Her arches were killing her and she could already feel a Charlie horse wanting to form in her right calf. Like a dumbass she'd given into her fear and had run as fast as she could from the house and into the forest. She had no idea how long she'd run, only that the sun had set almost completely and soon it would be full dark. Overhead the last of twilight brightened the sky and she almost moaned in despair.

Her ill-considered escape plan had not included the house being situated in the middle of nowhere. She'd been surprised the door had been unlocked when she made her escape, then reasoned that they'd never expected her to get away from Ivan. At the thought of the big, amazing, morally corrupt man who she wished was her Master she felt even worse.

She'd fallen for losers before, but this was a new low for her. When he'd touched her last night she'd been dying for him, encouraging him to take her harder. They'd made love three more times after their initial encounter, one of them rousing in their sleep to stroke the other and slide their bodies together. The third time, it had been her turning to Ivan as he slept, taking his deliciously thick cock into her mouth. Without a doubt, she'd wanted him more than she'd ever wanted anyone and her shame knew no bounds.

Pushing herself from the cold stone, she looked around for a place to sleep tonight. While she might be excessively stupid at times, she wasn't purposely suicidal. Walking around in the woods during the night was next to impossible. She'd be better off if she found someplace to curl up and keep warm until dawn. Wincing as her calves cramped up, she made her way over to a pine tree and looked down at the bed of needles beneath the thick branches. It looked relatively creature-free, so she went and grabbed a bunch of long wild fern stems and tried to lay them out enough so she wouldn't be covered in pine needles. With a grunt, she sat beneath the branches and took a deep breath.

She was cold, tired, hungry, and heartsick. The fact that she hadn't eaten since yesterday gnawed at her gut, adding to her misery. Tears began to fall, and she didn't stop them. A breeze blew through the forest, and the path of her tears cooled, then chilled. She ventured a little farther out to gather more ferns before the light was totally gone, hoping she could layer them over her like a blanket. There was enough illumination to see by as she crawled back beneath the tree and pulled as many leaves onto her as she could.

What happened over the next few hours were the closest thing to hell she'd ever felt. She was so, so very cold. Her body shivered in uncontrollable jerks. With her hands between her thighs, she tried to curl into a ball as tightly as possible. The forest was in almost complete darkness, and she swore she kept feeling bugs crawling over her. She berated herself a thousand times for doing this, wishing with all her might she was back with Ivan right now.

Yes, he was scary. Yes, he was a criminal, but he'd also been good to her—at least so far. While she was sure he'd be seriously pissed when he found her, she would endure anything to be warm again. Freezing to death had to be one of the most painful ways to die and she hoped the numbness of her toes didn't indicate frostbite. She'd lost feeling in her ears a couple times, but then she'd cup her hands over them until they thawed. But now her hands were becoming cold no matter where she put them on her body and she was afraid to fall asleep. She'd watched enough rescue shows to know that when a freezing person fell asleep, they didn't wake up.

Her thoughts slowed and her shivers began to wind down as well. She thought maybe she was dying because she swore she heard her name. Craning her neck toward the sound, she saw a bright light and was sure she was dead. But if she was dead, why did she still hurt?

The thoughts spun through her head like bubbles on the wind, insubstantial and fleeting. Someone called her name again and she recognized the rough accent.

Ivan.

"Here," she croaked out, her throat completely dry.

He came closer. "Gia!" His voice was rough and starting to break.

Taking a deep breath, she tried to sit up on numb arms. "Here."

The beam of light swung away from her and she cried out, a harsh and jagged sound that hurt her throat like nails. Terrified he wouldn't see her, she tried to scramble out from beneath the tree, but her limbs didn't want to respond. A burst of adrenaline lent her some strength and she moved a few feet out from beneath the branches.

A moment later the light hit her and stayed on her.

"Gia!" Ivan's voice held so much relief, she started to cry again.

When he reached her, he set his light down and immediately shrugged off his backpack before he picked her up. The shivers started again as she tried to tell him she was sorry, but she couldn't form words around the chattering of her teeth. In the harsh light of the flashlight, his face was all highlights and deep shadows, but the strain was obvious.

He was clearly worried about her.

The thought spun around in her head as he set her down. "Hold on, Gia. Let me get this set up and we'll get you warm."

She could barely keep her eyes open, the last of her energy exhausted. He then began to undress her and she wondered why he wanted to have sex now. Her shivers had stopped again and a comfortable fuzziness blanketed her skin. With a grunt, he lifted her against him and he slid them into some kind of gigantic foil bag. He must have put their clothing beneath the bag because there was a buffer in-between her and the ground. Next he drew a blanket over them and wrapped his big body around hers. With a rough gasp, she clung to him, turning her face on his chest to warm herself. She started to shake again, more like convulsions than shivers. He pulled her tight and she absently noted he was naked, but she couldn't care less.

He was warm.

Blissfully, wonderfully warm.

Though he startled at the touch of her cold skin, soon he was briskly rubbing her hands. "You are freezing."

For a moment he moved away from her and she stuttered out a protest. "I have heated packages."

Wondering what the hell he was talking about, she watched as he rubbed some kind of gel pack briskly before placing it in her hands. The instant heat felt like it was burning her skin, but she moaned, slowly becoming aware of how cold she still was as the numbness faded from her limbs. Little pinpricks of pain came from her hands, then Ivan placed another two gel packs down by her feet.

When he pulled her into his arms he resumed stroking her. "Gia, are you okay?"

She nodded, then snuggled closer to him.

"I'm so, so sorry. I didn't know you weren't aware this was all fake."

Her teeth chattered as she looked up at him, but she managed to stutter out, "What?"

"You aren't really kidnapped. I won you at the auction. I was trying to fulfill your capture fantasy, so I staged the kidnapping."

"You…asshole," she managed to stutter out. Anger warmed her blood and she gripped the gel pack, releasing another rush of heat to her frigid hands. "You fucking asshole!"

"Your throat sounds dry, let me get you some water."

She wanted to kick him in the nuts and cover him with kisses at the same time. Most of all, she was immensely relieved to know she wasn't going to die and wasn't losing her mind by falling for her captor. When he lifted her gently to help her drink, she could see the guilt and regret in his gaze.

After she was done, he recapped the bottle and helped her turn in the tight bag so her icy back was to his front. When she pressed her cold butt against his groin he yelped. "Shit!"

He brushed her hair to the side and began to kiss her icy ear, slowly warming it with his lips and breath. "I'm so sorry, Gia. I will return you immediately and pay for any therapy you need. I cannot begin to tell you how ashamed I am of myself and my actions. To know that I caused you fear is intolerable to me."

The way he rubbed his hand over her hip combined with his lips on her skin started a burning warmth of another nature. Fifteen minutes ago she'd been sure she was going to die alone out here, and now she had this big, gloriously warm male touching her with such tenderness. When her shivers subsided and heat continued to build within the bag, she finally let out a long sigh.

"I'm hungry."

He sat up, being careful to not let the heat escape from the bag. Now that her brain had thawed she watched him as he dug through the pack. He really was a handsome man, if in an unconventional way. While she was still pissed at him, she also felt bad for Ivan. He obviously felt terrible that he hadn't figured out she really didn't know what was going on. When he handed her the energy bar she quickly ate it and washed it down with big gulps of water. The air outside the bag was frigid, so she quickly snuggled up to Ivan.

"They will find us soon," he said in a low voice against the top of her head. "The helicopter is looking for me and it will see my flashlight shining through the trees."

Rubbing her face against the soft fur of his chest hair, she wrapped her arms around him as best she could. "I'm so happy you're not a criminal."

He stiffened, then laughed and relaxed against her. "Me too."

"Did you really not know I wasn't aware this was a fake kidnapping?"

He shook his head, the movement rubbing his face against her hair. "I thought you were a very good actress. Though I'm glad to say I know your climaxes weren't fake."

The way she'd orgasmed over and over for him, doing anything he wanted, giving herself to him made her sex contract. He smelled so good and he'd rescued her. She was going to live. That probably deserved some type of reward.

Moving her arm down his torso, she let her fingertips trace the firm sections of his muscles and marveled at how little body fat he had. When she reached the indentation of his belly button he grabbed her wrist. "What are you doing?"

In response, she moved her head until she could rub her lips over one of his hard nipples. "I'm thanking you."

"No, it is not necessary." She used her other hand to reach between them and cup his increasingly hard cock in her fist. He groaned then said, "Please, Gia, you don't have to do this. I don't deserve it. I'm a bastard."

She slung her leg over his hip and he tried to turn away from her, but that only made her roll on top of him. A cold breeze drifted into the bag and she leaned down closer to his body. In the weird half-light from the flashlight he watched her with narrowed eyes, but didn't try to move her body off of his.

The hot shaft of his erection rubbed against her butt cheeks and when she wiggled he groaned. "Gia, please…"

"Please what, Master?" she whispered against his lips.

He startled, then ran his thumb over her cheek. "I don't deserve you, but I don't care. You are mine."

With that, he captured her lips in a kiss that had her panting against him. With a shift of her hips, she trapped his erection between the solid muscle of his lower abdominals and her aching pussy. Her slit was wet enough that when she slid up his shaft to where it ended just past his belly button it was a wet and smooth glide. The sensation of his thick cock splitting her labia had her moaning low in her throat.

"You have such a wet, tight little pussy. I want my cock in it, now. Grip me in your fist then slowly lower yourself onto me."

The guttural tone in which he made his request had her whimpering as she reached between them. The steely length of his cock pulsed in her fist and she placed him at the entrance to her sheath. The broad head of his dick stretched her and she bit her lower lip, struggling to keep from slamming herself down on him. She was ravenous for him to fill her, to fuck her, to make her come hard and long as only he could do. For a while there she thought she'd never get to feel his touch ever again.

"Look at me," he growled.

She met his gaze and shivered as she slowly slid down his length. The strength in his eyes kept her mind from returning to dark thoughts and she blinked back tears.

He cupped her face and swept her cheeks with his thumbs. "*Lyubov moya*, why are you crying?"

"I thought I'd never see you again."

An incredibly tender look entered his gaze and she melted inside. "Then let me remind you that you are very alive."

With a low grunt, he slammed her down onto his cock and rocked her clit against his lower abdominals, which were clenched deliciously hard. A surprisingly quick orgasm almost overtook her, but she managed to hold it back and squeezed his cock inside of her as hard as she could. He groaned and gripped her ass with both hands, rocking her pelvis against him. "Fucking tight pussy, my pussy."

Her reply died as he tilted her hips and began to drive into her. Each thrust stretched her sheath, jolting his pelvis against her clit. The way he moved, the way he rocked against her had her scrambling to hold on to his broad shoulders. He grunted as he rammed into her, the bestial sound driving her higher until she was screaming out his name.

"Come for me, my Gia."

Every muscle in her body locked up and she could only keen softly at the pleasure saturating her body. Her pussy milked Ivan's cock as he slowly moved inside of her now, delicious drags that seemed to match perfectly with the fading contractions of her orgasm. Once she'd stopped twitching he shifted his hips and sat up the slightest bit, making the angle perfect for him to work her clit. She groaned as he coaxed her arousal back to life. He said something in Russian that sounded intense and passionate. When she managed to open her eyes past the sensations suffusing her she studied Ivan as he touched her. He had his eyes closed and his jaw was clenched tight. She began to move faster on him and he groaned, giving this sexy jerk of his head before opening his eyes. When he saw her looking at him he gave her a small smile.

"My Gia."

"My Master."

"Say that again."

"You are my Master."

He pulled her down until there wasn't an inch of space between them and wrapped his arms around her tight enough that she couldn't move. Not that she really cared at this point. Right now her mind floated in soft darkness, the strong beat of Ivan's heart beneath her palm reassuring her that she was safe and with a man who would do anything to keep it that way. The heat they generated together had her sweating and their skin slid as he took her. That's what he was doing. He wasn't having sex with her, or making love, or even fucking her. He was taking her like she was his.

Hard, slamming thrusts had her shaking as her overwrought body tried to absorb all the sensations rolling through her. A moment later he lifted her off of him with ease, then rubbed the slit of her pussy along his cock as he came. The warmth of his seed against her skin made her moan and she shuddered when he ran the tip of his cock over her sensitized clit. She wished he'd come inside her—they both had sparkling clean health records and she was on a hormone shot to prevent pregnancy—but she also liked the way his seed seemed to mark her as his.

Not saying anything, he grabbed the shirt she'd worn when she escaped and gently cleaned them both. She was so warm now she was sweating, so when the bag let out some of the heat as he repositioned her on her side and curled around her back, she let out a long, low sigh. She had food in her belly, warmth all around her, and the ever so pleasant full body hum of a really good orgasm.

Ivan kissed the back of her neck. "I was so worried about you."

She snuggled closer, suddenly very tired. "I'm sorry, I didn't mean to scare you."

"No, it is my fault. I meant what I said, Gia. I will send you home as soon as we get back and will make sure you have everything you need to get over what I did to you."

The sorrow in his voice hurt her heart. "Hey now. Let's not rush things. So maybe you scared me a little—okay, a lot, but it was also an amazing experience. Now that I know you're not some sleazebag, I'd really like to stay the rest of the week with you."

He turned her so he could study her face and whatever he found there seemed to satisfy him. "You're not afraid of me."

"No."

"But you were before."

"Yes."

Letting out a heavy sigh, he cradled her face with his big hands. "I will make this up to you. I swear it."

"Well, now that I know you're not going to kill me or cut off my ear in order to get ransom money, I have to admit, being held hostage by you was hot."

He raised his eyebrows. "Really?"

"Mmm hmmm."

His cock stiffened against her thigh and she wondered if he was even human. “What did you like?”

She shivered, memories of all the erotic things they’d done together blending through her mind until arousal spread through her in a slow, delicious wave of sensation. “Everything.”

He laughed. “We still have so many of your fantasies to attend to.”

“As long as you’re with me, Master, I can’t wait to see what the future holds for us.”

He got an evil glint in his eye, then he spoke in such a seductive tone that a nun would have thrown her panties at him. “Do you want me to push you?”

Slowly she nodded as her whole body burst into flames. “Just not my hard limits stuff, okay?”

The way he licked his lips made her press her hips against him with a moan. “Of course. You had a very, very long list of things you wanted to do, my beautiful girl.”

As she thought back on her list she flushed and looked at his chest, then began to play with his chest hair as she said, “I’ve lived a sheltered life.”

His startled laugh made her giggle and then they were almost gasping with laughter.

She looked up at him and attempted to speak. “You have no idea how fucked up this day has been for me. I mean, you fucking kidnapped me!”

“Evidently I did too good of a job,” he replied with a sad smile. “I’m sorry.”

Placing her hand over his mouth, she shook her head. “Save it, okay.”

He nipped her fingers hard enough she had to move her hand or lose some skin. “You do not get to tell me what to do, girl.”

It was hard to glare at him when she was naked and draped over him like a blanket, but she gave it her best shot. "Uh-uh, doesn't work like that. If, for any reason, I see you doing something I know is hurting you, I can tell you to stop being silly."

His eyes sparkled, but he didn't smile. "I am not silly. Terrifying, yes, intimidating, yes, a boxing champion, yes, but silly…never."

Sure now that he was teasing her, she grinned down at him. "You know, when you're not being terrifying you are really nice."

A pleased sound rumbled through his chest and straight into her heart, and other naughtier places. "Baby, I can be plenty mean."

To emphasize the point, he grabbed her ass and dug in with his fingers, sending sparks of fierce desire through her blood. His grip was so possessive and it reminded her of how big he was. How strong…holy hell, he was the hottest man she'd ever had the pleasure of even seeing, let alone being with.

Overcome with emotion and lust, she leaned over and gently kissed along his scar, working her way from his cheek to his lips. His hands gentled, but he began to play with the crack of her ass in a way that let her know he was thinking about playing with other more…forbidden places on her body. The thought of him breaking her in, of taking her ass, made her very, very wet.

"How did you get this scar?"

"Knife fight when I was seventeen."

"Yikes."

"I'm not sure what that word means, but I will assume you are startled. I was a stupid, arrogant boy who thought because he had hair on his balls he was a man."

"I can't imagine you that young. So what happened?"

"After a night of drinking I picked a fight with the wrong man. I was with my uncle and he let me get my ass beat."

"What? Why would he do that?"

"Because I deserved it. I was being an arrogant loudmouth with an attitude I hadn't earned. If my uncle had saved me, he would've only encouraged that behavior."

She stroked her finger over the scar. "But you could have been killed."

"I got accidentally punched through a window."

"How does that happen?"

"He punched me, and because I was so drunk I didn't fall like a normal person, but stumbled right through a window." He shook his head and she could see he found the memory funny. "When my mother came to the hospital she took one look at me and told me I had to keep this scar for the rest of my life to remind me every time I look in the mirror what an idiot I am. It worked and to this day I wake up every morning and the scar keeps me humble."

Laughing, she rubbed her thumb over the scar tissue on hischin. "Humble? Are you sure that's the right word?"

With a growl, he turned and nipped her arm hard enough to leave marks. "You are a brat just begging for a punishment."

Giving him wide, innocent eyes, she fluttered her lashes at him. "What are you talking about, Master?"

"Minx." Reaching between them, he began to twist and pull her nipples. "You like it rough. Just a little bit of pain and tension. Too much and you'll go cold, but just right and it will make you drip onto my cock, like you're doing now."

Embarrassment warred with desire and her inner slut won this round. She arched her butt into his hand, wishing he'd slide his fingers from her ass to her pussy. Fuck, she was like a cat in heat around him. They'd been together all of one day and she'd had sex with him five—no, wait, six times? He must be dehydrated. Then he pressed his thumb against her anus and she froze, grateful for any touch at this point, even if it wasn't quite where she wanted it.

Her body hummed with energy and she bent down to kiss him, then jerked up when she realized the sound was growing louder. Ivan muttered something in Russian, then moved quickly out of the bag. He threw his underwear and pants on, then tossed her his shirt.

"Put this on. We're about to be rescued."

Chapter

Gia held Ivan's hand as they walked back into the house and she groaned inwardly as she saw the assembly of people waiting for them in the main hall of the mansion. It was past three in the morning, so she was pretty sure they hadn't walked in on a late night party. Sure enough, the distinct smell of coffee filled the air, and she saw a submissive serving sandwiches to a very subdued group.

To her embarrassment, her stomach rumbled and Ivan looked down at her. "You need to eat."

One of the men, a little bit older but still very fit, strode up to Ivan with barely contained fury. "I will speak with you in a moment."

It surprised her that he'd spoken English in front of her, but what he said next shocked her.

Turning to her, his expression gentled and he took a deep breath and bowed before her. "Ms. Lopez, my name is Kiryl Blum. I'm so terribly sorry for everything you've suffered. If you would like to press charges against Ivan, we will contact the authorities and detain him."

Gia gaped at him, then reached out and clutched Ivan's hand. "No, absolutely not. You can't make me press charges against him. That's not fair. He didn't know I wasn't aware this was a ruse and he was so wonderful to me. Please, it was my mistake, so there is no need to contact the authorities."

Ivan pulled her back against his chest. "Calm down, *dorogaya.*"

Kiryl arched a brow. "Are you sure, Ms. Lopez? Ivan, why don't you release her so she can come stand by me."

"I'm speaking my own mind, thank you very much. Just because he's a Dom doesn't mean I'm his little submissive puppet."

Tilting his head, Kiryl motioned to Gia. "Still, I'd like you to come here. Ivan, release her."

Ivan laughed. "You really don't want me to do that."

Gia pushed at Ivan's arms. "He isn't influencing me! I like him, okay? He's a nice guy, so leave him alone. Can't we just go to bed? Please?"

Her voice broke on the last word and Ivan swept her up into his arms. "You are done questioning her. We are going to bed. Send someone by with a meal for her."

She curved her face against his chest, relieved beyond belief that she could finally go to sleep. Then she felt something scratching her forehead. She reached up and pulled out a pine needle. Groaning, she felt again and found four more.

"What's wrong?" Ivan asked in a soft voice.

"Do I have leaves and shit in my hair?"

"Well, you do have some of the forest with you."

He stopped, lowered her to her feet, then unlocked a door. It opened to her sumptuous suite and she almost wept at the sight of the bed. Fighting a yawn, she darted into the bathroom and answered the call of nature. When she finally looked at her reflection she moaned in acute embarrassment. At some point she must have gotten sap into her hair because she had a lovely almost dreadlock of the sticky stuff on the right side of her head. Various other bits of ferns and things she didn't even want to identify came to light as she turned her head in the mirror.

A shudder of revulsion washed through her and she ripped Ivan's shirt off before running into the shower. She turned it on full blast and got hit with the icy water and let out a high-pitched shriek at the top of her lungs. The water soon warmed enough so she wasn't gasping, and she sighed as heat enveloped her.

"Are you all right?" Ivan asked from right next to her.

She would have jumped if he hadn't held her against him. His erection slid against her skin and she melted in his arms. "Yes. The water was cold at first."

Turning, she reached for his erection, but he stopped her hand. "No. You are exhausted and you will sleep if I have to chain you to the bed."

She pouted, but he picked up the bottle of shampoo. "Turn around and lean your head back."

To her delight, he began to wash her hair, as skilled as any beautician had ever been. He had strong, firm hands and laughed when she sagged against him.

"Close your eyes."

Ivan rinsed her hair with gentle strokes of his fingers. They got stuck here and there, so he squirted out a palm full of conditioner and began to pick the debris out of her hair as gently as he could. He was so careful with her that she couldn't help the surge of intense emotions flooding her. When he was finally finished he washed her body, his slick hands rubbing over her. When he reached her pussy he paused and slowly slid a soapy finger between her labia.

She immediately groaned and tilted her hips. "Ivan."

Laughing, he removed his finger and washed her quickly. “Sorry, *lyubov moya*. I could not resist.”

“What does that mean?”

He turned her to make sure she was totally rinsed, lifting her arms to the water. “It means kind of like your American sweetheart.”

Pleased, she stepped out when he opened the door and let him dry her. After tending to her needs, he wrapped one towel around his waist and used another to dry off his back and chest while she twisted her hair up in a towel. She felt clean all over, except for her mouth.

“Do you have an extra toothbrush?”

“Why don’t you wait until after we eat? If my nose is right they brought us some Truffle *Shchi*.”

“What’s that?”

He walked into their bedroom and she followed, then stopped with a gasp. A lovely table service for two had been set up with beautiful china, a vase of flowers, and a rolling cart with covered silver trays on it. She’d expected a sandwich, not this amazing presentation.

He opened one of the covers and smiled, revealing two porcelain bowls.

“We travel with our own chefs. That way we know there will always be food we like and we don’t have to worry about going out to eat if we don’t want to. This is a traditional Russian soup. It has pork, truffles, and lots of delicious cabbage.”

She grinned. “Delicious cabbage, huh?”

He gave her a puzzled look and set the bowl before her. “You don’t like cabbage?”

The soup certainly smelled good and she picked up her spoon. “We never really ate it when I was growing up. If it didn’t come from a box or you could microwave it, my mom didn’t want to cook it.”

She took a sip of the soup and smiled. It was good, really good. Her appetite roared to life, and before she knew it, she was scraping the bottom of the bowl.

Watching her, Ivan took a bite then said, “Your mother did not like to cook?”

Weariness dragged at her and it became a race to see if she would finish her soup or fall asleep in it first. “After my dad died when I was eight, my mom slipped into a deep depression…except no one called it that. They said my mother had a broken heart that had never healed. She loved my father so much a part of her died with him. I think she was actually happy when that guy shot her, knowing she’d be with my father soon.”

“What happened?”

Bad memories assailed her and her stomach cramped up. “Look, I don’t want to talk about it. Just drop the subject, please. I’m really tired, Ivan, and I can’t take much more tonight.”

“I am sorry. I did not mean to add a further burden to you.”

“No, it’s okay. I’m not ashamed of my family or my past. I just don’t like to talk about the bad stuff. My mom loved me, I know she did, and she tried the best she could to raise me. She was a good woman and she always did her best to keep me and the other kids in our neighborhood safe from the drug dealers and gang bangers. My mother was broken, but fearless.” Her voice choked up at the end and she set her spoon down.

He watched her with such understanding that tears welled in her eyes. With a sniff, she sat back, but as soon as he opened the next set of lids, her mouth watered. Cuts of what she assumed were beef floated in a rich brown gravy, accompanied by some potatoes seasoned with what smelled like delicious roasted garlic, and there was a fancy sprig of vegetables tied to look like flowers on top.

Her appetite returned with a vengeance and she dug in, only sparing a moment now and then to tell Ivan how good this was. After filling the hole in her stomach, she sat back and sighed. Ivan watched her with amusement, and she narrowed her eyes at him.

"What are you laughing about?"

"You eat like you do everything else, with zest."

"Is that an insult?"

"No." He pushed back from the table and came over to her. Bending down, he swept her out of her seat and gently placed her on the bed. He began to kiss his way down her cheek to her neck. "You fascinate me. Being next to you makes life seem…brighter? I don't know the right English word."

With a sigh, she stretched out and curved into his kisses. "You make me feel brighter."

She yawned and Ivan smiled down at her. "Let's get you comfortable."

Soon she found herself naked beneath the sheets, watching the sunrise through the windows. Pink and gold frosted the horizon while the most beautiful blue began to inch into the darkness. It was pretty now, but she didn't want the sun in her eyes in an hour. She planned to sleep for at least the next two days. When she moved to go shut the curtains Ivan pulled her back against him. "So eager to run from me again?"

She rolled her eyes. "No, I just wanted to close the curtains."

"Allow me." He grabbed a small remote off the side table and pressed a couple buttons. The curtains closed and the lights turned off. The bed shifted as he put the remote back and she rolled closer to him. When he leaned back he gathered her against him with a very content sigh and pulled her closer until her head rested on his heavily muscled chest. The thump of his heart was deep and reassuring beneath her ear, as was the movement of his breath. Soon she found herself breathing the same time he did and when he began to gently stroke her hair she couldn't remember the last time she'd felt this loved.

Chapter

Gia stretched out in bed with a low groan and tried to remember what she'd done to make her legs so stiff. One of her feet touched something warm and solid beneath the covers. Her memories came back in a rush, and she turned as slowly as she could to look at the man sleeping next to her. He slept almost spread-eagle, and it amused her to realize not only was he a bed hog, he was also a cover hog. Thankfully, the bed they shared was oversized, or she would have been on the floor.

The need to use the bathroom became a pressing urge and she slowly got out of bed and crept naked through the bedroom suite. A thin sliver of light showed over the top of the curtains, and she wondered what time of day it was. Not that it really mattered. She was going to spend the next five days with one of the most amazing men she'd ever met and come out of it forty-two thousand dollars richer. That thought stopped her after she flipped on the bathroom light. The money wasn't as appealing as it had once been when she realized she would have to leave at the end of those five days.

In an effort to distract herself from that disturbing thought, she decided to rinse off in the shower. One of the main things Mistress Viola had impressed upon Gia was to always be fresh and appealing for her Master. And what a Master he was.

Just thinking about Ivan sent a rush of heat through her body. She actually giggled when she realized she didn't have to go to her trusty vibrator for relief. Something much, much better waited in the bedroom for her. While brushing her teeth with a new toothbrush she found in the vanity, she thought about how worried Ivan had been last night when he found her. Her heart beat a little harder as she thought about how he'd almost missed her curled up beneath the trees. Staring into the mirror, she remembered how close she'd come to dying.

Goosebumps erupted on her arms and she quickly spit then rinsed her mouth. No, she wasn't going to think of how badly everything could have ended. She was here, she was alive, and she owed her rescuer a big thank you. Fortunately, she had a pretty good idea about what he would enjoy.

She made her way across the dimly lit room and gently climbed back into bed. Ivan had rolled over with his big arms spread out on either side of him. As her eyes adjusted to the dim lighting, she took her time admiring his physique. He was a big man all over. Biting her lower lip, she tugged down the blanket so his hips and cock were slowly revealed. He shifted and grumbled something, and his breathing evened out again. Licking her lips, she bent down and took his soft cock into her mouth. Even when he wasn't aroused, he was a big boy and more than a mouthful.

Knowing there was no way in hell she'd be able to deep throat him all the way when he was hard, she took the time now to fit as much of him as she could in her mouth. His shaft began to fill with blood and she started to slowly bob her head up and down his length, taking her time and keeping her movements leisurely. He became too large to comfortably fit down her throat, so she gripped his shaft with her free hand, using the other to balance as she knelt next to him.

As she licked the little notch beneath the head of his dick, he stirred against her, those amazing stomach muscles of his shifting beneath his lightly furred skin. Unable to resist the temptation, she lightly touched his hipbone, then followed the tendon line that swept down to his pubic area in such a provocative way. The smooth skin of his balls felt delicious beneath her teasing fingertips. Ivan was such a big, masculine guy and she loved it.

He suddenly grabbed the back of her head and forced her mouth down onto his shaft. "Good morning, Gia."

She struggled to take him, to open her throat, but he was too much. When she gagged he slightly let up the pressure on her head. Shifting, he spread his legs and rocked his hips into her mouth. She jerked in time with her sucks and soon he was sitting up on his elbows to watch her. He smoothed her hair back from her face so he could get a better view and growled low in his throat.

That primal, delicious sound only made her work harder for him. She began to rub and twist her wrist as she stroked him, then leaned down to lick his balls. Taking one soft globe into her mouth at a time, she delicately tongued him as she'd been taught. One nice thing about having trained with an experienced Dom and Domme was she knew how to please men and women. The knowledge she'd gained gave her new self-confidence about sex, and as Ivan continued to make his lusty noises, pride surged through her.

Her own pussy was wet and swollen, aching to be filled. With a soft moan, she returned to licking his shaft and wiggled her bottom before moving a bit so she had her ass in the air, silently begging for his touch.

He gave a choked laugh as she attempted to deep throat him again. "Do you want me to touch you, *krasavitsa*?"

She loved it when he spoke Russian to her, even if she had no idea what he meant. He sat up a little more and reached forward, caressing the curve of her ass with his fingertips. The light, teasing way he touched her drove her crazy, and she redoubled her efforts to make him come. Her breasts shook as she moved her head quickly up and down his length while jerking the base of his shaft with a corkscrewing motion that had never failed to make her trainer, Master Mark, come.

Ivan slapped her ass, the loud sound as startling as the flash of heat. "I'm going to come. When I do, I want you to rub your face all over my cock. I want you to cover your pretty lips and cheeks with me."

The tight way he spoke let her know how close he was. She pulled back so the tip of her tongue lashed the swollen head of his shaft. He reached down and closed his hand over hers, jerking himself much harder than she'd been. His cock swelled and she moaned in delight as he trembled with the first explosion of his seed against her lips. Quickly turning her cheek, she rubbed his jerking dick against her face, spreading his essence around as he demanded.

He gathered her hair off her neck and gripped it in his fist hard enough so her scalp stung. In her needy state, feeling deliciously proud of being marked with his seed, the pain was just the right intensity to make her pliant in his grasp. He pulled her closer to him and with gentle, careful strokes licked himself off her cheeks. She fairly shook apart at the raw carnality of the act, of the way he was so soft with his mouth but so punishing with his grip in her hair.

Without releasing his grasp, he moved them so he stood next to the bed while she was parallel to him on the mattress. "On your hands and knees, ass in the air."

She did as he asked, yelping when he gave her ass a good swat. "Yes, Master."

“I said, ass in the air.” He pushed her lower back until she’d arched as much as she could, exposing the wet folds of her pussy to the cool air.

He gave what she could only describe as an evil laugh. “You like being told what to do, don’t you, my Gia?”

Cheeks flushing, she nodded. “Yes, Master.”

He adjusted his grip on her hair and turned her head so his lips were at her ear. In a soft voice he whispered, “I must admit, I enjoy it as well. I love knowing it makes you hot.”

Abruptly he stood and slid one long, calloused finger between the lips of her sex, making her wiggle against him. He slapped her ass hard. “Stay still.

She whimpered and tried to keep from giving into the natural urge to wiggle, to do something with all the intense sexual energy he was building in her. To her shock he raked his fingernails down her back hard enough that she wondered if he’d drawn blood. Her scream filled the room and her Master laughed at her misery.

“There. Now anyone who looks at you will know you are mine.”

She shuddered when he leaned over and began to gently lick the fiery paths he’d created on her skin. With his free hand, he began to thumb her clit, and she quickly lost herself in him. Warmth, need, and bright sparks of pain danced along her nerves. He finally released her hair, making her scream yet again at the sharp burst of pain. She’d never experienced this much discomfort during sex before. She moaned when Ivan moved behind her and spread her ass so he could have better access to her pussy.

“Does my little slut want me to lick her?”

She nodded emphatically while forcing herself to stay still. Normally, if someone called her a slut she’d be kicking their butt, but she could tell by the way Ivan said it he wasn’t being offensive. He was deep in the moment and his tone was in no way negative or mean. If anything he sounded very tender when he called her a slut, almost like a beloved pet name. Plus, she secretly liked the dirty little thrill of admitting she was his slut.

"I didn't hear you." He gave one ass cheek a hard bite.

"Please, Master, lick my pussy."

His hand cracked on her ass again, right on the area he'd bitten her. "Beg harder."

"Please, Master, please lick my pussy."

Another slap, this time to the other cheek. "Not good enough."

"Oh, fuck." She sucked in a deep breath as his talented tongue licked over the areas he'd spanked and abused. Need burned inside of her and she was pretty sure if she pressed her thighs together she would come. "Please fuck me, lick me, do something. Please!"

"Better."

When he latched his mouth on her pussy a hard shudder ripped through her body, making her arms collapse. The position opened her further to him and he made a greedy, almost growling noise against her sensitive flesh. Her muscles tensed and she whined as he only gave her clit a teasing stroke with his tongue. Then he started to lick at the entrance to her body and she groaned.

"Please," she whispered as she clutched at the blankets.

He held her open wider, no doubt getting a close-up view of every inch of her pussy and ass. His devil blessed tongue continued to tease the swollen nub of her clit until she was panting and biting the sheets. She wanted to come so bad, but he wasn't working her like she needed. Instead, he kept his touch soft, driving her higher and higher until she wasn't sure if she wouldn't stroke out. Her mind began to shut down, to focus only on the sensations of his touch, of his scent in the air, of how badly she wanted him.

When he pulled back she made a pleading whisper, then moaned as he cupped her whole sex in his hand. "This is my pussy. Say it."

“This is your pussy, Master.” Her words came out choked and she was surprised she could say them at all.

“Good.”

He stepped off the bed and she let out a small whimper, hoping he would finally finish her off. To her dismay, he walked across the room and pulled the curtains open. Standing in the bright sunlight, he stretched out, the muscles of his back art in motion. Her gaze traveled down to his tight ass and powerful thighs. He continued to look out the window and she made a little noise, hoping to draw his attention back to her.

“I know you’re there, Gia, and I know you’re suffering.” She was pretty sure she heard laughter in his voice. “Unfortunately, you won’t get any relief for a long time.”

“Why?” Her voice broke and she had actual tears filling her eyes.

“Because you did not ask for my permission before you sucked me off. I’m not in the habit of rewarding bad behavior.”

He turned, giving her his profile, which included his big, very hard cock—the perfect antidote to her needs. If he would just sheathe himself in her for a moment she would come all over his length. Her pussy clenched and unclenched, aching for some stimulation. He was so in control of the moment, and she wanted to please him with a desperation bordering on madness. Part of her, the part pissed off he wasn’t giving her an orgasm, insisted she argue the point with him, but the part that had been trained to submit knew better than to try and plead her case.

“Yes, Sir.”

He smiled, letting her know he could hear how irritated she was.

A knock came from the door and he scowled before picking up his pants and jerking them on. Getting his rampant erection to fit in them had her biting her lip. He met her gaze and the heat she saw in his eyes had her arousal dripping down her inner thighs.

She started to move and he snapped at her. “Stay there.”

“Stop! They’ll see me.”

He stalked across the room to her, giving her ass a brisk slap, then pulling her thighs further apart until her pussy was exposed in an almost obscene fashion. “Whose pussy is it?”

“Your pussy, Master.”

“That’s right. And if I want to show it off, I will. It is a beautiful, wet, swollen pussy. Everyone who sees you will know how aroused you are, how needy. It will make them not only aroused as well, but also envious that I have such a beautiful girl.”

She had no idea how she could be both embarrassed and proud, but she was.

“Put your face into the pillows, Gia. I do not want you to look no matter what happens.”

Confused, but eager to please, she did as he asked, arranging the pillows so she could hide her face, but still breathe.

A man’s voice, sounding vaguely familiar and speaking in Russian, filled the room, his tone obviously teasing. The strange man’s words cut off abruptly, and when the man at the door spoke next, there was a growl to his tone that was decidedly carnal in nature. Ivan replied and she wondered what the hell they were saying. A moment later, Ivan’s familiar hand touched her back, moving her around so he could shove pillows beneath her hips. Once she was arranged to his liking, he began to run his finger up and down her slit, easily gliding through her wetness.

She was glad the pillow stifled her loud moans.

Both men chuckled, and the hand playing with her pussy pulled her vaginal lips apart, showing the hard bud of her clit. Being so fully exposed to a stranger she couldn’t see made her sex clench, and the men laughed again. They exchanged words, again in Russian, and suddenly a face was pressed between her thighs—a face with a scratchy beard.

She startled, but Ivan pressed his hand down on her shoulder blades, easily pinning her. "You will not come, do you understand me, Gia?"

All she could do was frantically nod her head as the strange man lapped at her pussy like an ice cream cone. Big, long strokes that had her rocking against his face. Someone began to put their thumb into her pussy and she immediately clamped down on it, keening as her orgasm rushed toward her. She tried to hold back, tried to keep from going over, but it was an immense struggle.

The delicious, wonderful, torturous mouth on her pussy pulled away and she wailed in despair. The men laughed again and she gritted her teeth. Someone patted her bottom, then traced their fingertip around the pucker of her anus. Ivan said something in a low voice and she knew it was him when he gripped her ass. No one's hands fit her body quite the way Ivan's did.

The other man sighed and said something. A few moments later, the click of the door opening and closing made her startle. She was shivering, overwhelmed with need. Before this moment she would've never thought one of the greatest tortures she could experience was being denied an orgasm, but it was. She'd do anything at all for her Master to give her some relief.

The bed dipped as Ivan sat and pulled her onto his lap. She clung to him, rubbing her face against his chest as her whole body squirmed against him. A frantic need came over her and she began to lick and suck at one of his nipples, grinding her ass against his hard cock. If he would fuck her, make her come, make her break, she'd be able to think again. Right now, all her ability to think and reason focused on her need to have him inside of her.

"Easy, baby." He held her close and stroked her until her shivers ceased. "You are doing so well. I'm so proud of you."

To her dismay, she began to cry. It was the only outlet for her frustration, and he made soothing noises, rocking her as she wept. When her tears tapered off to sniffles, he gripped her chin and inspected her face. “You kill me when you look up at me with those big brown eyes of yours, Gia.”

“Please, I need to come so badly.”

Running his finger over her lower lip, he gave her a small smile. “I know.”

She clenched her teeth to keep from saying something very unflattering about his mother. He must have seen her ire because his grin grew bigger. “You know, when you look at me like that it makes me even harder. I like a little bit of defiance. Maybe if you're a good girl I'll let you try to wrestle me.”

“Maybe I'll go in the bathroom and finish myself off,” she countered.

His gaze grew dark and she swallowed. “Do I have to put you in a chastity belt? Parade you around wearing only it so people can see how little self-control you have?”

“No,” she said with a rather unflattering squeak to her voice.

“Good.” He moved her off his lap and onto the bed and gestured to the dresser. “Ilyena and Catrin donated some clothes for you to wear until I can take you shopping.”

She bit her lower lip, still pissy from being denied. “Who was that man?”

“Why? Do you want to know who I let lick that hot, wet cunt of yours?”

Flushing, she looked at the floor.

“I'm not going to tell you. I want you to look at every Master in this house and wonder which one offered me one hundred thousand dollars to fuck you.”

She gasped. “What?”

He sorted through the pile of clothes. "I told him no. I'm the only one who gets to fuck you."

"He tried to buy me?"

Ivan shrugged. "You sold your sexual favors for money at the auction, so he assumed you were a professional prostitute, a, what do you Americans call them, an escort."

The blasé way he said that sent a jagged shard of pain through her, and she suddenly wondered if he saw her as no more than a prostitute. His cell phone rang and he dug it out of his pocket. Without looking at her, he answered it and strode over to the other side of the room, speaking in Russian again. She dashed away the tears falling down her cheeks, unbelievably hurt by his statement. She thought he cared about her.

Without even looking, she grabbed the soft gold cotton halter dress he'd selected for her and stomped off to the bathroom, glaring at him. Ivan was oblivious, his expression stern as he spoke rapidly into his cell phone. She managed to stifle her tears until she had the door closed behind her, then she sank to the cool tile floor and cried. Stupid, stupid, stupid. She'd been warned not to become too attached to whoever bought her, but dammit she thought they had something together.

Obviously, she was wrong. It suddenly made sense to her why Ivan liked to share her so much. He wasn't attached to her. To him she was only an object, a warm body to be used as he saw fit. She suddenly felt dirty and didn't want to be here, at all. If it weren't for the money going to the shelter, she would have walked out the door and demanded someone get her the fuck out of here.

Her crying was interrupted by Ivan knocking on the door. "Are you all right?"

"Yes, just trying to get myself together. I'll be out in a moment."

No, she wasn't going to let him see her crying like some stupid, naive little girl. She hated crying, hated how weak it made her feel, and most of all hated that she'd let him get close enough to hurt her like this. The need to shore her defenses back up pushed away her pain for the moment and she concentrated on at least looking like she was okay.

He didn't answer and she was afraid he'd break the door down to come in, somehow sensing her unhappiness. To both her dismay and relief, he didn't and she began to question how good of a Dom he was. She knew plenty of decent Masters from her club back home and had always admired how they seemed to know every facet of their submissives' needs. Obviously Ivan didn't know her that well, and she didn't know him at all. She wondered if he'd been with escorts and suddenly wished with all her might she'd made him wear a condom. Then she remembered the rigorous health tests that all auction participants had to go through and calmed down.

Okay, so at least she was physically safe. She had to endure five more days with him and she'd be done. Maybe she should look at this like he was. Just sex. She would keep her emotions out of it and be his submissive, but she would never let him get near her heart like this again.

Chapter

Ivan looked across the dining room table to where Gia sat next to Nico and his submissive, Catrin. With over thirty people in residence, all the meals were casual affairs served buffet style in the solarium. Two large tables seating sixteen each had been brought in, and every seat was filled. Gia had barely touched her breakfast and had been coldly polite to him ever since they left their suite. He stared at her, trying to figure out what was going on. She had real warmth in her gaze when she smiled at Nico, and when she laughed with Catrin he could see her happiness. Then she would look at him and her face would shut down into that polite, cold mask he was starting to despise.

Nico looked over at him and grinned before asking in Russian, "Any reason why your submissive is giving you the cold shoulder?"

Ivan grimaced and jabbed a piece of sausage with his fork. "I have no idea. We were having a great morning, then she turned bitchy for no reason I can think of."

Catrin leaned over and whispered to Gia, which sent her into a fit of giggles. He wanted Gia to laugh like that for him, to look at him with warmth in her expressive eyes. He suddenly realized he was jealous. It was such a foreign emotion to him he wasn't sure how to handle it. He had women throwing themselves at him so often, he never really cared if a relationship went sour.

Then again, he'd never met anyone like Gia.

Nico shook his head. "I don't know what you did, but she is really pissed at you."

With a frown, Ivan sat back in his chair, giving up the pretense of eating. "I was doing some orgasm denial with her this morning, working her up then leaving her with no relief. Do you think she's angry about that?"

Nico shook his head. "I don't think so. She doesn't seem to be frustrated, just pissed."

He tried again to get Gia to talk to him. "Gia, would you like to go to the stables today?"

She turned to him and gave him a blank, cold look. "Whatever you wish, Master."

Several eyebrows were raised around the table from other Dominants and submissives chatting and having breakfast. While they might not understand her words, her 'fuck you' tone came through loud and clear. Real anger burned through him at her disrespect, and he longed to spank her until she lost that cold look, but he'd never, ever touched a submissive while he was really pissed.

Ivan threw his napkin on the table with a low growl. "Fuck this. Nico, look after her. I need to go work out some aggression."

Catrin gave him a sympathetic look that annoyed him even more, and when Gia refused to even give him a glance his temper almost snapped. He stared down the table and saw Pylar, one of his sparring partners. The tall submissive might look sweet with her long, curly dark hair and big blue eyes, but she was quick enough to keep up with him. She should be. Before she'd settled down with her Master, she'd been on the Russian Women's Olympic judo team and had a silver metal to prove it.

"Pylar, want to spar?"

She gave him a wide-eyed look, glancing between him and Gia before nodding. "Sure. Let me go get changed and I'll meet you in the gym."

He walked past Pylar and gave her a kiss on the cheek. "Thank you."

She smiled up at him, then frowned. "Your girl doesn't look very happy with you right now."

"That makes two of us," he muttered and stalked off toward the gym, refusing to look back at Gia and see the unearned anger in her eyes. He'd done nothing to deserve her ire and it really pissed him off that she was throwing such a public snit. Normally, he'd have her face down on the table, blistering her ass, but he didn't want to do anything to scare her after the trauma he'd put her through with the fake kidnapping gone wrong.

Gia watched Ivan stalk away and had to bite her lower lip to keep from crying. Nico stood and removed his plate. "I have something to attend to. Catrin, would you please keep Gia entertained?"

"Of course, Master."

When Catrin and Nico kissed Gia's heart ached in envy and she bit the inside of her cheek until she tasted blood, determined to keep from crying. She hated sitting here, knowing they all thought she was a prostitute. A couple women kept throwing snide looks her way and she wanted to yell at them that she wasn't a whore.

As soon as Nico left the table, Catrin leaned closer. "What's going on with you and Master Ivan? You were practically snarling at him."

With a low sigh, Gia rubbed her face, not sure how much she could trust Catrin. "It's nothing."

"Come on, something is bothering you. I won't tell Ivan, I promise."

The other woman's gaze shone with sincerity and Gia relented, eager to talk with someone about this mess. "Ivan called me a prostitute."

"What!" Everyone in the room looked at them and Catrin's cheeks turned red. "Come here."

Catrin dragged Gia over to the small hallway separating the kitchen from the dining room. The other woman smoothed the skirt of her red dress and gave Gia a stern look, which only made the short, curvy blonde look adorable instead of mean.

"Tell me exactly what Ivan said."

Gia briefly went over what had happened, and by the end of the story, Catrin was shaking her head. "I can't believe he said that."

"Is it true? Does he hire prostitutes?"

"Master Ivan? No, he doesn't need to. Women throw themselves at him."

Gia's stomach clenched again and she gave a stiff nod. "Well, he seems to have made an exception with me."

"I don't understand—"

Movement came from the corner of her eye and Gia turned and watched two big men walk into the hallway, each giving off that shivery vibe that made her bones hum. One was a tall man with a soft red beard, while the other man was a bit shorter, but stocker and had a deep brown beard with red highlights. They both stopped and looked at Catrin and Gia with amusement.

The man with the darker beard grinned at her. "Gia, so nice to see you again."

She blinked, unsure of what to say. He sounded familiar. She tried to think back to when she'd seen him before, and it suddenly dawned on her. He was the man who'd just eaten her pussy. Heat flooded her cheeks and his knowing grin had her stumbling back a step.

"Is she okay?" his friend asked.

"Yes. She's probably remembering me from when we airlifted her out of the woods. I was on the rescue team. It's probably traumatic for her."

Then he gave Gia a wink that could only be described as lecherous and she narrowed her eyes in indignation. Why didn't he scream out that he'd seen her writhing, begging, and moaning like a slut while he worked her over in front of Ivan? Most guys she knew would love to brag about something like that. Especially since he'd done it so well.

With a hard pound, her clit stiffened and desire flooded her. Fucking Ivan had her so primed for sex with his orgasm denial that all a man had to do was wink at her and she got wet. Really wet.

This was such bullshit.

Terribly embarrassed, she turned to Catrin. "It's a little warm in here. Can we go outside?"

Turning, Catrin grabbed Gia's hand and pulled her down the small hallway into the kitchen. A few people milled around, cleaning up from breakfast, but Catrin kept tugging on Gia until they were outside.

Catrin gave her a curious look. "Why was Dimitri making you blush?"

Sure she was going to pass out from the rush of blood to her head, Gia turned and pretended to inspect the ivy growing up the side of the mansion. She wanted to talk about this and needed help sorting her head out. Catrin was a good listener who wouldn't judge her for her personal kinks. At least she hoped not.

"Um, I…Ivan let him do things to me."

Catrin grinned. "Mmmmm, I've had Master Dimitri do things to me. He is very talented in oral sex."

Gia placed her hands on her burning cheeks. "This is so odd. I mean, I've never even seen his face before he said hi in the hallway. Ivan made me put my head in the pillows so I couldn't tell who he was. Only his voice gave him away. That and the fact that he has a beard. Shit…I think he was the man Ivan let eat me out on the helicopter."

"Dimitri was eyeing you like an ice cream sundae on a hot summer day." Catrin fanned herself. "*O bozhe moy*! Ivan was a fool to let him near you. Dimitri wants you and he's used to getting what he wants."

Giving a small snort, Gia looked around to make sure no one could hear them. "Well, he's going to be disappointed."

A bird flew overhead and Catrin turned her face up to the sun. "Ivan must be quite talented in bed for you to say that."

"You haven't had sex with him?"

Giving her a droll look, Catrin shook her head. "No. I know Ivan through Nico and Nico would never share me with his personal friend. We see Ivan in social settings all the time. It would be too weird. You know what I mean?"

"I do know." Gia smiled, relaxing as they laughed. "Your English is excellent."

"It should be. I'm the daughter of the former Russian Ambassador to the United Nations."

"Wow." Gia had to blink a couple times. "What the hell is a woman like you doing here?"

Gia flushed and stuttered an apology that Catrin waved away. "I know what you mean. I should be somewhere serving tea to a bunch of stuffy old women. No thank you. I married my husband because I love him and he is, quite simply, my world."

Envy moved through Gia and she sighed with yearning. “That’s so romantic.”

“Please don’t cry!” Catrin made a distressed noise. "I can’t stand tears.”

“I’m okay.” She sniffed and pulled herself back together. “Is it always like this?”

“What do you mean?”

“I’m not used to all this…excitement.”

“You mean drama? It’s like your American soap operas around here.”

Gia nodded, finding an absurd similarity to how crazy her life had become and the programs she’d watched with her friends when she was a teenager. “Yes. People aren’t like this where I’m from. I’m not a bad person and I’m not a prostitute, but you…all of you are way out of my league.”

“First, no one is in any league, so there isn’t anything for you to be out of. We are all human beings. And no, nobody thinks you’re a prostitute. Almost everyone here was at the auction! If you’re a whore, so are they.”

“Really?”

“Yes, really. Didn’t you notice how almost everyone at breakfast was speaking English? Wouldn’t that be odd in a house full of mainly Russian, German, Polish, and French people?”

“I thought they were being polite,” Gia muttered and looked down at her hands. “Ivan thinks I’m a prostitute.”

“No, he doesn’t.”

“Are you sure?”

“Absolutely.”

Licking her lips, Catrin dropped Gia’s hand and looked away. “Just remember this is only for a week. Ivan will show you the time of your life, but when your time is up he will be on a plane back to Russia without a second glance."

Gia's heart hurt, but she tried to play it off. "Don't worry. I know this is only physical."

"That's the problem. With BDSM it gets to be more than physical pretty quick. If you aren't connected with your Dom in that special way, you'll never get into subspace."

"So what should I do? Have sex, but don't let him top me? Pretend to be submissive? Fake subspace?"

"Goodness, you Americans certainly are…passionate."

Gia took a deep breath and let it out slowly when she realized she'd shouted the last word. "Sorry."

"Apology accepted. Now, you are a big girl who can make her own decisions. This is a once in a lifetime opportunity, so my advice would be to go with it."

"Just go with it?"

"Yes." Catrin reached out and grabbed her hand, giving it a squeeze. "Honestly, usually Ivan is a very nice man. He's not the relationship type, so don't get attached. He'll treat you like a queen, be the Master of your dreams, and still leave you."

Forcing a smile, Gia shook her head. "Don't worry about that. Ivan has quickly cured me of any desires for him other than physical. I'll chalk this up as a learning experience. And thank you for taking the time to talk to me."

"You need to talk to Ivan," Catrin said in a sure voice, a look of resolution coming over her sweet face. "Maybe he misspoke or something was lost in the translation."

"And say what? You think I'm a whore and technically I am?"

"You are not a whore, stop calling yourself that."

Rubbing her eyes, Gia nodded. "I'm sorry. I'm not like this. Usually I'm very calm and rational."

“You’re not in a very calm and rational situation, Gia.” Catrin smiled. “Go, talk to Ivan as a woman. Tell him what is on your mind.”

Guilt and apprehension tightened Gia’s stomach. “I don’t want to fight with him. He paid a lot of money for me.”

Catrin rolled her eyes. “He has more money than God. I’m sure whatever—”

“A little over four hundred thousand dollars. It’s going to the no-kill animal shelter I volunteer at, but still…”

With wide blue eyes, Catrin stared at her. “Wow…that is a lot.”

“I know,” Gia replied miserably.

Catrin got a contemplative look on her pretty face. “No man pays that much for a woman without wanting something more than her pussy.”

Gia snorted. “Right.”

“No, I’m serious. He could have any one or more of a dozen girls who travel with the Masters if he only wanted to have sex.”

“Then why did he kiss that woman at the table?”

“Because she’s his sparring partner. I know Ivan. When something bothers him, he fights.”

Thinking about how tall and slender the other woman had been, how delicate looking, Gia was afraid for her safety. While she didn’t think Ivan would purposely injure the woman, he was so big and strong.

“Is he going to hurt her? I mean, he’s so big and she’s so small.”

“Not likely.” Catrin snorted. “Come on, you need to see this. If you’re mad at Ivan, I think you’ll like watching him get his butt beat by a girl.”

They made their way back through the immense house. Normally, Gia would’ve been staring at everything around her, from the sumptuous furnishings to the exquisite people lounging around. She loved their language, how beautiful it sounded when the women spoke it and how guttural and masculine it sounded when a man said something.

They turned down a hall off the main living room and Catrin stopped. A woman, the same one Ivan had kissed at breakfast, was storming down the hall. She wore a pair of loose gray pants and a tight black tank top. Sweat dripped off her face and she let out a grateful sigh when she saw Catrin and Gia.

"Thank goodness you're here." The other woman's accent was thick, and Gia had to focus to understand what she was saying. "He is so full of anger. We barely started before he had to stop and start beating on some bags. He doesn't want to spar, he wants to fight."

Gia swallowed, knowing she was the source of his bad mood. Ivan had been obviously irritated at breakfast by her refusal to speak with him. He was totally overreacting. Then again, she was probably overreacting a bit as well if what Catrin said was true. Gia's pulse picked up as she looked down the hall and the sudden need to clear the air between her and Ivan flared to life. If he wanted to fight, she'd give him a fight. She didn't have a quick temper, but when she went off, she went off big time.

"Is he still in there?"

"Yes." Gia went to walk past her and the other woman reached out to stop her.

"No, you shouldn't go in."

"Why? He won't hurt me." Gia shook the other woman's hand off.

"I don't want *you* to hurt him. He is wounded. You were so cold to him and he's torturing himself about it. You are selfish."

"Excuse me?"

Catrin said something in Russian, and the other woman spoke fast, with lots of arm movement. After nodding a few times, Catrin turned to Gia. "She couldn't say what she wanted to say in English, so she switched to Russian. Ivan thinks he's hurt you, physically, and that he doesn't remember doing it. He fears he was so into you that he pushed you too far too fast. She is mad at you because she thinks it is selfish to make Ivan suffer instead of talking to him."

"What? No, that's not it at all. Look, Catrin, you tell her what's going on. I need to speak with Ivan. This is ridiculous. What, are we in friggin' high school?"

Both women stared at her, and Gia threw up her arms in disgust. The sooner she talked to Ivan, the sooner she'd let him know exactly how she felt about being called a prostitute. If he didn't like it, tough. She didn't care how much he paid for her, humiliation was a hard limit and she would not let him play games like this with her.

Pushing the door to the gym open, she stalked inside and froze in place as every single hormone in her body trembled with anticipation. The sight of Ivan punching a speed bag, clad only in a loose pair of silky shorts and his shoes, transfixed her. Every single muscle of his body gleamed as he beat the hell out of the bag. His expression was set in a savage snarl, made all the more fierce by the scar twisting his face. Perversely enough, that turned her on. She *liked* that he was scary.

The twist and turn of his torso made her weak in the knees. She swore she could smell his sweat in the air, and it made her nipples hard and achy. She longed to slide her hand between her legs while she watched him, to make herself orgasm while he destroyed that bag. He must have been in his own world because it took him a moment to notice she was there.

He stepped back from the bag and rocked back on his heels, stretching out his thick calf muscles. She wanted to grab his legs and bite his big, heavy thighs, to run her tongue along the tempting ridges of his abdominal muscles and basically devour him. Sweat dripped down his face and he grabbed a towel, the tape on his hands bright against his skin. “Hello, Gia.”

She blinked and tried to steady herself. The way he said her name made her feel like he’d just had his hand between her legs. Angry with herself for losing her mind around Ivan, she forced herself to spit out why she was here. “I. Am. Not. A whore.”

Chapter

Ivan stared at the woman he'd been obsessing about, pretty sure either she was insane or he was. "Excuse me?"

Her hands trembled with anger, but her nipples were rock hard as well. He'd blame that on an adrenaline rush, but she also kept checking him out. In fact, his little submissive was practically vibrating with need. The way she rubbed her legs together, no doubt in an effort to soothe her swollen cunt, then bit her lower lip while looking at his dick was like waving a red flag to a bull. She was daring him to take her, obviously needing him to be the aggressor. His Gia liked to pretend she had no control in a situation, and he was oh, so happy to fulfill her needs.

"Speak, girl."

She flushed, but she held her ground. "I'm *not* a prostitute. You said your friend offered you money for me and that I was a prostitute."

"Wait. What?" He blew out a frustrated breath, not understanding what in the hell she was talking about.

Taking another step forward, she fisted her hands at her side and said through clenched teeth. "You called me a prostitute."

"I would never call you that!" His roar was loud enough to wake the dead.

When she flinched in real fear he felt like an asshole. He hadn't meant to shout it, but her accusation really pissed him off. Did she really think he was that big of a bastard? Tears filled her eyes, making him groan. She obviously believed he'd called her that, and it hurt her, deeply.

Grabbing another towel, he continued to wipe himself down before donning his shirt. "Gia, come here."

Angrily dashing away a tear, she shook her head. "No."

Her lower lip trembled and she hugged herself even as she took a half-step toward him. Poor girl. She was so conflicted with her feelings, but he couldn't go easy on her. He could already see her withdrawing from him and retreating back into the icy silence. A mad and talking Gia he could deal with, a cold and silent Gia, he could not.

With a shrug, he said, "Fine."

Less than a second later he lunged after her, and she sidestepped with a small shriek, raising her hands. "Get away from me. I'm not in the mood for any of your spanking nonsense."

"Who said anything about a spanking?"

She licked her lips and he watched her gaze dart all over his body, but with special attention to his dick, which was rapidly filling with blood. "You know what I mean."

"Gia." He put a purr in his voice and had to hide his grin when her beautiful brown eyes grew wide. "I don't want to spank you. I want to fuck you. Hard."

"What!" She darted away from him and put a weighted bag between them. "You stay away. We're having an adult conversation here."

"Are you using your safeword?"

He saw her seriously consider it, then a pretty pink flush colored her cheeks, and she shook her head.

Before she could take a breath he dove at her, easily capturing her in his arms and rolling onto the floor, careful to cushion and protect her body.

"What are you doing?" She smacked his chest. "You will not distract me with sex. Let go of me right now. We are not doing this, do you hear me!"

He growled as she tried to scramble away from him. He knew for a fact she wasn't wearing underwear and he also knew the instant his erection pressed against her clit because she quivered and her pupils dilated. Then she ground her hips against his cock with a pained moan. Clamping his hands on her thighs, he kept her there, slowly shifting his hips until his cock split the lips of her sex. The material of his shorts was so thin it almost felt like they were skin to skin.

And her cunt was so, so hot against him, driving him insane.

"This isn't fair," she whispered as she braced her hands on his chest. "I'm mad at you."

She tilted her hips and was rewarded with a low moan as he increased the pressure of his strokes. Fire still snapped in her eyes, but she was no longer fighting him. No doubt his earlier orgasm denial had left her needy, something he planned to use to his advantage. True, it wasn't fair, but he found himself breaking his own personal rules for this woman who filled him with such need.

"I would never call you a whore, *krasavitsa*."

She began to rock herself against him, and he loved the way her body fit against his. "What does that mean? That word you called me?"

"It means beautiful. I think you are one of the most exquisite women I've ever seen."

Her smile seemed to light her from within, and she opened her eyes, once again filling his soul with warmth. Things were so very complex, and yet simple with Gia. It boiled down to the fact that when she was happy, he was happy. It was as if his emotions were tied to hers, and it felt too good to overanalyze. He simply accepted it and wanted more.

Then the joy dimmed and she looked down at his chest, avoiding eye contact. He didn't like the purposeful way she kept trying to break a connection with him. In an odd way, it hurt him. He'd felt something with her he'd never experienced before, something deeper that awoke the predator in him.

Rolling her off of him, he stood and hauled her to her feet. Her breath sped up, but once he fisted his hand in her silken hair, a little smile hovered around the corners of her sweet lips. He couldn't resist the temptation and turned her head so he could feast on her delicious lips. She softened against him, and as she opened for him, her moan was a sweet victory. She was soon making hungry noises and had a leg thrown up around his hip, grinding her pussy against his dick with sharp little jerks.

He pulled back and studied her, waiting until the moment when she was getting close to orgasming. When he took a step away she groaned and fisted her hands in his shirt like he'd fisted her hair.

"For fuck's sake, Ivan, I need to come!"

He growled, displeased by her outburst. She was being willful and she knew it. Not that he should be surprised. Gia was a high-powered submissive if he'd ever met one. She was the kind of woman who would have to know, without a doubt, that her Master was strong enough to earn her submission. No wonder it had taken two Dominants to train her. Luckily, Ivan liked a challenge and he looked forward to the sweet smile she got when she was drifting deep in subspace.

"On your hands and knees. You will crawl next to me." He waited while she clenched her jaw, no doubt holding back some rather choice words. "Gia..."

She glared at him, then looked away with a trace of guilt. "Yes, Master."

"Ah, you do know my name." He snapped his fingers like he would for a dog, earning a barely choked back growl from her.

Fighting a smile because she could see him in the mirrors surrounding the workout area, he led them across the room to the small weight lifting section. After a quick glance around, he found a couple of exercise bands that would work for what he had in mind. He wished he had some clothespins to try out on her, but then something much better suited for his little fighter came to mind. When anyone saw her body for the next few days they'd know to whom she belonged.

He would worry later about the power this small woman had over him. Right now he had a very aroused, very needy submissive begging for his touch.

She shifted restlessly next to him, and he ran his hand through her golden brown hair. He needed to seduce her, to make her as entranced with him as he was with her. Most of all, he wanted to make her happy. For Gia, happiness in the bedroom came in the form of submission.

An idea came to him, something that, as soon as he thought of it, he knew would be perfect for his girl in her current state of mind. She wanted an orgasm and he was going to give it to her, but not in the way she was expecting. "Gia, on the other side of the room are the locker rooms. Go into the women's and empty your bladder as much as you can."

Her cheeks turned so red it was almost comical, then she stood and sprinted into the locker room. Chuckling, he surveyed the equipment and tried to decide what he wanted to use. A few moments later the door to the women's locker room squeaked as Gia came out, looking at the floor. She started to walk toward him, stopped and went gracefully to her knees. The way her body moved as she crawled the rest of the way had him ready to chew nails. Without a bra, her breasts wobbled with her movements and the skirt was short enough that he got a glimpse of the wet almond shape of her pussy in the mirror behind her. It took every ounce of his self-control not to give into the almost overwhelming demand of his body to fuck her until she realized to whom she belonged.

He went over to the inner thigh muscle machine. The seat was situated so her legs would be spread wide open, one in each leg rest. In order to close her legs she'd have to lift the weights. He planned on making sure it was too heavy for her to lift.

"Up you go."

She hesitated then stood and sat, blushing furiously as she put her legs on the padded surface and placed her feet on the foot rests. Tugging her dress down, she tried to hide her sex from his view, but the wide open position didn't allow for that. Twice her mouth opened like she wanted to protest, but so far she'd managed to keep her composure. He'd let her have her false sense of security now, because he was about to give her as many orgasms as she could take.

He went back to the punching bag area and grabbed his large bottle of water. When he returned to Gia he handed it to her. "Drink."

Giving him an unsure look, she did as he asked, then handed the bottle back him.

"What is your safeword?"

"Damascus."

"Use it only if you need to. I'm going to give you so much pleasure you'll scream, begging me to stop. But I will not stop until you safeword out or I am satisfied. Do you understand?"

She nodded, her eyes wide as she watched him. After raising the weights on the machines to the point where she wouldn't be able to lift them, he began to bind her to the piece of exercise equipment with the elastic exercise bands. Legs first, one on each ankle and one on each thigh. He checked the fit, making her move so he could be sure she wouldn't be hurt. Then he tied a band around her stomach and the backrest of the chair. He debated for a moment tying her arms up as well, but she would need to hold on to him or the handgrips on the chair at some point if he did his job right.

Through it all, Gia watched him, but didn't say anything. He liked the way her breathing sped and how her nipples grew into hard points beneath the thin material of her dress. Taking a deep breath, he tasted her arousal in the air and smiled. The little bit of cloth from the bottom of her skirt still covered her sex, but he could see how her inner thighs were slick with her arousal.

After stripping off his shirt, he gathered up a mound of folded white towels, then returned to her side and placed them beneath her.

"What are you doing?" He gave her a cold look and she quickly added, "Master."

"You earned yourself another orgasm."

She blinked at him. "Is that a punishment, Master?"

Tracing his fingers up the insides of her deliciously muscled thighs, he nodded. "Yes, it is, *milaya moya.*"

"What does that mean, Master?"

He crouched between her thighs and leaned over, placing a line of gentle kisses along her neck. "It means 'my sweet'."

The way she relaxed beneath his touch warmed his heart. "Thank you, Master. I think you're sweet too."

He laughed against the sensitive skin where the neck and shoulder meet. "Mmmmm, I'll have to work on being a little more frightening with you, yes?"

She shook her head vigorously. "No, you're plenty scary, Master."

He rolled her skirt up so her mound was exposed. Spread open like this, her pussy made his mouth water. Cupping her sex, he whispered against her lips, "Whose pussy is this?"

She swallowed hard and her breath came out in a burst against his mouth. "Your pussy, Master."

"That's right." He rubbed her sex and loved the way she shuddered. "Have you ever experienced female ejaculation, my Gia?"

"What is that?"

"It is what you Americans call squirting, I think."

Her breath froze, then picked up again. "No, Master. There is a woman at my club who likes it, but I've never..."

"You've never what?"

"I've never trusted someone enough to do it to me. Some guys have tried, but it didn't work."

She tried to turn her head from his, but he gripped her chin and made her stay where she was, with their lips almost touching, breathing each other's air.

"It didn't work because you didn't trust them." He grinned, then nipped her lower lip. "We will not have that problem."

She stiffened. "I'll try, I promise I will, but please don't be mad if I can't."

"We will also not have that problem. There is something between us that makes our connection the strongest I've ever experienced as a Master. Do you not feel it?"

She slowly nodded, their lips barely touching but feeling better to Ivan than some blowjobs he'd received. "Yes."

“Then you will obey me, trust me, and I will tear you apart from the inside out until you are nothing but pleasure.”

“I don’t want to disappoint you if I can’t orgasm that way.”

“*Milaya moya*, if your body is not ready for it, I will not blame you. But if I see you fighting your release, I’ll be forced to go hard on you.” He pulled back enough to see her expression, intent on her reaction to his next words. “You don’t want that, Gia. I don’t think you can handle me full force yet.”

Her pupils dilated and she arched her back, silently offering herself to him even if she wasn’t consciously aware of it. He’d found that sometimes a submissive’s body reacted to what a woman truly wanted, even if her mind was fighting the idea. Evidently the idea of Ivan taking greater control aroused her. He wanted to remind her again about her safeword, but she was beginning to sink into subspace and he didn’t want to disturb that.

Having her mind and body focused on her pleasure would only make this more intense for her, and he wanted to be the best Master she’d ever had.

Reaching between them, he began to rub his finger up and down her slit, spreading her moisture, making her moan. She pulled against the restraints, but they held. When he began to stroke her clit with his thumb her shudder made him grin. She smiled weakly back, then closed her eyes and moaned as he rubbed that sensitive nub a little harder.

“When I say bear down, I want you to push out like you are urinating. If you’ve seen a woman climax from a G-spot orgasm before, you know it will merely be sugar water leaving you. A very sweet, delicious nectar I will love to clean off your swollen little pussy with my tongue.”

Bucking beneath his hand, she tried to get him to play harder as she moaned. Her eyes were closed and a lovely red flush spread over her chest. He leaned forward and took one of her nipples into his mouth, playing with the piercing through the cloth. Her pussy clenched beneath his hand and he gave her nipple a sharp nip, earning a shout then a moan as he slid his middle finger and ring finger into her waiting sheath.

He moved over to kiss the side of her breast, rousing her skin, flicking her clit with his thumb. She whimpered and he picked the spot for his first mark. No one would look at her body without knowing that she belonged to someone. He untied then tugged down the halter straps of her dress, bearing her pert little tits. After licking the stiff bud of her nipple, he kissed his way to the top curve of her breast. While he did this he began to massage her clit between two of his fingers. Then, after selecting the perfect spot for his brand, he bit her hard enough to leave a mark that would bruise up nicely.

The guttural sound she made and the way her legs stiffened let him know how aroused she was. Without removing his fingers, he moved around so he was standing next to her. While he wouldn't mind her squirting on him, he found it fucking hot as hell to watch. His cock was an iron bar in his pants, and he would be shoving it into her eager little mouth by now, but if she came hard enough, she might bite him on accident.

Instead, he satisfied himself with having her nuzzle against his shaft with her lips and nose through his shorts. The way she rubbed her face against him reminded him of a kitten. His heart grew full and the connection between them deepened. He began to feel inside her slick channel, searching for the slightly rougher skin indicating the position of her G-spot. Inside that spongy mass was a small amount of fluid. If he stimulated her the right way, that spongy mass would fill with fluid until it had to be expelled. At that point, if the woman went with it and did what her body naturally wanted to do, she would orgasm hard.

From what he'd been told, G-spot orgasms were very, very intense. Even better, a woman could have one after another, unlike clitoral orgasms where sometimes a woman was left so sensitive any stimulation became painful. He hoped he'd brought enough towels to clean up the mess he planned to make.

He began stroking that spot inside of her wet pussy with a hard, fast tapping motion. This wasn't a gentle caress. This was finger fucking his woman into submission. Soon enough, she began to twist and moan, crying out and clutching at his shorts with one hand and the chair with the other. When she began to grunt and that special spot in her was ready, he quickly removed his hand and said, "Push out, *milaya moya*."

She stiffened for a moment, and he was afraid she might have too much anxiety over the rush of fluid, so he pinched her clit and tugged. She came with a scream and her legs twitched in the restraints as she tried to move and pull away from the sensations. A small amount of clear fluid gushed from her and he reached down to rub his fingers through the warmth. For another good thirty seconds she continued to come as he played with her clit and pussy. Once she'd settled, she looked up at him with an utterly amazed expression.

"Holy crap."

"Again," he said in a firm voice. "Play with your breasts."

Her jaw dropped and she took a deep breath then nodded. She began to pinch and pull at her nipples as he slipped his hand back between her legs and into her eager cunt. Now that he knew what to look for, he swiftly brought her to orgasm. He wanted to rub his cock through the warm, sweet stream, but he wanted her begging him to stop. Something about forcing her to take him, making her come again even if she believed she couldn't, flat out did it for him. Of course, if she safeworded out he'd stop, but up until that point, he would use her trust to take her places she'd never imagined.

After giving her a few moments to recover, he checked her dazed expression and nodded. "Again."

Before she could protest he finger fucked her hard enough to make her breasts shake. She came with a wail, writhing in her bonds and fighting the restraints. He placed his hand on her chest to hold her down because this wasn't really bondage equipment and he didn't want her getting hurt. She clutched his arm with both hands and her little nails dug into his skin as she continued to shake.

She needed time to come down from the last one, so he kissed her long and deep, sucking her tongue into his mouth. The soft, slow way she kissed him back let him know exactly how dazed she was; he loved it, but he wanted more.

His greed for her pleasure knew no bounds.

"Again."

Her moan against his mouth was delicious and his cock throbbed so hard it hurt. "Noooo…"

He let her continue to hold his arm and gritted his teeth as her nails dug into a new section of his skin. As aroused as he was, the pain only added a sharper edge to his pleasure and made him want to exert even more control over her. He leaned down and began to lick slowly at her clit and stroked her G-spot, making her twitch and moan. Her clit was as stiff as he'd ever seen it and it took less than fifteen seconds of fingering her to make her orgasm again. This time he had the pleasure of catching drops of the ejaculate on his tongue as he continued to manipulate her quivering clit.

She wailed and reached down, trying to pull his head from her, but he growled and bit her clit.

Her hands fell away to grab the handles attached to the chair and she began to beg him to stop in little, breathy, broken sentences. His balls were pulled up tight and the taste of her sweet juices had him mad for her. With another growl, he released her clit and stood, quickly toeing off his shoes and socks before stepping out of his shorts and underwear. His cock was so hard it stood past his belly button, a throbbing shaft of need.

His gaze zeroed in on her wet, sweet, swollen pussy and he lunged at her. Crouching between her legs, he placed the head of his cock against her slit. "I'm going to fuck you hard. Hold on to my shoulders."

Sinking into her hot, tight depths was a pleasure like no other. While he invaded her body, she invaded his heart with her soft moans and the way she kept whispering his name. She was beautiful in her submission and the lovely little smile that indicated she was in her subspace curved her lips. He pushed in further and adjusted his angle. There was no way in hell he could resist the feeling of her tight pussy gripping him like a fist. He wanted at least one more orgasm out of her before he had his own climax.

Reaching between them, he began to manipulate her clit and she stiffened. "Too much!"

"No, it's not. This is my pussy, Gia, and I say when it's too much."

She went limp and he had to brace her with his arm as he began to slam his cock into her with enough force that she gasped with every thrust. He slid in and out and his balls drew up tight. At this angle, it wasn't hard to judge where her G-spot was and it wasn't long before he had her gearing up for another orgasm.

"No, no, no, no," she chanted even as her shoulders clutched him closer. "I can't, not again."

He didn't even bother to answer, her body's response easily showing her lie. The way her cunt tightened, then softened along with her almost hysterical cries let him know it was time to pull out. As soon as he did she began to squirt all over his cock, bathing him in wet heat that had him orgasming with a roar. He stroked his dick and it felt so good to shoot his seed all over her pussy. He shoved himself back inside with a growl, and her hands dropped from his shoulders. She moaned and turned her head back and forth, her lower half twitching hard enough in the restraints that the weight lifting machine shook.

As soon as he was able to move without his legs giving out under him, he slipped out of her. He had to grit his teeth at the overwhelming sensation of her slick pussy clutching at his shaft as if she wanted to keep him inside of her. The sounds she made were music to his soul, the whimpers and groans of a well-used submissive. He'd bet right now she'd totally forgiven him for his earlier blunder, and that made his heart lighter.

He didn't like that he'd inadvertently hurt her. He had to remind himself that women, especially submissives, had tender feelings that could be easily bruised. It looked like Gia, despite her naturally aggressive personality, had a very gentle heart. He'd have to make sure to give her lots of praise, although not so much that it lost any meaning, but enough that she would feel cherished…loved even.

He wanted to love her.

Dismissing that notion as an orgasm-induced thought, he freed Gia from her bonds. When he picked her up, she cried out as he gently put her on the ground and began to rub her stiff legs. Her muscles relaxed and she had one arm flung over her head, breathing deep enough that he wondered if she was asleep. Covering her with one of the towels, he quickly set about cleaning up their mess and spraying the equipment down.

When he turned around Gia was watching him with barely open eyes. "You're sexy even when you clean."

Her voice was slightly slurred, like she'd been drinking, and he grinned. He tugged his shorts on and threw the rest of his stuff in the locker room. He lifted Gia into his arms and looked down at her, his heart filled with tenderness for his girl. She reached up and traced his features with her fingertips, leaving a trail of tingles on his skin. The way she looked at him, with such open affection, was utterly addictive.

"You're amazing."

Part of him wanted to make her tattoo his name on her ass, but even he had to admit it might be rushing things…at least for her. He already knew that he wanted to know this captivating woman longer than the one week she belonged to him. His mind spun with ideas of bringing her back to Moscow with him and moving her into his house. While he wasn't foolish enough to rush into marriage, he'd like to see what it was like to live with Gia, to have her presence bring life to his world.

He'd need to call his uncle and have some special arrangements made to get her paperwork done for her visa ASAP. If she decided to come with him, he didn't want her to have the excuse of not having a travel visa for Russia. The thought of coming home to find Gia waiting for him sent a welcome sense of contentment through him. His mind tried to argue that there was no way he'd get Gia to come with him, that he barely knew her, but he didn't care.

The look of trust and devotion in her gaze, the way she made him feel, was something he could not live without.

She was his.

She just didn't know it yet.

He brushed his lips over hers. "Let's go back to our room and get some food and some sleep. We have a big evening ahead of us and I want you well-rested for what I have planned."

Chapter

Gia looked around the enormous bedroom Catrin shared with Nico and tried to keep from staring. The room had been transformed into some kind of couture fantasy store. Right now Gia, Catrin, and Ilyena were trying on different dresses, giggling while the sales associates fawned all over them. There was also a jeweler ready to accessorize any look they picked out. From the way Catrin and Ilyena acted, this was nothing unusual.

They found Gia's astonishment funny.

Ilyena turned slightly and cocked out her hip, looking into the full-length mirror with a fierce smile Gia wished she could copy. Gia's poor sales assistant seemed horrified that she didn't want to look at anything too expensive. The beautiful Russian woman had picked out a floor-length emerald gown that clung to her fantastic body like glittering paint and made her pale blond hair look almost white. While the dress was intensely sexy, it wasn't slutty and was so perfectly made it fit the tall blond woman like a dream.

Catrin had selected a lovely pink gown with a sweetheart neckline and had her honey blond hair done up in curls. The bodice of the dress was tight enough to support her large breasts, but layered with a sheer material in ruffling waves of fabric. The front of the skirt had been cut short, showcasing Catrin's lovely legs, while the back extended out into a subtle train. Gia felt a momentary flash of attraction to the other woman and hoped no one saw her blushing.

"You look fabulous," Catrin said to Ilyena. "Time to look for something sparkly."

They both turned to Gia, who still stood awkwardly in her underwear.

"Where are your clothes?" Ilyena said in surprise.

Catrin frowned. "Didn't you see anything you liked? If they didn't bring the appropriate outfits, I can have another shop come here at a moment's notice."

The sales associate helping Gia made a little whimpering sound and Gia felt guilty. It wasn't her money to spend, but she bet the woman helping her, who really had been kind, could use whatever bonus came from selling gowns worth thousands of dollars. Taking a deep breath, she tried to think of some way to salvage this situation.

"I—I feel weird spending Ivan's money."

Both women stared at her, then laughed until Gia crossed her arms and glared back at them. Even the other saleswomen had to hide their smiles.

Ilyena shook her head, once again turning to look at her reflection. "You've never had a man who likes to spoil you?"

"Well, kind of. But nothing like this." She rubbed her arms, chilled by the memories of some of the total losers she'd dated. More than one guy had 'forgotten' his wallet on a first, and last, date. "This is excessive. He doesn't need to do this."

"Did it ever occur to you that seeing you in beautiful clothes, wearing things Ivan provided for you, appeals to him deeply on some mysterious male level?" Ilyena tried on a necklace made of hammered gold embellished with diamonds. "I know Ivan. He likes you. He will want to see you in something amazing, and I know he will want you to be happy. So stop making this into something it isn't, and let your Master have the right to spoil you."

"However," Catrin added, "if you don't pick something expensive, he will worry you think he is too poor to afford you. Men are odd creatures. If you let them take the protector and provider role every once in a while, it does worlds of good for their ego."

When Catrin put it that way, it sounded so simple. Could Gia really just go with this?

Well, why the hell not.

If this wasn't a once in a lifetime experience, she didn't know what was.

"I'm not sure what to wear. Do you think you could help me pick something out? You're both so exquisite. I trust your judgment."

Catrin and Ilyena turned on her with a gleam in their gaze that was almost scary. Gia took a step back, but they advanced on her so quick she found herself surrounded by their sweet perfume and smooth skin as they touched her and examined her. To her irritation, they spoke in Russian while commenting about one aspect of her body or another. Embarrassment tightened her stomach, and she wished she'd never asked.

Catrin paused and looked at Gia. "Don't be so fearful. We're speaking in Russian because we're excited. Normally, we don't have someone who lets us play dress-up with them."

With a giggle, Ilyena ran her fingers through Gia's hair. "It's true. I've known Catrin since we were ten years old and we've always loved dressing up beautiful women."

Gia swallowed hard, wondering what the heck she'd gotten herself into as Catrin and Ilyena began to rapidly order around the staff.

An hour later, Gia cupped her hand over her mouth to smell her breath. They'd had a snack of meats and cheeses as well as fruit and some small tarts. They'd also split a bottle of really, really good champagne. The alcohol floating through her bloodstream relaxed her enough that she wasn't babbling or making herself sick with worry. Instead, a fine sense of anticipation hummed through her body. She was going to see Ivan, and she had to admit, she looked fabulous.

Ilyena and Catrin were like some kind of super awesome fairy godmothers. They'd put her into an outfit she never would have considered, but now that it was on her, she felt beautiful, sexy, and yet very classy. Having close to five hundred thousand dollars in antique Indian sapphires dripping off her body certainly added to the appeal of the outfit. There was even a jeweled hairpin fastened into her elaborately braided hair. The braid itself curled over one shoulder and sparkling sapphires had been added to the band at the bottom.

The way her hair was styled exposed her back, and for a good reason. The deep blue and silver beaded sari-inspired gown had an exquisite back. Gia may not have had great breasts, but she had to admit she'd never considered how nice her back was. The dress was actually two pieces. The embroidered top had a modest neckline and was tied in the back with a braided tassel at the top and a more intricate series of braided tassels at the middle of her back. The skirt started a few inches later, leaving a bit of her midriff exposed, but not enough so she'd be afraid to sit and have a pooch bulging past the waistband. A clever draping effect had been done to the rear portion of the skirt, and she loved the subtle weight of the train as she walked.

With Catrin on one side and a beaming Ilyena on the other, the women entered the main foyer of the home. Her heart pounded in her throat and Gia forced herself to meet Ivan's gaze, afraid she'd see disappointment. It was an unconventional outfit, but she was an unconventional looking woman, the result of America's great melting pot. She'd never be a classic beauty like Catrin, or a potential supermodel like Ilyena, but Gia had to admit she looked good.

Now she could only hope Ivan approved as well.

It disturbed her how much his approval meant to her, but with the champagne flowing through her system, she didn't dwell on that thought.

She met his gaze and his eyes went wide. It was actually comical, and she couldn't help but grin at him. He looked stunned and as his gaze traveled up and down her body she could see the slow, proud smile curving the edges of his lips. Tonight he wore a deep gray suit that brought out the blue in his amazing eyes. As if he couldn't wait to touch her, he strode across the foyer toward her. The men behind him chuckled, but he ignored them as he reached Gia.

Cupping Gia's cheek, Ivan whispered something in rapid fire Russian. She had no idea what he said, but the way he looked at her made everything south of her belly button contract. He made a pleased sound and brushed his knuckles down the side of her throat.

"You are exquisite. Beyond compare. I am so very proud to have you as my woman tonight."

Her heart lurched at the bitter reminder she wasn't really his woman, just his for these few days. The thought of leaving him hurt, and she tried to get a grip on her emotions, disturbed that he had so much control over her feelings, and very angry at herself for giving so much of her heart to him.

He must have sensed her mood shift because his hold on her face tightened. "My words displeased you? Didn't we have a discussion about you talking with me when you get angry?"

His voice was low, but the power in his words made her nipples hard. Still, he had a point. The memory of the intense series of orgasms he'd given her this afternoon ran through her mind and she shuddered. He smiled and brushed his thumb over her breast.

"Good girl. Now talk to me."

“I was thinking this week seems to be going by quickly.”

The lines around his mouth softened and something in his gaze shifted. It was almost like she could see his mood going from aggressive Dom to caring Master. She loved both sides of him, but right now, she was glad she got the caring Master. Her moods were a little fragile from being tipsy.

“Who says it has to end?” Ivan murmured in a low voice. “I’m open to considering something more permanent after our time here is done.”

She blinked at him, not sure what to say. “That’s…quite an offer.”

Frowning at her, he then sighed. “You are not ready to discuss this. That is fine.”

Nodding, she still felt like she’d somehow hurt his feelings. Not liking the guilt bringing her down, she reached up and cupped his cheek, mirroring his hand on her face. Unlike his possessive grip, her stroke was light and caressing. He gentled beneath her fingertips. She was amazed her touch meant so much to him. Stroking his face seemed to drain the anger out of him.

She looked into his eyes and willed him to see the truth of her words. “I’m flattered, I really am, but I’ve had a bit of champagne and I’m not in a position to discuss anything so serious right now.” She was proud of herself for sounding so mature, but couldn’t help adding, “Think we can sneak a quickie in before we leave for whatever mystery spot you’re taking me to?”

“You are insatiable.” He grinned, all male arrogance. “I like it.”

“Only for you, Ivan. You make me crazy.”

Slipping her hand over his arm, she caught a glimpse of them together as they passed the large mirrors in the foyer. For a moment she froze, unable to believe how good they looked together. In this outfit she hardly recognized herself, but Ivan was as fine as ever. What surprised her was how nice of a couple they made. He turned to see what she'd stopped for and followed her line of sight to their reflection.

"Is something wrong, Gia?"

"No, nothing is wrong." She flushed and tried to move away.

"Gia…"

"I was thinking we look good together."

He put her arm back around his and whispered into her ear, "Yes, we do."

With a lighter heart, she practically floated next to Ivan, then came up short at the sight before her. An army of helicopters filled the vast mowed field next to the house. Brilliant orange and deep purples streaked the clouds overhead, turning the rustic landscape into a fairytale image. Everywhere she looked, men and women in the most beautiful clothes got into the helicopters, laughing and smiling.

There was an energy in the air that made her heart pound, and she looked up at Ivan, needing to ground herself in him. She didn't know this world or how to act in it. He'd have to take care of her, make sure she didn't do anything stupid or shame herself with her lack of sophistication.

"Ivan?"

He smiled down at her. "Yes?"

"Will you…will you make sure I don't do anything to embarrass myself or you, please?"

"What are you talking about? Has someone offended you? Tell me who it is and I will deal with them immediately."

The protective growl in his voice and change in his stance from relaxed to ready to fight made her swallow. This was a powerful and aggressive man. She had to keep that in mind when dealing with him. She swallowed hard as her heart filled with his spirit, warming with his concern until she swore their hearts beat in the same rhythm.

“I meant, I’m not sure of the etiquette of high society. I’m asking if you’ll please make sure I behave in a way that won’t embarrass you.”

His gaze warmed and he swept her up into his arms, carrying her toward one of the waiting helicopters. “Gia, be yourself. You are an amazing woman. Know your own worth. I don’t give a fuck what anyone thinks. To me, you are my Gia and there is nothing you could do that would bring me shame.”

She sighed and wanted to rub her face against his chest, but her makeup had been so expertly done that it felt like a crime to mess it up. People all around them talked in excited voices, and her anticipation returned again. Ivan would take care of her and she knew he’d make sure she had a wonderful time. Happiness bubbled through her veins and she couldn’t think of anywhere she’d rather be tonight than with Ivan.

She found herself in a familiar helicopter and grinned at Ivan as she realized it was probably the one he’d used to kidnap her. He smiled in return and carefully buckled her into the seat next to him. The delicious musk of his cologne teased her senses as she leaned against him. She placed her hand on his thigh and gave him a small squeeze, loving the flex of the muscles beneath her hand.

Seemed like Ivan had awoken her inner nympho.

She couldn’t touch him without wanting him, without needing his big, thick cock deep inside of her. Swallowing hard, she tried to distract herself by examining the couple across from them. The woman was a very slender brunette with her hair in cute ringlets. She wore a daring amethyst velvet dress that flattered her lean figure and exposed the sides of her small breasts. The man Gia assumed was the other woman’s Master smiled at her and ran his knuckles down the woman’s cheek. His love for her was so obvious, Gia’s breath caught in her throat. The pure adoration for each other in their eyes made

Gia slightly uncomfortable, like she was spying on a very private moment.

She moved to shift away from Ivan, but he tightened his arm and whispered into her ear, "They are Margo and Olson, recently married and on their honeymoon. They are also exhibitionists and Margo asked if it was okay if they did a little bit of public play in front of us during our flight. Are you fine with this? If you aren't, I will find a couple to switch with us."

Gia took in a quick breath through her nose and tried to look away from the couple, but couldn't. At her local BDSM club she'd seen lots of crazy, hot, kinky shit, but not a lot of love. The physical exchange between the newly married couple was secondary to the emotional one. They were each other's world and it showed. Gia could practically feel their affection for each other, and when they began to kiss, her arousal went off the charts.

"Hell, it's their honeymoon. Who am I to say no?"

He chuckled and the cabin vibrated slightly as the helicopter geared up for liftoff. "Then just stay next to me and enjoy. Holding you has become one of my favorite pleasures."

Biting her lower lip, Gia tried to tell herself that ripping off these lovely clothes, messing up her perfectly styled hair, and maybe losing a twenty thousand dollar dangling sapphire earing were bad ideas. Unfortunately, at this moment, her libido thought bending over and begging Ivan to fuck her was the best idea she'd had in years, especially when Margo was lowered onto her back along the bench and licked her lips while slowly sliding her dress out of the way, revealing her incredibly toned and slender body. If Gia had to guess, she'd say Margo was a dancer of some sort. Two of Gia's cousins danced for a professional ballet company, and they had the same lean, strong build.

Olson kept his wife's seat belt on, but loosened it enough so she could move. He took off his seat belt and scooted back until he could comfortably lean over her body, a sinful smile hovering over his full lips. Margo lifted her leg and pointed her toe, wiggling her lovely silver high heels near his mouth.

When he began to lick her shoe Margo said in a warm, utterly sensual voice, “Worship me, my handsome bastard.”

Gia suddenly realized this wasn’t a Master and female sub couple but a Domme and male sub couple. Gia perked up and watched with renewed interest. Dommes fascinated her, and she loved to watch a hot guy get naked and aroused. Didn’t matter if this guy was a sub, he was hot. So was she. Memories of Gia’s training with Master Mark and Mistress Viola flashed through her mind, and she barely stifled a groan.

Ivan leaned down and ran his lips over her ear. She shivered and tried to find her voice, but he stole it with one bite on her neck. Even though it took a great deal of effort to keep her eyes open, she did so she could also watch Margo’s husband slowly licking his way up her leg. The man had a very big, very thick tongue. The way he moved it over Margo’s skin made Gia think his Mistress was one lucky bitch.

Ivan’s tongue was currently licking her neck, driving her out of her mind. She wiggled and shifted next to him, the need to touch and be touched making her crazy. She wanted Ivan’s face between her legs, now, but she knew that wasn’t going to happen. He liked to tease her too much. Well, other than that mind-blowing experience he’d given her in the gym. Those orgasms had been so fucking good she’d almost passed out at the end. It felt like she’d smoked a lot of really potent marijuana.

Her after-graduation present to herself had been a brief tour of Europe with the modest amount of money left over from the sale of her childhood home and the store after paying off some of her student loans. One of the places she’d visited during her brief vacation had been Amsterdam. There was no way she was going to miss the opportunity to legally try pot and she’d ended up spending the night with a very, very nice girl from Denmark. It had been the only time she'd ever been with a woman alone, but it had been a lovely experience. Plus, that girl could eat pussy like a fiend. The floaty sensation she'd had while making love to the woman after smoking a joint had been similar to this, but mellower somehow. While she was light-headed, she was also restless with arousal and her senses seemed to have sharpened.

Ivan took her hand in his and placed it over his rock solid cock. "This is what you do to me, Gia. Just tasting you makes my body want you. Keeping my hands off of you is going to be difficult. I want to stroke you until you come apart in my arms, soaking me with your arousal."

"You can touch me," Gia whispered with a soft shudder in her voice.

"Not yet. You'll want to look good for where we're going. There will be cameras."

She blinked up at him, apprehensive enough to be distracted from the sight of Margo's submissive licking the crease between her hip and pussy. The other woman had an almost full bush, trimmed enough to shape her bikini area. It had been a long time since Gia had seen a pussy that didn't have a fully shaved labia and she rather liked the contrast of the dark hair over the pale pink of Margo's sex. Her husband certainly liked it, because when he rubbed his lips over the fluffy down between her legs he moaned.

Gia gave Ivan's cock a squeeze and he bit her neck hard enough to sting. "Behave."

She could only whimper for the next hour or so as she watched Margo come over and over while she had to sit next to Ivan and behave. Her body was so aroused she feared she'd soaked through her panties to her skirt. If Ivan fucked her now, he'd slide right in and she *wanted* him inside of her.

Lights finally began to appear, and she smiled when she recognized the familiar skyline of Boston. Olson helped Margo up, both of them laughing as they tried to straighten each other's clothes. Ivan leaned over and looked out the window. "We've rented the top two floors of this hotel as well as the ballroom. We'll be attending an opera tomorrow night, but if it is all right with you, I'd like to spend the day exploring you in our bed."

She tried to keep the goofy grin off her face, but judging by Ivan's amused look, it didn't work. "I think I'm okay with that."

He laughed and gave her a very gentle kiss. The emotion behind his touch knocked her off her feet and she instantly relaxed. He gave her another soft brush of his lips, making her think of all the ways she wanted his lips on her body, and all the ways he used his mouth to bite, to lick, to suck.

He nipped her lower lip and growled low in his throat. He pulled back and she leaned closer to him, not wanting any distance between them. She craved his touch more than she craved cheesecake, and that was saying something. After studying her gaze, he cupped her cheek gently, his palm barely grazing her skin. He held her like she was precious and it melted her heart.

"I hope you will not hate me, but I've made the decision that I cannot fulfill one of your fantasies."

"What?"

"You had a fantasy of being penetrated by two men at once, but I will not share you like that. I hope you are not too disappointed."

She reached up and cupped his face like he was holding hers. "I don't have that fantasy anymore, nor the one about me sharing you with another woman. I would not like that. At all. Ever."

"What about me sharing you with another woman? I would not touch her. All the attention would be for you."

"Maybe. We'd have to discuss it."

With a soft laugh Margo said something in Russian and Ivan chuckled. “Margo said she would be more than happy to have you service her while her husband and I watch.”

Heat raced to her cheeks and she couldn’t believe she’d almost forgotten she and Ivan weren’t alone. That man got her so horny she literally lost her mind. She didn’t know if that was a good thing.

“Ummm…thank you?”

Margo giggled, the sound surprisingly girly. She said in halting English, “Only if you are comfortable. I want willing, not hesitant.” She looked at Ivan and said something in rapid fire Russian.

“Margo says she only desires someone who wants her just as badly. She likes mutual attraction, not just for show.”

Gia nodded and tried to slow her pulse as they joined what looked like a fleet of helicopters hovering around a tall glass building with a landing pad on the roof. With an expert touch, Margo fixed her makeup and winked at Gia. Grinning back, Gia wondered what Ivan had in store for her tonight.

Three hours later, she found herself in Ivan’s arms, over the moon with happiness. While there was sexual tension in the air, the evening had been a very traditional party. They’d had a delicious seven-course dinner, followed by drinks, and a live band played at the end of the ballroom. The floor-to-ceiling windows revealed the glittering city lights, and Ivan danced like a dream.

He’d seen to her every need all evening, and she had never felt this loved. It sure felt like love to her. She really had no idea what Ivan’s feelings for her were, but she hoped she wasn’t alone in her adoration. He looked at her as though he was seeing who she really was and liked what he saw. It was one of the best things in the entire world. Thoughts of how soon he’d be oceans away from her tried to intrude, but she wouldn’t let them. She felt like Cinderella with the clock ticking down toward midnight, but she was not going to let it fuck up her night with her Prince Charming.

Well, Prince Charming may not quite fit Ivan. He was more like a warlord than some spoiled prince. As attentive and caring as he'd been tonight, there was always the undercurrent of power and control, of a powerful and barely civilized male.

Like the way he was effortlessly leading them in a waltz. She didn't want to leave his arms, but nature was calling after her three glasses of wine with dinner. When the song ended she stepped out of his arms with a sigh.

"I have to take a break for a moment. I'll be right back."

He nodded and smiled. "I'll wait for you over at Catrin's table."

Blowing him a kiss, she hurried across the dance floor and tried to keep from grinning like a fool. When she was in Ivan's arms, letting him lead her across the floor, she felt...cherished. He looked at her like she was the most beautiful woman in the world.

After finishing her business, she inspected her makeup and was happy to find it was relatively intact.

Someone opened the door and a young, dark-haired woman in a maid's uniform came in. She smiled at Gia and walked up next to her with her bucket of cleaning supplies. A couple inches taller than Gia, and with much broader shoulders, the other woman continued to smile at her.

Unnerved, Gia cleared her throat and said, "Good evening."

The other woman suddenly grabbed Gia in a chokehold and whispered in her ear, "What's your safeword?"

"What?"

"Master Ivan wants to know your safeword. The city you went to as a little girl."

"Damascus."

"Ivan said to remind you this is all for your pleasure and you will not be harmed."

"Okay." Her pulse hammered in her throat and she hoped this wasn't really some attempt to kidnap her. Then logic kicked in and she doubted anyone would go to the trouble. Besides, the only thing worth money in this room was the jewelry she was wearing and that could be taken off easier than trying to steal her whole body. Despite her reassurances, her heart still raced and the nasty, metallic taste of fear rolled over her tongue.

The other woman nodded, then tightened her grip on Gia enough that she couldn't move, but could still breathe. "Come with me. Do everything I say and you won't get hurt. Fight me and I'll fight you back."

The melodramatic way the woman said that made Gia want to giggle. Trying to hide her grin, Gia let the big woman haul her out of the bathroom. As soon as they were outside she kicked off her shoes and twisted her hip, sending the other woman crashing to the floor. Unfortunately, Gia's kidnapper held on and Gia found herself quickly flipped over onto her stomach. The woman reached back, then something cold and thin pressed against Gia's neck.

"Don't fuck with me. I'm holding a knife to your throat and I will cut you."

It really did feel like a knife and Gia hesitated, torn between blossoming arousal and fear. She liked knife play, a lot, but she didn't know this woman. It was better to not do anything stupid until she was delivered to Ivan.

"Sorry."

The pressure withdrew and the other woman yanked Gia to her feet. "Move."

Gia was dragged down the hallway and into an elevator without passing anyone. Once inside the small space, the other woman switched her hold on Gia and something hungry glinted in her eyes. "You are a beauty. No wonder he is so enamored with you."

Getting into it, Gia lifted her head at a defiant angle. "You'll never get away with this."

The other woman slammed her against the wall and grabbed Gia's ass, pulling her forward until she felt the unmistakable bulge of a hard dick pressing up against her. Blinking rapidly, Gia came to the stunned realization that this beautiful woman was actually a beautiful man. She had no idea how to respond to this turn of events, but her kidnapper smiled at her. "That's right, Gia, I may be gorgeous, but I have a cock big enough to please any woman."

Arousal lit through Gia at his—or was it her—rough talk. Then again, Ivan had said no other men would get to touch her, so she pushed back. "He'll kill you if you try anything."

Her kidnapper frowned. "I know. Greedy bastard. He isn't usually like this. There must be something special about you. Dimitri says you have the sweetest pussy he's ever tasted. I wonder if you'd enjoy watching me suck your juices off your Master's cock."

They arrived at their floor and all Gia could do was gape at her kidnapper. The maid laughed and grabbed Gia by the back of the neck. "Come along, my naive little captive."

Chapter

Gia was rudely shoved into a dimly lit room and someone grabbed her the second she got through the door. He, at least she thought it was a man by the size of his hands, gently placed a really good blindfold on her. She tried to fight a smile, but that had to be Master Ivan touching her. She could smell his cologne.

"Thank you for bringing her to me, Jessica."

The cross dressing man who'd kidnapped Gia chuckled from somewhere behind her. "I think I might have shocked her."

"What did you say?"

"I told her that since you were being such a stingy bastard with her sweet pussy that I wanted to taste her on your cock."

"Look at her blush." Ivan laughed and she wished she could see so she could stomp on his foot.

"She is lovely, Ivan," a woman's voice said from somewhere to Gia's right. She wondered how many people were in the room with them.

The thought at once excited and embarrassed her. Ivan would be reducing her to a shivering puddle of twitching nerves while others watched. She wondered if they'd become turned on and touch themselves while Ivan dominated her. The idea made her arousal quickly warm to a burning need.

"Margo, help me get her undressed."

A renewed surge of desire had Gia squirming and pressing her thighs together. The beautiful Domme was going to play with her tonight. While Ivan helped. Oh, God, she wasn't going to survive this. They were going to break her and she'd never be the same. Despite the threat to her heart, she couldn't bear the thought of not pleasing her Master or missing out on his touch.

"With pleasure."

Gia shivered as Margo's soft hands slowly untied the stays at the back of her top. With unhurried, lingering caresses, she lowered the shirt off of Gia's arms, leaning around her and nuzzling her mouth against Gia's throat. When Margo bit her Gia groaned, wondering if Ivan was enjoying the view.

Her answer came as his rough hands grasped her breasts. "Whose body is this?"

"Yours, Master."

The words left her in a rush as he continued to knead and shape her now aching breasts. His coarse fingers combined with Margo's soft mouth kissing along Gia's shoulder stroked her exactly the right way. She relaxed between them, accepting their hold, their right to touch her as they wished. They were the Dominants and she was a submissive. Giving over the control to someone she trusted gave her a feeling of relief almost as good as an orgasm.

Margo said something in Russian and Ivan answered back in a low voice. The other woman made a happy sound before reaching down Gia's back then slowly unzipping her skirt. They both helped her step out of her clothing until she stood before them in her black lace panties and black garter belt. Ivan and Margo once again pressed her between them and she became overwhelmed with the sensation of their hands roaming all over her body.

Margo said something with a husky purr in her voice and made a questioning sound while gripping Gia's ass, hard.

"Gia, Margo would like to flog you." He must have seen her apprehension because he quickly added, "It would be a sensual flogging. For pleasure."

"If it is my Master's pleasure, it is my pleasure." She was proud of herself for remembering that bit of her training, even as her body was sinking further and further into her floaty space.

"Such a good girl," Ivan said before he brushed his lips over hers. "I will enjoy fucking you with your ass all red and burning to my touch."

"Oh, please," she moaned without shame.

Someone gave her nipple a sharp pinch that seemed to go straight to her clit. "Is that how you address your Master?" Margo said in a sharp voice.

"No, Ma'am. I'm sorry, Master."

Cloth rustled over skin, and a moment later, Ivan lifted her against his body. He'd removed his shirt, and when she slid down his front, she noted he was still wearing his pants, but his cock was a nice, thick bar against her body. She wanted him inside of her, pounding her, fucking her, taking her.

"Come with me, Gia."

He led her a dozen steps forward and lowered her hands to something smooth, round, and cool to the touch. "This is the bed post. Hold on to it."

With efficient movements, he bound her hands to the post with what felt like nylon rope. She instinctively pulled at her bonds, then relaxed further as she realized she was well and truly tied up, in a room with people she couldn't see watching her every move. In a way, it was flattering to have all of their attention focused on her. The thought of arousing so many people with her submission was a heady thing. She spread her legs and tilted her ass, providing Margo with a better target.

The other woman gave a pleased murmur, and a moment later the long, soft falls of a flogger trailed over Gia's skin. She let out a silent sigh of relief that the woman wasn't using a particularly harsh flogger. To her surprise, Ivan began to stroke and play with her breasts. His knowing touch soon had her dancing to the slap of the suede over her ass, thighs, and upper back. Margo wielded the flogger with consummate skill, and Gia cried out as the strikes burned across her sensitive skin.

People around her talked in Russian, but she really didn't care what they were saying. All she cared about were Ivan's hands playing with her hipbones, almost close enough to touch her needy sex but not quite. She lost herself in the sensations overwhelming her and fell into an almost trance-like state. He dipped his hands between her inner thighs to play with the moisture there.

"Mmmm, nice," he murmured against her cheek. "So wet for me."

"Please, Master, take me."

He said something and the thudding falls of the flogger against her buttocks stopped, leaving her panting and squirming.

Margo's soft perfume tickled Gia's nose right before the other woman placed a gentle kiss on her cheek. "You mark beautifully. Thank you for letting me play with her."

Ivan began to run his hands over Gia's back, pressing his fingers into the light welts and making her moan for him. "It was a pleasure to watch you work her."

Other voices spoke from around the room and Gia struggled to place how many people were here. Then the voices faded and she was sure most of the people had left already.

Margo gave Gia's ass a brisk slap, making Gia go up on her toes and hiss. "Let me know when she arrives in Moscow."

"I will."

Gia wanted to ask him what he was talking about, but Ivan picked that moment to start rubbing on her clit. She was so close to orgasm, all it took was several hard flicks and she was coming hard. Her body broke and shook, the mixture of pain endorphins from the flogging and pleasure chemicals from her orgasm rocketing through her nervous system and blowing her mind. She moaned and twitched, collapsing against Ivan as he kept rubbing her. He was relentless and he worked her until she begged him to stop. He ignored her pleas and trapped her between his strong legs, then rubbed her clit until arousal replaced her discomfort. Soon he had her bucking beneath his touch and she wanted to scream.

"We are alone now, my Gia. Just you and I."

Abruptly he removed his hands and she sagged against the bedpost, crying from the overwhelming onslaught of sensations. He removed her blindfold and looked down at her, full of stern disapproval. "You orgasmed twice without permission."

Trying to blink back her tears, she looked at the ground. "I'm sorry, Master."

He wrapped his hand in her hair, holding her head back at a sharp angle and exposing her throat. "Five spanks for each climax."

A whimper became trapped in her throat as he rubbed her ass, his big hands making her already burning skin sting. The thought of a spank on her abused bottom had her crying harder.

"Shhhh, Gia. You will take your punishment."

The first smack was light, but holy *fuck* it hurt. She couldn't hold back a sharp cry and his grip on her hair tightened.

"You should see how beautiful your bottom is. All red and hot."

Then he began to spank her in earnest and she lost all of her dignity. Thank God they were alone because having anyone besides Ivan see her like this would have been too much. She arched, screamed, begged, and sobbed her way through the spanking, the throbbing of her abused flesh secondary to the need ridding her hard. It seemed the more he spanked, the more savage she became, twisting in his grip and fighting him as much as she could.

He laughed and pinned her between his legs again. "Two more, my wild girl."

She snarled at him, then dropped her head and moaned while he smacked her with both hands at once. Pain radiated through her and soon the sympathetic reaction started to kick in. The discomfort faded a bit and when Ivan dropped to his knees behind her and began to lick her ass, she was in heaven—an ouchy, hurty heaven. He licked her like the lion soothing his mate, long, slow strokes that made her sag against the bedpost. His touch was so gentle she lost control of her emotions again and began to cry.

"Oh, Master."

He gave a pleased growl and spread her aching butt cheeks apart. She had no shame at this point; there wasn't room for it in her head. Instead, she followed her body's directions and tilted her hips to him, submitting and offering herself. When he gave her pussy a leisurely lick, her toes curled and she keened at the intense sensation. She'd been wound up all night, but it was worth it if the overwhelming sensual feelings running through her were the result.

He gathered up some of her abundant arousal and spread it over her anus, gently pressing at that nerve laden opening and adding a new facet to her pleasure. The gentle pressure of his tongue laving her clit was beyond amazing and she moaned and trembled for him, taking everything he had to offer and begging for more. Her world narrowed to her Master, and it took what little control she had left to try to keep from coming.

At first it wasn't too bad, then he began to suckle on her clit and she gripped the bedpost as hard as she could, fighting the natural reaction of her body to her Master.

"Please, I can't stop. Please, Master, please have mercy on me."

His response was to plunge his thick thumb into her anus and slowly begin to fuck her as he ate her. The unusual sensation of her muscles being stretched back there had her sagging, her knees unable to hold her anymore as her entire body tensed for orgasm. Ivan muttered something in Russian and stood, removing his thumb from her ass.

"Stay standing, Gia. I'm going to fuck you and I want you to take it."

Under the rapid panting of her breath, Gia could faintly make out Ivan pulling his pants down. She looked over her shoulder and was treated to the pussy clenching sight of Ivan staring at her body like he wanted to devour her. His lips were peeled back in a slight snarl, and when he fisted his cock and rubbed it against her sex, his nostrils flared.

Then he began to push in and she lost herself in the endless length of him sliding into her wet, welcoming body. Once seated all the way inside of her, pinning her to him, he reached around and she caught a flash of silver before he cut through the ropes with a large knife. Keeping himself inside of her, he moved them so she was bent over the mattress with her feet on the floor and her chest on its soft surface. The ability to go limp while he fucked her was lovely and when he began to trace the tip of the knife over her back, all she could do was groan.

Cool and deadly, the tip of the blade pulled over the welted skin of her bottom and she moaned in protest.

"You are so beautiful, my girl. I love to see your body wrapped around mine, my cock deep in your hot pussy. You are mine, Gia. No one else's. Who do you belong to?"

She knew what he wanted to hear. “This is your pussy, Master.”

His savage growl made her smile, and as he began to move against her, thrusting his cock in and out of her needy body, she became lost in him again. The slide of his flesh against hers, the rasp of his breath on her neck, the weight of his body pinning hers to the mattress. He stood and pulled her back so her feet dangled from the floor as he pounded into her.

His voice was almost guttural as he ground out, “Come for me, Gia.”

She’d been holding back for so long it was hard to let go, but when she did, she climaxed in the most amazing way. Every single inch of her body vibrated with her cries as she came over and over again all over his cock. Through it all, he kept thrusting into her, grunting each time he bottomed out and holding her hips hard enough to bruise. All of her energy gone, the best she could do was moan softly as his movements became jerky.

“Please, Master, come inside of me. I want to feel you.”

She wasn’t even sure if he heard her because her voice came out so soft, but a few seconds later, he gasped her name and shoved himself as far into her body as he could get. Tremors raced through him and into her, making her poor, abused body twitch in his harsh grasp. His deep, low groans of pleasure made her smile and filled her with a warm joy knowing she’d pleased her Master.

Her Ivan.

After gently pulling out and wiping them both with his shirt, he dragged her up the bed and into his arms. Once he had her positioned the way he wanted, he worked on taking the sapphire pin out of her hair and pulling out the numerous bobby pins. His touch was surprisingly gentle, and he kept making sure he wasn’t hurting her. It seemed somewhat ironic when she thought about how he’d spanked the hell out of her still burning ass.

She giggled and tried to hide it, which ended up making her snort, which only lead to more giggles. Soon she was clinging to him, laughing like a loon. His touch paused and he smiled down at her.

"Are you all right?"

She snickered, then laughed again. "Yes, it's just that you're being so careful not to pull my hair and hurt me, but you beat the hell out of my ass."

He grinned and resumed taking out the last of the pins. "I don't think pulling your hair out would make you as wet as getting flogged, then spanked did."

His fingers felt like heaven as they combed through her hair. "Mmmm, good point. That was wonderful."

With a smile, he stood and pulled her to her feet. "Come, let's shower. Your makeup has been…abused."

Embarrassment rushed through her and she gave him a horrified look. "Oh no. How bad is it?"

He smiled, then outright grinned. "I think it's hot. Seeing your tear tracks, remembering how I made them happen, how hard you came, how well you obeyed me. It makes me want to fuck you again."

Flustered, she darted forward to what she was guessing was the bathroom. His chuckle followed her, but she tried to ignore him. She probably looked like some kind of clown whore right now. Oh, God…all that mascara. And she wore false eyelashes!

Reaching around on the wall, she located the light switch and rushed to the first mirror she spotted. With a low moan, she walked up to the glass and tried to wipe at her face. Her mascara had indeed melted down her cheeks in dark tracks from her tears. She dabbed at her smeared eye shadow with a tissue until she didn't resemble a clown on meth. Her lipstick was long gone and she had swollen lips from Ivan's firm kisses.

With a wince, she turned so she could see her butt. As soon as she saw the bruising starting to rise up in places she bit her lip. Sitting would be an issue for the next few days, and there were a couple very visible bite marks. Bending, she swore she could actually see the bruising imprint of Ivan's big hand blooming quite nicely on her ass.

There was no doubt she hurt, and would hurt more tomorrow, but she absolutely loved the way he'd marked her. In her experience, a man only marked a woman if he wanted a very visible stamp of ownership. For fuck's sake, she had his teeth marks all over her. Can't get more obvious than that. Turning slowly, she looked at her front and traced her fingertip on one particularly dark imprint of his teeth on the mound of her breast. The bite would easily show if she wore a shirt that revealed any kind of cleavage.

Ivan had come into the bathroom, and the way he smiled when he found her playing with his bite mark made her knees weak. Open affection shone in his face as he strode forward, gloriously aroused and nude, then swept her into his arms. With a low groan, he lifted her high enough to lick at the bite mark on her breast. Once again, she was reminded of the lion, or the wolf licking his mate, or considering Ivan's size and his wonderfully furry chest, a bear. His touch brought a warm wave of comfort that left her sighing in pleasure.

He lowered her to her feet, then turned on the water in the shower. It was a beautiful green and silver marble affair with multiple chrome showerheads, and warm amber light bathed them in a soft golden glow. Turning, he took her hand and pulled her into the water with him. The way he held her so gently made her heart melt, and she cupped his face with her hands, wanting to tell him her feelings but scared of his reaction. They only had a few days left, but she was sure if she didn't tell him how she felt, she'd regret it for the rest of her life.

She almost said something, but fear made her bite back the words and turn away from his gaze. "Thank you for tonight."

Holding her closer, Ivan placed a sound kiss on the top of her head. "I have never had such a good time with anyone, Gia."

Blinking back the water from the showerhead, she searched his face. "Me, too."

His expression became serious and thoughtful. "Would you like to come to Moscow with me?"

"What?" She would've stumbled back if he wasn't holding her so securely. "Are you crazy?"

His expression shut down and she swore a chill raced down her spine. "I'm sorry, I misread your interest in me."

When his hands slipped from her waist she pushed him back against the shower wall. "No, you didn't. I...I really like you, Ivan, a lot. Like more than I should and it scares me. But I can't go to Moscow with you."

"Why not?"

"Well, for one thing, don't you have to get like special permission to go there or something?"

"You have your passport. In fact, I have it in a safe along with your other papers, a set of your clothes, and your purse."

She blinked at him, trying to rationalize why she couldn't do this when her heart was begging her to say yes. "We don't know each other."

"This is true. Which is why, when we arrive in Moscow, I will give you your own space. I own vast amounts of real estate in Russia." He got a rather savage gleam in his eye. "In fact, I'm the top ten percent of private property owners in Moscow. Or at least my corporation is. Do not worry about any papers you might need. My family has connections and I will take care of it."

She frowned, wishing they weren't having this conversation in the shower. His hard cock pressed against her, and as usual, her hormones went crazy at his touch. Her hunger was already rising for him, and she wondered if there would ever be a time when she could be around Ivan without wanting to jump his bones. But all the best sex in the world wouldn't keep her happy.

She needed love.

"Why do you really want me to come with you, Ivan? You have your choice of any woman in the world. No offense, but I won't be any man's mistress, not even yours."

His lips thinned. "I do not want you as a mistress. I want you to come with me because it makes me feel good to have you near me. That is, until you get that stubborn little frown on your face, which I also find cute. You're like an angry puppy."

The need to have him inside of her grew, but so did her temper. "I'm serious."

He sobered. "I know you are. The truth is, I don't know. None of this makes sense to me either. I hope you will believe me when I say I'm in uncharted waters with you. No one has ever made me feel like this. It is like the world is better when you are with me."

She wanted so much to believe him, but she'd been sweet talked more than once by some asshole. Having her heart broken more than a couple times made her instantly suspicious of charming men. At least, it usually did. Ivan seemed so sincere, and she knew she wasn't misreading the heavy emotions in his gaze. In fact, she felt like she knew him better than she'd ever known anyone, in a weird way.

"What about my job?"

"What about it? You don't have to work when you're with me."

"Uh-uh, buster." She pushed herself out of his arms and put her hands on her hips. The effect was slightly ruined because of her wet and naked state. "I'm not anyone's house pet."

"What are you talking about?"

"I worked my ass off for my degree. Do you know how many times I had to choose between eating and paying for books? I worked two part-time jobs while I was in school and usually averaged five to six hours of sleep a night. Why in the world would I give it up now, when I've finally started to achieve my dreams?"

Instead of answering her, he took down a bottle of body wash and poured it into his palm. The sweet scent of oranges and the perfume of bergamot filled the steamy air. "Come here, my Gia."

God, she loved it when he said her name like that, all growly and sexy. She took a reluctant step forward. Ivan closed the distance between them with a sigh and began to gently wash and massage her left hand.

"That feels good, but I'm still mad."

"You do have a temper."

She started to protest, but he hit a tense muscle in her palm that had her sighing. "I do."

He grinned, moving up to wash her arm now. The callouses on his big hands gently rasped over her skin, making her shiver. He washed her in silence for a few minutes and she didn't try to break it. Her mind spun with the implications of his words, and for a brief moment, she allowed herself to indulge in the fantasy of being his woman. Then reality stepped in and brought up all the scary things about moving across the world to be with a man she barely knew. The part of her mind that loved a good fairy tale when she was a little girl was urging Gia to go for it, but she'd stopped believing in fairy tales a long time ago.

Ivan gently turned her and tilted her head back. "I'm going to wash your hair."

He tucked her closer to him and she enjoyed the sensation of his big, solid mass pressing against her and his hard dick nestled between them. Ivan was such an intensely sexual man, she wondered if he had it in him to be monogamous. Of course, being into BDSM didn't make him a swinger, but for all she knew, he wanted a submissive at home to play with on the nights he didn't feel like going to a club.

His thick fingers massaged her scalp and she tried to relax into his touch, but it was hard. "Gia, I apologize."

"For what?"

"For assuming you'd want to stay at home and live a life of pampered leisure."

She relaxed somewhat against him as she grinned. "When you put it like that I feel silly for being mad."

"No, I think I understand. You are like me. We both sacrificed much to get where we are and we love what we do. I tried to put myself in your place." He tipped her head back so he could rinse the soap out of her hair. "It is something I do when I'm making business deals. I try to see the world through your eyes. If I can do that, I can usually figure out what I need to do next."

She shook her head beneath the shower. "I love my job. I really do. If I didn't, I wouldn't have spent the last seven years busting my ass for my degrees. It's not just a job to me, it's my passion. I love to design buildings. Seeing my vision come to life is…it's like watching a part of my soul put up for the world to see."

He uncapped another bottle, this time conditioner, and worked it through her hair. Ivan was, by far, the best bath time buddy she'd ever had. If this was what he meant by pampering her, she could get used to this treatment, especially when he was sounding so rational and logical while she was a hot emotional mess. She'd never wanted anyone as badly as she wanted Ivan, and it scared her. On the other hand, imagining a future with him was all too easy, a sure sign he'd managed to fuck her stupid. She was absolutely sure of one thing about herself, she was not some hopeless romantic. In fact, most men she knew were more romantic than she was. With Ivan, though, all she wanted to do was share her heart with him.

"So, what do you see when you try to put yourself in my place?"

He rinsed her hair, then turned her around so she faced him. The intense look in his eyes definitely made him look like he could either read her mind, or he'd be really good at hypnotizing someone. Either way she found herself drowning in him and she couldn't summon the strength to resist.

This moment was everything she'd been looking for, complete surrender to a Master. She opened herself to him, offering her heart in her gaze, trying to make him see how vulnerable she was to him. His lips curved into a smooth, warm smile.

"There we go. You want to make this work with me, but you're apprehensive, and with good reason. You are not a stupid woman and you are not weak-willed. I will have to respect your opinion, but I will not tolerate any shit from you in the bedroom. Once we're in our private space together, you become mine completely. I will not be content with just having you, Gia. I will want to own you. Already the urge to see you in my collar eats at me and I struggle to hold myself back."

His open honesty and pretty correct presumption of her state of mind had her smiling even as she sighed and gave him an irritated look. "What am I going to do with you?"

"Kiss me?"

Giggling, she splashed water at him. "No."

"Want me to kiss you?"

"You're crazy."

"Ahhh. I know exactly what you need." The lusty gleam in his eye should have warned her. When he spun her around so her back was against the shower wall and sank to his knees, she almost passed out from a fierce onslaught of desire. Her clit hardened and her arousal began to make her sex slick for his entry. "You want me to kiss your pussy like I kiss your beautiful mouth. This is what you need."

His complete confidence was quickly backed up when he began to gently kiss her sex like he was seducing her mouth. All she could do was to try to remain standing. Then he began to French kiss her, sliding his tongue through her folds in a way that had her grasping onto his shoulders. The big muscles beneath her hands reminded her of how strong he was.

Which allowed her to do things like this.

"Hold me. You're too good. I'm going to fall."

His pleased growl against her pussy did take the last of the strength left in her legs, but she didn't move an inch. He held her against the wall, his arm supporting her ass while he ate the fuck out of her. The way he sucked on her clit, then began to rub his tongue over it had her screaming out his name as her climax hit hard and fast. He pulled back and began to lap at her sex, then thrust his tongue in deep enough to make her pussy clench again in a mind-numbing rush of need. There was no way it should be physically possible for her to want him again mere seconds after coming, but she did. The orgasms he gave her drained her emotionally and physically, leaving her feeling so damn good inside and out.

When he stood back up, she was pleasantly aroused and languid from her release. He lifted her into his arms and dipped his head for a kiss. She wrapped her arms around his neck and kissed him back, delighted she didn't have to worry about being too heavy. Ivan was so strong, she knew he could hold her like this all day.

He broke their kiss and slid her down his body. "Come, you need to get dried off. I took the liberty of ordering some dessert for us. You'll need your energy."

She giggled and managed to make it out of the shower on shaky legs without falling and killing herself. Ivan shut the water off and she grabbed two lush gray towels off the nearby rack. To her pleasant surprise, they were warm and she grinned at another perk of living the high life. She'd never have to dry off with a chilly towel again like a peasant. That silly thought sent her off into another fit of giggles.

Ivan wrapped his arms around her. "Give me those towels."

She handed one to him and sighed as he wrapped her up. After securing the other towel around his waist, he began to pat her with a gentle, but firm touch. He placed a trail of kisses over her skin as he went, in a way that brought tears to her eyes. He made her feel too much. She didn't know how to handle her emotions around him. In a way, he made her feel like an awkward teenager with her first boyfriend. This was so different from anything she'd ever done, all she could do was react.

Ivan glanced up and gave her an understanding look. "Come on. Let's wrap you up and get you fed."

He stripped off her towel and helped her into a thick, comfortable black robe. The plush fabric made her feel like she was being hugged by a stuffed teddy bear. He tried to wrap her hair up for her in a towel, but he couldn't quite get it to stay. Finally, he blew out a frustrated breath.

"I must admit, I've never tried to do this for a woman before."

"Dry her hair?"

"Yes."

She turned and took the towel from him, flipping forward so she could do it. "Why?"

"I've never felt the need to take care of someone as much as I want to take care of you."

She flipped back up and secured the towel. "Can we not talk about serious stuff for a little bit? I mean, I'm kinda shell-shocked here. I'd like to eat and cuddle if that's okay."

He held out his hand, but he couldn't quite hide the hurt in his eyes. "Of course."

When they entered the bedroom she let out a soft gasp. A lovely, romantic display of milk, cookies, and cupcakes graced the table in the dining area. A vase of colorful flowers accented the meal, and the lighting had been turned down to give the room an intimate atmosphere. She flushed and tried to remember if Ivan had closed the door to the bathroom. Well, even if he hadn't no one could have seen anything through the heavily frosted glass, but they sure as heck would have heard her.

Suddenly famished, she grabbed a giant oatmeal and raisin cookie, grinning when she found it was still warm from the oven. Her first bite was bliss and she shook her head as she chewed. "I could eat everything here, so you better grab something before I do."

Ivan laughed and took a chocolate cupcake. "I find that hard to believe. You need to gain weight, so I definitely encourage you to have a bite of everything."

She grinned at him, then took a sip of her milk before saying, "I love food. Love it. But I also love running, so it balances out. I can eat like a pig then go clear my mind with a good eight-mile run."

"I like to run as well, but I usually only manage to get five miles in. It's hard to find time for a good run."

"Unfortunately, or fortunately, depending upon your perspective, I am a dreadfully boring person. I work all the time and hardly ever go out."

"What about your local BDSM club?"

"Oh, I go there a dozen or so times a month." He raised his eyebrows and she flushed. "What? There's no judgment there. I can talk with people and be myself. I'm not always there to play, but sometimes I do."

"I don't like hearing about another man touching you."

She had to resist rolling her eyes. While dominant men were wonderful in so many ways, they had quirks that made her want to kick them in the ass. Like being uber possessive. She didn't want to make Ivan mad, but he needed to know she would only let him take it so far.

"Ditto. Are there any girlfriends of yours I need to be aware of?"

“I was dating a few women, but nothing serious.”

She took another drink to wet her suddenly dry mouth. “Am I something serious?”

He studied her and her heart threatened to break if he rejected her now. “Yes, Gia, you are.”

His words scared her, while at the same time, her soul relished the idea of being Ivan’s ‘something serious’. Her mind was spinning a thousand miles an hour, and she took a deep breath and blew it out. While it wasn’t a declaration of everlasting love, which would have sent her running out the door, it was nice to know she meant something to Ivan. She really was too tired for more drama tonight, so she said one word that summed up all her chaotic feelings.

“Good.”

She grabbed a cupcake with yellow frosting and what looked like sugar snowflakes on it. Intrigued, she took a bite and moaned in bliss. “Oh my God, this is like some kind of crazy good vanilla mint. You have to try this. It’s like it has a hint of birthday cake to it.”

He obediently opened for her, the fine lines around his eyes deepening with humor. They spent the next hour eating and talking about their lives. She learned Ivan was one of three children. He had a younger brother living in Kazan, Russia, and a sister living in Japan with her husband and two children. His parents passed away a few years ago from different illnesses, and he had an uncle he was very close to, who was like his surrogate father.

She told him about growing up poor and her own extended family as well as the area where she’d grown up. When he asked her a question it was obvious he was really paying attention to what she said and cared about her response. That warm, fuzzy feeling enveloped her again, and by the time she’d taken her last bite, she was nodding off. Ivan laughed and hauled her next to him.

“Come, let’s brush our teeth and go to bed.”

She stumbled after him; her body pretty much on autopilot while her mind waved the white flag of surrender. After rinsing her mouth out, she didn't even wait for Ivan, instead lurched toward the bed. Before she reached it Ivan was there, turning down the covers.

"How many pillows do you like beneath your head, Gia?"

"Two," she mumbled as she shrugged out of her robe. The food and milk sat heavy in her belly, lulling her further until she was sinking into the darkness.

Ivan eased her down onto the bed and the sigh she gave when her head hit the pillows made him laugh. Beyond even caring, she wiggled into her usual sleeping position on her stomach. After that her mind just drifted while her body buzzed.

Ivan got beneath the sheets and rolled over onto his side. He pulled her next to him, curving her back against his front. Once he had her positioned as he wished, he kissed the back of her neck and began to whisper to her in Russian. She had no idea what he was saying, but he kept repeating one word over and over *'lyubit'*. Her world narrowed down to his voice, and when she dreamed, she dreamed of Ivan.

Chapter

Ivan woke up with Gia's hand over his face and her leg thrown over his hip. He was at the very edge of the enormous bed. He removed her hand and looked up in disbelief, wondering how such a tiny girl took up so much space. With a sigh, she rolled away from him and he got a nice view of the top curve of her bottom. He laughed when he saw she was spread out like a starfish on the bed. Light came through the edges of the curtains, but it was muted, like it was a cloudy day outside.

Moving slowly, he got out of bed and used the bathroom, pausing to quickly brush his teeth. When he came back into the bedroom Gia was sitting up and yawning, stretching her arms out wide and giving him a marvelous view of her breasts. He growled low in his throat and she looked at him with wide eyes.

"Hold that thought."

She scurried past him into the bathroom and shut the door. He grinned at the click of the lock and looked around the room. He found his black toy bag sitting in the bottom of the closet and brought it out. He put it prominently on the small chaise lounge at the foot of the enormous bed. Then he tugged on a pair of pants and had an evil thought. He quickly called Ilyena and he was waiting for Gia when she came out.

Her hair was slightly damp, so she must have showered, and her skin had that beautiful rosy glow from the hot water. She was completely nude and her amazing body made his cock ache to possess her. She leaned against the doorway and crossed her arms beneath her breasts, tempting him to bite her dark nipples with their gold piercings until she screamed.

"What's in the bag, Master?" she asked in a saucy voice.

Her teasing smile made him want to grin in return, but he kept his face stern. She needed to understand him, to know how kinky he liked his sex. While he would never violate her trust by sleeping with another woman as long as they were together, and he expected the same from her regarding men, Gia agreed that she liked women, and he heartily enjoyed watching two smooth, warm bodies wrap around each other. Two women kissing had to be one of the most sensual things he'd ever experienced, a visual pleasure he'd like to share with her.

He'd called Ilyena instead of Catrin because he sensed a true friendship happening between Nico's wife and Gia. When Gia agreed to come to Russia, and he would make sure that she did, it would help her to have Catrin as a friend. The other woman would take Gia under her wing and introduce her to people who wouldn't care that Gia was an American. He never wanted Gia to feel alone even if he had to travel on business. Maybe he'd get her a couple of pets to keep her warm at night when he couldn't be there with her.

Ilyena, on the other hand, was one of Alex's passing girlfriends. Ivan didn't see her lasting very much longer with his friend. He could already see the signs of them drifting apart and that made her perfect for Gia to experiment with. And he happened to know Ilyena had a very special skill she loved to use on women.

He'd sit back, wait until Gia was a sweaty, crying, orgasmic mess, and then take her.

Hard.

But he needed to focus on the here and now, which included a naked, fresh submissive begging for him.

"Come here. I want you to bend over and hold on to the bed post."

She swallowed and took a hesitant step forward. "Um, I'm not sure if you noticed, but my ass is a little tender."

"I know, that's why I'm going to soothe you."

When she bent over the bed, she licked her lips and looked at him over her shoulder. "How bad is it?"

Ivan strode over to the window and opened the curtains onto a dreary day. The gray skies made staying in bed all day with his submissive sound like a perfect idea. As he came closer and inspected her ass, he felt a twinge of guilt. She had distinct marks from his hands spread across each of her cheeks. He placed his fingers over one mark reaching toward her hip and sighed as the bruise perfectly matched his hand.

"I did not mean to mark you so much. I forget that you still have a virgin ass."

She snickered. "Hardly."

He reached into his bag and brought out a jar of a special balm that would help her heal quicker. "What I mean is, you're not used to being spanked and flogged for hours."

"Hours?"

"How long do you think we played with you before I took you?"

"Umm…" Her gaze went distant. "I don't know. I kinda lost track of things for a while."

"Two hours."

"What?" She almost jerked up from her position but stopped herself. "No way. There is no way I could have handled it for that long. The most I've ever lasted was fifteen minutes."

"Yes, but you weren't in your subspace at that time."

"Oh." She grinned at him and wiggled her butt. "You do that to me, you know."

He wanted to smack her for her sass, but at the same time, he did enjoy occasionally having his ego stroked, especially by the woman he wanted so badly to be his and his alone. Emotions threatened to burst through his careful control and he exerted his iron will. He was becoming as soft as a woman around Gia and it bothered him.

His parents had been very physically and emotionally cold people. He didn't really understand her open affection and easy joy, but he wanted to. In watching her live her life he found his true happiness.

Reminding himself of the task at hand, he rubbed the balm into her bottom, barely resisting the urge to grab handfuls of her supple ass and squeeze. He'd never seen a butt as round and firm as hers. When she came to Moscow with him, he would have sculptures of her nude form done, something to forever capture the perfect balance of hard and soft that made up her body.

It wasn't long before he had her wiggling beneath his touch and he put the jar down. Shifting over her, he began to gently kiss each and every bite mark on her body that he could reach. She sighed and the smile that curved her full lips was a reward like no other. That intense possessive feeling reared its head again, and he felt a slight panic at the idea she might not want to come with him.

No, that was an unacceptable thought. She would be his. He would do whatever it took to make her happy, so that she would never want to leave his side.

A moment later, there was a knock on the door.

"Come in."

Gia went to cover herself with a shriek, but he pressed her down to the bed with his chest on her back. "Easy, it is just Ilyena."

The tall, lithe blond woman entered the room. She wore a pretty white summer dress that showed off her lean figure. After shutting the door, she came over to Gia's side and stroked her fingertip down Gia's flank. "Beautiful."

Ivan grinned at the other woman. "Thank you."

Ilyena switched to Russian, "You really like her, don't you?"

He narrowed his gaze. "What business is it of yours?"

Smiling, Ilyena continued to carefully stroke Gia. "She is a nice girl and she adores you."

It took a great deal of effort, but he tried to remain calm. "Good, because I plan on keeping her."

The grin Ilyena gave him had an answering smile tugging at his lips. She was a very nice woman, but she didn't want to settle down right now and he could respect that. Hell, up to this point the thought of having a woman in his life was pleasant, but not necessary. He needed Gia like an alcoholic needed a drink.

"So, what would you like me to do?"

"Do you feel like topping today?"

"Of course." A hungry gleam entered her gaze and she licked lips.

He went over Gia's list of hard limits and what turned her on. Gia was getting impatient and kept glancing over her shoulder at them with a barely concealed frustrated expression. When he caught her peeking again he raised an eyebrow. "Feeling restless?"

She bit her lower lip and nodded.

"Ilyena is going to top you for my pleasure."

"I thought she was submissive?"

"She's a switch. I want you to obey her as you would me, Gia. I'm going to watch you, and if you please me, I'll spill my cum into one of your holes. Which one is up to me. If you act like a brat and shame me, I'll jerk off into a napkin and make you wear it as a gag for a few hours."

Gia arched her back, the scent of her arousal making his nostrils flare. "Mmmmm."

He looked away from Gia's face and back to her body to find Ilyena playing with Gia's wet cunt. She had the long, slender fingers of an artist and her attention was all on Gia.

Ilyena looked up and gave him a slow smile. "I don't think you'll ever have to worry about Gia wanting to have some Domme time. This beautiful girl is submissive to the bone. Look at how well she gives into me, all because you told her to. She genuinely gains pleasure from submitting to you."

Ivan gestured to the bag at the end of the bed. "I have a strap-on in there with a variety of dildos. Pick whatever you'd like, but nothing too large. I'd still like to be able to fuck her and feel how tight her little pussy is."

He moved up the bed until his legs were sprawled and he was resting against the sturdy headboard and a mound of pillows. "Gia, I want you to come here and kneel between my legs."

She scrambled up to him, her breath coming out in harsh pants, her gaze filled with desire. Once she was close enough, he grabbed her and pulled her up until her lips met his. He began to kiss her slowly, thoroughly, enjoying the way she softened for him. When she braced her hands on his shoulders he made no objection, enjoying how she kneaded at his muscles like a kitten. He knew the moment Ilyena touched her because Gia stiffened.

"Easy, baby," he whispered against her lips. "This is all for your pleasure, for being such a good girl and pleasing me so much. It is my gift to you."

A second later she grunted, then sucked in a harsh breath. "Oh fuck, she has a vibrator. Master, I won't be able to last long. I don't want to disappoint you but…ohhhh."

To his great pleasure, Gia began to undulate in his arms and he looked over her shoulder to find Ilyena fucking her. The other woman still wore her innocent summer dress, but had rolled it over her hips so she could don the strap-on. Ilyena watched the fake cock slide in and out of Gia and Ivan knew how sweet of a sight it was. Gia's pussy would grip his cock like it was trying to keep him inside of her, and sliding out was the most exquisite agony.

His dick demanded it be up inside of Gia, now, but he tried to keep his own passions under control. He needed to seduce Gia, to make her his willing slave. Plus, he flat out got off on watching another woman fuck his girl.

Ilyena moaned as Gia slammed her hips back against her. "If she keeps that up she's going to make me come."

Unable to resist, Ivan pulled Gia's hair aside and whispered in her ear, "If you make Ilyena come first I'll eat your delicious little pussy while you lick hers."

"Oh, God. You are so dirty."

He grinned and nibbled on her neck, having to sway with her as she moved with Ilyena. The other woman grabbed Gia's hips and pounded into her. With a long, low moan, Gia met her every thrust, then began to grind her ass against the strap-on. Knowing the vibrating cock was stimulating Ilyena as well, he couldn't help but smile as she wailed and jerked against Gia.

His little submissive whimpered and groaned, begging him to soothe the ache.

Unable to resist any longer, he snapped at Ilyena, "Take the harness off and ride Gia's face."

He flipped Gia over onto her back and spread her thighs wide, feasting on the sight of her soft, swollen, very wet pussy. The way the skin of her labia darkened with her arousal drove him crazy, but not as much as the glimpse of her pink within. As he watched, her pussy clenched and he leaned down. After blowing a hot breath on her thigh, he began to tongue fuck her while nuzzling his nose against her clit.

With a low sigh, Ilyena crouched over Gia's mouth, giving him a nice view of tempting female ass and Gia's magnificent little breasts. He'd never been that big a fan of body piercings, but Gia's fiercely aroused him. He was pretty sure he could spend hours playing with them and never grow tired of how responsive her tight little nipples were thanks to those gold bars.

He let his eyes close and enjoyed having Gia open and available to him. She moaned and twitched at the lightest strokes of his tongue. Ilyena had begun to grunt and grind her hips against Gia's willing mouth. She looked over her shoulder at Ivan.

"Fuck. She can eat pussy. You lucky man."

He began to lick Gia's sweet cunt from the crack of her abused bottom all the way up to her clit, which was hard and swollen with her need. After placing a tender kiss there, he gently ran his teeth over the bud. Gia tensed and moaned, and he thought his girl might come, but Ilyena chose that moment to have a very loud and visible orgasm. Through it all, Gia kept her mouth on Ilyena's pussy, even gripped her hips to hold her in place. Soon Ilyena was twitching and pleading for Gia to stop.

Ivan pulled back and hauled Ilyena off Gia. He glanced at her. "Please leave us now. And thank you."

She giggled and rose on shaky legs. "Thank you. I love going back to Alex after being with a woman. It drives him crazy."

Gia wiggled on the bed and said in a rough voice, "Goodbye, and thank you."

"If I do not see you again, Gia, I want you to know that you are a priceless treasure. Don't settle for anything but the best."

Ivan shot Ilyena a glare, but she was already out the door.

He was the best for Gia.

End of story.

He smiled, then turned his attention back to Gia. She radiated sexual need as she stared back at him, her breath coming out in harsh pants. Her lips shone with the proof of Ilyena's climax, almost like lip gloss. He helped her up onto his lap and she immediately clung to him with her head against his chest and her arms wrapped around him. The long sigh she let out was so full of relief that Ivan could only grin.

"Easy, baby. I will take care of you."

She whimpered and began to lick his chest, covering every inch of his skin she could reach with her warm, wet mouth. In an odd way, he felt like she was marking him. He reached behind her and slid his finger down to the tiny star of her anus. She groaned and pushed against him, obviously eager for any kind of relief.

"You would like me to fuck you here, wouldn't you?" He spread some of the abundant wetness from her pussy to her ass. Then he began to press his finger in, teasing the tense ring of muscle that would squeeze his cock when he took her here. "Gia, do you want me to put my thick cock up your round, tight ass?"

"Anything you want, Master." She leaned back and looked him in the eye. "I want to please you."

His heart swelled at her words, his careful defenses around his emotions showing signs of major stress fractures. She overwhelmed him with desire and he felt fiercely protective of her. If he possessed her, she would never know another moment of fear, sadness, or insecurity.

This was his woman. The sooner she admitted it, the better for both of them.

“You should not say such things if you don’t mean them, Gia,” he admonished in a low voice, trying to warn her from forcing him to establish his dominance over her. “I know a million ways I want you to please me. I could keep you here, fucking you day and night for ten years and never grow tired. You are mine.”

Her breath came out in a low shudder and tears filled her eyes. She swallowed hard and tried to look away, but he grabbed her chin and stopped her. “Please don’t say things like that.”

He’d never met a woman with such volatile emotions. It was so foreign to him he wasn’t sure how to react. So he went with his gut and prayed he was right. “I mean it, Gia. No lies between us. I want you as my woman. I want to spend the next few years traveling the world and getting to know each other. There are so many things I want to do with you, to show you.”

Gently, she placed her fingertips over his lips. “Shhh, Master. Just touch me, please. Make love to me.”

“Gia, my version of making love may be very different from yours. My passion is dark, it is who I am. Can you deal with that?”

She smiled at him and a couple tears slid down her cheeks. “I can deal with that. Take me, Ivan. Make me yours. Own my body. Please.”

With a low sigh, he leaned back and crossed his arms behind his head. “Touch me, Gia, explore my body. Because if you agree to be mine this will be the only male body you get to touch.”

Biting her lower lip, she rubbed her wet sex against his thigh through his pants. “Really?”

“Yes.”

To his surprise, she did touch him, on every inch of his body except for where he wanted her touch the most. She made short work of his pants and soon had her chest pressed against his as she touched and nuzzled him until he thought he might lose his mind. Her soft, hesitant caresses were making his dick hurt with the need to come, and his balls felt like two boulders between his legs.

Finally, she began to lick his inner thigh, working her way toward his cock. She gave him a little teasing flick right across the tip of his shaft with her tongue. Sensations tore through him and his control broke.

Gripping her by the hair, he quickly had her up and on his lap, facing away from him. She had the most perfect, bitable ass, and he loved fucking her and looking at his marks. The bruising imprints of his fingers stoked him just right and he growled low in his throat as Gia gripped his cock and positioned it at the soaking wet entrance to her hot, snug pussy.

Unable to hold back, he brought her down as quickly as he could on his cock, her tight body arching and clenching up, fighting his entrance. He loved tearing through her like this, using his superior strength to drive himself into her. Gia screamed and bucked in his grip, crying out his name and coming all over his cock in a hot, wet rush. In this position, he could hit her G-spot just right, and he planned on making her soak the bed with her arousal. The sensation of her hot release dripping down his balls had him lifting and slamming into her as she screamed and cried.

He grabbed her arms and held them behind her back, using the position to hold her still while he fucked her. He'd once been told he could fuck like a machine if he put his mind to it, and he did that now, hammering into her without mercy, making her come again and again. It was only when her voice broke that he finally slowed and let her collapse. She melted back against him, his cock barely in her pussy as she twitched and moaned in a boneless heap.

He eased her off of him and onto her back, bending to take a quick lick of her pussy before slowly thrusting his aching shaft into her. She was probably very sensitive right now and he intended to make her feel every inch of him. When her lips curled into a silent snarl he bent and captured one of her nipples in his mouth, sucking hard.

"Oh, Master…"

Her beautiful words were music to his soul, the whisper of a very content slave. Pride filled him and he found himself rapidly approaching his own climax. Gia stroked his chest and arms, slowly rousing beneath him.

"You are so big and strong," she whispered in her raspy voice. "I love the way you take me, Ivan."

He groaned and thrust harder, trying to hold back because he didn't want to hurt her bruised ass in this position. With an agonized grunt, he pulled himself from her hot cunt. "I want you to suck my cum out of me."

She grasped him and went down on his cock like it was her favorite thing in the world to do.

He didn't stand a chance.

Within seconds, the cum boiled out of him in bone shaking rushes. His thighs twitched and his breath came out in harsh bursts as he whispered Gia's name. Sucking down every spurt, she coaxed more from him by rubbing her thumb along the vein on the underside of his cock. She eased him down with gentle licks, and by the time his ability to think had returned he couldn't believe how intense that had been and still was. Aftershocks of his climax sparked through his blood like bomb blasts.

Without a word, he dragged Gia over onto the side of the bed that wasn't soaked with her release. She curled around him and nuzzled her lips against his neck, making a happy, almost purring sound. It was a low, little growl that was as unique as Gia and he found it adorable.

Gia yawned and rolled off the bed for a moment, stumbling before she found the strength to stand. "Damn. I thought you crippled me."

He smiled and lifted himself so he could pull the covers down. "Come back to bed. I want a nap and then I will take you out for lunch and maybe to a museum."

For a moment she pretended to consider his offer, her body still glowing from her orgasms. "I think I can live with that."

She dove back into his arms and kissed his face with an easy affection that stole his heart. As he turned the kiss slow and seductive, he began to plan his attack. He'd always been a good strategist, in both the military and the corporate world, and he would use those skills now to lure Gia into coming back to Russia with him. If he could get her on the plane willingly, he had no doubt he could make Gia so happy she'd never want to leave him.

Chapter

Gia woke up with a long, low moan as her body tried to figure out where she was. When she opened her eyes she saw that she was in a hotel suite of some kind, obviously five star, but where? Next to her Ivan grumbled something in his sleep and slung an arm around her waist. She smiled at the way he cuddled up to her like she was his favorite teddy bear.

With his nose buried against her back, he slipped back into a deeper sleep, his body surrounding hers like the world's most comfortable blanket.

A little bit of light shone around the curtains and Gia wondered what Ivan had in store for her. They were in Washington DC today after flying in from New York City last night on yet another luxury helicopter. The memory of the flight out snuggled in his arms as he kissed her over and over, had her brushing her fingers over her still swollen lips.

Moving slowly, she eased his arm off of her and left the bed to order up some room service. She knew how she wanted to wake her Master up today. He'd given her so much and she wanted him to know that she appreciated it. No one had ever been this nice to her, and she found the thought incredibly sad.

After slipping on a robe and letting room service in, she took the tray she'd requested and made her way back into the bedroom. One thing she already knew about Ivan was that when he slept, he slept like the dead. She could probably do jumping jacks on the bed and he wouldn't wake up.

Fortunately, she had a much better idea in mind.

Placing the tray next to the bed, she opened up the curtains just a sliver to let more light in. Ivan's ferocious body was a work of art, and she wanted to fully appreciate him in the little time she had left. Sadness pushed away her desire and she shook her head, not letting herself dwell on the inevitable. This was all about savoring every moment she had with him.

Currently he slept on his side, away from her, so she had to improvise her plan a little bit. Slipping her robe off, she opened the large silver serving tray and smiled at the assortment of jellies, honey, whipped cream, and fruit. Each small, elegant dish had its own tiny silver knife and she picked up one in what looked like strawberry jelly.

Easing the sheet down his hip, she spread a thin line of the jelly from the muscled curve of his ass up to his hip.

Then she licked, sucked, and nibbled it off.

By the time she reached his hip, Ivan was awake and making the low, hungry growl that drove her crazy.

"What are you doing, my Gia?"

"Having breakfast."

With a grunt, he rolled over and captured her with one big arm, pulling her down onto the bed with him while she laughed and struggled against his hold. He nipped at her ear and said in a rough voice, "I want you for breakfast."

A pleasant warmth raced through her body and settled into her sex in a low throb. “Not fair. I want you first.”

He laughed and smoothed her hair back from her fast. “Fine, you will have what you want and I will have what I want.”

“Wha—”

Before she could question him further he had her spun around so her face was next to his big, thick cock while her pussy was near his chin. “Hand me the whipped cream.”

She gave his dick a small lick before obeying his command, liking the way his stomach muscles clenched beneath her.

After handing him the whipped cream, she grabbed what looked like some peach jelly. The cool, light feel of the whipped cream being spread around her pussy had her groaning low in her throat. His touch was so sure and the sight of his thick erection, now beaded with a drop of pre-cum, had her reaching eagerly for him.

Ivan had already started his breakfast…with gusto.

Not trusting herself with the knife, she dipped her fingers into jelly and spread it over his cock with an unsteady hand. Tremors of desire moved through her and over her skin, awakening her senses to the healthy male animal beneath her. He smelled so good in a way a man had never appealed to her before. Something about his natural, musky scent made her hormones ratchet up into overdrive and her body go into heat.

Grasping his cock by the sticky shaft, she slowly licked up and down, cleaning him with her tongue. There was something very erotic about feeling his reactions beneath her as she serviced him, the taste of sweet peaches mixing with the salt of his precum. Because he waxed his pubic area she was able to clean him all the way down to his sensitive pubic bone and was even able to lick at his balls a little bit before he gripped her ass and pulled her back to his wicked tongue.

They started a slow rhythm together of give and take, her sucking down his cock with eager little moans and him flexing his hands on her ass as he began to fuck her with his tongue. She became lost in him and gave herself over to his expert touch. It was different than when they were deep into a heavy BDSM scene together. Now she was more aware and just as absorbed in him. Bracing her hands on his firm thighs, she began to suck him in a rhythmic manner that soon had him thrusting up to meet her lips. Not hard enough to choke, but with enough strength to make her moan and quake while he tilted her hips to get better access to her clit.

He latched onto that little bud with his gentle lips and when he suckled she arched and yelled around his hard length in her mouth. Frantic to bring him over with her, she moved one of her hands and began to gently stroke and roll his balls. Ivan had very sensitive testicles and she let out a little satisfied hum as they tightened beneath her touch. Soon her sucking became disjointed as Ivan put first one, then two fingers in her and fucked her with them in time to his suckling on her clit.

With a long, low moan, she pulled her mouth off his cock enough so that she was just drawing on the tip while continuing to jack him off. Her orgasm started to ramp up and she rubbed her pussy against his mouth like a shameless slut, dying to come as he hooked his fingers and began to press on her G-spot. It wasn't hard enough to make her squirt, but it was hard enough to have her stiffening as all her muscles drew taut.

The vein on the underside of his cock throbbed and she tried to concentrate and focus on his needs, but doing anything other than moaning and crying out around his hard flesh became impossible. Her breath froze in her lungs and an excruciating pleasure racked through her as she began to come. Ivan snarled and removed his fingers, covering her whole pussy with his mouth and lashing it with his tongue as she came hard.

As she was just beginning to coast down, the first hot blast of his seed splashed into her mouth and she eagerly swallowed him down, teasing the slit of his cock with her tongue as she used her thumb running up the underside of his erection to try to coax more of his cum out.

Ivan gasped and rolled her off of him with her body still quivering from her orgasm.

"Enough."

They lay there, panting in each other's arms until Gia's heartbeat returned to something nearing normal. With a long sigh, she stretched out and cuddled into him, arranging her pillows so she was on her side and looking into his eyes. The emotion, the gentleness she saw in his expression made her swallow hard. He looked at her like she was something special.

He reached out and brushed some hair back from her face. "Why do you fix old houses?"

Disconcerted by his question, she shrugged. "It's just something I love. Why do you sell them?"

Being this close to him, she could read the subtle nuances in his expression. For a moment his face went blank, then he sighed. "I don't really know why I love buying and selling real-estate so much. I think part of the reason is because I like to take care of people."

She leaned up on her elbow and looked down at him. "How is selling real-estate taking care of someone?"

"I mostly buy residential properties, places in established neighborhoods where families have lived for generations. Good places where neighbors take care of each other. That way, when I hand them over to my team I know that our client will be moving into a home where they will be safe and happy. I also like owning buildings around the world and renting them out to different businesses. It puts me in touch with some very smart and interesting people. You never know when having a contact in a particular field would be helpful."

"True." She studied him. "I guess I just can't picture you showing someone a house."

When he laughed the deep rumble of it vibrated through her like quiet thunder. More felt than heard. "I do not show houses. My mother's family has been in the property owning business for a very long time."

Oddly enough, the thought of him growing up with a silver spoon in his mouth didn't appeal to her that much. She liked a man who worked, who earned his way in the world. "So you started working for them after high school?"

"No, after I left the military and then another career. My personal assistant likes to say that I never left the military. I enjoy conquering things and adding them to my hoard too much." He looked up at her with a small smile curving his lips. "I answered your question, now you answer mine."

She blew a short breath out through her nose. He'd given her a pretty honest and detailed answer, taking away the option of giving him some fluffy bullshit in return.

"We were poor growing up after my dad died. He was the one who brought the money home and my mom had no education beyond high school. My mom had to fix a lot of things around the house to keep them working. With no man around, there was no one to tinker with things when they went wrong. When I was fourteen, I heard Mom on the phone with one of my aunts, wondering where she would get the money to fix the concrete steps in front of our house that were starting to crumble. She was already going through a rough spot and in my child's heart I felt like if maybe I fixed the steps it would help fix her."

He began to slowly stroke her hip, his touch more comforting than she wanted to admit. "I went to our local hardware store, which back in those days were still small mom and pop shops, and told Mr. Benson, who owned the place, that I needed to know how to fix some concrete steps."

"He taught you how?"

"Even better. He hooked me up with his brother who worked in construction."

Ivan's grip on her thigh tightened and he said in a low, cold voice, "He gave you to his brother to date when you were fourteen?"

"What? No, no. I mean, hooked up, like introduced us. Manuel has twin daughters a few years older than me and he'd never do that to a kid." She frowned at Ivan, offended on her mentor's behalf.

"I'm sorry. Language barrier." His shoulders eased and he returned to stroking her. "So he taught you?"

"Yeah." She looked away and blinked back tears. "He was such a nice man and I think he kinda knew I needed a father figure in my life. Not only did he show me how to fix the steps, that summer he gave me a job doing office stuff at his construction company. It wasn't a big place, he only had five men working under him, but he took pride in his work. His specialty was restoring antique homes."

He smiled at her and the way his eyes brightened had her automatically smiling back. "So that is how you came to be an architect."

"Yes. Every summer until graduation I worked for him. I even worked some school holidays as well for extra spending money. He helped me a lot when I was growing up."

With a low sigh, Ivan pulled her to his chest and kissed her on the forehead. "You are a remarkably strong woman."

She shrugged. "Not really. People do what they have to do every day. I didn't have it as bad as some of my friends. At least my mom wasn't a drug addict or a prostitute."

For a long time he was quiet, but he never stopped touching her. It wasn't a sexual touch, rather, a soothing one that had her relaxing against him. With the strong, steady beat of his heart beneath her ear, she traced patterns in his chest hair.

"What was it like growing up in Russia?"

"Cold," he said with a small smile.

"Come on. I need more than that. I want to know more about you, Ivan. You fascinate me."

She hadn't meant to be so honest, but the words just slipped out. The warmth that suffused his face helped chase back any embarrassment. He looked like someone had just given him his favorite type of cookie.

"Why?"

She rolled her eyes. "Fishing for compliments?"

"I will assume that means you are asking if I need you to stroke my ego. I do not. I want to know what you find interesting about me so I can keep doing it."

"Ivan, I find everything about you interesting. I mean, look at you."

In an unexpectedly gentle move, he picked her up as if she weighed no more than a feather and draped her over his chest as he lay back on the bed. The solid, warm, strong feeling of him beneath her sent a wave of satisfaction coursing through her body. On some base, animal level she knew she had the strongest wolf in the pack protecting her. Placing her hands on his chest so she could play with his chest hair, she tilted her head and wiggled her hips.

"Ready for round two, Master?"

He smiled and put his arms behind his head on the mound of pillows. "Did you know that this is my first vacation lasting more than a week in six years?"

Her body stilled and she studied him. "Seriously?"

“Seriously.”

“What’s the point of having all the money in the world if you don’t enjoy it? I mean, come on, Ivan, you can give yourself two weeks off. No one would care.”

When he shrugged the muscles of his body did a lovely dance that distracted her as he said, “For the past six years I was in a different phase of my life. My empire building years.”

“Empire building, huh?”

Instead of smiling back he nodded. “Isn’t that what you’ve been doing? Going to school, working two jobs and still managing to donate time to the animal shelter once a month? How many vacations, real vacations have you gone on in the last six years?”

“We’re not talking about me, we’re talking about you.”

“Let me guess.” He stared intently at her and studied her face. “Three. And two of those were business trips.”

She gaped at him. “How did you know?”

He averted his gaze and tensed beneath her. “You will not like the answer.”

“Ivan.” She curled her fingers in his chest hair and tugged hard enough to get those amazing Caribbean blue eyes back on her. “How did you know that?”

“The same way I know you don’t have an arrest record, any mysteriously missing husbands, or were ever involved in any type of criminal activity that could harm me, my family, or my company. I had a background check done on you.”

She tried to pull away, but he jerked her back to the hard mass of his chest. “That is a huge invasion of my privacy!”

“I know, it is, and I apologize.”

Her feelings were really hurt, and she had to battle tears. “Why?”

"Gia, please believe me when I say I have had women try to establish a relationship with me for criminal purposes. Blackmail, bribery, outright theft. More women than you can count on both hands have tried to infiltrate my life. You...you are different." Cupping her face between his hands, he leaned up and brushed his lips against hers, draining her anger with his touch. "You are a good woman, inside and out. You have no idea how rare that is today."

"That's still bullshit." She shoved at his chest and got absolutely nowhere. "Let me go."

"Wait. I understand you feel your privacy was invaded, but please consider it from my position. I had a woman I was dating try to seduce my eighty-two-year-old father before he passed away. Do you know how furious I was, how ashamed and embarrassed that I'd brought her into his home?"

Her heart hurt for him and she traced her fingers over his lips, trying to gentle the irate look that had come over him. "I understand. But this means I get to do as many Internet searches on you as I want."

His lips twitched beneath her fingers in a small smile and his body softened, just a bit, beneath her. "All the nude photos are fakes."

A giggle bubbled up from her stomach and she tried to swallow it and failed. "Dammit, Ivan, I'm mad at you. Don't make me laugh."

Running his hands gently through her hair, he nodded. "I know you are upset, but I hope you will forgive me. I could have lied to you, but I don't want that between us. I want to be able to trust you, and for you to trust me."

"I do trust you." She narrowed her eyes at him. "At least I think I do. I won't know until I get access to a computer."

Beneath her belly, his stomach growled loud enough that it rumbled against her skin. She snickered, then leaned forward and placed a quick kiss on his lips. "Come on, Master, I have the primal female need to feed you and care for you."

He rubbed his face against her cheek like a big cat, scratching her with his early morning stubble. "Are you sure we can't stay in bed?"

Pushing off of him, she gently moved out of his grasp and stood next to the bed, all too aware of her naked state as his eyes gleamed with hunger. "You promised me we'd see some tourist stuff. I've never been here before."

"I did." He reached out and grasped her wrist, bringing it to his mouth so he could lick and nip at the pulse beneath her skin. "But you said you needed to feed and care for me."

"I meant eating food, Ivan. One cannot survive on love alone."

His lips stilled for a moment, and she hoped he didn't notice her sudden tension. She hadn't meant that the way it sounded. Okay, so she was pretty sure she was falling in love with him, but that didn't mean she had to tell him that. If she hadn't had that talk with Catrin about Ivan being an international playboy, she would have thought the conversation they'd just had changed things between them, taking their relationship to a whole new, more intimate level.

When he pulled her into his arms she didn't protest, and much later, when he was moving deep inside of her, she thought her heart might break at the reverent way he said 'My Gia' as he climaxed, over and over again.

Chapter

Gia laced her fingers through Ivan's hand and leaned her head against his shoulder as they slowly strolled through the National Mall in Washington DC. The wardrobe people had arrived after Gia and Ivan's long morning nap and had clothed her in an absolutely lovely orange and white summer dress that fit her like a dream. It was comfortable enough to walk around in and expertly made to enhance her body.

Her shoes were so well crafted it felt as if she was walking in sneakers instead of cute, strappy orange sandals. She didn't know the label, but they were amazing. Ivan would have a hard time getting her out of them tonight. The thought of tilting her ass up to him as she bent over a couch in these shoes had her pressing her thighs together. She needed to watch herself. The tiny scrap of frothy white lace that barely covered her mound and didn't cover her ass at all was going to be soaked with her arousal soon. That would be uncomfortable, but she couldn't help it.

Her heart soared as she held his hand and simply enjoyed being with him. It had to be some kind of hormonal thing that resulted from frequent and utterly devastating fucking, and boy, did she feel good.

Everywhere they went women looked at him with longing while many of the men looked away. A few stared back; it was like witnessing two wolves snarling at each other as they passed.

And those men who dared to look back, looked at her with barely concealed hunger.

Ivan glanced down at Gia, then led them over to the vast stone steps of the Lincoln Memorial. He sat and pulled her onto his lap, turning them for a better view of the lights shining on the reflecting pool stretched out before them.

As he enveloped her she pushed at his chest. “Ivan! There are children around.”

“No, there aren’t. It’s late, Gia, almost nine-thirty.”

She blinked up at him in surprise. “Wow. Time sure flies when you’re having fun.”

Stroking her cheek, he grazed his thumb over her lips. No one could see because of how he held her, and she shivered in his arms. His gaze darkened, but she swore it was with sadness instead of heat. Her heart gave a funny thump as she examined his face.

“It does. Unfortunately, my time with you is shorter than you think…unless you come to Russia with me.”

“What are you talking about your time is getting shorter? We have two more days.”

“No. I have to leave tomorrow.”

“What?” Her soul shattered and she tried to push her way out of his arms. “Why?”

“There is a delicate company matter I must deal with at home. I swear I would not leave unless I absolutely had to, but I have over three thousand employees depending on me to make the right business decisions. I’m responsible for their livelihood, so I will always have matters I have to personally attend to.”

“I understand,” she whispered as she turned her head into his chest.

Inside, she was screaming and crying as her heart refused to accept the loss. It didn’t help that he was here, now, in her arms as she breathed in his scent and felt his heat. Ivan was perfect, everything she wanted all wrapped up in one yummy package, but she was scared. The commitment he was asking for was astonishing, a monumental leap of faith and trust.

“Come with me,” he urged in a low voice. “Please, Gia. I will not live without you.”

“Please don’t ask this of me,” she said as she pushed herself away and stood before him.

He grasped her hands in his. “Give us a chance. I know I can make you happy. Just come with me, Gia.”

Even standing she still looked him in the eye as he sat. His size, his raw masculinity pushed at her and she pulled her hands from his, then wrapped her arms around herself, trying to keep her from reaching for him. The sadness in his gaze deepened until she felt as if she was drowning in his sorrow. She’d thought him cold, his face a perfect mask, showing nothing. His eyes told the story of his soul, and his pain tore her apart.

She couldn’t do this to him. She couldn’t do this to herself.

God help her for making what was, without a doubt, the stupidest and most foolish decision of her life.

“One week,” she whispered.

He tilted his head, the fading light catching the scar on his face and casting harsh shadows over the planes and ridges of his cheekbones. “I do not understand.”

“I have another week of vacation owed to me at work. I can only go for that long.”

She'd seen many expressions on Ivan's face, but never the shock that was now widening his gaze. "You will come with me?"

"Yes." She leaned over and put her hands on his shoulders and brushed her lips against his. "I'll come to Russia with you."

His face closed down and he said in a low voice, "Thank you. I promise you will not regret this."

The enormity of what she just said raced through her. She sat next to him and stared out over the National Mall. Couples strolled through an unusually warm fall evening, arm in arm beneath the mellow lights. She took a deep breath and let it out, willing her heart to slow down. Without another word, he stood and helped her to her feet again. A sick feeling descended into her stomach. She looked up at him, but he ignored her.

His indifference had certainly not been the response she'd been looking for.

He'd been so passionate about her coming with him that she imagined she saw something more in him than was there. Instead of hugging her, swinging her into his arms and kissing her, or even smiling, all he was doing was holding her hand as they walked through the National Mall at a brisk pace while he talked on his cell phone.

They made it all the way to their waiting limo without him ever pausing to do more than glance at her. Worse yet, he spoke Russian, so she had no idea what he was saying. If he hadn't been gripping her hand so hard, she might have thought he'd forgotten about her.

She got into the limo silently, wishing she'd never agreed to go with him. If his indifference hurt now, what would it feel like if she was trapped over in Russia with him? What if she wanted to leave and he wouldn't let her? Okay, that last thought was pretty dumb. One thing she was sure of was that Ivan wouldn't hurt her. Plus, there would be a trail of documents and stuff. She would also call her best friend and let her know where she was going and who she was going with.

If she was still going. Maybe it had all been some kind of mind game. There were men out there who really got off on breaking women, on winding a woman around their finger then shattering her heart.

A sudden silence filled the car and a moment later Ivan threw his phone across the limo with one hand and grabbed her with the other. She squeaked in surprise when he hauled her onto his lap and began to kiss her senseless. If she'd thought she'd experienced every kind of kiss she could with this man, he proved her wrong. He kissed her like he was touching her soul and she loved the way his hands clenched on her hips, holding her there while he undulated his pelvis against hers.

When they came up for air she was panting and his gaze glittered with lust. "I've made the arrangements. We'll be flying out on my private jet. My personal shopper in Moscow is assembling a wardrobe for you and I'll show you the homes you can pick from for us to stay in."

She blinked rapidly. "Is that what you were doing on the phone?"

"Yes. I wanted to get everything done as quickly as possible so you could not change your mind." His voice deepened and a hard pulse of need wet her inner thighs. "You are mine, Gia, and I will not let you go without a fight."

He slipped his hand beneath her dress and slid his fingers against the lacey froth of her panties. His nostrils flared as he played with the wet fabric, pinching and massaging her pussy until she thought she might come without anything other than his gentle rubbing to get her off. He slid two fingers beneath the lace and teased at the soaked entrance to her sheath. That tender skin contracted hard, earning a deep chuckle from Ivan.

"Your body is begging for my cock."

"Yes, it is," she agreed with a desperate gasp. "Please take me."

His mouth tilted in an arrogant grin and he leaned back, putting his arms behind his head. "Well, I was planning on taking you out dancing."

"Dance naked with me," she moaned as she ground herself against his cock through his shorts.

The feel of his warm, firm muscles beneath her was driving her crazy and she wanted to tear at his clothes.

"If you want my cock in that hot pussy, you're going to have to earn it, my Gia. Show me how much you want me. Seduce me."

Reaching between them, she cupped his straining erection and had to hide a smirk. She was pretty sure he wanted her as much as she wanted him, but if he wanted to be seduced, she was more than eager to give it a try. Ivan responded to her like no other man, and it made her wanton to pleasure him, to make him feel the burning fires that licked through her body, tightening her for him, readying her pussy for the thick head of his shaft.

He wore a button-down blue shirt that she made quick work of, the smooth fabric parting to reveal his sculpted torso.

Leaning over while she was doing this, he pressed a button and said something in Russian. Then he leaned back and smiled at her. "The driver will take us around DC until we are finished. I rather like the thought of fucking you here. I want you touch me, but only with your mouth."

A delicious shiver went through her as she moaned and grasped her hands behind her back. It was either restrain herself or she would forget and touch him. She frowned down at his shorts and his brown leather belt. "Master, could you assist me with those?"

"Normally I would ask you to pay the price of being spanked with it, but your ass is still too tender." He unbuckled the belt and unbuttoned his shorts, sliding them down enough that his cock was trapped inside but pushing at the fabric. "Now the price is coming down your throat. You will not be able to breathe, Gia, only suck and hope I finish coming before you pass out."

A hard shudder of desire sparked along her nerves like bolts of erotic lightning. Breath play had always intrigued her, but she didn't like having someone flat out choke her. At least externally. Having his cock block her throat as he came was so naughty and she loved the illicit thrill it gave her. She imagined what she'd look like to him as she took him down her throat and her pussy clenched.

Starting at his face, she covered every inch of him that she could with soft kisses. When she lost her balance he held her so she could continue, his eyes closed and his lips slighty parted, an almost blissful expression covering his rugged face. As she worked her way over his body, kissing every exposed inch of skin, she realized Ivan had completely relaxed beneath her. When she'd peek at him she would find him watching her with a look of almost wonder on his face. Well, wonder for Ivan. The small smile on Ivan's lips wouldn't mean much on other men, but on Ivan, it made her heart sing with contentment. The feeling she'd made the right decision grew until she started to get excited about going to Russia with Ivan.

He was hers. At least for another seven days.

She used her teeth and freed his erection from his deep blue boxer briefs as she nudged the material down under his balls. He lifted himself slightly to help her and once he was free she smiled up at him, then lightly traced the tip of his cock with her tongue, lapping at the pre-cum gathered there. His essence slid over her taste buds and she groaned. He was delicious and his taste instantly invoked thoughts of drinking down her Master's seed. She was rapidly becoming addicted to him.

She had to rely on his grip to steady her as she took him in her mouth, softly licking and teasing him the best she could. Soon, he was thrusting his hips into her wet heat and all she could do was take as much of him as possible.

"Brace your hands on my thighs. I will be watching you. If you think you might pass out, I want you to squeeze my thighs three times. Do it now."

She complied, unable to answer because right now she was teasing the slit of his dick with her tongue. The way he twitched and the throb of his shaft between her lips let her know he wasn't as unaffected as he seemed. Ivan had mastered his body to the point where nothing was revealed he didn't want to show. But he couldn't hide from her.

Giving him a wink, she flicked her tongue over the sensitive skin on the underside of his shaft. He chuckled and groaned, a smile breaking his mask of indifference and revealing the warm man beneath. "You are nothing but trouble. But you're *my* trouble."

She hummed in agreement, then began to ease her way down his cock as far as she could. She didn't get very far before she was choking.

"Easy, Gia. This is a bad position for deep throating, especially since we're in almost constant motion." He gripped her by the hair and pulled her off his cock. "Besides, I've changed my mind. I want to fuck you. I want to use my pussy."

She shuddered with need and her desire for him to be inside of her increased exponentially. "Yes, Master."

"Turn around and scoot forward until you reach the other bench. Then bend over and flip up your skirt."

Sweet anticipation hummed through her veins and she quickly did as he commanded, enjoying the feel of the cool air on the overheated skin of her ass. Eager for him, wanting him, she tilted her butt high and set her legs wide, making herself as available to him as she could. The smell of her musk flavored the air and Ivan let out a low groan.

"Mine."

He palmed her ass and rubbed his hands over the still-tender surface. Sitting wasn't comfortable for long periods of time, and she winced when he'd given her a gentle pat earlier. He dipped his fingers between her legs and grunted. "You are so wet, my Gia. I wish we had more time, but I'm going to have to fuck you hard and fast."

"Yes, please, Master," she said in such a sultry voice even she was surprised by it.

He slipped a finger between her soaking panties and her sex, moving the lace to the side instead of taking them completely off. A rush of chills raced over her at his touch and she moaned in anticipation. The fat head of his dick pressed against her sensitive entrance, and her body tried to suck him in. He began to push and gripped her hips, his fingers over her bruises, holding her tight enough to slightly hurt. Then, true to his word, he slammed into her and she screamed his name. He fucked her, hard and raw, until she came again and again. Each orgasm seemed to bind her closer to him, and by the fourth one, she was beyond spent. He rocked inside of her and growled low in his throat. "Suck me."

Pulling out, he jerked her around by her hair and shoved his prick into her eager mouth. With a low moan, she used her hands to jack him off as she sucked. It took less than a minute before he began to say something in Russian that sounded like it was probably really dirty as his dick jerked in the tight confines of her mouth. She took a deep breath through her nose and carefully swallowed as much of him as she could.

The effect was instantaneous. He roared and began to come, the hot throbs of him in her throat making her reflexively swallow. It must have felt really good because, every time she did it, he made something close to a snarling sound. When she finally released him from her mouth she was gasping for breath and immensely proud of herself.

They both leaned against the bench, panting and staring at each other. She began to giggle, then outright laugh. "This is insane!"

"What?"

More laughter spilled out as she tried to smooth her dress back in place and wondered if she should take off her ruined lace thong. At some point while he'd ravished her, he'd snapped one strap and the other had been stretched out. "This! I mean, look at us! Look at what we just did in a limo in the middle of Washington DC. You are such a bad influence."

He gave her an amused smile. "I can't even begin to tell you all the kinky things I want to do with you. All the places I want to take you, or all the people I want you to meet."

Zipping himself up, he sat back and motioned her forward. "Come here. I messed up your makeup."

She groaned. "I need to stop wearing it around you. I just sweat it off."

"True, but you know that makes me hard."

Her giggles resurfaced as he carefully cleaned her face with a pristine handkerchief he took from his pocket. "Who carries around a hankie?"

"A hankie? What is a hankie?"

She touched the ultra-soft fabric he was using to clean her face. "This."

He shrugged as he pulled her next to him and cuddled her close. Melting into him was easy, almost natural, like her body knew she had nothing to fear while in his arms and she could relax. Plus, four really good orgasms had left her feeling all giggly.

"There are many things about my culture that are different than yours."

"I'm sorry, I didn't mean to offend you."

Smiling, he surprised her by kissing the tip of her nose. "Never worry about me being offended if you have a question. There is no such thing as a stupid question. My mother used to like to say that."

The sparkle in his gaze dimmed and she felt his sorrow. It was like she was so attuned to him that his pain became her pain and her heart ached for him. "I'm sorry, Ivan."

"For what?"

"That your mother passed away."

He pulled her close and rested his head on hers. "I wish my mother was still alive, that she could see all I've done and accomplished."

She sighed. "Me too. My mom would have loved to see me graduate from college. It had always been her dream for me."

"When did your mother pass?"

"Four years ago. She was murdered."

His arms tightened around her and his voice deepened. "What happened?"

"My father used to own a convenience store in a not so nice part of town in Atlanta, but it was all we had. When he passed, my mother kept it running, using the money to take care of me. It's hard to explain, but our store was like a part of the neighborhood family. Not everyone living in the ghetto is bad. Some really good people got caught up in bad situations and others just couldn't afford to move. My mom was a very kind woman, despite being clinically depressed. For her, working in the store was like visiting with extended family. There was always someone coming in to talk." She let out a pained sigh. "After I moved out to go to college at the University of Georgia, things got worse back home. The economy went down the shitter, and people started to get real desperate. Our store was robbed at gunpoint three times before I could convince my mom to take the money she'd put away for college for me and buy one of those bulletproof glass booths. I'd rather work a second job and take out a bunch of student loans than think about her being held up."

He stroked her back. "You are a good daughter."

“Not good enough. She was still working there when a drug addict decided to rob it. She had all these security measures in place, but the robber took a hostage and threatened to shoot the guy unless she came out of her booth.” Staring out the window at the passing lights, she curved into Ivan. “The man he took hostage, Darshel, was a good family friend. My mom had known Darshel since he was six years old. A neighborhood kid who beat the system and became a police officer, Darshel would stop by while on duty and make sure my Mom was all right. She would have remained safe, if she’d just stayed behind the glass.”

“Did Darshel perish as well?”

“No, but he’ll never walk without a limp. He got shot twice in the back and four times in the leg as he tried to overpower the robber.” She took a watery breath. “At least my mom didn’t suffer. She got shot in the head, so her death was almost instantaneous.”

Ivan stiffened next to her. “The man who did this, is he in your American jail?”

She let out a sigh and brushed aside a tear. “Can I see your hankie again?”

He handed it to her without comment and began to stroke her back, and his touch comforted her immensely. Had she known being held like this could ease her grief, she could have saved herself a lot of heartache. Then again, she’d never felt this way about anyone, but Ivan.

“Yeah, the guy’s in jail. Probably for the rest of his life.”

He studied her face in the shafts of light from passing stores and streetlights. “Do you wish he was dead?”

Blinking at him, she slowly shook her head. “No. God will take care of him in the end.”

“I can make him pay for what he did to you.”

The look in his eyes scared her a bit and she cupped his face with her hands. “Really, it’s okay. I’ve made peace with it and I know my mom wouldn’t want anything bad done in her name.”

The car pulled to a stop, and the side door opened a moment later. She stared out in confusion as a low, roaring sound filled the air. The scents of oil, gas, and something she couldn’t quite identify filled the car. Ivan wiped her face again and gave her a gentle kiss on her lips before he slid out of the limo and helped her out as well. She clenched her ass to keep the destroyed thong from falling down off her leg as she walked.

Then she saw Ivan’s jet and her mouth dropped open.

Sleek, huge, and black with silver accents, the jet reeked of wealth and she glanced at Ivan as they walked. This wasn’t a small corporate jet, this monster was the size of a commercial liner. She knew Ivan was loaded, but seeing something like this put him into a whole new light and made her wonder once again what the hell he was doing with her. More than likely, they’d get over there and he’d be ready to move onto his next woman in a week’s time. Before she could get too embroiled in those negative thoughts, she had to navigate her way up the stairs to the entrance while trying to keep her underwear in place.

By the time they reached the top she was clenching her ass with all her might. Ivan gave her an odd look, but the perky and smiling flight attendant waiting for them inside of the jet held a tray with two glasses of what looked like champagne. “Welcome, Mr. Eshov and Ms. Lopez.”

“Thank you,” Ivan said and took a glass before handing it to Gia. He looked back at the flight attendant. “I’d like a meal as soon as we are at cruising altitude. Nothing heavy.”

“Of course, sir.”

Ivan led Gia past crew berthing, through a door and further into the opulent interior of the plane. She let out a soft gasp as she took in how the top one percent flew. Two groups of sumptuous cream leather chairs with seat belts were arranged around ebony wood tables and made up the front part of the passenger section. On either side of the plane there were couches big enough for five people to sit on and a wall of some kind of beautiful dark wood divided the room with a small door to one side. The majority of that wall was taken up by a huge flat screen TV and right now it was showing a map of the world with a small plane to indicate where they were currently located, their final destination, and how long it would take to get there.

She wandered toward the map and took a sip of her champagne before handing it to Ivan. "Hold this for a second, please."

He did as she asked with a curious look, and after checking that no one was watching, she quickly took off her ruined thong and shoved it in his pocket.

Grinning, he put his hand in the pocket with her panties. "How in the world did these not fall off already?"

"I have a strong butt," she said with a slight flush as she took her drink.

He let out a little growly sound that made her all shivery. "That you do. Come, we need to be seated for takeoff."

After pulling her over to the couch, he sat and had her snuggle next to him as he belted her in. The flight attendant came back and asked if they would like a cashmere throw to keep them warm. Ivan nodded and soon Gia wasn't only belted in, she was snuggled close. It was actually really nice to have him holding her. She didn't like takeoffs and landings—they made her skin crawl. Normally she'd be on a regular plane and trying to disguise her panic, hoping the person sitting next to her didn't hear her accelerated breathing. When Ivan felt the change he held her closer.

"Are you scared of flying?"

"No. I love flying. It's the getting up and going down that I don't like. It feels wrong to my body to go up and down so quick."

The big engines hummed to life behind them, the vibration thrumming into her bones and ramping up her anxiety.

Trying to distract herself, she asked him a question, “Why do you want me to come with you, Ivan?”

He held her gaze and said something in Russian. She had no idea what it was, but the flight attendant approaching them stopped in her tracks and gaped at Ivan.

With a soft lurch, the jet began to move and she drew in a quick breath. “What did you just say? It better have been complimentary.”

His features started to close down, but his eyes opened to her, letting her see the truth in his words. “I told you I was very glad you were coming with me, that I could not wait to show you my city and my life, and that you are the most amazing woman I’ve ever met. I am blessed to have you with me.”

The engines started to ramp up and she clutched at his hand while the flight attendant went up front to the crew berthing after making sure they had everything they needed. The jet taxied to the runway and Gia tried to keep her anxiety under control. When the engines began to rev up and they moved forward she braced herself for the g-force, but Ivan held her tight and she barely shifted. Then that horrible, wonderful moment when the wheels left the ground and they were flying. For her, it was akin to magic and she let out a low breath.

“I’m very glad I came too. Even though I have no idea where we’re going.”

With a laugh, he turned and pointed at the wall. “Just look at the image. It’s in both Cyrillic and English.”

Biting her lip, she turned to him. “Ivan, I’m a little frightened about going to a country where I know nothing of the language.”

“You will never be in a situation where that will be a concern. I will always take care of you. Besides, immersion is the best way to learn a language. It is how I learned English.”

"Really?"

"Yes. I spend a great deal of time in both the United States and Canada attending to business." He smiled slightly, his gaze distant. "You Americans are an odd people. I watched a great deal of American television to try to help learn the language. It took me a long time to realize that most of you are not like those reality television programs your people are so fond of."

She laughed and held his hand, rubbing her thumb over the thick veins on the back. "Well, I can't argue with that."

A second later the captain's voice came over the speakers in Russian. Ivan translated for her. "We've reached cruising altitude and have a long flight over the Atlantic ahead of us with good weather."

A few minutes later there was a lovely light dinner set out for them consisting of fresh fruits, small sandwiches, and absolutely amazing chocolate croissants.

As usual, Ivan watched her eat with a small smile, but she ignored him. This was good, really good. With all the marathon sex she'd been having with Ivan, she'd burned off a ton of calories, so she didn't feel too guilty about cleaning her plate. Besides, he liked to watch her eat. It made him happy, and if something as simple as watching her eat made him smile, then she figured things were going pretty good between them. Noticing he hadn't eaten much, she grabbed a croissant and strode over to his seat, easily spinning his chair so he faced her. The flight attendant had retreated to the crew's compartment to give Gia and Ivan privacy.

She held the treat to his lips. "Eat."

Taking a slow bite and moaning in his throat, she swore he fucked the food right in front of her as he ate. Lucky croissant. Then he began to chew and she watched the flex of his jaw, admiring the lines of him, the changes in his expression as he enjoyed the sweet pastry. When he took another bite, he nipped her finger with a low growl, making her giggle.

She liked this playful side of him.

"Does that couch fold out into a bed?"

He shook his head. "No. Are you tired?"

"I won't lie, I could sleep for around fifteen hours right now. You're a lot to keep up with."

He gently eased her off his lap, then took a drink of his water. She followed suit, knowing that a flight this long could lead to dehydration if she wasn't careful. Then he led her further into the plane, past the partition, and through a door. On the other side she found an actual queen-sized bed tucked beneath the windows. Mounds of fluffy white pillows graced the brass headboard and a thick, soft earth toned comforter completed a space of pure luxury.

"Wow. I've never slept on a bed in the sky."

He smiled and began to unbutton his shirt, grabbing her immediate attention. "The bathroom is to your right. There is a small shower in there. I want you to take one and then I want you in bed."

She put her hands on her hips. "Awfully bossy, aren't you?"

With a grin, he tugged his shirt off, the ripple of his muscles making her wet. "Yes. But you love that about me."

She snorted, but didn't dispute him. Sick as it might be to some people, she liked being ordered around…in certain situations. Like being told to shower and the way his gaze had glinted with the promise of retribution if she bratted out on him. In fact, she was so sure his hand was coming to smack her ass that she slammed the door after her and engaged the lock. Ivan's muffled laughter came from the other side and she stuck her tongue out at him. The shower was small and completely enclosed in glass, but big enough to do what she had to do. Black marble and chrome accents highlighted the bathroom and as she washed herself she couldn't help the occasional giggle at the thought that she was showering at 37,000 feet.

After drying off with some deliciously thick towels, she sniffed at each of the four different kinds of body lotion offered in a small basket on the sink. She picked one that smelled faintly like apples and lotioned herself up, shaking her head with a rueful grin as she counted the bite marks decorating her body. She slipped on a white silk robe that hung next to the door and yawned. There was something about a warm shower that made her instantly tired and her jaw cracked as she yawned again.

As soon as she stepped out, Ivan went in and shut the door behind him after giving her a brief kiss. She made sure her hair was as dry as she could get it before she jumped on the decadent, wonderful bed. For a moment she just lay there, on top of the comforter and sprawled out. She sank the slightest bit into the mattress and it gave her the feeling of being gently held. The heat from the shower, the food in her belly, and the vibrations of the plane lulled her to sleep.

Chapter

Gia sipped her coffee and settled back into her seat on Ivan's plane. She was eating a delicious brunch and wondering how many miles she needed to run to work off all this over indulgence. Speaking of over indulgence…

"Ivan, do you really need seven homes in Moscow?"

He smiled at her and sipped his orange juice. "Why? Do you think I need eight?"

Shaking her head, she pointed at the screen on the wall, which now displayed his properties, so he could give her tours of each. A part of her was appalled at the amount of money it would have taken to purchase these homes, but the architect in her was blown away by the beauty of the buildings. She had to admit, having her choice of seven top-notch, very different homes was kinda cool in an over-the-top sorta way.

Ivan owned everything from a six-story townhome, to an estate on the outskirts of Moscow complete with stables and a great deal of land. It made her feel very poor and out of place. Most of all it made her ashamed of her ghetto roots. He'd obviously been born into money, while she came from one step above poverty.

"Gia, why do you look so sad? Did I say something to offend you?" His voice deepened. "You promised you would tell me if I hurt your feelings."

She blinked and took a long drink of her coffee, then said, "No, no, you didn't say anything. I was thinking my own thoughts, okay?"

The fine lines around his mouth deepened as he frowned. "What does that mean?"

With a tired sigh, she flopped back in her chair. "Tell you what. You answer one of my questions and I'll answer yours."

A shrewd light came to his eyes. "I'd like to hear the question first."

"Uh-uh. That's not how we play this game."

He suddenly lunged from his chair and she fell out of hers with a yelp as he started for her. Before she managed to crawl more than a foot, he grabbed her and flipped her over. Heat suffused her as her body remembered his touch, how blindingly good he made her feel. She hated how her wits fled around him, but adored the way he pinned her to the carpet.

Giving him a little growl, she spread her legs and bucked her pelvis. Her legs were actually really strong, and Ivan looked surprised as she almost dislodged him. Then he growled back and slammed his body into hers. The way he distributed his weight left her helpless beneath him.

Helpless and aroused.

"This is not a game to me, girl. I believe I am far more serious about you than you think."

She twisted beneath him. "Come on, Ivan. We both know your track record with women isn't exactly stable."

"Do you really want to talk about our sexual pasts? Because I'd bet you've done some things most people would consider perverted."

Flushing, she tried to ignore the way her nipples scraped against his chest. Today she wore a lovely cream silk shirt while he wore a soft gray cotton shirt that clung to his heavily muscled frame. The sensation of his warm, hard body sliding over her sent her hormones into overdrive. Still, she couldn't make this easy for him. While her hormones might be completely at his mercy, she was still her own person with her own demands and needs.

There was no way in hell he was going to bulldoze over her.

"Fine. You ask your question first, then I'll ask mine. Deal?"

"If it is insulting, I will not answer it."

"Don't be such a baby. Ask your question."

He gazed into her eyes. "Why are you alone? Why do you not have a man in your life?"

Swallowing hard, she looked away. "That's two questions."

He didn't move, but his weight lightened on her and he stroked her face with one hand.

Embarrassed and vowing she was going to get him back for this, she shrugged. "I never met the right guy. My first real boyfriend turned out to be a man-whore."

"A what?"

"A man-whore. He cheated on me, constantly."

His lips softened and he bent down and gave her lips a soft kiss. "He was a fool."

Melting, she nodded. "He was. Then there was just a string of guys who turned out to be losers for one reason or another. I guess that's why I've been kind of playing the BDSM scene for the last two years. There is an honesty there you don't get in most vanilla relationships. A trust. I can go in, have my needs taken care of, and leave without getting my heart butchered."

"I will not hurt you."

To her shame, tears filled her eyes. "How do I know that?"

He stood, then scooped her up in his arms, carrying her back to the bedroom. "Because I said so."

Then he grinned at her and she couldn't help but smile back. "So bossy."

"Take your clothes off and get on the bed. Except for your stockings. Leave those on."

The demanding tone in his voice made her shiver. She turned and made a long, slow production of drawing her shirt over her head and her skirt down her hips. When they were alone like this, she wanted to serve him, to bring him pleasure, to always be aware of him in everything she did. While it was true she'd been trained in how to submit, she'd never actually felt the bone deep need to actually do it before she'd met Ivan. Soon she was clad only in her nude stockings with their fringe of white lace at the top.

Turning slowly, she sauntered over to the bed and climbed on it, sure he could see her arousal wetting her inner thighs. When she lay on her back and raised her arms overhead, stretching out, she turned to look at him and smiled. His total attention was on her and it felt like a caress as warm as the sun coming through the windows of the plane.

"Since you are in the mood to entertain, I want you to touch yourself. Show me what you do when you are masturbating for your pleasure. I don't want some bullshit porn show. I want your honest reaction. Give me your passion."

She licked her lips and cupped her breasts, tweaking her nipples with a sigh. Touching herself had never been this much fun. Having Ivan watch her, hearing his sharp inhalation as she pulled her nipple piercing, then twisted it, had her pussy throbbing with need.

"Master, may I come?"

"You may."

Closing her eyes, she smiled and slipped one hand between her legs as she continued to play with her breasts.

"What are you thinking about?"

"You." She circled her clit with the tip of her finger, spreading her arousal over the tight bud.

His pleased murmur made her body flush with need. It was almost as if his approval fed her arousal, made her burn hotter. The additional heat in her blood had Gia sliding two fingers into her pussy and bringing her other hand down to play with her clit. Strong hands spread her thighs wide and she opened her eyes to find Ivan, still dressed, staring down at her body.

"Whose pussy is this, Gia?"

"Yours, Master."

Just saying that brought her orgasm within shouting distance. She furiously worked her body, wanting to come, needing to share her pleasure with him. If she pleased him, he would reward her. He always did and in ways she never imagined.

The world spun as he pulled her around so her ass was at the edge of the bed. Sinking to his knees, he began to lick her inner thighs where they met her pussy. The feeling of his face against her fingers, his lips on her thighs, had Gia tightening in exquisite pleasure so intense it was almost painful.

"Come for me," he whispered against her skin and she obeyed.

As she started to orgasm, he licked at her fingers, sucking at her pussy and sensitizing her until she was trying to push him away. With a low growl, he slung her legs over his shoulders and gripped her ass, holding her captive as he devoured her sex. The more she tried to get away the more he sucked on her oversensitive nub and soon he had her shuddering and saying incoherent things.

When he finally released her swollen clit she groaned low in her throat, fisting the sheets and writhing. Her whole body was one big, oversensitive bundle of nerves. A moment later Ivan's naked skin moved against hers like a balm for her pain. His warmth pressed into her as he pulled her up so she was lying on her side, facing him. He lifted her leg over his hip and the tip of his erection pushed into her an inch or two, just enough to torment her.

"Ask me your question, Gia."

She gripped his shoulders and tried to push him further into her with a whimper. "You want to talk now?"

"Ask me your question so I can fuck you hard and deep."

"You're insane." She tried to fight back another moan as he began to torment her nipple. "Why do you do this to me?"

"Because you think too much. You're more honest when I'm inside of you. There, question answered."

Before she could protest that what she'd said hadn't been her real question, Ivan slammed himself into her sheath hard enough that he hit her cervix and she winced, then moaned. He filled her so completely, and when he kissed her as he began to stroke in and out of her body, she lost herself in him.

"I do this to you," he whispered against her lips, "because it makes me feel joy."

She rubbed her cheek against his and raked her nails gently over his back. The affection she felt for him swamped her senses, spilling huge amounts of hormones and chemicals into her bloodstream until she could only scream out her pleasure. Ivan really began to fuck her then, hard thrusts like a machine that tore her apart as she orgasmed deep and hard. Feeling her sex clench around his cock as she rode each wave of pleasure was one of the best things she'd ever experienced. She could totally let go and simply feel, trusting he would take care of her, not having to worry about anything but her pleasure.

He stiffened and shoved himself inside of her with a low grunt that vibrated through his body into hers. She swore she was so sensitive to him she could feel the hot pulse of his release deep within her. He held her closer, running his hands over her body as his hips finally stilled. They were both damp with sweat and Gia didn't want him to leave her body yet.

"Cuddle me, please."

"There is nothing I would rather do. Sleep, *moya lyubov*."

He twitched every time her pussy gave an involuntary pulse and she let out a contented sigh.

Gia tried to keep from noticing how people stared at them as she and Ivan walked through Moscow's Sheremetyvo Airport with his entourage in tow. Instead of his comfortable traveling clothes, he now wore a smart black suit with a blue and green tie that made his turquoise eyes stand out. Gia was similarly dressed in an elegant black skirt and shimmering pale yellow top cut to accentuate her toned arms, now adorned with matching gold bracelets that resembled BDSM cuffs. When Ivan put them on her he made a little growling noise that made her laugh. She discovered that when Ivan was alone with her, he was playful and open with his affection, but when they were around others, he almost always kept his cold, commanding mask in place.

And he was certainly doing that silent 'You don't want to fuck with me' thing right now. He radiated confidence and strode through the airport like he owned it, but he was constantly sneaking glances at her. Their eyes would meet and his gaze would warm before he turned off his emotions again and looked away. She found his confidence compelling and very sexy.

Gia smiled at a pair of cute little girls as they passed, and their mother frowned at her and gave her a suspicious look. She squeezed

Ivan's hand. "Why do people give me weird looks when I smile at them?"

"It's a cultural thing." They walked past a group of Chinese tourists and Gia smiled as they parted for Ivan to pass. "The Russian people do not smile as easily as in America. Russians tend to distrust people who smile too much. They think anyone who smiles that much is fake, or what you call a phony. Like your smiling used car salesmen."

She stopped smiling right away and looked up anxiously at him as they took an escalator. "I don't know if I can stop smiling at people. It's so much a part of who I am. I mean, I don't think about smiling, I just do it."

"Do not worry. Give people a chance to get to know you and they will see what I already know."

"What's that?"

He looked down at her, then rubbed his thumb over her hand. "That you have a beautiful soul."

She was surprised when she didn't melt into a puddle of goo and ooze through the grates of the escalator.

The rest of their trip through the airport passed by in a haze as she floated along next to him. He was so sweet and sincere, but only with her. To everyone else he was intimidating or downright scary. When a man had accidentally bumped Gia Ivan glared at him and that had the poor guy dropping his gaze and moving so quickly away from them he almost ran.

When they reached the baggage area they met up with two big, hulking men who silently screamed hired muscle. She wasn't the least bit surprised when she found out they were Ivan's bodyguards. The men spoke halting English, but they treated her with great respect and deference. After their luggage had been collected, they'd gone outside and Gia found a silver Rolls Royce sedan waiting for them and another bodyguard who would sit up front with the driver. The other two would follow in the black SUV.

All three men were huge, and she tried not to stare at them.

She slipped her hand into Ivan's as he spoke with his bodyguards in Russian. People were openly gawking at them now and she subtly tried to check her outfit to make sure she was appropriately covered. Everything looked in place and her kick ass black and gold wedge heels by Ruthie Davis didn't have any toilet paper stuck to them.

Ivan looked down at her and she motioned for him to come closer. "Why are people staring at us?"

"Because I am well-known in Moscow."

She gave one of the women watching a hesitant smile and received nothing in return.

Ivan gently tugged at her hand and escorted her into the waiting car. As she sat back in the lush interior, she looked out the window at the traffic. It was early evening in Moscow and as they left the airport, she turned to the window and eagerly looked around. In all the chaos of getting here, she hadn't really considered how excited she was to just be here. Moscow was one of the best cities in the world and she couldn't wait to explore it with Ivan...and his bodyguards.

"Why do you need so many bodyguards?"

Ivan shrugged. "Normally, I only have one, but I wanted extra security for you."

"I'm not sure if that's sweet or scary." She settled back into her seat and turned to face him. "Are people trying to hurt you?"

He tapped his finger against the side of the door, his gaze distant. "Russia is different from the United States, and far older. We do things differently. Bribing and embezzlement are part of my culture."

She blinked at him. "Do you bribe people?"

"Of course. I paid a bribe yesterday to a building official to make sure our permit gets done in a timely manner. Like I said, it is standard business."

"That's…different. Anything else I should know?"

"My people may be slow to warm to you. Do not be offended if they appear a bit cold and standoffish. Also, trust your bodyguards before you trust the police and never leave the house without them or your passport."

"Why?"

"Kidnapping is not unknown and I would be surprised if your picture with me at the airport is not already in the gossip pages on the Internet. Plus, you are required to carry your papers with you at all times or face arrest."

"Oh."

She really wasn't sure if she liked that. She was a private person by nature and the thought of so many strangers looking at her made her skin itch. Unease clenched her stomach and she looked through the raised glass partition at the front of the car. "So they have to go everywhere with us?"

"In public, yes. You will not always see them, but they will be there."

"What about in your home?"

"My buildings are very, very secure. There is no need for them to guard me in any of my homes." He held her closer to him. "I do not like you so far away from me. Why do you seem sad?"

"I'm not sad, I'm just…overwhelmed. This is a lot to take in."

Ivan's cell phone began to play a melody from his pocket. He pulled it out and began to speaking in Russian while cuddling her close to him on the seat. That was another thing that bugged her, she didn't know what people were saying. Maybe she should take Ivan up on his Russian tutor offer.

When he hung up he stroked her cheek. “Why don’t we stay in tonight? Your jet lag will be catching up with you soon and I want you to feel rested. You can nap while I go to work.”

“You have to work today?”

“Unfortunately, yes. I wish I didn’t, but there are things I must attend to.”

She understood, she really did, but at the same time she felt a pang of loneliness. “Okay.”

“There is food prepared by my chef in the refrigerator if you are hungry. If you need anything, I’m leaving my numbers with you. I will also secure your own phone and bring it home with me.”

“I’ll miss you.”

He cupped her face in one hand and kissed her. “I will miss you as well. Though I admit it is nicer than I had imagined to know you will be waiting for me when I get home.”

She kissed him back and nuzzled his neck with her nose, a warm glow filling her at the sincerity of his words. The car stopped in front of an impressive building with matching door guards out front. As they approached the car Ivan caressed her cheek. “Welcome to our home, my Gia.”

After settling in and doing a cursory exploration of Ivan’s fabulous four-bedroom six-bath apartment, she wandered back into his bedroom—no, *their* bedroom. Ivan had cleared out close to half his enormous walk-in closet for her and had it stocked with more beautiful outfits than she’d ever seen in her life. He’d also bought her over a dozen pairs of shoes, including some hot pink running sneakers and a couple pairs of comfortable walking sandals and loafers.

When she opened the lingerie drawer her whole body clenched with hot desire at the sight of all the feminine, silky garments he’d bought her. Now she dug through the drawer below it, the one filled with elegant silk nightgowns and sleep sets. She picked out a pale blue nightgown with spaghetti straps and slits up both legs. It slid over her body like a dream and she sighed at the caress of expensive silk over her skin.

Turning to look in the mirror in Ivan's closet, she almost didn't recognize herself. Her eyes sparkled and her lips were still kiss swollen from Ivan's adoration. The nightgown fit her like it had been made for her. Even though pale blue wasn't a color she usually wore, she had to admit it looked great on her. A little bit of lace across the bodice sparkled with some kind of silver thread, and another section of lace graced the bottom of the nightgown. It was so pretty she almost hated sleeping in it.

She left the closet and moved across the hushed quiet of Ivan's bedroom, admiring the massive Persian carpet that took up much of the room. She'd drawn back the thick gold velvet curtains, giving her just enough light to see by as she climbed across the broad expanse of his bed. This room smelled like him, and she wondered if this was his main home. As she pulled the embroidered burgundy comforter over her body, she sighed at the smooth feel of the sheets and the softness of her pillows. While the mattress was a little bit firmer than she was used to, it was also extremely comfortable.

She had no idea how long she'd been asleep before Ivan's body curled around hers. He was nude and aroused, but when she went to turn in his arms he held her tight and whispered, "Go back to sleep, my Gia."

With his warmth enveloping her, she drifted in his firm embrace, the feeling of safety and contentment dragging her into unconsciousness.

When she woke next it was still dark outside. She glanced at the little digital clock and read that it was four-thirty in the morning and she couldn't go back to sleep. Ivan was completely out next to her, so she scooted from the bed and donned her robe. Her stomach growled and she decided to see what Ivan had to eat in his modern and massive kitchen. She finally figured out how to use Ivan's microwave and heated up the little pitcher of maple syrup to go on some pancakes she found in the warming box. There was a silver dish of sliced strawberries in the fridge and even a little mesh bag full of powdered sugar to sprinkle on top.

Thankfully, Ivan had a single cup coffee maker that she could figure out. Two cups later, she was antsy as she watched the sunrise over Moscow ten stories below from Ivan's living room. Normally, she went for a run in the morning and the urge to move filled her. She wondered if Ivan included running clothes in addition to the hot pink running shoes she'd seen in his closet. Moving as silently as she could, she made her way to the bedroom closet and started looking through the drawers for some running gear.

"Good morning, my Gia."

She turned to find Ivan standing in the doorway, fully nude, aroused and completely unashamed. It took her a few seconds to look away from his thick shaft, up the rippled muscles of his abdomen, and then to his amused gaze.

"Morning. I was going to go for a run." Her voice came out low and husky and Ivan's lips curved into a grin.

"Give me a minute and I will join you, if you don't mind."

Looking at his perfectly toned and muscular body, she tried not to drool. "Okay. You need some help with that?"

He looked down at his erection and grinned. "I do, but first, I want to show you some of the city. As tempting as it is to keep you permanently in my bed, you need to see what Moscow has to offer. Just keep in mind this is not the United States. If you can accept Russia for what it is, you will begin to love it as much as I do."

She pursed her lips while she made sure her socks were on right. “That makes sense. I mean, if I expect people to respect my culture while visiting America, I should do the same.”

His voice held a great deal of warmth as he said, “Exactly.”

She grabbed her clothes and quickly changed into them, trying to keep her tongue in her mouth as Ivan strode out in a pair of black sweatpants and a dark blue tank T-shirt with something written on it in Cyrillic. He placed a quick call, then began to stretch out. The smooth flow of his muscles, the delicious curve of his ass as he bent over made her want to take a bite out of him in the worst way.

Trying to distract herself, she began to stretch out as well. “How do you stay in such great shape?”

He grinned at her and flexed, obviously showing off. It was such a male thing to do and she tried to keep from giggling. “When I was younger I was in the Russian military. I started boxing for them and continued as a professional fighter after I got out.”

“Were you good?”

“I was very good.” He gave her a pleased smile. “Enough that after three years of fighting I retired and bought my first six properties.”

Well, that explained the broken nose and other injuries she’d noticed on him. It also explained the way he was beating the hell out of those weighted bags back at the lodge. A pang of homesickness ran through her and she sighed as she bounced on her toes. She usually ran on the long boardwalk along the ocean and she missed her sunrise run and the smell of the surf. It was comfortable, familiar, and safe.

Ivan led her down to the main floor of the building where they met up with two bodyguards, also dressed up in workout gear. They kept their expressions impassive and she almost felt as if two statues were guarding her. After conferring briefly with them, Ivan turned to her.

“We are going to go running along the Moscow River.”

"Sounds good to me."

After a short car ride through some of the craziest traffic she'd ever seen and through and around numerous pedestrians, she found herself running beside Ivan past some beautiful buildings alongside the river. The sun had begun to rise and the evening chill was receding. It took them a bit to coordinate their running styles, but once they got their rhythm down she lost herself in the first burn of her muscles waking up, the scent of the river, and Ivan running next to her.

They got strange looks as they passed other people and she turned to Ivan after a couple of guys that looked pretty wasted laughed and raised what looked like a beer in their direction as they jogged past and yelled something.

"What did they say?"

"They said if they had a woman as beautiful as you are they'd go running around like an idiot as well."

"Why is everyone staring at us? And were those guys drunk?"

"Jogging isn't very popular in Moscow and, yes, they were drunk."

"Really?"

"Well, running is more popular than it used to be." He shrugged. "Most people belong to gyms for their exercise. I ran as part of my training and I still like to do it. Running helps to clear my mind. Plus, our winters are not tame and definitely not the kind of weather you want to jog in."

"No, I meant about the drunk part."

His big shoulders rolled as he shrugged and she couldn't wait to get him home and between her legs. "Drinking is an epidemic in my country according to some people. To others it's not a concern."

She nodded and they continued their trek down the river, passing a couple of stray dogs and more staring people. When they jogged past,

Gia tried to keep from staring back at the men and women, watching them as they walked to what were probably their jobs. Most people wore business clothes of some kind and more than one eyebrow was raised as they ran past. Soon the pedestrian traffic thinned out a bit and she breathed easier.

"How long have you lived here, Ivan?"

"I grew up outside of Moscow. My family has lived here for generations, since the 1600s."

"Wow."

Ivan stopped and turned around.

"Hey, I can run farther. You don't need to stop for me."

"Yes, we do. You are wearing new shoes."

She glanced down at her feet. "You know, I totally forgot. They fit really, really well."

As they jogged back she caught him looking at her out of the corner of his eye. "Would you like to go to the ballet tonight, Gia?"

Her breath was starting to come a little faster now. "I'd love to."

"After, I'd like to take you to my BDSM club."

"Sounds like the perfect date to me."

He laughed and they ran the rest of the way in comfortable silence.

Chapter

Gia looked down at her floor-length crimson silk couture evening gown and back up at Ivan as they pulled into the secure parking lot adjacent to his home BDSM club. To say she was nervous was a complete understatement. She was about to go meet a bunch of Ivan's closest friends and probably have sex in front of them. Maybe even with them.

Shit.

She licked her lips and touched Ivan's leg, drawing his attention from looking out the window to her. "Ivan, about tonight…I have a request."

"You look so serious. What is wrong, my Gia?"

Nervously rubbing her hand over his knee, she took a deep breath. "If we involve another girl tonight, I don't want her touching you."

He tried to hide a grin, but failed. "That is fine. I admit I find your jealousy cute."

“Cute? Yeah, well, you wouldn’t find it so cute when I’m boiling your bunny.”

“What?” He gave her a confused look. “I do not understand that phrase.”

The driver parked the car and got out. She waved her hand away. “It’s American slang from a movie. Never mind. Just believe me when I say I can turn into a total crazy woman.”

Ivan shook his head. “I would not betray you like that. Besides, I don’t want any woman in that building. I want you.”

“You’re so sweet.” She gave him a quick kiss on the lips, some of her earlier anticipation returning.

“I want you to do something for me.”

“What?”

He reached into the pocket of his tux and drew out a choker of beautiful champagne-colored pearls interspaced with thin diamond encrusted bars and what looked like a gold ring in the middle. A medallion dangled from it and said something in Cyrillic. It took her another second before she realized it was a beautiful BDSM collar made of pearls and gold. “Oh, oh my…Ivan, it’s lovely.”

Her hair was already in an updo for the ballet they’d attended earlier in the evening and it was easy for him to secure the collar around her throat.

“I want you to wear this, so everyone inside knows you’re mine.”

“What does it say?”

“Roughly translated it says ‘Ivan’s Property’, but property isn’t really the right word. More like Ivan’s most valued and cherished possession. Ivan’s treasure.”

From his other pocket he took out a long leash made of gold links with a black leather hand strap at the other end. When it snicked onto her choker he gave it a gentle tug, pulling her closer, and sending all kinds of erotic sensations through her, which settled into her lower belly in a melting burn. Her sex contracted as he jerked her closer still, then captured her lips in a long, probing, amazing kiss. He kissed her with such passion that her panties were damp by the time he was done fucking her mouth with his tongue.

He held the leash in one hand and reached between her legs with his other to press against her sex. "Whose pussy is this?"

Instant liquid warmth raced through her blood and her clit was begging for his attention. "Your pussy, Master."

"The rules for this club are a bit strict. It is not what you Americans call high protocol, but it is close. You will not speak to a Dominant without my permission. If you wish to speak with a submissive, ask me and I will inquire if it is allowed."

"Understood." She reached up and traced the collar with her fingertips, loving the feel of the cool pearls slowly warming against her skin. "Thank you for this, Ivan. I know it's only temporary, but I've never seen such a beautiful collar."

He frowned. "There is nothing temporary about it, Gia. You are mine."

She blinked at him, unsure of what he meant by those words. Her mind immediately rejected the thought that he might want something more permanent with her, or that she could even give it to him. This was one fantasy week she planned to enjoy to the fullest, and that meant not getting any more attached to Ivan than she already was. To do otherwise would be opening herself up to heartbreaking pain. She'd seen what happened to her mother when she lost the man she loved. The memory of how she'd lost the will to live and suffered through continuous bouts of depression made Gia's stomach churn.

Gia had no urge to ever love someone so much that their loss would slowly kill her.

Ivan knocked on the glass of his window twice, and one of his bodyguards opened the door. They went to a side entrance of the imposing stone building somewhere on the outskirts of Moscow. As they got closer she noticed the massive stained glass dome on the building and the intricate detail work of the earth-toned glass.

Ivan held her tightly as they crossed the parking lot to reach the entrance. The door was made of highly polished stainless steel, and Ivan looked up into the camera before pressing his thumb on the pad next to the door. A moment later, the door swung open and Gia followed Ivan inside. They were in a dimly lit foyer with black painted walls and gold chased black marble floors.

Golden sconces held real flaming torches and a lovely, svelte blond woman with big blue eyes greeted them at the door. She wore a little black dress that fit her perfectly, and a black leather collar with something written on it in gold Cyrillic text.

Ivan greeted her in Russian and gestured to Gia a few times. The other woman nodded, then her eyes got really big and she gave Gia a double take. Unsure of what the hell they were saying, Gia took a half step closer to Ivan and he slung his arm around her waist, hugging her to his side.

The woman nodded again and said something in a soft voice. Ivan turned to Gia with what she'd come to think of as his public face. Closed, cold, and intimidating. But when he looked at her, his turquoise gaze warmed and a small smile hovered at the corners of his scarred lips. "Club rules are you must be barefoot inside. Remove your shoes and give them to Willa. She will store them for you in my personal locker."

"Okay." She slipped out of her cute gold Gucci heels and handed them to Willa, who smiled and went through a door to their left to return a few moments later with a black leather bag.

Gia immediately knew it was Ivan's toy bag and a shiver of anticipation went through her. After Willa handed it to him, Ivan looked down at Gia and gave her a small, terrifying, and oh so fucking sexy smile. Before he could say something that would no doubt make her dumb with hormones like a horny teenager, she leaned up to whisper in his ear.

"Master, could it just be you and I tonight, please?"

He rubbed his face against hers like a cat, marking her with his scent. "Why?"

"I want you all to myself. I know that makes me a selfish submissive, but I want to lose myself in you tonight, Master, and have all of your attention. You make me feel safe."

His chuckle vibrated against her as he pulled her to him, trapping her with his impossibly hard bicep to his equally chiseled chest. Ivan was almost unfairly hot and she couldn't blame Willa for drooling. As hot as he was, he was hers and she didn't want to share…at least not tonight.

"I must confess, I want you all to myself as well." He hauled her up easily with one arm around her waist until their lips met. "And I will always keep you safe, my Gia."

To her shock, she instinctively made a happy, almost purring sound of pleasure. He let her slide down his body and she sighed in contentment. She rested her head against his chest and listened to his heartbeat with her eyes closed and whispered, "I'm scared of going inside."

His arms tightened, and she had to thump his chest to get him to loosen up so she could breathe.

"No one will hurt you, ever, while I'm around."

Her inner cavewoman loved that her man was strong enough to defend her, and a rush of warmth glided through her veins. "I know that. I'm not used to such a large club. My club back home has around forty members. If this entire building is the club, you must have thousands."

He cupped her face with his firm, calloused hands and brought his lips down to hers, softly kissing her and slowly demanding entrance to her mouth by licking across the seam of her lips. When she gasped he stroked his tongue against hers in a long, smooth motion that had her ready to take him right here. He smelled so good, felt so good, and her body associated pleasure with him like Pavlov's dog associated a bell to food.

Ivan broke their kiss and looked into her eyes. "I don't care about how many people are here tonight, you are the only one who matters. Your pleasure is my only concern."

Her knees turned to water and he chuckled, holding her in place. "Easy, my Gia. We have a long night ahead of us."

After the strength returned to her legs, she held Ivan's hand as he led her into the club.

It was fucking huge.

Walking into this room was like walking into a giant cavern. The dome above was made up of massive pieces of stained glass and the lighting from outside made it glow. BDSM equipment done in black leather and pale wood stretched out before her in a massive wave of arousal and need. The air was saturated with pheromones and her body flared to life. Her club at home had a similar scent, a heady mixture of sweat, sex, perfume, and desire.

Ivan released her hand and looped her leash around his wrist. Being led by him was the first step of slipping into subspace. And she wore his collar. Being leashed was about as clear an indication of Ivan's dominance over her as just about anything.

Hoping he didn't notice, she stroked her fingers over the warm pearls at her throat and touched the medallion. Her fingertips tingled and she swallowed back a smile, not wanting the club members to think she was untrustworthy or fake. That thought sobered her enough to return her hand to her side and walk behind Ivan with the elegant, rolling stroll Mistress Viola had taught her.

She followed behind him, keeping her eyes lowered, sneaking peeks as they passed different people and things. The ebony wood floors were so smooth that it felt like she was walking on satin. Out of the corner of her eye, she caught sight of a middle-aged woman giving her fit, young Dom a blowjob as he sat in his chair with an indulgent, adoring look in his eyes as he ran his fingers through her hair.

They reached their destination and Ivan stopped her. She looked up through her lashes and found that they were standing before a group of sofas and chairs, mostly full of Doms and their subs along with a few Dommes and their submissives. Every single one of the Tops made her nipples hard. She was pretty sure there was enough dominant energy here to keep her aroused for the next twenty years. It made sense. Ivan was a very powerful man and he would be drawn to the same for friendship.

The subs were, for the most part, stunning, but there were a few men and women here and there who wouldn't have looked out of place at a PTA meeting, if it wasn't for the fetish wear. Ranging from chains to leather, to lace, every conceivable type of clothing was displayed. And the jewelry was beyond amazing. These women were dripping in diamonds, emeralds, sapphires, and rubies—a pirate's treasure chest worth of jewels. She glanced up at Ivan and the proud look on his face made her heart thump.

To her surprise, he spoke in English, "Everyone, I would like you to meet my Gia."

The emphasis he put on the word 'my' screamed ownership and she tried to hide her grin. She wasn't sure if she was allowed to speak, so she gave a very small smile and a hesitant wave. Reactions ranged from genuinely happy smiles to sullen looks from the single submissives hanging out on the fringes of the group, and a few who, Gia assumed, were with their Masters. Gia made note of the women who appeared pissed so she could avoid them in the future. If Ivan decided Gia needed a female lover for the night, she didn't want it to be one of those bitches shooting daggers at her with their eyes.

Ivan led her by her leash over to a large black leather chair. At the other end of the group the circle of friends opened up to the light of a massive black onyx fireplace. Two submissives, a male and a female, were posed on either side, bound to the marble in a manner that kept them confined, but wouldn't be too hard on their bodies. The male, tall and hung had been rubbed down in glittering gold paint and wore a sun mask. The female, short and pleasantly plump, had been rubbed down in silver paint and wore a moon mask. At the top of the mantle hung a huge mirror, which reflected the room behind her in an almost panoramic manner.

Her gaze focused on her own image and she was startled at how elegant she looked despite the leash and collar, or maybe because of the leash and collar. She was falling into submissive mode and began to hold herself as she'd been trained. In her case this meant perfect posture at all times and she liked how sophisticated it made her appear in her dress and elaborately styled hair. Add the image of Ivan standing behind her, and she felt like Belle in *Beauty and the Beast*.

If she was elegant sophistication, he was raw masculinity. Ivan rocked a tux like no man she'd ever seen. He couldn't hide his nature and didn't even try. His possession of her was blatant, unapologetic, and animalistic.

Ivan curled his big hand around her wrist and broke her gaze with the mirror, reminding her of how delicate she was compared to him. The gentle way he handled her, the restraint he used to keep from injuring her, made her feel cherished, a previously unknown feeling she found to be very undervalued. The sensation of knowing someone gave a shit about you, that they did everything they could to make you happy, was an all-encompassing emotion that struck her just right. He took a seat, then hauled her up onto his lap. She let out a small sigh, grateful for his surrounding warmth. He was so nice to her and the way he took care of her made her feel dangerously close to falling in love. She couldn't help it and she certainly needed his comfort right now.

Speaking in Russian, Ivan was arguing with a man who wore a pair of black leather pants and a loose white silk shirt. His hair was carefully styled and his body was thick with muscle. A tiny redhead at least ten years his junior sat at his feet with a blissfully content look as she leaned her head against his thigh.

Ivan raised his voice and the other man pointed at Gia, and then at Ivan. She stared up at him and he sighed, then sat her up higher on his knee. "That loud mouth over there is Karl. He wants to do some shots of vodka with you. It is a traditional welcome to the club."

Karl laughed and said in halting English, "It is tradition to get drunk, but Ivan is too protective of you."

He said something in Russian that had Ivan scowling and the rest of the group laughing.

Ivan growled at the other man. "If she's drunk, I cannot play with her. That is unacceptable."

The man's lips twitched with another smile, but he didn't say anything more.

A second later a woman yelled, "Gia!"

She turned in Ivan's arms to find Catrin coming over to them. Tonight, the delightfully curvy blond woman wore a pink corset that cinched her waist down to a tiny size and barely covered her breasts. She also wore a sheer pink skirt, and it was obvious that she wasn't wearing any underwear beneath. Nico trailed behind her and gave Gia a wink.

Gia almost moved off of Ivan's lap, then looked up at him through her lashes. "Master, may I speak with Catrin?"

Chuckling, Ivan set her off to the side at his feet. "Yes, but I want you kneeling at my feet while you talk."

Nico joined them and a spot was made for him in the circle. He was greeted warmly and seemed at ease with everyone. Ivan reached out casually as he talked to rub his fingers over the back of her neck and upper shoulders, almost as if he was petting her. Regardless of his intent, the soft stroke of his hand helped ground her and gave her the strength to ignore one particularly stacked brunette who kept giving Gia shitty looks. The other woman snarled something and stalked off.

Catrin bounced over to her and received a gentle spank on the butt from every Dominant she passed. Gia really wanted a chance to speak alone with the other woman, but she had a feeling Ivan wouldn't want her out of his reach. Catrin stepped past a pair of outstretched Dom's legs and knelt next to Gia with an easy grace.

"Darling! What are you doing here?"

Gia smiled and gave the other woman a quick hug. "Ivan convinced me to extend my vacation and come to Moscow with him."

Catrin's eyes grew wide and she flicked a glance up at Ivan, who was now speaking to the group in Russian again, then back at Gia. She leaned in to whisper in an excited tone, "Gia, I think he really likes you."

Barely whispering, Gia leaned closer to Catrin's ear. "You said he likes lots of women."

"He does, but nothing like this. I came over because word is going around the club that Ivan is bringing the woman he plans on collaring. Permanent collaring."

Gia barely resisted the urge to cover her pearl clad throat with her hand. "He said that?"

"Yes. I couldn't figure out who it could possibly be. No offense meant, but this is so out of character for Ivan that it never occurred to me he'd manage to get you to come back to Moscow with him." Catrin dropped her voice further. "There are some women here tonight who are not very happy with you. If you have to go to the bathroom, tell me so you can avoid an incident."

"An incident?"

“Many of these women are rich, bored, and spoiled. And you just took away their favorite toy.”

“He’s my toy now,” Gia grumbled.

Catrin giggled and Gia couldn’t help but smile back. Ivan was giving them a suspicious look, so Gia leaned back and started talking about normal things like shopping and places to visit. Soon the shots arrived and Gia downed hers with everyone else, gasping at the strong drink and blinking back tears as everyone laughed.

With a hard look on her face, Catrin stood and pulled Gia to her feet. “Come on, I have to use the restroom.”

Ivan said something to Catrin and she said something back in a heated rush that made Ivan slip the leash over Gia’s wrist. “Take care of her, Catrin.”

“I will, Master Ivan.”

Catrin turned and practically dragged Gia across the crowded sitting area to the ladies’ rooms. Once inside the other woman started chatting again as if nothing was wrong. Gia quickly went about her business, then confronted Catrin as they washed their hands. “Why did you drag me away from Ivan?”

Giving her a suspiciously innocent look, Catrin tiled her head, her blond curls and blue eyes giving her the look of complete innocence. Gia wasn’t fooled for a minute. “What are you talking about?”

“Catrin, I’m not dumb.”

The other woman sighed and dried her hands. “One of Ivan’s ex-submissives was headed our way. He dated her a year ago for a couple months, then broke it off because she’s a manipulative bitch. She loves drama and is no doubt making a scene out there right now in order to get everyone’s attention on her.”

“About what?”

“About the fact that Ivan is introducing you as ‘my Gia’, his submissive.”

“He always calls me ‘my Gia’. It’s a cute name he has for me. Like sweetheart or baby.”

“No, he is calling you his.” Catrin touched at her lipstick with a frown. “This is hard to translate because there are no English words for it, but he called you his submissive, his woman. Like he owns you.”

“But I’m leaving in a few days,” Gia said faintly as she stared at Catrin in the mirrors over the sink.

Catrin gave Gia a small smile. “Not if Ivan has his way. He can be very persuasive.”

Gia pretended to touch up her makeup around her eyes as she scrambled to find her emotional footing. “Well, as persuasive as he can be, I have a job and a life back in the United States. I’m not giving it up to be any rich man’s plaything.”

“I hope you will at least consider his offer. See what he has to say before you shoot him down.”

Leading them out of the restroom, Catrin stopped as soon as she was out the door. Gia joined her and gaped at the sight of an enraged, very pretty brunette with skin the color of cream, who was almost nude except for a teal thong, yelling at Ivan while he watched her with a bored expression.

She yelled something again and Ivan laughed, then replied in Russian and in a cutting tone that made everyone around them laugh, except for the crazy woman glaring at him.

Gia elbowed Catrin. “What are they saying?”

“Tila, the woman with the fake tits, says he belongs with a true Russian woman and he’s betraying his country for a little American bitch. Then Ivan said she’s getting bitter in her old age. He called her a dried-up, moldy, old fruit while you’re a fresh, ripe peach.”

Gia stared at Ivan, watching him closely, trying to see if he was interested in this woman at all. He had his cold, cruel mask on and the look in his eyes was like that of a shark. Flat, emotionless, and deadly.

The woman continued to throw a tantrum until Ivan abruptly made a cutting off gesture with his hand and snarled something. Catrin gasped and translated. "He said that you are his woman and if anyone disrespects you they disrespect Ivan and his entire family, that an insult to you is an insult to him, and everyone knows what he does to people who dishonor him."

"Wow," Gia whispered, aware of heads turning her way and people talking about her. "What does he do to people that dishonor them?"

"Destroys them," Catrin said in a faint voice.

Before Gia could ask Catrin what she meant by that, Tila had thrown herself to her knees before Ivan, her hands clasped together as she wailed something out like a B movie actress. More people had gathered to witness the scene, and a few gave Ivan smug looks from the shadows. Gia made note of them as well and promised herself that she'd warn Ivan before he trusted any of them.

Catrin said in a tight, angry voice, "Now Tila is saying she wants to be Ivan's kept woman, his mistress, and he can have sex with her on the side, and she'll be and do whatever he wants."

"Oh, hell no, she didn't!"

Gia pushed Catrin to the side and quickly made her way across the room. Tila had thrown herself at Ivan's feet and began to lick his shoes. With a disgusted look, Ivan pulled away, then said something to the woman in a cold, cruel voice that Gia had never heard before.

Ivan might not be her permanent Master, he might not even be her boyfriend, but for tonight, he belonged to her and there was no way in *hell* she was letting some bitch throw herself at him. To Gia's horror, the woman started to reach for Ivan's crotch, but before she could reach it, Gia smacked Tila's hands away with enough force that the other woman yelped and clutched her hand to her chest with a stunned expression.

"Sorry, honey. This seat is taken."

She plopped herself down on Ivan's lap and glared at the other woman before turning back to him with a sweet smile. "Hello, Master."

Ivan looked down at her with a bemused expression. "Hello, my Gia."

His ex-girlfriend said something in Russian that didn't sound at all complimentary, but Gia ignored her.

The already hard muscles of Ivan's body stiffened and he roared something that had the other woman falling back on her ass. Extremely uncomfortable at seeing the woman's goodies spilling out of her thong between her spread thighs, Gia looked away and began to kiss Ivan's neck. Shit, as territorial as she was feeling right now, she would have written her name on his forehead in permanent marker if he'd let her.

Determined not to give in to the other woman's drama, Gia concentrated on the softness of Ivan's breath, the sensitive skin of his ear, and the way he tasted. So clean, so good, so masculine. She could lick his entire body and still be hungry for more. Ivan said one last thing, then gripped Gia's chin and kissed her. It wasn't a gentle kiss by any means. It was a branding kiss, a meeting of tongues and lips bordering on savage. His cock surged beneath her ass and she moaned in response.

Fire, burning heat, and desire so fierce it was almost pain, had her pussy soaked in anticipation of his touch. Nothing mattered but him, and she sighed against his mouth as he cupped her breast and began to play with her nipple through her gown. Tila shouted something, but Ivan and Gia totally ignored her, consumed by their kiss. He didn't dominate her, he owned her, and Gia still couldn't believe she surrendered to him like this. It took men years to earn her trust, and then they always broke it soon after.

As illogical as it was, Ivan had her trust from the moment their eyes first met after the auction.

She didn't think Ivan would betray her. No, she knew he wouldn't cheat on her the first chance he got. The chemistry between them was off the charts, and she'd never felt this way about anyone. Evidently Ivan was experiencing the same if he was calling her his woman and defending her honor. She laced her arms around his neck and softened her kiss, trying to tell him with her willing body how much she appreciated him.

He made a pleased sound against her lips and began to tug at her nipple ring through her dress. The sensation of his clever fingers manipulating her stiff nub had her squirming against him and moaning into his mouth.

She wanted him.

Now.

When she tried to reach between them, Ivan pulled back and nipped her lower lip. "Are you feeling needy, my Gia. Is that soft pussy all wet and swollen for me?"

"Mmm, yes, Master."

God, when he talked dirty to her it made her mindless with lust. His accent was the cherry on top and when he called her his Gia she felt like her heart might pound out of her chest. Joy filled her soul and she took in a shuddering breath as an intense emotion, stronger than anything she'd ever felt, overwhelmed her.

He'd said an insult to her was an insult to him and his family.

That was the most romantic thing anyone had ever said about her.

She pulled back enough to look into his eyes and it took everything she had to not tell him she was falling in love with him. This was a brief fling, nothing more. But oh how she wished she could stay with him. If they'd been dating for a while she'd consider it, but she couldn't move her life out here for a man who was a stranger, even if he was becoming the center of her world.

Her stomach clenched as she thought about leaving him, never seeing him again, never feeling his touch or his arms around her.

Ivan must have seen something in her gaze because his whole face softened. "You, my beautiful girl, are thinking too much. Let's shut that brilliant mind down. I only want you to feel me. Tonight I'm going to give you harsh pleasure."

When she shivered he gave her a small smile and stroked her pulse, then set her down. She noticed Tila was gone, and that people were watching them, but she didn't really care. He'd ditched the jacket and bowtie, leaving him in his crisp white dress shirt that clung to his broad shoulders. Her gaze was focused on Ivan's tight ass in his tuxedo pants as he walked with her leash once again wrapped around his hand.

Where it belonged.

He was such a man. There was nothing soft or giving about him. His control and domination rolled off of him in almost visible waves, leaving her trembling with need. Not just her own physical needs, but the bone deep desire to please him, to make him proud of her. She wanted to be worthy of the devotion he'd shown her. In a really odd way, Ivan's domination made her want to be a better person, the kind of woman he would be proud of.

How strange was that?

The more they moved into the play area the louder the music got until it was a deep bass pounding through the air, making the scenes look like moving art. The fall of the lash, the grimace of ecstasy twisting a woman's lips, and the wail of release all blended together and into the music. After walking past at least a dozen different scenes on various pieces of BDSM equipment, Ivan led her to a stone wall with thick chains bolted into it. He held out his hand and pulled her gently to his side, rubbing his face against her cheek as he whispered, “You do not have any problems with being restrained, correct?”

“No, Master, no problems there.”

He kissed the tender lobe of her ear, stealing her breath. “And knife play?”

She swallowed hard as her juices flowed from her, preparing her body for him. “I love it.”

The happy, growling sound he made had her wishing he was inside of her, taking her while he rumbled with desire. She drew back enough so she could brush her lips over his. He indulged her for a few moments, then gave her ass a gentle smack and stepped back. As soon as he was out of her line of sight she was greeted with the view of more than a few people watching them intently. Shit, she was right. Because of who Ivan was, and the rumors floating around the club about her, they were sure to be under a great deal of scrutiny.

“Take your dress off.”

Licking her lips, she nodded and turned, trying to ignore everyone around them who would soon be judging her. The unease filling her was almost like stage fright. Sure, some of them would be watching for the pleasure of it, but she could feel this was a big moment in the politics of the club. It was something to see because Ivan was doing it. She had a feeling anything he did was a big deal.

And she was his woman.

Warmth heated her limbs and let her release some of her nerves.

A movement in the crowd caught her attention and she watched Catrin blow her a kiss before she and her Master took a seat on a wide black leather chair facing Gia. The pretty blonde had a bright flush on her chest and when Nico pulled Catrin onto his lap, he spread her legs wide open and Gia could plainly see the big dildo held in the other woman’s wet sex by a harness. Gia looked back at Nico’s handsome face and he winked, then brushed Catrin’s lovely blond hair aside and bit on her neck. The contrast of his dark lips and her pale flesh warmed the banked embers of Gia's desire almost as much as the thought of what it must feel like to be stuffed that full of cock while her Master cuddled her.

She turned just a bit and gave Ivan a coquettish look over her shoulder. "Master, can you help me unzip?"

He stepped behind her and slowly lowered the zipper on the back of her dress, then let it fall to her feet in a puddle of expensive silk. The sensation of his calloused hands rubbing over her shoulders did a great deal to ease her anxiety. Clad now only in her white lace panties and strapless bra, she quickly unhooked it and slid it down her arms. People were talking around them, but only in Russian. She tried to figure out what they were saying by their tone of voice, but Ivan chose that moment to give her right breast a stinging slap.

"Are you here for them or for me?"

"For you, Master."

"Then I want your attention on me."

Someone laughed at his words and she flushed, quickly removing her panties. She stepped out of her dress and put her undergarments on top. Now, clad only in his collar with the chain hanging between her breasts, she looked at him and felt powerful. For all his being one of the most influential men in Russia, he was riveted by the sight of her naked body. His gaze slowly traveled over her frame and she stood as she'd been instructed, arms at her sides, palms facing forward, standing at the slightest of angles. He grabbed his dick and adjusted it with a growl.

"Up against the wall, *lyubov moya*."

When her palms hit the cool stones she took a deep breath and used some techniques from her submissive training to get into her version of 'the zone'. She let the voices become a background hum, focusing instead on the music and the feel of the air on her skin, to concentrate enough so she only focused on the moment and her Master.

"Raise your hands higher."

She did as she was told, and he slipped one of his hands between her legs, giving her swollen sex a very proprietary stroke. Her wetness coated his fingers and he chuckled low in his throat. A deep, masculine tone that made her insides clench with desire.

"Whose pussy is this, Gia?"

"Your pussy, Master."

"You make me very happy, my Gia. What is your safeword?"

"Damascus." He let out a low, purring hum and bit her bare shoulder hard enough to make her gasp and quickly add, "Master."

He then licked her skin where he'd bitten her, big sweeps of his tongue soothing away the ache and starting a whole new kind of burn to flare through her body. The walls of her sex clenched and she wanted him inside of her. Needed him inside of her.

"Please take me," she whimpered.

"No. First, I want to play with you. Keep your hands where they are, no matter what I do. If you break form at any time without my permission, I will shackle you and that will limit the positions I can fuck you in. I don't want to be limited. I want to fuck you until I can no longer get hard…" He made a growling noise that had her arousal dripping down her inner thighs. "And trust me when I say that since you are my submissive, that could be a long time."

She swallowed as her clit tightened. "Don't hold back, Master, if that is your pleasure. I'm yours."

His breath stilled then came out with a low sigh. "Yes, you are. My Gia."

The need for his kiss consumed her, but he'd said not to break form. This particular type of play had always been a challenge for her. When she was with him she lost control of her body to his skilled touch, writhing for him and unashamedly fucking him back with everything she had. Their couplings were primitive, visceral. To fight her natural urges was going to be really hard, but she would not embarrass Ivan in front of his friends. Besides, so far he hadn't done anything she didn't now crave like a drug. Every single kinky thing they'd done together had been amazing.

She just had to let go and trust him.

His warmth left her side and she took in a deep breath through her nose, held it, and slowly let it out through her mouth. She'd done this three times before he was back, rubbing his hand over her hip as he stood behind her. The hard edge of his energy caressed her, creating little electrical sparks to dance along her skin. He cupped her breasts with both hands and she startled, almost looking down before she stopped herself. Painful and soft, harsh and gentle, each of his hands was sending a different signal to her nervous system.

Ivan chuckled. "That was close. You almost looked."

Whimpering, she tried to steady her voice as she said, "Master, what is that? It feels like you're touching me with a bed of nails on your palm. And on the other side it feels so…soft?"

He removed one hand and held it where she could see. He'd donned a black leather glove that had tiny spikes all over the palms. Not sharp, but pointy enough that if he spanked her with them she would probably need to go to the hospital. A vampire glove. Then he brought up his other hand and she saw that it was a glove made of black rabbit fur.

"We will start out slow. I remember your high pain threshold when you're in subspace. The last thing I want is for you to pass out on me." He moved his lips over the side of her neck, teasing her skin with his gentle touch. "There are so many things I want to do with you. It would take me the rest of my life just get through half of that list. But we'll make a start tonight."

“Yes, Master.” She would’ve been embarrassed by the audible tremble in her voice if she hadn’t been so wrapped up in his spell.

Ever so slowly, he began to drag the hand with the spikes across her back, going on either side of her spine and making her flinch the tiniest bit. He wasn’t pushing hard enough to cut, only scratch. It felt similar to someone drawing their nails lightly down her back. Then he did it again, and again, an insidious awakening of her skin and making her burn. Sweat beaded on her upper lip as he kicked her legs wider, exposing her body to him and his wicked glove. Instead of going right for her pussy, he scratched her inner thighs, sending a chill through her and making her nipples ache.

Part of her feared what it would be like when Ivan used the vampire glove on her delicate sex, but the darker side of her soul hoped it would hurt…just a little bit—enough to give her that huge endorphin punch that would come from her orgasm. Every bit of pain he gave increased her arousal until she was panting and straining to keep from moving the tiniest bit.

He removed his other hand from where he had it pressing into her pubic bone and she held her breath.

When the soft stroke of the rabbit fur smoothed over her body she flexed her fingers into the stone, trying to hold on, struggling to not lose herself in the decadent, yet painful stroke of the rabbit fur across her overly sensitized skin. He returned his other hand to her pussy and gently cupped it, the spikes cool against her overheated flesh.

“You are so hot, so wet. Fucking you is heaven. Keep holding your position while I slide my cock into your greedy cunt.”

“Oh, Master,” was all she could manage as her sex clenched and released.

A moment later he positioned himself at her back so the curve of her ass fit against his pelvis. He slid his rock hard erection between her legs, but not inside of her, instead tormenting her clit and labia with slow, steady thrusts. A long, almost continuous pleading sound came from deep inside of Gia as she ached to tilt her hips enough to fit him inside.

Then he did three things at once that made her break her form with a scream. She might have been able to resist the urge to move if he'd just pressed a spike directly onto her clit, she might have been able to keep from bucking beneath him if it had only been his fur-covered hand gripping her throat, but when he shoved his cock into her at the same time she came apart in a million, screaming pieces.

He must have known it would be too much for her, because his hold on her throat tightened, constricting her air the slightest bit in warning before he released her. "Bad girl."

"I'm sorry, Master," she gasped and began to thrust her hips back at him with each fading wave of her orgasm.

He froze, a fine tremor going through his thighs pressed to the back of hers. "I'll punish you in a bit. Right now I want your hot little pussy to suck the cum out of me."

With a low groan, she squeezed and contracted her inner muscles, loosening when he pushed in, but squeezing tight as he pulled out, creating delicious friction. Behind her Ivan said something in Russian that rubbed across her skin just like the fur glove at her chest. So far, he'd been gentle with the vampire glove on her pussy and she grunted as she took Ivan from an angle that made him hit deep inside of her.

Abruptly Ivan grabbed her breast with the vampire glove and her pussy with the fur one. He simultaneously punished and pleasured her, reducing her to nothing but his slave.

He began to massage her clit with the fur glove and she arched against him. "Master, may I come?"

"Beg."

"Please, Master, please let me come."

"More," he said in a growling voice as he curved closer to her, surrounding his body with hers.

"Master, please let me come on your cock. Please!"

"You may."

A shiver of delight raced through her as he gave her a fierce, bone jarring pounding. Everything inside of her tightened, then tightened more until all she could do was keen. He bit her shoulder and she began to climax.

Hard.

It was so damn good, so intense. Her sex gripped Ivan like a fist and she could feel him throb inside of her, shooting his seed deep into her body while he joined her as she nearly died from pleasure. He kept slowly stroking in and out of her, driving her higher until her voice broke.

He rested his chest against her back for a few moments. Her pussy twitched around his still hard cock. Slowly, gently, he began to slide in and out of her again, and she sighed in contentment. Something about the thought of him sliding through his climax inside of her, his passion lubricating the devastating stroke of his dick, made her go to pieces beneath him.

Oh, God, he was going to fuck her to death.

Chapter

With every stroke, Ivan had to bite his cheek as the sensitive tip of his cock dragged through Gia's clutching pussy. He was still hard, and the urge to take her again was building at an almost alarming rate. She felt so good, so soft and wet. Her body fit him perfectly.

A sigh of regret lifted from his lips as he pulled out of Gia. "And now, time for your punishment."

Gripping her by the hair, he then grabbed his bag and pulled her across the room to a large, black leather-covered table. After helping her up, he pulled a pair of leather restraints lined with black fur from his bag. "On your back."

He grabbed her ankles and pulled her down to the edge of the table. With her feet dangling off the edge, he moved her forward further until her ass hung half off the table. He then moved around to her side and placed the cuffs around each of her delicate wrists. She watched him with such trust he couldn't stop himself from stealing a kiss. As always, she came alive beneath his touch and moaned into his mouth while he secured her hands together without breaking contact as he ate her moans from her lips.

The low throb in his balls returned and he wanted to cover her in his come. Mark her as belonging to him before every man and woman in this room who wanted her. All around them, people watched and people fucked, but none of them had someone as special as his Gia.

Ivan caught a couple of submissives he'd played with in the past watching him with longing. He made sure to meet each of their gazes and warn them off with a look that made more than one woman flinch. He was off the market. As much as Gia belonged to him, he belonged to her. Now, he needed to seduce another week out of her, then another month, and another, until she agreed to never leave him.

From his bag he took out a large hunting knife with a bone hilt in a tooled brown leather sheath.

Gripping the smooth bone handle with its cool gold pommel, he pulled the long blade out slowly, letting the light catch the surface. Gia responded immediately, her thighs clasping together and her back arching up. The way her pupils dilated and her nipples stiffened stroked his ego as a Dom. The control he had over her passion, over her body and heart humbled him. He'd never had a woman give herself to him like this. There was no artifice, no game playing. He simply touched her and she responded like she was made for him.

He slowly withdrew the knife from the sheath and watched her gaze grow wider and her breath halted in her chest. Her breasts moved slightly with the beat of her heart, and when he licked down the dull edge of the knife, she groaned and went limp. The evidence of her arousal scented the air and he smacked her thigh. "Spread your legs."

Jerking slightly at the restraints that held her hands over her head, she complied. Once her sex was open to him, he took the knife and ran it down her cheek, using some sleight of hand so it seemed to her like he was using the sharp edge, but it was actually the dull one. He wanted to pleasure her, not harm her, and this knife had been specially made so he wouldn't accidentally catch her with the sharp edge. The gold piercings in her nipples gleamed as she let out a shuddering breath.

His beauty responded so well to mind games.

"Do I have to tell you to stay still?"

She started to shake her head, then froze as the knife pressed into the delicate skin of her cheek. The elegant makeup she'd worn this evening had smeared into dark circles beneath her eyes, making her gaze seem all the more vulnerable. Fuck, she looked unbearably sexy like this.

He was losing himself in her and he couldn't be happier.

The club faded around them, the screams and wails, the laughter and dirty talk becoming nothing to him. All that mattered was his Gia. He laid the knife down and smoothed her sweat-dampened hair back from her face before picking up the blade again. She smiled, a gentle curve of the lips that he returned.

He was still smiling when he drew a thin line down her neck from her jaw, circling her throat hard enough to scratch but not deep enough to mark. In no rush, he enjoyed the way her dark caramel skin paled then flushed beneath the tip of his knife, how her thighs clenched when he traced the tip of the blade along the pulsing vein at the side of her neck. Instead of going straight for her breasts, he ran the knife down first one arm then the other, pausing at her wrist. She didn't flinch, just held still and watched him with fathomless, dark eyes. He felt like she could see him in a way no one had before. Something in her touched his soul.

Unable to express the emotions he was trying to keep off his face, Ivan had to satisfy himself with telling her simply how much he enjoyed her.

"Gia, look at the way you trust me. Your hands are uncurled, your sensitive and vulnerable palms open even as I hold a knife sharp enough to end your life to your wrist. One wrong turn on my part and you would be in real danger."

She closed her eyes and laid her head back, completely relaxed. "I trust you, Master."

With a growl, he worked the knife back up her slender limbs, noting places that made her shiver when the flat of the blade brushed over the swell of her right breast. Moving between her thighs, he lifted her leg and wrapped it around his waist. This opened her sex to him and he got to enjoy the sight of her wet, dusky pussy with its bright pink interior. Some of his cum had dripped out, a dash of cream mixed with her own release. Such a beautiful cunt.

His beautiful cunt.

Running the tip of his knife over her breast, he gave himself over to the caress of steel against silken skin, the goosebumps running over her, and the way she kept whispering his name. By the time he reached her navel she was sweating, and when he parted the sparse curls guarding her mound she let out a breathless whimper that went straight to his cock.

"Gia, look at me."

She opened her eyes and raised her head. Her dark eyes were glazed and out of focus, sure signs his girl was flying in subspace right now. Not to the point where she was incoherent, but pretty close. Evidently, she enjoyed the implied violence of this type of play.

A deep bass note hit the room and Ivan gritted his teeth, fighting the urge to fuck her to the hard throb of the music. Instead, he pressed the knife between her legs, sliding the dull side of the blade across her pussy. She cried out his name in an agonized shout and he allowed himself a small smile. Her eyelids began to flutter shut, so he slapped the flat of the blade on her pussy, hard.

"Oh, God!"

Her voice joined the chorus of submissives and Dominants around the room enjoying themselves. His club didn't have any private rooms and he liked it that way. There was no place for his woman to hide from the overwhelming pleasure. People stood around, watching him work over his girl and it aroused them, which in turn made his dick ache now to slip into her wet sheath. But he wanted her to burn hotter first. There was nothing as sexy as Gia when she was out of her mind with need, begging him to let her orgasm. The desperation in her gaze, the way she screamed out his name, and the abundant flood of her liquid arousal all fed his soul.

She struggled to meet his gaze, and when she did, he used the tip of the knife to scoop up some of her arousal. He brought the blade to his mouth and began to slowly lick her juices off the smooth surface. Jerking at her chains, she tried to reach out to him and struggled. Soon, he would let her touch him, ride him until she was sated, but he wanted her hotter.

After the blade was clean, he gave her what was no doubt an evil grin and lowered the knife down, moving it once it was out of her sight so it was hilt first, until it pressed at the entrance to her sheath. Sweat blossomed all over her body and she whimpered again, but this time in real fear.

"Easy, my Gia. It is the hilt of the knife. Smooth and cold gold pressing against my sweet pussy."

Then he pressed the hilt into her and she shuddered, hard.

"Close your eyes. Let go. You can't control this. I will do to your body as I wish. You are mine to torment and pleasure, Gia. Only mine, and I protect what is mine."

He added the last remark as a warning to those witnessing their scene. If anyone touched Gia, he would bring down his wrath on them in biblical proportions. Considering his mother's family ran one of the oldest criminal networks in Russia, and on his father's side he came from a long line of KGB agents and politicians, Ivan had connections for pretty much anything he needed. But he'd never considered using those resources to protect the woman in his life, until now. He would do anything to make sure no one ever harmed her.

With a start, he realized he'd break his own personal moral code to keep her safe. A surprisingly strong possessive streak went through him and he withdrew the knife from her gripping cunt, fighting her strong pussy muscles to pull it out. His dick wanted inside of her, now, but he needed to free her first.

Kissing his way up her stomach, licking the clean, ocean salt sweat from her skin, he took his time tormenting her breasts. Sucking hard on each aroused nub in turn, he growled low in his throat as Gia rocked her pelvis against his cock. It would be so easy to slip into her welcoming heat, but he wanted all of her passion right now.

By the time he'd licked and sucked his way up to her mouth, she was grinding hard against him, lifting her pelvis against his by wrapping her strong legs around his waist. She snarled at him when he went to kiss her and he smiled against her lips.

"Feeling a little feral, my Gia?"

She tried to nip his lips and he frowned at her. "Bad girl."

Anger and frustration burned hot in her gaze and she bared her teeth at him. He loved it when she let go like this, when she let her primal instincts drive her. This woman would never be truly tamed. He would have to seduce her into submission every time and the challenge of it, the energy that drove him higher until his mind entered that crystal clear realization of Top space. The best description of the feeling was that he was like a predator looking at his prey, watching her body, waiting for her to try to flee or strike.

Before she could react, he grabbed her by the throat and held her tight. When she continued to struggle, he tightened his grip, nowhere near enough to hurt her but just enough so she would feel collared by him. She swallowed and the fight went out of her abruptly. Not trusting her to remain passive, he removed the pins from her hair with his free hand until it spread around her in a silken veil of honey brown waves.

So beautiful with her deeply tanned skin and dark golden hair. He released her throat and she leaned up, licking his chest while he caressed her wrists, her cuffs still in place. His erection slid against her arousal soaked sex and he gripped a handful of her hair, stretching her neck open to him. When he bit her hard in the sensitive place where her neck and shoulder met beneath the pearls, she shivered and began to lick and suck his nipple.

He lifted his head and looked over at one of his friends watching them. “Get me a couch with a blanket.”

Gia ran her nails lightly down his back, then gripped his ass. The happy, purring sound she made had his dick twitching against her pussy. After he unhooked her arms from the chain holding her to the table, he brought her wrists, still cuffed together, to his mouth and kissed both her palms. She gave a beautiful whimper that went straight to his cock, driving his urgency to truly possess her higher.

He scooped his arm beneath her ass and threw her over his shoulder. She let out a little shriek that he found exquisitely feminine. Giving her hip a smack, he walked them over to the couch his friend had secured for them. He almost stumbled when she began to lick his lower back, and he bit her hip.

Little minx.

When he reached the couch he slid her off his shoulder and made sure she was okay to stand on her own before he sat. A soft, thick red blanket had been placed over the couch to protect it from body fluids and with Gia he would need it. No doubt she would soak his balls with her orgasm. The way she got so wet for him had him pulling her forward until she straddled his lap with an eager growl.

“Ride me. I want you to come all over my dick.”

She practically jumped him and he found himself with an armful of hot, aroused, squirmy girl on his lap. Without preamble, she lined his cock up with her slit and began to slowly lower herself on him. She adjusted her stance so her legs were better situated outside of his. As she eased him into her ever so tight little pussy, she met his gaze and now it was his turn to shiver.

The intense emotions he saw there made his chest hurt. She looked at him like she loved him and he found it impossible to keep his feelings hidden from her. With one look, she stripped away all the formidable walls he kept in place around his emotions and made them vanish like dew on a hot summer morning. Pleasure raced through his nervous system and the need to own her completely overwhelmed him.

He could never let her go.

She had to stay.

He would die without her.

She was riding him, her face tensing as she neared her orgasm. He tilted her hips, the delicious slide of his dick in and out of her clenching cunt making his vision dim. Not wanting any distance between them, he pulled her close and began to kiss her. She gasped against his mouth and began to grind her amazing pussy against his lap. Feeling how close she was, he gripped her ass hard, awakening the still bruised flesh.

She jerked back enough to almost break his hold and screamed, her back arching as she ran her nails down his chest hard enough to draw blood. When the first milking contraction of her orgasm hit, Ivan slammed himself into her, drawing out her orgasm as he raced toward his own. Ecstasy exploded in his veins and he roared as the blinding climax ripped through him.

Through it all, Gia kissed his neck, whispering how amazing he was, how good he made her feel, and how much she adored him. As the last staggering blast of his release faded he held her to his chest and whispered to her in Russian how important she was to him, how much better his life was with her, and how he was never letting her go. Then he leaned in even closer and whispered low enough so that no one could hear him confess his love for her, how his life goals now included having her with him as his wife, the mother of his children, and how he wanted to grow old with her at his side.

They continued to cuddle and pet each other for a long, blissful time. Someone put a blanket over Gia's shoulders and Ivan looked up to find Nico watching him closely. Before he could say anything, Nico handed him a damp towel and said in Russian, "Don't let her go, Ivan. She loves you."

He moved his girl enough to dab at the blood seeping from the scratch marks on his chest.

She looked groggily at his motions and made a soft, pained noise. "I hurt you."

"No, *miliy*, you marked me with your passion."

He handed the towel to an attendant wearing latex gloves, who stood nearby. Another club submissive handed Ivan a container of baby wipes. Moving Gia as little as possible, he cleaned her sore pussy, then used more wipes and cleaned his blood from her chest where it had smeared while she rode him. Once that was taken care of, another attendant handed him a clean towel and he laid it on his chest before pulling Gia back against him without the risk of getting more of his blood on her.

Gia snuggled against him, making sleepy humming sounds. Contentment, peace, and happiness warmed him almost as much as the way Gia was nuzzling his neck with her lips. He nodded at the attendants to signal that he didn't need anything else, then stroked Gia's hair, trying to figure out how he was going to possibly convince this fiery, stubborn, smart, amazing woman to leave behind everything and everyone she knew to live with him in Russia. No matter how hard he tried, he couldn't think of a way to prove to her that he was sincere.

Looking at it from a logical point, he could hardly blame her. They'd known each other for a handful of days. Asking her to give up her life and her family, and move to a totally unfamiliar country thousands of miles away because he loved her only worked in fairy tales. He would have to compromise with her and figure out what kind of offer she wouldn't be able to refuse. While it would have been nice to just be able to buy her some expensive jewelry to get her to stay, he knew that wouldn't work with Gia.

One of the things he loved about Gia was her appreciation of the luxuries of life. She wasn't someone who believed they were entitled to things. And she definitely wasn't the kind of woman who would enjoy being a housewife. She needed something to sink her teeth into, a job where she would have a chance to work and grow as an artist. And she was an artist, one of the most talented he'd ever seen. Her work had a beautiful flow and symmetry to it with a distinct style that was all her own. Some people might look at her blueprints and find them boring, but he looked at the homes she'd changed and had been in awe of her skills.

A plan began to form, a compromise that would change his world forever, but in a good way. The idea was by no means rational, but he hadn't been acting rationally since the moment he saw her on the stage at the auction, trembling with fear, and everything inside of him roared out to possess her, because she was his. When he'd claimed her after the auction and she looked up at him with those big, dark eyes, he had the insane thought that this was her, the woman he'd been waiting for. The time they'd spent together since then only reinforced that notion, and after the way she looked at him tonight, he knew his affection wasn't one-sided.

It was time for him to begin a new phase of his life. He'd done his empire building and had amassed a large enough fortune that neither he, nor his future children and grandchildren would ever have to worry about having a place to live and food to eat. He would protect her, love her, and cherish her. For a brief moment he tried to imagine what his and Gia's child would look like and his heart gave a heavy thud.

They would make beautiful babies.

Gia was soon in a deep sleep on his chest. He motioned to one of the submissives who worked at the club to bring him his bag. The employees had already cleaned the stations and put the equipment back in place. A middle-aged male sub with short blond hair placed Ivan's bag next to him on the couch and left.

Taking care not to move Gia too much, he pulled his cell phone from his bag then began to text his uncle Petrov. If Petrov couldn't assist Ivan in convincing Gia to stay with him, no one could. What Ivan had in mind wasn't easy. He would need his family connections to smooth the way for Gia. There were a number of people in Russia who wouldn't work with Americans, and he didn't want their ignorance to touch his woman. She couldn't know he was behind her job because he knew she wouldn't accept anything handed to her. Gia had to work hard to get where she was and she deserved a chance to really show the world what she could do.

That would never happen for her at the small firm where she currently worked. Ivan had looked into it and the top earners of the firm were all related. Gia's chance of advancing within that company was next to nothing no matter how hard she worked. The thought of her getting screwed over like that made him angry for her and even more determined to convince her that her place in the world was at his side.

Chapter

Gia looked around Ivan's unfamiliar kitchen and realized she had no idea what half the products were. She'd normally use her cell phone to take a picture and do an Internet search, but the battery was dead and she didn't have a European charger. Ivan had a computer in his study, but it was set up in Cyrillic and she had no clue how to do anything on it. He was having a new laptop delivered to her tomorrow so she could video chat with her friends and family back in the States. Her cousins had been thrilled that she was in Russia and bought her excuse of being here for business. She'd felt bad lying to them about it, but the last thing she needed when she came home was being interrogated by her well-meaning, but nosy relatives, not to mention her girlfriends who would probably smack her on the back of her head for leaving Ivan.

Her heart constricted and nausea gripped her at the thought of never seeing him again. Placing a hand to her stomach, she tried to close her emotions off, something she'd been able to do effectively in the past, but for some reason right now all she could do was try and hold herself together enough to keep from crying. A need to connect with Ivan swept through her and she placed her hand on the wall next to the gas range. This was his home, she was here right now, so she was going to make the absolute best of it.

Turning to her right, she looked out the floor-to-ceiling tinted windows that revealed a breathtaking view of Moscow. To her delight, Ivan also had a large patio outside of the kitchen that was tastefully decorated with comfortable lawn furniture that encouraged one to sit and relax. There were also a great variety of potted plants that lent a softness to the clean, ultra-modern lines of his kitchen.

When she'd arrived at Ivan's apartment a few days ago, she had been so stunned by the size of the place she didn't really hear half of what Ivan had said. She picked the apartment near the American embassy because Ivan said there were lots of ex-pats in the neighborhood. He also said it had a good deal of culture and she would get to see a different side of Russia.

Her stomach rumbled, reminding her that she'd promised her man a home cooked meal.

Turning back to the cupboard, she mused that she was seeing a different side of Russia all right, the one where she had no idea what the hell the boxes in the pantry held. Her first thought had been to do a good spaghetti dinner. It was a stick-to-the-ribs food that every man she'd made it for appreciated. While it wasn't one of the gourmet meals he constantly delighted her with, it was home cooking, and her aunts had taught her well. Ivan had given his personal chef the night off at her request and she didn't want to let him down. Some primitive female part of her psyche got a great satisfaction from the idea of feeding and caring for Ivan.

Now she was trying to figure out which can had SpagettiO's in it.

"Pardon me, do you happen to know where my nephew might be?" It was the voice of an older man who spoke in lightly accented English.

Gia jumped back with a small scream, looking for the phone, then remembered the emergency button beneath the edge of the countertop that would summon security. The man staring back at her with one eyebrow raised didn't appear threatening, but he had a dangerous vibe that she couldn't ignore. His gaze was just…cold. But he'd called Ivan his nephew.

"He's at work." Internally wincing at her blunder, she said, "I mean, he's upstairs. He'll be down any second. Why don't I go get him?"

She tried to slow her breathing as he walked closer and slowly closed the cupboard.

Leaning on the black marble counter, Ivan's supposed uncle studied her. He still cut a trim figure in his heavy gray sweater and had only a touch of silver in his dark hair. Overall, he had the same powerful, almost deadly vibe as Ivan and she swallowed hard. For all she knew, he could be one of those kidnappers.

She darted a glance at the security button beneath the table. "I'm sure he'll be down any second."

The man almost smiled, and he did have the same expressive eyes Ivan did, but in a colder shade of blue. She studied Petrov's features and could see the physical similarities that clearly marked him as being related to Ivan. Her tension dissipated and she gave him a hesitant smile.

He tilted his head and watched her intently. "Gia, my name is Petrov. Ivan called me last night to let me know he was back home and I wanted to stop by to visit with him. I mean you no harm. If you like I can call him and you can speak to him so you can verify who I am. Or you can call security and ask one of them to come up and stay with us while I'm here."

"No, no, that's okay. You just startled me. I didn't expect anyone to be here and you must walk like a cat because I didn't hear you at all. Ivan's at work right now, but he said he would be home in time for dinner."

Flushing, she pulled at the edges of the ultra-comfy top of her pink cashmere lounge clothes. The shirt was a cute, tight racer back tank top. She hadn't worn a bra, expecting only Ivan later tonight. Now she was standing in front of his uncle and her nipples were hard from the adrenaline rushing through her system and the bumps of her piercings were clearly visible.

Trying to casually cross her arms to hide her breasts, she cleared her throat. "It's very nice to meet you."

"And you." His look was more curious than aggressive now. "So, Ivan tells me you're an architect? That you restore old buildings?"

Pleased that Ivan had mentioned her profession, she nodded. "Yes. Though I mostly gut the interiors, renovate all the electricity, plumbing, take out asbestos, clean out any bats from the attic, replace old toilets, take care of any mold or water issues, and I usually put in central air and heating. Oh, and last month I installed my first solar grid. Then I put the house back together again better than before so you can hardly tell it was even touched."

He gave her a surprised look with a slight raising of the eyebrows. "It sounds like you're a busy woman."

She laughed nervously. "Usually I am. But I'm afraid your nephew is trying to spoil me with a life of leisure on my week's vacation here."

His gaze sharpened and the lines around his mouth deepened. "Only a week?"

She tilted her head and looked closer at him. Something about the way he said that, the genuine surprise in his voice, made her inner alarms go off. "Yes. Just a week. Why?"

He gave her a charming smile much like Ivan's when he was going to try to sweet talk her, or manipulate her, or both. "I am trying to imagine all the wonders of Moscow and seeing them in a week. Is my nephew boring?"

To her surprise, he actually sounded offended. Like she'd insulted him somehow. "Oh, no. It's not that. Ivan is wonderful. It's just that I don't have any more vacation time at work. I need to get back and start on a bunch of projects."

"Understood."

She glanced at the cupboard. "If it wouldn't be too much trouble, could you translate some of the food packages for me? I'd like to make Ivan dinner, but I don't know how to read Cyrillic."

"You're making him dinner?"

His surprise confused her. "Yes. Is that okay?"

He nodded and gestured toward the stove. "Come, I want to teach you how to make a dish Ivan's mother made for him. She was my sister and in addition to being a wonderful cook, she was also an English professor at the Moscow State University Language Center. A brilliant woman. She spoke nine languages fluently and could read ancient Greek."

"Nine languages?" He nodded and she blinked in surprise. "Ivan mentioned something about her teaching him English, but I had no idea."

Petrov shrugged. "He does not like to boast."

Thinking back to how amazed she'd been to realize just how powerful of a man he was in the world, she nodded. "He doesn't need to boast."

"What do you mean?"

She flushed. "Just that you can look at Ivan and know he is a man in control of his destiny."

"Very well put." His lips turned up just the slightest bit. "Now, would you like me to teach you this dish?"

“I would really like that. I can figure out what some of the boxes and cans are by their labels, but others are a complete mystery.”

He removed his sweater and rolled up the sleeves of his button-down cream-colored dress shirt. “That is a nice outfit. I would not want it to get ruined by the cooking. Why don’t you put something else on?”

While he said it with a straight face, she saw a twinkle in his eye that made her cheeks heat. “Okay.”

After she returned to the kitchen in jeans and a comfy peach sweater, she found that Petrov had poured them both a glass of chilled vodka. He taught her how to sip it as he had her measure and chop up ingredients. They were making *zharkoe*, which looked to her like a traditional stew. They browned the potatoes, carrots, and onion in a little butter. Next came the slices of pork, which were browned a bit as well. All of this went into a crock and into the oven. Gia’s stomach was growling for food.

While they cooked Petrov told her about Ivan’s family and she found out that Ivan had over two hundred cousins living in Moscow. From what Petrov said the family reunions were mad houses with people getting drunk, singing, and weeping over the old days. It was nice to know that, despite Ivan’s perfection, his family was as crazy as her own extended family back in the States. A soft pang of homesickness went through her, but she wasn’t looking forward to going home. At all. The thought of leaving Ivan was unbearable, so she tried to ignore it and pretend she had all the time in the world with her handsome, dashing Master.

She was also feeling a little tipsy, not the point of slurring words or anything, and she really enjoyed talking to Petrov. He had a brilliant mind and his insight to the world was different than any she’d ever known. It wasn’t that he was a pessimist about things, but he was an unflinching realist. He didn’t try to gild anything, but at the same time, his pride in his country was obvious.

As the time drew closer for Ivan to come home, she checked her reflection in the living room mirror to make sure she looked all right.

Petrov caught her finger combing her hair. "Go, go fix yourself up for your man. I will take care of things down here." He paused and took in her jeans and sweater. "I'm not sure how things work for young women in your country, but I do have three daughters, and I would like to give you the advice I gave them. When your husband or boyfriend comes home from a hard day at work, seeing his woman looking beautiful makes all the stress and worry worth it. And, when family is visiting, it always does a man's heart proud when his wife looks her best. It shows that he can take care of you, that he is a good provider, a responsible man. It is our job as men."

He said the last part so vehemently that she really didn't want to tell him her feelings about being able to take care of herself. After all, it wasn't like she was going to be here forever. She could play nice and respect the older man's views.

"Should I put on a dress? Maybe some heels and curl my hair?"

It came out with a little more snark than she intended, but to her surprise, Petrov laughed. "And that is pretty much what my daughters tell me. But hey, what do I know? I've only been happily married to the same woman for over thirty-four years."

He winked at her and she grinned. "I'll be right back."

She hurried up the stairs, thinking about Petrov's advice. Being here with Ivan was uncharted territory for her. Aside from all the insanity of even being here, she'd never lived with a man before, and that was what she was doing. For the next week she'd be playing house with Ivan. Why not go all out and indulge her inner Donna Reed? It wasn't like she was going to get the chance to do this again.

Sorrow tried to sink its claws into her, but she brushed the negative thoughts off. No, she wasn't going to have a good cry in the closet right before Ivan got home. That was simply too pathetic and she wasn't going to indulge herself in an emotional meltdown. Besides, she got all puffy when she cried.

She'd have plenty of time for that once she was back home, alone, longing for his body against hers and his voice calling her 'my Gia'.

She switched her outfit, picking out a tight tan suede skirt and pairing it with a gold off the shoulder blouse. Smoothing her hand over the skirt, she mused that it was kind of fun to dress up for dinner. Not that she'd ever give up her pizza and jammies suppers, but it gave the meal a sense of anticipation. And she was proud that she'd made Ivan food he'd actually like. Feeling slightly naughty, she switched out her cotton thong for a white lace and crystal studded pair of high cut panties. She liked the way it looked against her tanned skin and knew Ivan would adore it.

She braided her hair back and added a little eyeliner and mascara, then threw on some gold jewelry that she tried to tell herself was just costume, that Ivan couldn't possibly have brought her what looked to be a king's ransom in gold and jewels.

Giving her lashes another coat of mascara, she had to smile at her reflection. While she had no interest in staying at home all day awaiting her man's return from work, she had to admit she did enjoy the thought of having everything welcoming and comfortable for when Ivan came home. Who knew she had such a hidden domestic streak, and that she'd enjoy it so much.

Making her way back to the living room and kitchen area, she found Petrov and Ivan having an intense conversation. She had no idea what was being said, but as soon as the men caught sight of her they broke apart with an almost guilty look. Then Ivan smiled in her direction and she forgot her concern in a rush of passion and pure joy. He looked so happy to see her, and he sure as hell filled out that black suit nicely. It clung to his big figure and she wanted to rip it off of him.

"I must be going now," Petrov said in an amused voice. "The wife gets irritated when I disappear. It was a pleasure meeting you, Gia."

"You as well. And thank you so much for all the help."

"You are welcome." Petrov looked over at his nephew and his expression grew stern. "Think about what I said, Ivan. Push too fast and we will lose this acquisition."

Ivan's gaze narrowed. "I'll consider it, but I'm set on my course of action."

Petrov sighed and shook his head. "I'm telling you, the situation is not what you think it is."

Muttering something in Russian, Ivan closed the door after Petrov and leaned against it. He slowly took her in, from the shoes on her feet to her hair back in a simple braid, and smiled. "I don't think I've ever been so happy to be home from work."

He stepped away from the door and held his arms open. Right away Gia cuddled close to him, loving how protected and cherished he made her feel. "I'm happy to see you too."

With a long, slow stroke, he rubbed his hand down her back to cup her bottom. "I cannot wait for this to heal so I can spank you again. Maybe a little bit of a cane, but only if you're a good girl."

Heat raced through her and she took a step back and shook her head. "No way. Hands off. I made you dinner. You will at least try it before whisking me off."

He held out his arm in a formal gesture, his posture straightening and drawing her eyes to his big frame. "If you will."

She slipped hers through his, and while she felt silly being escorted across the living room, it was also very nice.

Ivan let out something between a happy purr and a growl as he saw what was for dinner. "My favorite."

As he sat her in her chair at the dining room table she smiled at the elaborately beautiful birds his uncle had made using cloth napkins.

Ivan noticed as well and raised his eyebrows. “It appears my uncle likes you.”

“Why do you say that like it’s a surprise?”

“He is a very…hard to get along with person.”

“I thought he was really nice. He scared the crap out of me by sneaking up on me in the kitchen, but he was nice after that.”

Ivan took his first bite of the meal and moaned. “So good.”

Laughing, she shook her head. “Hey, that’s the same voice you use during sex.”

He grinned, then tucked into his stew like nobody’s business.

She had to admit it was good and had second helpings as well. Something about the searing beforehand really locked a lot of flavors into the stew. When Ivan finally put his spoon down, he leaned back in his chair with a contented sigh.

“Wonderful.”

“I’m glad you liked it.” She beamed at him with what was no doubt a goofy smile, pleasure and satisfaction sinking into her bones.

They cleared their plates, and as soon as she set the last glass down, Ivan spun her around and lifted her so that her legs were wrapped around his waist and her hands around his neck. His healthy erection pressed against the softness between her legs and she gave a little wiggle.

“Hi.”

“Hello, my Gia.” His voice deepened. “You make me feel very…content.”

She rubbed her nose against his, loving how he held her like it was no big deal. “Content? Is that all?”

With a frown, he turned and walked them into the living room with its view of a lovely pond and park space ten stories below. It was around seven p.m. in Moscow right now, but her body was still trying to get used to the time zone difference. It made her feel really exhausted and awake at the same time.

Ivan sat on the long, wide hunter green couch and adjusted the yellow and green silk throw pillows behind him until he was lying on the couch with her draped over him like some kind of blanket. Belly to belly like this, she was reminded of how much smaller she was than him, of how feminine. It made her want to rub her hands all over his naked body.

"Content…I don't know if that is the right word," Ivan said with a faint frown. "I want to tell you that I feel like my home has a heart when you are here. You bring my life into a new focus and I see things differently when you are with me. You are my light, Gia. My warmth."

She blinked at him, her playful mood vanishing beneath the weight of his stare. He was so sincere. Her heart ached and she cursed herself for coming here. She knew this would happen, that things would become emotionally more intense, but she had hoped that maybe somehow she could protect her heart.

Stupid her.

"Ivan, we can't do this."

His brows drew down and the soft smile faded from his lips. "Do what?"

"We can't get serious. I'm leaving in three days."

His arms wound around her, pulling her closer to his chest. "Stay with me."

"I can't." She really, really wanted to, but her practical mind wouldn't let her. "I couldn't live here. I don't know anyone. I have a life, a job back in the United States and I love it there."

He shrugged. "Then I'll come back with you."

The idea shocked her and she tried to picture Ivan living her ordinary, mundane life. He'd get bored to tears and leave her within a month. "No, that won't work."

Suddenly he sat up and set her on the couch, away from him. "You mean you don't want it to work."

His grim expression frightened her, but the sorrow and hurt in his gaze made her own pain double. "No, I mean we are from two different worlds. You will get bored with me, Ivan, I know it, and then I'll be all alone in a foreign country trying to pick up the pieces of my life. Do you have any idea how hard it is to get a job in the US right now? Especially for an architect?"

"You have it all figured out, don't you?"

The chill in his voice froze the blood in her veins. Here was the dark, commanding, terrifying man who had built an empire. Being on the receiving end of his cold indifference was terrible. She pressed back into the couch and crossed her arms.

"I can't risk my heart with you."

"It wouldn't be a risk, Gia. Don't you understand that?" His hands clenched into fists and his whole body tensed.

"Ivan, I'm not stupid."

"Yes, you are."

Her discomfort and fear morphed into anger and she suddenly hated him for making all these false promises, for trying to manipulate her. How dare he make her feel like the guilty party for trying to protect them both? And how dare he call her stupid?

"You know what? I'm done with this conversation."

He stood as well, fury coming off of him in waves. "We are not done."

"Oh, yes we are." She turned to walk away and he grabbed her arm. His hold was gentle and she easily threw his hand off. "Don't touch me."

"Then listen to me! Stop being such a bitch and hear what I am saying."

She whirled on him. "Oh, I'm a bitch now? I see how it is. You don't get your insane way and I'm suddenly a bitch."

"I didn't say you were a bitch, I said you were being one." His eyes glittered and he lifted his chin. "I want you in my bed."

"You are fucking crazy if you think I'm going anywhere near your bedroom right now."

"Gia, you need to calm down so we can talk."

"So, what? You're going to use sex to try to change my mind? Sorry, Ivan, you're good, but you're not that good."

"I said get in my bed."

"Damascus," she snapped, throwing her safeword at him. Fucking asshole. Trying to manipulate her with sex. "I want my purse, now."

"No."

"No? Fine." She marched over to the door and went to turn the handle, but he came up behind her and put his hand over hers.

"Where are you going?"

"To the American embassy. You don't want to give me my things, I'll go to them and get a new passport."

"What are you talking about? You are being very irrational."

"No, irrational is trying to keep me a prisoner in your home. This isn't a sex game, this is real life, and in real life, don't you *ever* fucking *dare* to try to trap me in your house."

He snatched his hand away with a grunt. "I was very wrong about you. You are a coward."

Hurt seared her heart and sent pain rocketing through her chest like she'd been punched. "Give me my purse and get the fuck out of the way. I am done with you. Do you hear me? Done!"

Without another word, he strode toward the bedroom. He came back quickly and gave her the purse. Her hands trembled as she shoved it beneath her arm, then removed the earrings and gold necklace she'd put on. She tried to hand them to him, but he was totally ignoring her at this point and would not even look at her. So she set them on the small table next to the door. The metallic click of the links of the chain hitting the wood seemed very loud in the tension-filled hush of the apartment.

An incredible pain ripped through her heart and she tried to steel herself, to remember all the reasons why this wouldn't work. She couldn't end up like her mother, falling so deeply in love with one man that his departure from her life basically ended it.

"Goodbye, Ivan."

"Where are you going?"

"Don't worry about it."

She could actually hear his teeth grind. "Regardless of what you may think about me, I can assure you that wandering around Moscow would be a bad idea."

The protective note in his voice made her want to cry. "I'm going straight to the airport, okay? I just want to go home. I don't want to be here anymore."

"I will take care of it."

Sadness crashed over her at the instant trust she felt in him. He opened his phone and had a couple of long conversations. During the entire time, he kept his back to her and her soul hurt from being frozen out.

"My uncle will be here to help you get the documents you need to leave."

"Okay."

The silence stretched between them and she wanted desperately to stay but couldn't think of any logical reason. It was better to end this now before either of them got hurt any more than they already were. "I'll miss you."

He turned on her, his gaze fierce. "Do not say those things if you do not mean them."

"But I will miss you." To her horror her voice broke on the last word and tears filled her eyes.

"Then stay."

The blatant agony in his tone added a new level of pain to her already overburdened heart.

"Ivan, this is all going too fast for me. I barely know you. Even if we lived in the same town I would want to take things slow, get to know you first before we discussed living together."

Ivan's cell phone rang and he answered it with a frown, speaking Russian. After a few minutes he handed the phone to her, his jaw clenched in anger. "It is my uncle. He wishes to speak with you."

She took the phone, the brush of his fingertips burning her skin. "Hello?"

"Hello, Gia," Petrov said in a kind voice. "I understand my nephew was an idiot and did exactly what I told him not to do. He scared you off, didn't he?"

Clearing her throat, she wandered away from Ivan, all too aware of the way he watched her. "Yes."

"That is what I thought." He sighed heavily. "I love Ivan like my own son. My sister, God bless her soul, wasn't a very warm person and his father was about as loving as a stone pillar. Ivan spent much time with me when he was growing up."

"Why are you telling me this?"

"Because you need to know that you are the first woman Ivan has ever been serious about."

She laughed, and it sounded forced and choking even to her ears. "I find that hard to believe."

"It is true. I would not lie about this. He worships you, Gia."

"No, he doesn't," she said in a sad voice.

"Yes, he does. He invited all our family to his estate outside of Moscow for dinner so they could meet you."

Her heart lurched and she moved farther away from Ivan. "Why would he do that?"

"Because he is serious about you."

"Don't you see how crazy this is? I hardly know him."

"I understand. But you will never get to know him if you run away."

She bit her lower lip and considered his words. "What am I supposed to do?"

"Come work for me."

"What?"

"I've recently bought two properties, old homes that are in deperate need of massive renovations. I'd like to hire you to work on them."

She shook her head in disbelief, looking at a lovely impressionist work of a fall day without really seeing it as she talked. "You don't even know me."

"Actually, I do. Before I arrived at Ivan's apartment I had you researched. I know how hard you've worked and struggled to rise above the situation you were born into. I admire you and I've seen your portfolio. You have excellent taste and I really would like you to help me in renovating my properties. Pardon me for a moment." He said something in Russian and a woman's voice responded, then she laughed. "My wife said that I needed to tell you I bought these properties for my two youngest daughters to try to encourage them to live closer to me. She warns you that they may burn the places down in order to avoid having me as a neighbor."

Gia smiled and took in a deep breath, then let it out. “I’m not sure. This is a lot to take in.”

In the background the woman spoke again and Petrov translated. “My wife wanted to add that part of your benefits package, if you take the job, is housing of your own as well as your own driver. We will also find a translator that you like and who also has experience in the building world. If you and Ivan get married someday and give us beautiful brown-eyed babies, wonderful. If you do not wish to see him anymore it will in no way affect our business relationship. This will, however, look wonderful on your résumé.”

She clutched the phone and tried to still her racing heart. “I’d like to see a contract first.”

“Of course.”

“And I’ll need to go back to the States for some of my things.”

“Agreed.”

“And I’d like a Russian tutor as well. I need to be able to speak to my workers.”

“Smart woman.”

“Why are you doing this?”

“Because Ivan loves you and he doesn’t love easily.”

Shock had her swallowing hard and trying to still the trembling in her legs. She lowered her voice to a whisper, “Do you really think he loves me?”

“Gia, I had to talk him out of proposing to you tonight.”

Her knees went weak and she stumbled. “Oh…wow. But he doesn’t even know me.”

“I didn’t know my wife for more than two weeks before we got married. Sometimes you look at someone and know you can’t sleep another night without them at your side.”

“Oh.”

The words rang true in her soul and she realized that despite her best efforts, she'd fallen in love with Ivan as well. The thought of not sleeping in his arms tonight was unbearable. He was her man, her Master, and if she let him go she was beyond stupid.

The thought of marriage terrified her, but at the same time a part of her, becoming stronger with each beat of her heart, really liked the idea of growing old with Ivan. Her life wouldn't be dull, that was for sure. She'd never taken a leap of faith like this for anyone.

She stole a glance at Ivan, finding him watching her with such intensity her nipples hardened to points. Her body was certainly onboard for being around Ivan as much as possible. The thought of having her own place here, hopefully near Ivan, was nice. More than nice, it was awesome. Like his uncle had said, even if things didn't work out between them, she'd still have the experience of working in Russia on her résumé.

And Ivan loved her.

A silly giggle tried to escape while at the same time she fought back tears. She shook her head at her own foolishness. Damn Ivan for making her just as crazy as he was.

"Now talk to my nephew before he throws himself off a bridge. He is beside himself, even if he doesn't show it. Unlike the men of your American culture who weep like a woman when they break a fingernail, Russian men are strong and we endure. That does not mean we do not hurt."

They said their goodbyes and she turned to face Ivan with her pulse beating hard enough to thud in her ears. Across the room stood the man who could someday be her husband, the father of her children, and her partner in life. She slowly looked him over, putting together what she knew of him and what she suspected. When her gaze reached his face and she saw the pain eating up his soul bit by bit, she decided to make Ivan pay for turning her world wonderfully upside down and inside out.

Ivan wasn't the only one who got to act all irrational in this relationship.

She hoped his uncle was right that Ivan loved her because if Ivan said no her heart would break into a million, jagged pieces and cut her soul to ribbons.

Chapter

Ivan held his breath as Gia strolled back toward him, the golden light of the sun setting over Moscow painting her features in delicate shadows and giving her skin a delicious bronze glow. Amber highlights glittered in her eyes and she reminded him of a lioness with her graceful walk. Her hair was back in a braid he wanted to hold on to while he fucked her, but she was leaving him. There was something about her expression he couldn't read, and he wanted to kick himself in the ass for pushing her too quick.

Petrov had warned him, but Ivan was so sure Gia loved him that he moved too soon and frightened her off. His anger certainly hadn't helped the situation. Plus, Gia was right. He was trying to seduce her so she wouldn't leave him. To capture just another five hours with her, to have her taste imprinted on his mind so he would be able to remember her long after she'd vanished from his life.

His gut clenched and every muscle in his body screamed at him to stop her.

She set his phone on the table and let out a long, low breath. The anger had gone from her eyes and she seemed more relaxed. For a second, he thought that his uncle had talked her into staying, but he didn't dare hope. Not again. Not after she shot him down so brutally.

After she took a few more deep breaths, he began to worry that she might be getting faint.

So when she looked up at him and said, "Ivan, will you marry me?" *he* almost passed out.

He tried to make his lungs work so that he could speak, his lips move so that he could shape words, but the raw emotion tearing through his mind had him momentarily paralyzed. Searching her face, he found amusement, passion, a little bit of sadness, and the first beautiful gleam of love. So extraordinary…he could stare into her eyes for the rest of his life and never tire of it.

Unable to stop himself, he crossed the room and brushed his lips over hers. "Do you love me, Gia?"

"Yes."

The truth of her words could be heard in her voice. Then she added something that convinced him she was being honest. "It's totally insane, I know it is, but I can't seem to think rationally around you. I see you and all I want to do is kiss you. I kiss you and all I want to do is touch you, I touch you and then I can't remember my own name. I become so lost in you I forget myself and that scares me."

He gently ran the tips of his fingers down her neck in a light caress, enjoying the way she swayed toward him. "You consume me. I can't be around you without wanting to feel you beneath me, your little nails prickling my back while you scream my name, the ways I can make you purr for me."

She shivered as his fingers gently ran down her chest, stroking her breasts. "Wait. Before you steal my will, I want us to have a long engagement and I will have my own home."

The joy of someday having Gia as his wife gave Ivan the strength to bite back his initial impulse to demand that she stay here with him.

Demanding things of Gia only made her get all snarly. He would try to soothe her instead. While he loved his woman's strong spirit, a purring Gia was much easier to deal with.

"I haven't said yes, yet."

Her eyes grew wide and she clutched at his shirt. "Ivan?"

"Of course I will marry you, and I agree to your terms. Now, here are mine. I want to be able to travel with you, to show you the world. My company has reached the point where I can start delegating work to people I trust more, which means I'll have time to do all the things I've wanted to do. I would ask that you work a similar schedule. Six months on, six months off. I believe it would be in your best interest to start your own company, here, in Russia."

"My own company?"

"Yes. That way it is something that you have. I will help you work through the details and get the right permits, but it will be completely your business."

"My own company." She got a dreamy look that made satisfaction surge through him. "That would be awesome. Of course it would be a company of one, but I'll be busy with your uncle's project long enough for me to really think about how I want to do this."

He placed a soft, tender, heartfelt kiss on her neck and began to gently lick her skin.

The tremble in her voice was audible as she sighed out, "Do you think we can spend three of those six months in the United Sates? I still want to see my friends and family."

Lifting his lips for a moment, he said, "Of course. Find an older home in the area you would like to live. Preferably one with some land around it, then we can make our home base in the United States there."

She let out a long sigh, the tension leaving her body in a visible wave of relaxation. "Well, I guess when you're richer than God it's pretty easy to live anywhere you want."

"It is."

He didn't try to defend his extravagant lifestyle. Nothing came easy and he worked his ass off for every bit of success he had. The memory of all the nights he'd stayed awake until dawn, trying to close one deal or another, flew through his mind. He was infinitely grateful that he'd met Gia after that period of his life, during a time when he could treat her in the way she deserved and spend time with her in the way she needed.

"This could work."

"It will work."

He tried to make her see how much she meant to him because he couldn't put it into words, willing her to acknowledge that they were meant to be together.

Suddenly she smiled. "Hey, you're my fiancé."

Caught up in the light filling her gaze, he smiled back. "Yes, I am."

That made her giggle and he watched her, bemused as happy and tender emotions flew across her expressive face.

Licking her lower lip, she stepped back and gave him a sultry look. "Want to celebrate our engagement, fiancé?"

"Come to me, my Gia."

Gia couldn't help but shiver. When Ivan said her name like that she went all warm and fuzzy inside. He said it like she mattered to him and he made her feel as if she actually belonged with someone for the first time since her mother died. It was a good, comforting feeling. The kind of warmth that could only come from someone you loved and loved you in return.

She took his hand and he led her through the apartment to the corner room of his penthouse. It had floor-to-ceiling windows looking out over Moscow as the lights began to come on in the softly falling twilight. The sun was nothing more than a burning orange sliver on the horizon and the beauty of the city made her breath catch in her throat. The floor of this room was made up of pillows and she'd been surprised to find out that Ivan liked to meditate in here.

Now he placed her among the pillows in the slowly darkening room. He still wore his suit and she grinned up at him. "Hey, fiancé?"

He gave her a happy smile. "Yes?"

"Do you think we could do a little role playing? Seeing you in this suit has reminded me of a fantasy I have. And you fit it perfectly."

His smile turned predatory, making her feel like he was thinking about eating her.

"What is it?" He grabbed her hand and pressed it against his straining erection. "Feel what you do to me when you tell me your dirty secrets? I find it incredibly arousing."

Fuck, he was so carnal he reduced her to a hormonal mess beneath him. Wanting him. Her Master. Her fiancé, and someday, her husband. She had a feeling the wedding was going to happen before she knew it if Ivan had his way. As soon as she could she'd move into her own place…and probably have him over constantly.

"Gia?"

"Sorry, Master, I was thinking about having you sleep in my bed."

"Mmm, that is a nice thought, but I don't think it is your fantasy."

He abruptly leaned down and locked his teeth on her shoulder. A rush of excitement filled her and she squeezed his cock, loving how he throbbed in her hand. "Okay, let me start out by saying that if you ever treat me like this out of the bedroom, I'll kick your ass and I don't care who I have to do it in front of."

He growled against her before removing his mouth from what was, no doubt, a new bruise. In a strange way she felt like it was his way of establishing dominance over her. The sore spot of her bruise certainly sent a confusing stream of low-level pain through her, but the big handful of his cock had her wanting him inside of her.

Now.

She looked at his chest and stroked his tie with her free hand. "I'd like it if you would pretend to be my boss. You're going to blackmail me for stealing office supplies."

"What favors will you do me, my Gia, to keep your job?"

She slowly licked her lips and gave him big, innocent eyes. "Anything you want."

Beyond Ivan the sky had darkened, but the lights of Moscow made it impossible to see any stars. "When we're on vacation, can we go places where we can see the stars?"

"We can go anywhere you want, Gia. The world is now yours."

Happiness filled her to overflowing and she scooted away from him with a giggle. Then she tossed her braid over her shoulder, put her hands on her hips, and tapped her foot. "Mr. Kozlov, I don't know what you're trying to do here, but I will not be bullied into submitting to your perverse desires. I'm not going to jail for stealing pens."

Ivan studied her with a predatory look that reminded her of a tiger stalking its prey. In a way he reminded her of a big cat, all dark menace and heavily muscled grace. Then he straightened his jacket and wandered over to the window, looking out over the city as he said, "Yes, but the pictures I have of you masturbating in my office chair will get you in trouble."

"What?" Oh, he was good at this. She let herself sink further into her role.

"Tell me, Ms. Lopez, were you thinking about me when you slid your fingers through your pussy?"

"I don't know what you're talking about."

"I have pictures of all of it. Every delectable bit of your cunt exposed while you frantically fucked yourself. What had gotten you so hot? Surely it wasn't from sitting in my chair. Then again, the way you give me those hungry, needy looks all the time is testing my patience."

She wanted him in the worst way, but looked forward to pretending to fight him off. She wanted him to have to fight for her submission tonight, to see how far he would indulge her kinks. Keeping this policy of honesty with each other was important to her and she wasn't going to give herself time to think about it too much.

"The only way you're getting that big cock in me is to hold me down and force me to fuck you," she spat out.

Ivan finally turned, and the lust blazing in his eyes almost frightened her. "Is that a challenge, Ms. Lopez? Do you want to fight me so you can pretend you don't want this?"

"I don't want you."

"Liar. It was my name you were whispering as you came."

She was one thigh press away from her orgasm. "I don't know what you're talking about."

"Come here, Ms. Lopez, before I lose my patience."

"No."

He strode across the room and she fell back with a shriek. As he dove for her she rolled to the side and shoved a big pillow at him, then tried to scramble away. His hand locked on her ankle, pulling her back to him. She grunted and strained to reach something she could use to anchor herself, but all she could grab were useless pillows.

"Get back here, Ms. Lopez."

"No!" she shouted and pretended to kick at his face as he hauled her back.

Soon she found herself partially pinned beneath him with his enormous erection poking at her ass. The thought of him fucking her in that forbidden place had her juices wetting her inner thighs. There would be pain, but there would also be pleasure.

He moved so he was kneeling behind her with his legs on the outside of hers. He grabbed her braid and jerked her head up. "I get to fuck any hole on you I want. Don't I?"

"Go to Hell," she whispered even as her mind began to slip away.

His weight lifted off of her back and she tried to move, but his massive legs held her in place. She could feel him shifting behind her and strained to see what he was doing. Before she could get a good look he had her hair in his fist again, pulling with a delicious tug. "Open that smart mouth again and you'll regret it."

"Fuc—"

Before she could finish the word he had his tie shoved between her lips and wrapped around her head in a gag. Mad, she chewed at the fabric, the faintest taste of his cologne filling her mouth. A moment later he held her hair again and forced her to look at his hand where he had a small, but very sharp pocketknife lifted toward her face. She froze as anticipation sang through her blood.

When he'd played with her last night the sensation of the knife on her skin had made her insane for him. Just the memory of it had her relaxing in his grip, eager for his touch. She lifted her ass and rubbed it against his heavy erection.

"I'm going to cut your clothes off. If you fight me I will nick you. Nod if you understand." She nodded and he lifted fully off of her.

"Not a wiggle, my Gia. This beautiful skirt clings to your ass and it will take a very steady touch to cut it without harming the delicate skin beneath the fabric."

She nodded again and got into a comfortable position, using one of the pillows to prop herself slightly up. Ivan lifted her so her ass stuck up in the air and his growl of desire made her smile behind her gag. In taking away her ability to talk he also freed her to immerse herself in his touch. And the very real danger the knife represented to her made her arousal sharp and intense.

He began at her feet, cutting the skirt and letting it fall to either side of her body. When he reached the curve of her ass he blew out a harsh breath. "I need a taste of you first."

With that, he set the knife to the side and grabbed her ass, licking at the exposed line of her soaked thong. When he pulled back she cried out, but then he slapped the flat of the blade on her lower butt cheek. "Still."

He continued to cut and cool air enveloped her lower half as he sliced through the final inch of fabric. Then the blade slid between her skin and the thong. With a flick of his wrist, he sliced first one side, then the other. The ruined fabric fell from her sex and she moaned, aching for him.

"I'm going to fuck your pussy, then come in your ass Ms. Lopez."

She gave a bunch of muffled protests, then bit down on the gag as his thick fingers teased the lips of her sex.

"I love how wet you get for me," he said in a dark voice filled with passion. "It makes me want to spend the rest of my life inside of you."

He scooped up some of her slippery arousal and began to work it into her anus. She relaxed for him, her breathing deepening even as her heart beat harder. There was an art to anal sex and she had a feeling Ivan knew exactly what he needed to do to make this insanely good for her.

The only thing she had to do was relax and trust him.

"I'm not even going to play with you first, Ms. Lopez. You're so aroused for me that I think you'll come rather quickly."

He pressed the thick head of his shaft against her sex and she dug her fingers into the pillow beneath her as he slowly entered her, making her feel every inch. When he finally pressed all the way to where her ass met his pelvis she felt his pants and realized he'd just unzipped himself and pulled his cock out, staying otherwise fully dressed.

How fucking sexy was that.

Next time they did this she'd have to make sure there were mirrors for her to watch him.

He placed his thighs outside of hers and she closed her eyes and rocked beneath him, meeting his thrusts, taking him as deep as she could even though it hurt. The pain only added spice to her arousal now and she craved that little hint of danger from Ivan.

She had no idea why she found it so hot that he could hurt her but chose not to, but she did.

He gripped her ass with his hands and began to slam into her. Almost against her will, her arousal built until she was screaming out his name as she came with his cock stroking hard into her. When Ivan put his strength into taking her she had no more choice in how her body responded than a doll. Her orgasm stretched out until she was sobbing into the pillows, overwhelmed and overstimulated.

Still, he didn't relent.

When he began to press two of his big fingers into her ass she mewled in distress, but didn't have the strength to fight him. Another orgasm was on its way and she couldn't make him stop the punishing, amazing way he was fucking the hell out of her. When his fingers breached her anus she tightened around him and he swore softly.

“Relax and take me. I will be fucking your tight little bottom tonight. How hard I fuck it depends on how well you listen to me.”

She nodded and let her body ease around his finger while he stroked in and out of her dripping sex at a slow, mind-numbing pace. Every inch of his cock seemed to stimulate more nerve endings inside of her until her clit began to stiffen again. His scent filled the air and he pumped his fingers in and out of her bottom while doing the same with his dick in her pussy.

A third finger pushed its way into her and he pulled out long enough to gather more of her arousal, then pushed his massive erection back into her while he lubricated her ass with her own fluids. The sensation of three of his fingers in her was intense and painful. She gave a distressed moan and he shushed her.

“When I put my cock in this tiny hole I will take care of you.”

Now she wasn’t sure if she should be eager or afraid of him taking her back there. He pulled all the way out of her pussy and removed his fingers from her ass.

“Turn around, I want you on your back.”

She rolled over as best she could, her shaking limbs not responding very well at the moment. She finally managed to get into the position he wanted and she watched as he lifted her legs over his shoulders. This opened her ass to him and when he leaned forward and pressed his erection against her bottom she moaned and pushed back.

“There, that’s a good girl. Slow and easy, fill yourself with me.”

Biting her lower lip, she involuntarily arched when he was halfway in as a shock of pleasure tightened her muscles. He lowered one of her legs and reached between them, manipulating her clit as he slid into her at a pace that had her wiggling against him. That made him pause and he smiled down at her.

“So eager to be violated. You make me lose control. Not fucking you hard is testing my patience right now.”

She lowered her other leg, then wrapped both legs around his waist. He was so strong that he stayed in a pushup position over her while she raised and lowered her body against his, helping to work his cock into her all the way. Once he was inside of her ass, filling her, she groaned and rotated her hips, trying to get her clit to rub against his rock hard lower abs.

With a low growl, he pulled out and moved back in, slow at first, then faster until they were both panting. He began to fuck her with short, jabbing thrusts that made her scrape her nails down his jacket covered back. She wanted to come so damn bad.

His breath hissed out through his teeth and slammed into her.

"Yes!" She couldn't help her shout muffled through her gag any more than she could stop her building orgasm.

Playtime was over. Ivan took her now the way he liked to take her, hard and deep. He used every inch of his formidable cock to tease her and she raked his back again with her nails. This time he pulled her hands from his shoulders and held them over her head.

"No, little wild cat, you will not get your way. You'll come when I let you come."

She wanted to scream in frustration as he stilled within her, his cock throbbing so hard she could feel it. Squeezing down, she shivered at the edge of pain and her toes curled when Ivan pressed his body against hers, grinding into her clit. Needing more of his skin, she reached up and ripped his shirt open, the small buttons flying about the room. As soon as his chest was exposed she leaned up and suckled his small, dark nipple.

With a low grunt Ivan froze and his dick twitched inside of her.

"You'll pay for ruining that shirt, Ms. Lopez."

He pinned her hands and resumed taking her, but he moved so slow now that it was torture. Fighting his hold, she bucked and writhed beneath him, meeting his unhurried thrusts with twists of her hips that ground her sensitive nub against his body and gripped the man within her. He picked up his rhythm and sweat dampened their bodies as he took her. Moving one arm at a time, he managed to drag his suit coat off and his ruined shirt, leaving him blissfully bare chested. She ran her fingers through his chest hair, whimpering each time his abs scraped her clit.

"My Gia," he groaned out as his fingers found her clit and he began to rub it in a way that had her toes curling. "Come for me."

He resumed his slow in and out plunge, but the way he stroked her sensitive bundle of nerves, rubbing it in a firm circle with his thumbs, destroyed her ability to think. Pleading with him, she begged him to make her come. She arched into his touch, her lungs seizing up as shocking pleasure tore through her. She didn't come, she exploded. Lights flashed behind her closed eyelids and she took in a gasping breath as her body shook and contorted beneath Ivan as her climax spun through her and wrecked her, reducing her to nothing but sensation.

She was dimly aware that Ivan was achieving his own orgasm, but even breathing right now was a struggle. A few moments later, he gently pulled out and he used something to clean them both. Then, he collapsed onto the pillows next to her.

"I'm so glad I bid on you," he panted out.

She giggled. "Is that your version of pillow talk?"

He pulled her on top of him where she lay limp and sated. "I love you, Gia, more than I ever thought I could love anyone."

Emotions overwhelmed her and she whispered, "Hold me."

"I'll do better than that."

He easily picked her up and carried her through the apartment to the master bathroom. After turning on the water, he washed her quickly and gently, then himself as she sat on the small bench in the shower. Her body throbbed and she was just so damn happy. He toweled them both off, then carried her to his bed.

“You know, you don’t have to carry me everywhere.”

“Hush, woman, I like to carry you.”

“What about when I’m big and fat from being pregnant?”

He paused and looked down at her with such tenderness that tears filled her eyes. “When you are carrying my child you will not be big and fat. You will be as beautiful as you are now, maybe even more so because you will have our child inside of you. And you will be an amazing mother. The best any baby could ask for.”

“Oh.” She nuzzled her face against his furry chest, overwhelmed by the sincerity of his gaze. “I’m in no hurry to have kids yet, but when we’re ready, I think you’ll make a wonderful father.”

“Thank you, my Gia.”

He resumed walking and soon they were beneath the covers, both on their sides facing each other. She reached out and stroked his face, running her finger over the scar and down to his lips.

“I love you, Ivan. More than I thought I could ever love anyone. And that scares me.”

His eyes flashed in the dim lighting of the bedroom. “I will never hurt you.”

She smiled at him and the shadows left his gaze. “I know.”

As she snuggled against him she let out a long, easy breath and melted into his arms. He held her close, his big body guarding hers as his breath whispered over her neck. She thought of all that had happened, all the highs and lows they’d been through together, and wouldn’t change a single thing because it all led up to this perfect moment of being in the arms of the man she’d been waiting for her whole life.

THE END

The story continues with Dimitri's Forbidden Submissive available now! Keep reading for a sneak peek!

Thank you so much for reading **Ivan's Captive Submissive**! I hope you enjoyed the book, and would love it if you would please consider leaving a review. Not only does a review spread the word to other readers, it also lets me know if you have fun visiting with my hot Russian Doms. I love to hear from readers and you can reach me through my website and through my Facebook and Twitter accounts. As always, thank you so much for giving me the chance to entertain you!

Dimitri's Forbidden Submissive

As the daughter of an outlaw biker, Rya DeLuca is used to living a wild life, but nothing could prepare her for the danger of falling in love with Dimitri Novikov. To Rya he's a warm, loving, sexy as hell Dom who gives her exactly the kind of bondage and discipline she craves in the bedroom, but to the rest of the world Dimitri is a feared man, a cold-blooded, heartless killer who is at the top of the Russian Mafia food chain.

While her hard and Dominant Master is her perfect match in every way that matters, their love can never last longer than a few days at most. Every moment Rya spends with Dimitri puts her life in jeopardy from rival gangs and Dimitri's own family.

Dimitri will have to decide if he loves Rya enough to walk away from her in order to save her life, or if their love is worth starting a war that could change the world of the Russian mafia forever.

ABOUT THE AUTHOR~

With over forty published books, Ann is Queen of the Castle to her husband and three sons in the mountains of West Virginia. In her past lives she's been an Import Broker, a Communications Specialist, a US Navy Civilian Contractor, a Bartender/Waitress, and an actor at the Michigan Renaissance Festival. She also spent a summer touring with the Grateful Dead-though she will deny to her children that it ever happened.

From a young Ann has had a love affair with books would read everything she could get her hands on. As Ann grew older, and her hormones kicked in, she discovered bodice ripping Fabio-esque romance novels. They were great at first, but she soon grew tired of the endless stories with a big wonderful emotional buildup to really short and crappy sex. Never a big fan of purple prose, throbbing spears of fleshy pleasure and wet honey pots make her giggle, she sought out books that gave the sex scenes in the story just as much detail and plot as everything else-without using cringe worthy euphemisms. This led her to the wonderful world of Erotic Romance, and she's never looked back.

Now Ann spends her days trying to tune out cartoons playing in the background to get into her 'sexy space' and has accepted that her Muse has a severe case of ADD.

Ann loves to talk with her fans, as long as they realize she's weird and that sarcasm doesn't translate well via text.

Other Books by Ann

Prides of the Moon Series

Amber Moon

Emerald Moon

Onyx Moon

Amethyst Moon

Opal Moon

Club Wicked Series

My Wicked Valentine

My Wicked Nanny

My Wicked Devil

My Wicked Trainers

My Wicked Masters

Virtual Seduction Series

Sodom and Detroit

Sodom and the Phoenix

Submissives Wish Series

Ivan's Captive Submissive

Dimitri's Forbidden Submissive

Alexandr's Cherished Submissive

Alexandr's Reluctant Submissive

Long Slow Tease Series (FemDom)

Still

Penance

Emma's Arabian Nights (FemDom)

First Kiss

Second Touch

Third Chance

Fourth Embrace

Bondmates Series

Casey's Warriors

Jaz's Warriors

Paige's Warriors(Novel Coming Soon)

Iron Horse MC Series

Exquisite Trouble

Exquisite Danger

Exquisite Redemption

Exquisite Karma(Coming Soon)

For the Love of Evil Series

Daughter of the Abyss

Princess of the Abyss

Chosen by the Gods

Blessed

Dreamer

Single Titles

Blushing Violet

Bound for Pleasure (FemDom)

Sensation Play

Peppermint Passion

The Breaker's Concubine

Guarding Hope

Scandalous Wish

Pursued by the Prisoner

The Bodyguard's Princess

Summer's Need

Wild Lilly

Diamond Heart

Sam and Cody

Made in the USA
Middletown, DE
16 May 2017